FIONA McARTHUR

Lighthouse Bay

MILLS & BOON

CONTENTS

A Month To Marry The Midwife

Books by Fiona McArthur

Harlequin Medical

Christmas in Lyrebird Lake

Midwife's Christmas Proposal
Midwife's Mistletoe Baby

A Doctor, A Fling & A Wedding Ring
The Prince Who Charmed Her
Gold Coast Angels: Two Tiny Heartbeats
Christmas with Her Ex

Visit the Author Profile page
at millsandboon.com.au for more titles.

Dear Reader,

Lighthouse Bay is the best place to find caring and spirited midwives, fabulous townspeople and the most gorgeous docs around. I love lighthouses, I adore moms and babies and I thrive on strong women and men who make me laugh.

In this first of three books set in Lighthouse Bay, midwife Ellie Swift has been told the ultimate lie and vowed to dedicate herself to her love of midwifery and nurturing her friends. She won't be trusting a man any time soon.

Obstetrician Sam Southwell, a man dealing with the loss of his wife and babies, didn't plan on staying in Lighthouse Bay; he's just doing his dad a favor. But then he met Ellie.

The Midwives of Lighthouse Bay series is the place to come when your heart needs healing and your soul needs restoring. You just might find true love.

I wish you, dear reader, as much emotion and fun reading about Ellie and Sam as I did writing their story. Then you can look forward to Trina's and Faith's stories, too. We have some hot twin-brother Italian docs who have no idea what these feisty Aussie midwives have in store for them under the guiding beam of the lighthouse. I can't wait to share those stories with you and would love to hear from you as we celebrate love in Lighthouse Bay.

Fi McArthur xx

FionaMcArthurAuthor.com

Dedicated to Rosie, who sprinted with me on this one;
Trish, who walked the beach with me;
and Flo, who rode the new wave and kept me afloat.
What a fab journey with awesome friends.

PROLOGUE

THE WHITE SAND curved away in a crescent as Ellie Swift descended to Lighthouse Bay Beach and turned towards the bluff. When she stepped onto the beach the luscious crush of cool, fine sand under her toes made her suck in her breath with a grin and the ocean breeze tasted salty against her lips. Ellie set off at a brisk pace towards the edge of the waves to walk the bay to the headland and back before she needed to dress for work.

'Ellie!'

She spun, startled, away from the creamy waves now washing her feet, and saw a man limping towards her. He waved again. Jeff, from the surf club. Ellie knew Jeff, the local prawn-trawler captain and chief lifesaver. She'd delivered his second son. Jeff had fainted and Ellie tried not to remind him of that every time she saw him.

She waved back but already suspected the call wasn't social. She turned and sped up to meet him.

'We've got an old guy down on the rocks under the lighthouse, a surfer, says he's your doctor from the hospital. We think he's busted his arm, and maybe a leg.'

Ellie turned her head to look towards the headland Jeff had come from.

Jeff waved his hand towards the huddle of people in the distance. 'He won't let anybody touch him until you come. The ambulance is on the way but I reckon we might have to chopper him out from here.'

Ellie worked all over the hospital so it wasn't unusual that she was who people asked for. An old guy and a surfer. That was Dr Southwell. She sighed.

Ten minutes later Ellie was kneeling beside the good doctor, guarding his wrinkled neck in a brace as she watched the two ambulance women and two burly lifesavers carefully shift him onto the rescue frame. Then it was done. Just a small groan escaped his gritted teeth as he closed his eyes and let the pain from the movement slowly subside.

Ellie glanced at the ocean, lying aqua and innocent, as if to say, *it wasn't my fault*, and suspected Dr Southwell would doggedly heal and return to surfing with renewed vigour as soon as he could. The tide was on the way out and the waves weren't reaching the sloping plateau at the base of the cliffs any more where the lifesavers had secured their casualty. The spot was popular with intrepid surfers to climb on and off their boards and paddle into the warm swell and out to the waves.

'Thanks for coming, Ellie.' Dr Southwell was looking much more comfortable and a trifle sheepish. 'Sorry to leave you in the lurch on the ward.'

She smiled at him. He'd always been sweet. 'Don't you worry about us. Look after you. They'll get you sorted once you've landed. Get well soon.'

The older man closed his eyes briefly. Then he winked at Ellie. 'I'll be back. As soon as I can.'

Ellie smiled and shook her head. He'd gone surfing every morning before his clinic, the athletic spring to his step contradicting his white hair and weathered face, a tall, thin gentleman who must have been a real catch fifty years ago. They'd splinted his arm against his body, didn't think the leg was broken, but they were treating it as such and had administered morphine, having cleared it with the helicopter flight nurse on route via mobile phone.

In the distance the *thwump-thwump* of the helicopter rotor could be heard approaching. Ellie knew how efficient the rescue team was. He'd be on his way very shortly.

Ellie glanced at the sweeping bay on the other side from where they crouched—the white sand that curved like a new moon around the bay, the rushing of the tide through the fish-filled creek back into the sea—and could understand why he'd want to return.

This place had stopped her wandering too. She lifted her chin. Lighthouse Bay held her future and she had plans for the hospital.

She looked down at the man, a gentle man in the true sense of the word, who had fitted so beautifully into the calm pace of the bay. 'We'll look forward to you coming back. As soon as you're well.' She glanced at the enormous Malibu surfboard the lifesavers had propped up against the cliff face. 'I'll get one of the guys to drop your board at my house and it will be there waiting for you.'

Ellie tried very hard not to think about the next few days. *Damn.* Now they didn't have an on-call doctor and the labouring women would have to be transferred to the base hospital until another locum arrived. She needed to move quickly on those plans to make her maternity ward a midwifery group practice.

CHAPTER ONE

FOUR DAYS LATER, outside Ellie's office at the maternity ward at Lighthouse Bay Hospital, a frog croaked. It was very close outside her window. She shuddered as she assembled the emergency locum-doctor's welcome pack. Head down, she concentrated on continuing the task and pretended not to see the tremor in her fingers as she gathered the papers. She was a professional in charge of a hospital, for goodness' sake. Her ears strained for a repeat of the dreaded noise and hoped like heck she wouldn't hear it. She strained…but thankfully silence ensued.

'Concentrate on the task,' she muttered. She included a local map, which after the first day they wouldn't need because the town was so small, but it covered everywhere they could eat.

A list of the hours they were required to man the tiny doctor's clinic—just two in total on the other side of the hospital on each day of the week they were here. Then, in a month, hand over to the other local doctor who had threatened to leave if he didn't get holidays.

She couldn't blame him or his wife—they deserved a life! It was getting busier. Dr Rodgers, an elderly bachelor, had done the call-outs before he'd become ill. She hummed loudly to drown out the sound of the little voice that suggested she should have a life too, and of course to drown out the frogs. Ellie concentrated as she printed out the remuneration package.

The idea that any low-risk woman who went into labour would have to be transferred to the large hospital an hour away from her family just because no locum doctor could come was wrong. Especially when she'd had all her antenatal care with Ellie over the last few months. So the locum doctors were a necessary evil. It wasn't an onerous workload for them, in fact, because the midwives did all the maternity work, and the main hospital was run as a triage station with a nurse practitioner, as they did in the Outback, so actually the locums only covered the hospital for emergencies and recovering inpatient needs.

Ellie dreamed of the day their maternity unit was fully self-sufficient. She quite happily played with the idea that she could devote her whole life to the project, get a nurse manager and finally step away from general nursing.

She could employ more midwives like her friend and neighbour Trina, who lived in one of the cliff houses. The young widowed midwife from the perfect marriage who preferred night duty so she didn't lie awake at night alone in her bed.

She was the complete opposite to Ellie, who'd had the marriage from hell that hadn't turned out to be a marriage at all.

Then there was Faith who did the evening shifts, the young mum who lived with her aunt and her three-year-old son. Faith was their eternal optimist. She hadn't found a man to practise heartbreak on yet. Just had an unfortunate one-night stand with a charismatic drifter. Ellie sighed. Three diverse women with a mutual dream. Lighthouse Bay Mothers and Babies. A gentle place for families to discover birth with midwives.

Back to the real world. For the moment they needed the championship of at least one GP/OB.

Most new mums stayed between one and three nights and, as they always had, women post-caesarean birth transferred back from the base hospital to recover. So a ward round in maternity and the general part of the hospital each morning by the VMO was asked to keep the doors open.

The tense set of her shoulders gradually relaxed as she distracted herself with the chore she'd previously completed six times since old Dr Rodgers had had his stroke.

The first two locums had been young and bored, patently here for the surf, and had both tried to make advances towards Ellie, as if she were part of the locum package. She'd had no problem freezing them both back into line but now the agency took on board her preferences for mature medical practitioners.

Most replacements had been well into retirement age since then, though there had also been some disadvantages with their advanced age. The semi-bald doctor definitely had been grumpy, which had been a bit of a disappointment, because Dr Rodgers had always had a kind word for everyone.

The next had been terrified that a woman would give birth and he'd have to do something about it because he hadn't been near a baby's delivery for twenty years. Ellie hadn't been able to promise one wouldn't happen so he'd declined to come back.

Lighthouse Bay was a service for low-risk pregnant women so Ellie couldn't see what the concern was. Birth was a perfectly normal, natural event and the women weren't sick. But there would always be those occasional precipitous and out-of-the-ordinary labours that seemed to happen more since Ellie had arrived. She'd proven well equal to the task of catching impatient babies but a decent back-up made sense. So, obstetric confidence was a second factor she requested now from the locums.

The next three locums had been either difficult to contact when she'd needed them or had driven her mad by sitting and talking all day so she hadn't been able to get anything done, so she hadn't asked them back. But the last locum had finally proved a golden one.

Dr Southwell, the elderly widower and retired GP with his obstetric diploma and years of gentle experience, had been a real card.

The postnatal women had loved him, as had every other marriageable woman above forty in town.

Especially Myra, Ellie's other neighbour, a retired chef who donated two hours a day to the hospital café between morning tea and lunch, and used to run a patisserie in Double Bay in Sydney. Myra and Old Dr Southwell had often been found laughing together.

Ellie had thought the hospital had struck the jackpot when he'd enquired about a more permanent position and had stayed full-time for an extra month when the last local GP had asked for an extended holiday. Ellie had really appreciated the break from trying to understand each new doctor's little pet hates.

Not that Dr Southwell seemed to have any foible Ellie had had to grow accustomed to at all. Except his love of surfing. She sighed.

They'd already sent one woman away in the last two days because she'd come to the hospital having gone into early labour. Ellie had had to say they had no locum coverage and she should drive to the base hospital.

Croak... There it was again. A long-drawn-out, guttural echo promising buckets of slime... She sucked in air through her nose and forced herself to breathe the constricted air out. She had to fight the resistance because her lungs seemed to have shrunk back onto her ribcage.

Croak... And then the *cruk-cruk* of the mate. She glanced at the clock and estimated she had an hour at least before the new doctor arrived so she reached over, turned on the CD player and allowed her favourite country singer to protect her from the noise as he belted out a southern ballad that drowned out the neighbours. Thankfully, today, her only maternity patient had brought her the latest CD from the large town an hour away where she'd gone for her repeat Caesarean birth.

It was only rarely, after prolonged rain, that the frogs gave her such a hard time. They'd had a week of downpours. Of course frogs were about. They'd stop soon. The rain had probably washed away the solution of salt water she'd sprayed around the outside of the ward window, so she'd do it again this afternoon.

One of the bonuses of her tiny croft cottage on top of the cliff was that, up there, the salt-laden spray from waves crashing against the rocks below drove the amphibians away.

She knew it was ridiculous to have a phobia about frogs, but she had suffered with it since she was little. It was inextricably connected to the time not long after her mother had died. She knew perfectly well it was irrational.

She had listened to the tapes, seen the psychologist, had even been transported by hypnosis to the causative events in an attempt to reprogram her response. That had actually made it worse, because now she had the childhood nightmares back that hadn't plagued her for years.

Basically slimy, web-footed frogs with fat throats that ballooned hideously when they croaked made her palms sweat and her heart beat like a drum in her chest. And the nightmares made her weep with grief in her sleep.

Unfortunately, down in the hollow where the old hospital nestled among well-grown shrubs and an enticing tinge of dampness after rain, the frogs were very happy to congregate. Her only snake in Eden. Actually, she could do with a big, quiet carpet snake that enjoyed green entrées. That could be the answer. She had no phobia of snakes.

But those frogs that slipped insidiously into the hand basin in the ladies' rest room—no way! Or those that croaked outside the door so that when she arrived as she had this morning, running a little late, a little incautiously intent on getting to work, a green tree frog had jumped at her as she'd stepped through the door. Thank goodness he'd missed his aim.

She still hadn't recovered from that traumatic start to her day. Now they were outside her window… Her hero sang on and she determined to stop thinking about it. She did not have time for this.

* * *

Samuel Southwell parked his now dusty Lexus outside the cottage hospital. His immaculate silver machine had never been off the bitumen before, and he frowned at the rim of dust that clung to the base of the windscreen.

He noted with a feeling of unreality, the single *Reserved for Doctor* spot in the car park, and his hand hovered as he hesitated to stop the engine. *Doctor.* Not plural. Just one spot for the one doctor. He couldn't remember the last time he'd been without a cloud of registrars, residents and med students trailing behind him.

What if they wanted him to look at a toenail or someone had a heart attack? He was a consultant obstetrician and medical researcher, for heaven's sake.

At that thought his mouth finally quirked. Surely his knowledge of general medicine was buried miraculously in his brain underneath the uteruses? He sincerely hoped so or he'd have to refresh his knowledge of whatever ailment stumped him. On-line medical journals could be accessed. According to his father it shouldn't be a problem—he was 'supposed to be smart'!

Maybe the old man was right and it would do him good. Either way, he'd agreed, mainly because his dad never asked him to do anything and he'd been strangely persistent about this favour. This little place had less than sixty low-risk births a year. And he was only here for the next four weeks. He would manage.

It would be vastly different from the peaks of drama skimmed from thousands of women and babies passing through the doors of Brisbane Mothers and Babies Hospital. Different being away from his research work that drove him at nights and weekends. He'd probably get more sleep as well. He admired his father but at the moment he was a little impatient with him for this assignment.

'It'll be a good-will mission,' Dr Reginald Southwell had decreed, with a twinkle in his eye that his son had supposedly inherited but that his father had insisted he'd lost. 'See how the other half live. Step out of your world of work, work, work for a month, for goodness' sake. You can take off a month for the first time in who knows how long. I promised the matron I'd return and don't want to leave them in the lurch.'

He'd grinned at that. *Poor old Dad.* It dated him well in the past, calling her a matron. The senior nurses were all 'managers' now.

Unfortunate Dad, the poor fellow laid back with his broken arm and his twisted knee. It had been an accident waiting to happen for his father, a man of his advanced age taking random locum destinations while he surfed. But Sam understood perfectly well why he did it.

Sam sighed and turned off the ignition. Too late to back out. He was here now. He climbed out and stretched the kinks from his shoulders. The blue expanse of ocean reminded him how far from home he really was.

Above him towered a lonely white lighthouse silhouetted against the sapphire-blue sky on the big hill behind the hospital. He listened for traffic noise but all he could hear was the crash of the waves on the cliff below and faint beats from a song. *Edge of Nowhere.* Not surprising someone was playing country music somewhere. They should be playing the theme song from *Deliverance.*

He'd told his colleagues he had to help his dad out with his arm and knee. Everyone assumed Sam was living with him while he recuperated. That had felt easier than explaining this.

Lighthouse Bay, a small hamlet on the north coast of New South Wales at the end of a bad road. The locum do-everything doctor. Good grief.

Ellie jumped at the rap on her door frame and turned her face to the noise. She reached out and switched her heroic balladeer off mid-song. The silence seemed to hum as she stared at the face of a stranger.

'Sorry, didn't mean to startle you.' A deep, even voice, quite in keeping with the broad shoulders and impeccable suit jacket, but not in keeping with the tiny, casual seaside hospital he'd dropped into.

Drug reps didn't usually get out this far. That deeply masculine resonance in his cultured voice vibrated against her skin in an unfamiliar way. It made her face prickle with a warmth she wasn't used to and unconsciously her hand lifted and she checked the top button of her shirt. Phew. Force field secure.

Then her confidence rushed back. 'Can I help you?' She stood up, thinking there was something faintly familiar... But after she'd examined him thoroughly she thought, no, he wasn't recognisable. She hadn't seen this man before and she was sure she'd have remembered him.

The man took one step through the doorway but couldn't go any further. Her office drew the line at two chairs and two people. It had always been small but somehow the space seemed to have shrunk to ridiculous tininess in the last few seconds. There was a hint of humour about his silver-blue eyes that almost penetrated the barrier she'd erected but stopped at the gate. Ellie was a good gatekeeper. She didn't want any complications.

Ellie, who had always thought herself tall for a woman, unexpectedly felt a little overshadowed and the hairs on the back of her neck rose gently—in a languorous way, not in fright—which was ridiculous. Really, she was very busy for the next hour until the elderly locum consultant arrived.

'Are you the matron?' He rolled his eyes, as if a private thought piqued him, then corrected himself. 'Director of Nursing?' Smooth as silk with a thread of command.

'Acting. Yes. Ellie Swift. I'm afraid you have the advantage of me.'

The tall man raised his eyebrows. 'I'm Samuel Southwell.' She heard the slight mocking note in his voice. 'The locum medical officer here for the next month.' He glanced at his watch as if he couldn't believe she'd forgotten he was coming. 'Am I early?'

'Ah...'

Ellie winced. Not a drug rep. The doctor. *Oops.*

'Sorry. Time zones. No Daylight Saving for you northerners from Brisbane. Of course. You're only early on our side of the border. I was clearing the decks for your arrival.' She muttered more to herself, 'Or *someone*'s arrival...' then looked up. 'The agency had said they'd filled the temporary position with a Queenslander. I should have picked up the time difference.'

Then the name sank in. 'Southwell?' A pleasant surprise. She smiled with real warmth. 'Are you related to Dr Southwell who had the accident?' At the man's quick nod, Ellie asked, 'How is he?' She'd been worried.

'My father,' he said dryly, 'is as well as can be expected for a man too old to be surfing.' He spoke as if his parent were a recalcitrant child and Ellie felt a little spurt of protectiveness for the absent octogenarian. Then she remembered she had to work with this man for the next month. She also remembered Dr Southwell had two children, and his only son was a consultant obstetrician at Brisbane Mothers and Babies. A workaholic, apparently.

Well, she certainly had someone with obstetric experience for a month. It would be just her luck that they wouldn't have a baby the whole time he was here. Ellie took a breath and plastered on a smile.

First the green frog jumping at her from the door, then the ones croaking outside the window and now the Frog Prince, city-slicker locum who wasn't almost retired, like locums were supposed to be.

'Welcome. Perhaps you'd like to sit down.' She gestured at the only other chair jammed between the storage cupboard and the door frame. She wasn't really sure his legs would fit if he tried to fold into the space.

He didn't attempt to sit and it was probably a good choice.

There was still something about his behaviour that was a little...odd. Did he feel they didn't want him? 'Dr Southwell, your presence here is very much appreciated.'

It took him a couple of seconds to answer and she used them to centre herself. This was her world. No need to be nervous. 'We were very relieved when someone accepted the locum position for the month.'

He didn't look flattered—too flash just to be referred to as 'someone', perhaps?

Ellie stepped forward. Bit back the sigh and the grumbles to herself about how much she liked the old ones. 'Anyway, welcome to Lighthouse Bay. Most people call me Swift, because it's my name and I move fast. I'm the DON, the midwife, emergency resource person and mediator between the medical staff and the nursing staff.' She held out her hand. He looked at her blankly. *What?* Perhaps a sense of humour was too much to hope for.

His expression slowly changed to one of polite query. 'Do they need mediation?' He didn't take her hand and she lowered it slowly. Strange, strange man. Ellie stifled another sigh. Being on the back foot already like this was not a good sign.

'It was a joke, sorry.' She didn't say, *'J. O. K. E.,'* though she was beginning to think he might need it spelled out for him. She switched to her best professional mode. The experience of fitting in at out-of-the-way little hospitals had dispatched any pretensions she might have had that a matron was anyone but the person who did all the things other people didn't want to do. It had also taught her to be all things to all people.

Ellie usually enjoyed meeting new staff. It wasn't something that happened too often at their small hospital until Dr Rodgers had retired.

Lighthouse Bay was a place more suited to farming on the hills and in the ocean, where the inhabitants retreated from society, though there were some very trendy boutique industries popping up. Little coffee plantations. Lavender farms. Online boutiques run by corporate women retreating from the cities looking for a sea change.

Which was where Ellie's new clientele for Maternity rose from. Women with considered ideas on how and where they wanted to have their babies. But the town's reliable weekend doctor had needed to move indefinitely for medical treatment and Ellie was trying to hold it all together.

The local farming families and small niche businesses were salt-of-the-earth friendly. She was renovating her tiny one-roomed cottage that perched with two other similar crofts like a flock of seabirds on the cliff overlooking the bay. She'd found the perfect place to forget what a fool she'd been and perfect also for avoiding such a disaster again.

Ellie dreamed of dispensing with the need for doctors at all. But at the moment she needed one supporting GP obstetrician at least to call on for emergencies. Maybe she could pick this guy's brains for ways to circumvent that.

She glanced at the man in front of her—experience in a suit. But not big on conversation. Still, she was tenacious when there was something she wanted, and she'd drag it out of him. Eventually.

In the scheme of things Lighthouse Bay Maternity needed a shake up and maybe she could use him. He'd be totally abreast of the latest best-practice trends, a leader in safe maternity care. He should be a golden opportunity to sway the sticklers to listen to the mothers instead of the easy fix of sending women away.

But, if he wasn't going to sit down then she would deal with him outside the confines of her office. She stood and slipped determinedly past him. It was a squeeze and required body contact. She'd just have to deal with it. 'Would you like a tour?'

Lemon verbena. He knew the scent because at the last conference he'd presented at, all the wives had been raving about the free hotel amenities and they'd made him smell it. It hadn't resonated with him then as it did now. Sam Southwell breathed it in and his visceral response set off rampant alarm bells. He was floundering to find his brain. There was something about the way her buttoned-to-the-neck, long-sleeved white shirt had launched a missile straight to the core of him and exploded, and now the scent of her knocked him sideways as she brushed past.

The way her chin lifted and her cool, grey eyes assessed him and found him wanting, giving him the ultimate hands-off warning when he hadn't even thought about hands on—hadn't for a long time until now—impressed him. Obviously a woman who made up her own mind. She wasn't overawed by him in the least and that was a good thing.

He stared at the wall where 'Swift' had stood a second ago and used all of his concentration to ram the feelings of sheer confusion and lust back down into the cave he used for later thought, and tried to sound at least present for the conversation. She must be thinking he was an arrogant sod, but his brain was gasping, struggling, stumped by the reaction he was having to her.

She was right. Being jammed in this shoebox of an office wasn't helping. What an ironic joke that his father had thought this isolated community would help him return to normal when in fact he'd just fallen off a Lighthouse Bay cliff. His stomach lurched.

He turned slowly to face her as she waited, not quite tapping her foot. He began to feel better. Impatience wasn't a turn-on.

'Yes. A tour would be excellent,' he said evenly. She must think he was the most complete idiot but he was working to find headspace to fit it all in. And he could work fast.

The place he could handle. Heck, he could do it in his sleep. He had no idea why he was so het up about it. But this woman? His reaction to her? A damnably different kettle of fish. Disturbing. As in, deeply and diabolically disturbing.

'How many beds do you have here?' A sudden picture of Ellie Swift on a bed popped into his head and arrested him. She'd have him arrested, more likely, he thought wryly. He was actually having a breakdown. His dad was right. He did need to learn to breathe.

CHAPTER TWO

SAM HADN'T SLEPT with a woman for years. Not since his wife had died. He hadn't wanted to and in fact, since he'd used work to bury grief and guilt, with all the extra input, his career had actually taken off. Hence, he hadn't had the time to think about sex, let alone act on it.

Now his brain had dropped to somewhere past his waistline, a nether region that had been asleep for years and had just inconveniently roared into life like an express train, totally inappropriate and unwelcome. Good grief. He closed his eyes tightly to try and clear the pictures filling his head. He was an adolescent schoolboy again.

'Are you okay?' Her voice intruded and he snapped his lids open.

'Sorry.' What could he say? He only knew what he couldn't say. *Please don't look down at my trousers!* Instead he managed, 'I think I need coffee.'

She stopped. Dropped her guard. And as if by magic he felt the midwife morph from her as she switched to nurture mode in an instant. No other profession he knew did it as comprehensively as midwives.

'You poor thing. Of course. Follow me. We'll start in the coffee shop. Though Myra isn't here yet. Didn't you stop on the way? You probably rushed to get here.' She shook her head disapprovingly and didn't wait for an answer but bustled him into a small side room that blossomed out into an empty coffee shop with a huge bay window overlooking the gardens.

She nudged him into a seat. Patted his shoulder. 'Tea or coffee?' It had all happened very fast and now his head really was spinning.

'Coffee—double-shot espresso, hot milk on the side,' he said automatically, and she stopped and looked at him.

Then she laughed. Her face opened like a sunburst, her eyes sparkled and her beautiful mouth curved with huge amusement. She laughed and snorted, and he was smitten. Just like that. A goner.

She pulled herself together, mouth still twitching. 'Sorry. Myra could fix that but not me. But I'll see what I can do.'

Sam stared after her. She was at least twelve feet away now and he gave himself a stern talking-to. *Have coffee, and then be* normal. He would try. No—he would succeed.

Poor man. Ellie glanced at the silent, mysterious coffee machine that Myra worked like a maestro and tried to work out how much instant coffee from the jar under the sink, where it had been pushed in disgrace, would equate to a double shot of coffee. She didn't drink instant coffee. Just the weak, milky ones Myra made for her from the machine under protest. Maybe three teaspoons?

He'd looked so cosmopolitan and handsome as he'd said it—something he said every day. She bit back another snuffle of laughter. Classic. *Welcome to Lighthouse Bay.* Boy, were they gonna have fun.

She glanced back and decided he wasn't too worthy of sympathy because it was unfair for a man to have shoulders like that, not to mention a decidedly sinful mouth. And she hadn't thought about sinful for a while. In fact she couldn't quite believe she was thinking about it now. She'd thought the whole devastation of the cruelty of men had completely cured her of that foolishness.

She was going to have to spend the next month with this man reappearing on the ward. Day and night if they were both called out. The idea was more unsettling than she'd bargained for and was nothing to do with the way the ward was run.

The jug boiled and she mixed the potent brew. Best not to think of that now. She needed him awake. She scooped up two Anzac biscuits from the jar with a napkin.

'Here you go.' Ellie put the black liquid down in front of him and a small glass of hot milk she'd heated in the microwave.

He looked at it. Then at her. She watched fascinated as he poured a little hot milk into the mug with an inch of black coffee at the bottom.

He sipped, threw down the lot and then set it down. No expression. No clues. She was trying really hard not to stare. It must be an acquired taste.

His voice was conversational. 'Probably the most horrible coffee I've ever had.' He looked up at her. 'But I do appreciate the effort. I wasn't thinking.' He pushed the cup away. Grimaced dramatically. Shook his whole upper body like a dog shedding water. 'Thank God I brought my machine.'

She wasn't sure what she could say to that. 'Wow. Guess it's going to be a change for you here, away from the big city.'

'Hmm...' he murmured noncommittally. 'But I do feel better after the shock of that.'

She grinned. Couldn't help herself. 'So you're ready for the walk around now?'

He stood up, picked up the biscuits in the napkin, folded them carefully and slipped them into his pocket. 'Let's do it.'

Ellie decided it was the first time he'd looked normal since he'd arrived. She'd remember that coffee trick for next time.

'So this is the ward. We have five beds. One single room and two doubles, though usually we'd only have one woman in each room, even if it's really busy.'

Really busy with five beds? Sam glanced around. Empty rooms. Now they were in with the one woman in the single room and her two-day-old infant. Why wasn't she going home?

'This is Renee Jones.'

'Hello, Renee.' He smiled at the mother and then at the infant. 'Congratulations. I'm Dr Southwell. Everything okay?'

'Yes, thank you, doctor. I'm hoping to stay until Friday, if that's okay. There's four others at home and I'm in no rush.'

He blinked. Four more days staying in hospital after a caesarean delivery? Why? He glanced at Matron Swift, who apparently was unworried. She smiled and nodded at the woman.

'That's fine, Renee, you deserve the rest.'

'Only rest I get,' Renee agreed. 'Though, if you don't mind, could you do the new-born check today, doc, just in case my husband has a crisis and I have to go at short notice?'

New-born check? Examine a baby...himself? He glanced at the midwife. Who did that? A paediatrician, he would have thought. She met his eyes and didn't dispute it so he smiled and nodded. 'We'll sort that.'

Hopefully. His father would be chortling. He could feel Ellie's presence behind him as they left the room and he walked down to the little nurses' alcove and leaned against the desk. It had been too many years since he'd checked a new-born's hips and heart. Not that he couldn't—he imagined. But even his registrars didn't do that. They left it to Paediatrics while the O&G guys did the pregnancy and labour things.

'Is there someone else to do the new-born checks on babies?'

'Sorry.' She shook her head. 'You're it.'

He might have a quick read before he did it, then. He narrowed his eyes at the suspicious quirk of her lips. 'What about you?'

Her hair swished from side to side. He'd never really had a thing for pony tails but it sat well on her. Pretty. Made him smile when it swayed. He'd faded out again.

'I said,' she repeated, 'I did the online course for well-baby examination but have never been signed off on it. One of those things I've been meaning to do and never got around to.'

Ha. She thought she was safe. 'Excellent. Then perhaps we'd better do the examinations together, and at least by the time I leave we'll both be good at them. Then I can sign you off.'

She didn't appear concerned. She even laughed. He could get used to the way she laughed. It was really more of a chortle. Smile-inducing.

The sound of a car pulling up outside made them both pause. After a searching appraisal of the couple climbing out, she said, 'The charts are in that filing cabinet if the ladies have booked in. Can you grab Josie Mills, please?'

When he looked back from the filing cabinet to the door he could hear the groans but Swift was already there with her smile.

He hadn't seen her move and glanced to where she'd stood a minute ago to check there weren't two of her. Nope. She was disappearing up the hallway with the pregnant woman and her male support as if they were all on one of those airport travellators and he guessed he'd better find the chart.

Which he did, and followed them up the hall.

Josie hadn't made it onto the bed. She was standing beside it and from her efforts it was plain that, apart from him, there'd be an extra person in the room in seconds.

Swift must have grabbed a towel and a pair of gloves as she came through the door, both of which were still lying on the bed, because she was distracted as she tried to help the frantic young woman remove her shorts.

In Sam's opinion the baby seemed to be trying to escape into his mother's underwear but Swift was equal to the task. She deftly encouraged one of the mother's legs out and whipped the towel off the bed and put it between the mother's legs, where the baby seemed to unfold into it in a swan dive and was pushed between the mother's knees into Swift's waiting hands. The baby spluttered his displeasure on the end of the purple cord after his rapid ejection into a towel.

'Good extrication,' Sam murmured with a little fillip of un-expected excitement as he pulled on a pair of gloves from the dispenser at the door. Could that be the first ghost of emotion he'd felt at a birth for a long while? With a sinking dismay it dawned on him that he hadn't even noticed it had been missing.

He crossed the room to assess the infant, who'd stopped cry-ing and was slowly turning purple, which nobody seemed to no-tice as they all laughed and crowed at the rapid birth and helped the woman up on the bed to lie down.

'Would you like me to attend to third stage or the baby?' he enquired quietly.

He saw Swift glance at the baby, adjust the towel and rub the infant briskly. 'Need you to cut the cord now, John,' she said to the husband. 'Your little rocket is a bit stunned.'

The parents disentangled their locked gazes and Sam heard their indrawn breaths. The father jerked up the scissors Ellie had put instantly into his hand and she directed him between the two clamps as she went on calmly. 'It happens when they fly out.' A few nervous sawing snips from Dad with the big scissors and the cord was cut. Done.

'Dr Southwell will sort you, Josie, while we sort the baby.' Swift said it prosaically and they swapped places as the baby was bundled and she carried him to the resuscitation trolley. 'Come on, John.' She gestured for the father to follow her. 'Talk to your daughter.'

The compressed air hissed as she turned it on and Sam could hear her talking to the dad behind him as automatically he smiled at the mother. 'Well done. Congratulations.'

The baby cried and they both smiled. 'It all happened very fast,' the mother said as she craned her neck toward the baby and, reassured that Swift and her husband were smiling, she settled back. 'A bit too fast.'

He nodded as a small gush of blood signalled the third stage was about to arrive. Seconds later it was done, the bleeding set-tled, and he tidied the sheet under her and dropped it in the linen bag behind him. He couldn't help a smile to himself at having done a tidying job he'd watched countless times but couldn't actually remember doing himself. 'Always nice to have your underwear off first, I imagine.'

The mother laughed as she craned her neck again and by her smile he guessed they were coming back. 'Easier.'

'Here we go.' Swift lifted the mother's T-shirt and crop top and nestled the baby skin-to-skin between her bare breasts. She turned the baby's head sideways so his cheek was against his mother. 'Just watch her colour, especially the lips. Her being against your skin will warm her like toast.'

Sam stood back and watched. He saw the adjustments Ellie made, calmly ensuring mother and baby were comfortable—including the dad, with a word here and there, even asking for the father's mobile phone to take a few pictures of the brand new baby and parents. She glanced at the clock. He hadn't thought of looking at the clock once. She had it all under control.

Sam stepped back further and peeled off his gloves. He went to the basin to wash his hands and his mind kept replaying the scene. He realised why it was different. The lack of people milling around.

Swift pushed the silver trolley with the equipment and scissors towards the door. He stopped her. 'Do you always do this on your own?'

She pointed to a green call button. 'Usually I ring and one of the nurses comes from the main hospital to be on hand if needed until the GP arrives. But it happened fast today and you were here.' She flashed him a smile. 'Back in a minute. Watch her, will you? Physiological third stage.' Then she sailed away.

He hadn't thought about the injection they usually gave to reduce risk of bleeding after the birth. He'd somehow assumed it had already been given, but realised there weren't enough hands to have done it, although he could have done it if someone had mentioned it. Someone.

As far as he knew all women were given the injection at his

hospital unless they'd expressly requested not to have it. Research backed that up. It reduced post-partum haemorrhage. He'd mention it.

His eyes fell on Josie's notes, which were lying on the table top where he'd dropped them, and he snicked the little wheeled stool out from under the bench with his foot and sat there to read through the medical records. The last month's antenatal care had been shared between his father and 'E Swift'. He glanced up every minute or so to check that both mother and baby were well but nothing happened before 'E Swift' returned.

An hour later Sam had been escorted around the hospital by a nurse who'd been summoned by phone and found himself deposited back in the little maternity wing. The five-minute cottage hospital tour had taken an hour because the infected great toenail he'd been fearing had found him and he'd had to deal with it, and the pain the poor sufferer was in.

Apparently he still remembered how to treat phalanges and the patient had seemed satisfied. He assumed Ellie would be still with the new maternity patient, but he was wrong.

Ellie sat, staring at the nurses' station window in a strangely rigid hunch, her hand clutching her pen six inches above the medical records, and he paused and turned his head to see what had attracted her attention.

He couldn't see anything. When he listened, all he could hear were frogs and the distant sound of the sea.

'You okay?' He'd thought his voice was quiet when he asked but she jumped as though he'd fired a gun past her ear. The pen dropped as her hand went to her chest, as if to push her heart back in with her lungs. His own pulse rate sped up. Good grief! He'd thought it was too good to be true that this place would be relaxing.

'You're back?' she said, stating the obvious with a blank look on her face.

He picked up the underlying stutter in her voice. Something

had really upset her and he glanced around again, expecting to see a masked intruder at least. She glanced at him and then the window. 'Can you do me a favour?'

'Sure.' She looked like she could do with a favour.

'There's a green tree frog behind that plant in front of the window.' He could hear the effort she was putting in to enunciate clearly and began to suspect this was an issue of mammoth proportions.

'Yes?'

'Take it away!'

'Ranidaphobia?'

She looked at him and, as he studied her, a little of the colour crept back into her face. She even laughed shakily. 'How many people know that word?'

He smiled at her, trying to install some normality in the fraught atmosphere. 'I'm guessing everyone who's frightened of frogs.' He glanced up the hallway. 'I imagine Josie is in one of the ward rooms. Why don't you go check on her while I sort out the uninvited guest?'

She stood up so fast it would have been funny if he didn't think she'd kill him for laughing. He maintained a poker face as she walked hurriedly away and then his smile couldn't be restrained. He walked over to the pot plant, shifted it from the wall and saw the small green frog, almost a froglet, clinging by his tiny round pads to the wall.

Sam bent down and scooped the little creature into his palm carefully and felt the coldness of the clammy body flutter as he put his other hand over the top to keep it from jumping. A quick detour to the automatic door and he stepped out, tossing the invader into the garden.

Sam shook his head and walked back inside to the wall sink to wash his hands. A precipitous human baby jammed in a bikini bottom didn't faze her but a tiny green frog did? It was a crazy world.

He heard her come back as he dried his hands.

'Thank you,' she said to his back. He turned. She looked as composed and competent as she had when he'd first met her. As if he'd imagined the wild-eyed woman of three minutes ago.

He probably thought she was mad but there wasn't a lot she could do about that now. Ellie really just wanted him to go so she could put her head in her hands and scream with frustration. And then check every other blasted plant pot that she'd now ask to be removed.

Instead she said, 'So you've seen the hospital and your rooms. Did they explain the doctor's routine?'

He shook his head so she went on. 'I have a welcome pack in my office. I'll get it.'

She turned to get it but as she walked away something made her suspect he was staring after her. He probably wasn't used to dealing with officious nursing staff or mad ones. They probably swarmed all over him in Brisbane—the big consultant. She glanced back. He was watching her and he was smiling. She narrowed her eyes.

Then she was back and diving in where she'd left off. 'The plan is you come to the clinic two hours in the morning during the week, starting at eight after your ward round here at seven forty-five. Then you're on call if we need you for emergencies, but most things we handle ourselves. It's a window of access to a doctor for locals. We only call you out for emergencies.'

'So do you do on-call when you're off duty?' He glanced at her. 'You do have off-duty time?'

Ellie blinked, her train of thought interrupted. 'I share the workload with the two other midwives, Trina and Faith. I do the days, Faith does the afternoons and Trina does the nights. We cover each other for on-call, and two midwives from the base hospital come in and relieve us for forty-eight hours on the weekends. We have a little flexibility between us for special occasions.'

'And what do you do on your days off?' She had the feeling

he was trying to help her relax but asking about her private life wasn't the way to do that.

She deliberately kept it brief. Hopefully he'd take the hint. 'I enjoy my solitary life.'

She saw him accept the rebuke and fleetingly felt mean. He was just trying to be friendly. It wasn't his fault she didn't trust any man under sixty, but that was the way it was.

She saw his focus shift and his brows draw together, as if he'd just remembered something. 'Syntocinon after birth—isn't giving that normal practice in all hospitals?'

It was a conversation she had with most locums when they arrived—especially the obstetricians like him. 'It's not routine here. We're low risk. Surprisingly, here we're assuming the mother's body has bleeding under control if we leave her well enough alone. Our haemorrhage rate per birth is less than two percent.'

His brows went up again. 'One in fifty. Ours is one in fifteen with active management. Interesting.' He nodded. 'Before I go we'd better check this baby in case your patient wants to go home. I borrowed the computer in the emergency ward and read over the new-born baby check. Don't worry. It all came back to me as I read it.'

He put his hand in his pocket and she heard keys jingle and wondered if it was a habit or he was keen to leave. Maybe he was one of those locums who tried to do as little as possible. It was disconcerting how disappointed she felt. Why would that be? Abruptly she wanted him to go. 'I can do it if you like.'

'No.' He smiled brilliantly at her and she almost stumbled, certainly feeling like reaching for her sunnies. That was some wattage.

Then he said blithely, 'We will practise together.' He picked up a stethoscope and indicated she should get one too.

Ellie could do nothing but follow his brisk pace down the corridor to Renee's room. So he was going to make her copy him. Served her right for telling him she'd done the course.

In Renee's room when he lifted back the sheet, baby Jones lay like a plump, rosy-cheeked sleeping princess all dressed in pink down to her fluffy bloomers. Ellie suppressed a smile. 'Mum's first girl after four boys.'

'What fun,' he murmured.

He started with the baby's chest, listening to both sides of her chest and then her heart. Ellie remembered the advice from the course to start there, because once your examination woke the baby up she might not lie so quietly.

Dr Southwell stepped back and indicated she do the same. Ellie listened to the *lub-dub, lub-dub* of a normal organ, the in-and-out breaths that were equal in both lungs, nodded and stood back.

He was right. She'd been putting off asking someone to sign her off on this. Before Wayne, she would have been gung-ho about adding neonatal checks to her repertoire. A silly lack of confidence meant she'd been waiting around for someone else to do it when she should really just have done this instead. After all, when she had the independent midwifery service this would be one of her roles.

By the time they'd run their hands over the little girl, checked her hips didn't click or clunk when tested, that her hand creases, toes and ears were all fine, Ellie was quite pleased with herself.

As they walked away she had the feeling that Dr Southwell knew exactly what she was feeling.

'Easy,' he said and grinned at her, and she grinned back. He wasn't so bad after all. In fact, he was delightful.

Then it hit her. It had been an action-packed two hours since he'd walked in the door. This physically attractive male had gone from being a stranger standing in her office, to coffee victim, to birth assistant, to frog remover, to midwife's best friend in a couple of hours and she was grinning back at him like a smitten fool. As if she'd found a friend and was happy that he liked her.

Just as Wayne had bowled her over when they'd first met. She'd been a goner in less than an evening. He'd twisted her around his finger and she'd followed him blindly until he'd begun his campaign of breaking her. She'd never suspected the lies.

Oh, yes. Next came the friendly sharing of history, all the warm and fuzzy excitement of mutual attraction, pleasant sex and then *bam*! She'd be hooked. The smile fell off her face.

Not this little black duck.

Ellie dragged the stethoscope from around her neck and fiercely wiped it over with a disposable cleaning cloth. Without looking at Sam, she held out her hand for his stethoscope. She felt it land and glanced at him. 'Thank you. I'll see you tomorrow, then, Dr Southwell.'

She watched his smile fade. Hers had completely disappeared as she'd looked up at him with the same expression she'd met him with this morning. Polite enquiry. He straightened his shoulders and jammed his hand back in his pocket to jingle his keys again.

'Right,' he said evenly. 'I'll go check into my guesthouse.' Without another word, he strode away to the front door and she sagged with relief.

Lucky she'd noticed what she'd been doing before it had gone too far. But at this precise moment she didn't feel lucky. She felt disheartened that she couldn't just enjoy a smile from a good-looking man without getting all bitter, twisted and suspicious about it. Wayne had a lot to answer for.

She did what she always did when her thoughts turned to her horrific marriage that really hadn't been a marriage—she needed to find work to do and maybe Josie or her baby could give it to her.

CHAPTER THREE

THREE NIGHTS LATER, alone in her big oak bed on top of the cliff, Ellie twisted the sheets under her fingers as the dream dragged her back in time. Dragged her all the way back to primary school.

Her respirations deepened with the beginning of panic. The older Ellie knew what the dream Ellie didn't. Her skin dampened.

Then she was back.

To the last day of compulsory swimming lessons she'd used to love. Now school and swimming lessons made her heart hurt. Mummy had loved helping at swimming lessons, had even taught Ellie's class the first two years, but now all they did was remind young Ellie how much she'd lost, because Mummy wasn't there anymore. Daddy had said Mummy would be sad that Ellie didn't like swimming now, but it made her heart ache.

And some of the big boys in primary school were mean to her. They laughed when she cried.

But today was the last day, the last afternoon she'd see the grey toilet block at the swimming pool for this year, and she pushed off her wet swimming costume with relief and it plopped to the floor. When she reached for her towel she thought for a minute that it moved. Silly. She shook her head and grabbed for it again so she could dry and get dressed quickly, or she'd be last in line again and those boys would tease her.

Something moved out of the corner of her eye and then she felt the cold shock as a big, green frog leaped towards her and landed on her bare chest. She screamed, grabbed the clammy bulk of it off her slimy skin and threw it off her chest in mindless revulsion, then fought with the lock on the change-room door to escape.

The lock jammed halfway. Ellie kept screaming, then somehow her fingers opened the catch and she ran out of the cubicle, through the washroom and outside through the door—into a long line of stunned primary school boys who stared and then laughed at the crying, naked young Ellie until she was swooped on by a scolding teacher and bundled into a towel.

She wanted her mummy. Why couldn't she have her mummy? It should be her mummy holding her tight and soothing her sobs. She cried harder, and her racking sobs seemed to come from her belly, even silencing the laughing boys...

Ellie sat bolt upright in bed, the sob still caught in her throat, and shuddered. She didn't know why frogs were so linked with her mother's death. Maybe it was something she'd heard about her mother's car accident, coupled with her childhood's overwhelming sense of loss and grief—and of course that incident at the swimming baths hadn't helped—but she couldn't hear a frog without having that loneliness well back up in her again. It had become the spectre of grief. All through her childhood, whenever she'd been lonely and missed her mother, she'd had the frog nightmare. She'd eventually grown out of it. But, after Wayne, it had started again.

She hadn't had the dream for a while. Not once since she'd moved here a year ago—and she hoped like heck she wasn't going to start having it repeatedly again.

She glanced at the window. It was almost light. She'd have time for a quick walk on the beach before she'd have to come back and shower for work. Find inner peace before the day.

Then she remembered the new doctor. Sam. Day four. One more day and then she'd have the weekend off and wouldn't have to see him. Was that why she'd had the dream? The problem was she liked him. And every day she liked him more. He was lovely to the women. Great with the staff. Sweet to her. And Myra thought the sun shone out of him.

Ellie didn't want to like Sam. Because she'd liked the look of Wayne too, and look where that had ended up.

Of course when she went down to the beach the first person she saw was Dr Sam. Funny how she knew it was him—even from the spectacular rear. Thankfully he didn't see her because he was doing what his father had done—watching the ocean. Sam's broad back faced her as he watched the swells and decided on where to swim. Then he strode into the water.

She walked swiftly along the beach, her flip flops in her hand, waves washing over her toes while she tried not to look as his strong arms paddled out to catch the long run of waves into the shore that delighted the surfers.

She couldn't even find peace on 'her' beach. She stomped up the curve of sand and back again faster than usual, deliberately staring directly in front of her. If she hadn't been so stubborn she would have seen that he was coming in on a wave and would intercept her before she could escape.

He hopped up from the last wave right in front of her. 'Good morning, Ellie Swift.'

She jumped. She glared at his face, then in fairness accepted it wasn't his fault she was feeling crabby. 'Morning, Sam.' Then despite herself her gaze dropped to the dripping magnificence of his chest, his flat, muscled abdomen, strong thighs and long legs, and her breath caught in her throat. Even his feet were masculine and sexy. *My goodness!* Her face flamed and she didn't know where to look.

Sam said, 'The water's a nice temperature,' and she hoped he hadn't noticed her ears were burning.

'Um…isn't it warmer in Queensland?' Her brain was too slow to produce exciting conversation.

He shrugged and disobediently her eyes followed the movement of his splendid shoulders despite her brain telling her to look away. He said, 'Don't know. I haven't swum in the ocean for years.'

That made her pause. Gave her a chance to settle down a little, even wonder why he hadn't been to the beach back home. She needed to get out of here. Create some space. Finally she said, 'Then it's good that you're doing it here. I have your father's surfboard up at my house. I'll arrange to get it to you. I'm late. See you soon.'

Sam stood there and watched her leave. He couldn't help himself and he gave up the fight to enjoy the sight. She had a determined little walk, as if she were on a mission, and trying hard to disguise the feminine wiggle, but he could see it. A smile stretched across his face. Yep. The receding figure didn't look back. He hadn't expected her to. But still, it was a nice way to start the day. Ellie Swift. She was still doing his head in. He had to admit it felt novel to be excited about seeing a woman again. Could it be that after only these few days here he was finding his way to coming back to life?

He hadn't made any progress as far as breaking through her barriers went. Maybe he was just out of practice. But the tantalising thing was that, despite coming from different directions, he sensed the rapport, their commonalities, the fact that inherently they believed in the same values. And he was so damnably attracted to her. He loved watching her at work and would have liked to have seen the woman outside work hours. He didn't understand her aversion to having a friendly relationship with him, but that was her right and he respected it. Thank goodness for work. He'd see her in an hour. He grinned.

Ellie disappeared from sight and Sam strode up the beach to

scoop up his towel from the sand. He rubbed his hair exuberantly and stopped. Breathed in deeply. Felt the early sun on his skin, the soft sea breeze, and he glanced back at the water. The sun shone off the pristine white sand and the ocean glittered. He'd needed this break badly. He hadn't enjoyed the world so much as he had since he'd come here. Life had been grey and closed off to him since Bree's death.

The only light in his long days had been the progression of his patients' pregnancies to viable gestation—so that, even if the babies were born prematurely, it was later in the pregnancy and, unlike his and Bree's children, they had a fighting chance. Other people's surviving children had helped to fill the gaping hole of not having his own family.

Now this place was reminding him there was a whole world outside Brisbane Mothers and Babies. He really should phone his dad and thank him for pushing him to come here.

Thursday night, the nightmare came back again and Ellie woke, breathless and tear-stained, to the phone ringing.

That was a good thing. She climbed out of bed and wiped the sweat from her brow. She grabbed for the phone, relieved to have something else to drive the remnants of the nightmare away. 'Hello?' Her voice was thick and wavered a little.

'Sorry, Ellie. Need you for a maternity transfer. Prem labour.'

Her brain cleared rapidly. 'Be there in five.' That sounded much more decisive. She was in no fit state to walk in the dark but she'd have to. Hopefully a frog wouldn't do her in. Ellie dragged off her high-necked nightdress and pulled on a bra and trousers. Her shirt was in the bathroom and she stumbled through to get it, glancing at her face in the mirror. Almost composed.

But her hands shook as she buttoned her shirt all the way up. Damn nightmares.

She dragged her thoughts away from the dream. 'Who's in prem labour?' Ellie muttered as she ran the comb through her hair. The fringe was sweaty and she grimaced. It wasn't a fashion show and she'd find out who soon enough.

When she reached the hospital, swinging her big torch, she saw the Lexus. Dr Southwell. Trina had called him in as well.

If she thought of him like that, instead of as Sam, there was more distance between them and she was keeping that distance at a premium. That was what she liked about midwifery—nothing was about her. She could concentrate on others, and some 'other' must be well established in labour for Trina to call the doctor as well as Ellie.

She made a speedy pass of the utility vehicle parked at an angle in front of the doors as if abandoned in a hurry. Her stomach sank.

She recognised that car from last year because it had the decals from the fruit market on it.

Marni and Bob had lost their first little girl when she'd been born in a rush, too early. It had all happened too fast for transfer to the hospital for higher level of care, too tragically, and at almost twenty-three weeks just a week too early for the baby to have a hope to survive. Marni had held the shiny little pink body on her skin, stroking her gently, talking through her tears, saying as many of the things she wanted to say to her daughter as she could before the little spirit in such a tiny angel's body gently slipped away.

There had been nothing Ellie could do to help before it was too late except offer comfort. All she'd been able to do was help create memories and mementoes for the parents to take home because they wouldn't be taking home their baby.

Ellie had seen Marni last week. They'd agreed about the fact that she needed to get through the next two weeks and reach twenty-four weeks, how she had to try not to fear that she was coming up to twenty-three weeks pregnant again. That a tertiary hospital couldn't take her that early if she did go into labour. This was too heartbreaking. When Ellie walked into the little birth room her patient's eyes were filled with understandable fear that it was all happening again.

She glanced at Bob chewing his bottom lip, his long hair tousled, his big, tattooed hand gripping one of Marni's while the other hand dug into the bed as if he could stop the world if only it would listen. Old Dr Rodgers would have rubbed their shoulders and said he was so sorry, there was nothing they could do. So what *could* they do?

Marni moaned as another contraction rolled over her.

Sam looked up and saw Ellie, his face unreadable. He nodded at the papers. 'We're transferring. Marni's had nephedipine to stop the contractions and they've slowed a little. I've given IV antibiotics, and prescribed the new treatment we've just started at our hospital for extreme prematurity with some success, but we need to move her out soon before it hots up again. Are you happy to go with her?' There was something darkly intense about the way he said it. As if daring her to stand in his way.

'Of course.' What did he mean? If he was willing to try to save this baby and fight for admission elsewhere, she'd fly to the moon with Marni. But he knew as well as she did that most of the time other hospitals didn't have the capacity to accept extremely premature labour because they wouldn't be able to do anything differently when the baby was born. Too young to live was too young to live. 'They've accepted Marni?'

His face looked grim for a moment. 'Yes,' was all he said, but the look he gave was almost savage, and she blinked, wondering what had happened to him to make him so fierce.

'Ambulance should be here soon,' Trina said. She'd been quietly moving around Marni, checking her drip was secure, removing the used injection trays. She kept flicking sideways glances at Sam, as if he was going to ask her to do something she didn't know how to do, and Ellie narrowed her eyes. Had he done something to undermine her friend's confidence? She'd ask later.

Her gaze fell on the admission notes and she gathered them

up to make sure she had the transfer forms filled out. She heard the ambulance pull up outside and didn't have the heart to ask Bob to move his car. They'd manage to work around it with the stretcher.

She rapidly filled in the forms with Trina's notes, added the times the medications were given and waved to the two female paramedics as they entered.

'Hello, ladies. This is Marni. Prem labour at twenty-three weeks. We need a quick run to the base hospital. I'm coming as midwife escort.'

One of the paramedics nodded at Marni. 'Hello. Twenty-three?' Then a glance at Sam that quickly shifted on. 'Okey-dokey.' She said no more.

Ellie finished the transfer forms and disappeared quickly to pluck the small emergency delivery pack from behind the treatment room door just in case Marni's baby decided otherwise. She sincerely hoped not.

Four hours later Sam watched Ellie for a moment as she filled in paperwork at the desk. He had slipped in the back door from the main hospital and she hadn't seen him arrive, which gave him a chance to study her. Her swanlike neck was bent like the stalk of a tired gerbera. His matron looked weary already and the day had only just started. *His* matron? *Whoa, there.*

But he couldn't help himself asking, 'What time did you get back?' He knew the answer, but it was a conversation opener.

He watched the mask fall across her face. Noted he was far too curious about the cause of that wall around her and kept telling himself to stop wondering. Dark shadows lay beneath her eyes and her skin seemed pale.

She said steadily, 'Five-thirty. It was a lovely sunrise.'

Sam had thought so too—a splash of pink that had blossomed to a deep rose, and then a bright yellow beam soaring out of the cluster of clouds on the horizon over the ocean. The bay itself had already captured him, though he preferred to walk down on the pristine sand of the beach rather than along the cliff tops.

He hadn't been able to sleep after the ambulance had left so he'd sat well back from the edge on the small balcony that looked over the road and across to the headland. He'd spent time on the creakingly slow Internet catching up on his email.

By the time the ambulance had returned past his boarding house to drop Ellie back at the hospital, the sky had been pinking at the edges. She still had an hour before she started work and he'd wondered if she'd go in or if someone else would replace her after a call-out.

Now he knew. He was ridiculously pleased to see her and yet vaguely annoyed that she didn't have backup.

'How was Marni after the trip?'

Her face softened and he leant against the desk. Watched the expressions chase across her face whenever she let the wall down. He decided she had one of the most expressive faces he'd seen when she wasn't being officious. No surprises as to what she was thinking about because it was all out there for him to see.

'Of course, she was upset it was happening again. But the contractions slowed right off.' Concern filled her eyes and he wondered who worried about her while she worried about everyone else. He doubted many people were allowed to worry about her.

Her voice brought him back. 'How do you think she'll go?' She looked at him as if he could pull a miracle out of his hat. It was harder doing it long distance but he'd damn well try. Marni would have the benefit of every medical advance in extreme premature labour from his resources he could muster, every advance he'd worked on for the last four years, or he'd die trying. He wouldn't let *her* down.

'My registrar will arrange for the new drug to be forwarded to Marni and they'll start her on that. The OG at the base hospital will put a cervical suture in tomorrow if she's settled. And she'll stay there in the hospital until she gets to twenty-four weeks, and then after a couple of weeks if everything stays settled she can come home and wait. I'll phone today and confirm that plan with the consultant, and will keep checking until she's settled and sorted.'

'What if she comes in again then? After she comes home?'

Then they would act as necessary. 'We transfer again. By then the baby will be at an age where he or she can fight when we get a bed in a NICU.'

'We didn't get to twenty-four weeks last time.' Worry clouded her eyes.

He resisted the urge to put his hand on her shoulder and tell her to stop worrying. He knew she'd push him away. But the really strange thing was that he even wanted to reach out—this need for connection was new in itself.

He had this! He'd never worried about a response from a woman he was trying to reassure before and wasn't sure how to address it. Or even if he wanted to. Instead he jammed his hand into his pocket and jiggled his keys while he kept his conversation on the subject she was interested in. 'With treatment and persistence, we will this time.'

'Then they're lucky you're here.' Now she looked at him in the way he'd wanted her to since he'd met her. But this time he didn't feel worthy.

But he forced a smile. 'Finally—praise. And now I'm going.' The sooner he did the clinic, the sooner he could come back and check on her.

Ellie watched him walk away. Marni was lucky. She didn't feel so lucky, because a nice guy was the last thing she needed. Why was he being so friendly? She couldn't trust him no matter how nice he was. He'd be here in her face for another three weeks, that was all. Then he'd never come back. Why had his father had to break his arm and send the son?

She closed the file with a snap. Life was out to get her.

She heard the plaintive thought even though she didn't say it out loud and screwed her face up. *Stop whining*, she scolded herself and stood up. *We are lucky to have him. Very lucky.*

But she couldn't help the murky thoughts that were left over from the nightmare. The next day was always a struggle when she'd had the dream. And sometimes it meant she'd get some form of contact from Wayne, as if he was cosmically connected to her dream state so that she was off-balance when he did contact her.

'Hello, my lovely.' Myra's cheerful voice broke into her thoughts and thankfully scattered them like little black clouds blown away by a fresh breeze. Then the smell of freshly brewed coffee wafted towards her from the stylish china mug Myra was holding out for her.

'I hear you had a call-out so I've brought you a kick-start. Though it's not much of a kick.' She grimaced with distaste at the sacrilege of good coffee. 'Half-strength latte.'

Ellie stood up and took the mug. The milky decoration on top looked like a rose this morning. Ellie blew a kiss to the silver-haired lady who always looked quietly elegant in her perfectly co-ordinated vintage outfits. She reminded Ellie of the heroine from a nineteen-twenties detective show, except with silver hair. Myra had said that the only things she'd missed when she'd moved to Lighthouse Bay from Sydney were the vintage clothes shops.

Ellie sipped. 'Oh, yum.' She could hug her friend and not just for the coffee. Myra always made her feel better. 'Just what I need. Thank you. How are you?'

'Fine. Of course.' Myra seated herself gracefully in the nurse's chair beside Ellie. 'I'm going away for the weekend, this afternoon—' she looked away and then back '—and I wondered if you'd feed Millicent.'

'Of course.' Myra's black cat drifted between both crofts anyway and if Myra was away Millicent would miaow at Ellie's front door for attention. 'Easily done. I still have tinned food from last time.'

'Thank you.' Myra changed the subject. 'And how are you going with our new doctor?'

Ellie took another sip. Perfect. 'He seems as popular with the women as old Dr Southwell.'

Myra looked away again and, despite her general vagueness due to lack of sleep from the night before, Ellie felt the first stirrings of suspicion. 'I know you like him.'

'Sam and I have coffee together every morning. A lovely young man. Very like his father. What do *you* think of him?' There was definitely emphasis on the 'you'.

Myra was not usually so blunt. Ellie's hand stilled as she lifted it to have another sip. 'He seems nice.'

'Nice.' Myra rolled her eyes and repeated, 'Nice,' under her breath. 'He's been here for nearly a week. The man is positively gorgeous and he has a lovely speaking voice.'

Ellie pulled a face. Really! 'So?'

For once Myra appeared almost impatient. 'He's perfect.'

Ellie was genuinely confused. The cup halted halfway to her mouth. 'For what?' Maybe she was just slow today.

Myra's eyes opened wide, staring at her as if she couldn't believe Ellie could be so dense. 'For you to start thinking about young men as other than just partners of the women whose babies you catch.'

'As a male friend, you mean? You seem awfully invested in this doctor.' A horrible thought intruded into her coffee-filled senses. Surely not? 'Did you have anything to do with him coming here?'

Her friend raised one perfectly drawn eyebrow. 'And what influence could I possibly have had?'

It had been a silly thought. Ellie rubbed her brow. She tried to narrow her eyes to show suspicion but suspected she just looked ludicrous. The glint of humour in Myra's eyes made her give up the wordless attempt. So she said instead, 'You seemed pretty cosy with his father last time I saw you.'

Myra ignored that. 'And what have you got against young Dr Sam?' She produced a serviette, and unwrapped a dainty purple-tinted macaroon and placed it precisely on the desk in front of Ellie. She must have retrieved it from the safety of her apron pocket. The sneaky woman knew Ellie couldn't resist them.

'Ooh, lavender macaroon.' Briefly diverted, Ellie put down her cup and picked up the macaroon.

Myra was watching her. She said again, 'He seems a conscientious young man.'

Ellie dragged her eyes from her prize. 'Think I said he was nice.' She looked at the macaroon again. She'd had no breakfast but was planning on morning tea. 'He's too nice.' She picked it up and took a small but almost vicious bite. Sweetness filled her mouth and reminded her how she could be seduced by pretty packages. Wayne had been a pretty package... Her appetite deserted her and she put the remainder of the biscuit back on the plate with distaste.

'Poor macaroon.' There was affectionate humour in Myra's voice. 'Not all men are rotten, you know.'

Ellie nodded. Myra always seemed to know what she was thinking. Like her mother used to know when she'd been a child. Ellie didn't want to risk thinking she was a part of Myra's one-person family. Myra would move on, or Ellie would, and there was no sense in becoming too attached. But she suspected she might be already. It was so precarious. Ellie could manage on her own very well. But back to the real danger—thinking a man could recreate that feeling of belonging. 'I've met many delightful men. Fathers. And grandfathers. The other sort of relationship is just not for me.'

'It's been two years.'

This was persistent, even for Myra. 'Are you matchmaking? You?' She had another even more horrific thought. 'Did you and old Dr Southwell cook this up between you?'

'I hardly think Reginald—whom I would prefer you didn't call *old* Dr Southwell—would break his arm just to matchmake his son with the midwife at the hospital.'

Ellie narrowed her eyes. 'So neither of you discussed how poor Ellie and poor Sam could be good for each other?'

Myra threw up her hands in a flamboyant gesture that was a little too enthusiastic to be normal. 'For goodness' sake, Ellie. Where do you get this paranoia?'

She hadn't answered the question, Ellie thought warily, but she couldn't see why the pair of them would even think about her that way. She was being silly. Still, she fervently hoped Dr Southwell Senior hadn't mentioned her as a charity case to his son. That would be too embarrassing and might just explain his friendliness. A charity case...please, no.

Myra left soon after and Ellie watched her depart with a frown. Thankfully, she was diverted from her uncomfortable suspicions when a pregnant woman presented for her routine antenatal visit, so the next hour was filled. Ellie liked to add an antenatal education component if the women had time. She was finding it helped the women by reducing their apprehension of labour and the first week with the baby after birth.

Then a woman on a first visit arrived to ask about birthing at Lighthouse Bay instead of the base hospital where she'd had her last baby and Ellie settled down with her to explain their services. Word was getting out, she thought with satisfied enthusiasm.

The next time Ellie turned around it was lunchtime and she rubbed her brow where a vague headache had settled. She decided lack of sleep was why she felt a little nauseated and tried not to worry that it could be one of the twelve-hour migraines that floored her coming on.

Renee's husband arrived, armed with a bunch of flowers, and with their children hopping and wriggling like a box full of field mice, to visit Mum. The way his eyes darted over the children and the worried crease in his forehead hinted that Renee might decide to leave her safe cocoon early and return to running the family.

Ellie suspected the new mum was becoming bored with her room anyway and could quite easily incorporate her new princess into the wild household and still manage some rest.

It proved so when a relieved father came back to the desk to ask what they needed to do before discharge.

'It's all done. Renee has a script for contraception, baby's been checked by the doctor, and she's right to go.'

The relief in his face made Ellie smile at him despite the pain now throbbing in her head. 'Did you have fun with the kids, Ned?'

He grimaced. 'Not so much on my own. They've been good, but...'

Ned carried the smallest, a little carrot-topped boy, and an armful of gift bags out of the ward doorway with a new purpose and possibly less weight on his shoulders. Two more toddlers and a school-aged boy carrying flowers appeared from down the ward, with Renee bringing up the rear with her little princess in her arms, a wide smile on her face.

The foyer in front of the work station clamoured with young voices, so Ellie missed Sam as he returned from clinic and stood at the side of the room.

'Thank you, both,' Renee said. 'It was a lovely holiday.' She was looking past Ellie to the man behind her.

Ellie turned in time to see her new nemesis grin back. She didn't have the fortitude to deal with the 'charity' overtones left from Myra, so she turned quickly back again.

'I think you may be busy for a while,' Sam said to the mother.

Renee nodded calmly and then winked at Ellie. Lowering her voice, she confided, 'It does Ned good to have them for a day or two—lets him see what it's like to be home all day with the darlings in case he's forgotten.'

CHAPTER FOUR

THE AUTOMATIC DOORS closed behind the big family and they both watched them disappear. Sam turned and Ellie saw that flashing smile again. 'Imagine juggling that mob! It wouldn't be dull.'

There was a pause but she didn't say anything. She couldn't think of anything to say, which was peculiar for her, and had a lot to do with the fact that her vision had begun to play up. Small flashes of light were exploding behind her eyes. Migraine.

He filled the silence. 'Do you enjoy watching the women go home with their new babies?'

'Of course. That's a silly question!' He was looking at her with a strange, thoughtful intensity but she was too tired to work it out. She really wasn't in the mood for games. 'Don't you?'

'It isn't about me.' He paused, as if something was not right. 'I'm wondering why a young, caring woman is running a little two-bit operation like this in a town that's mostly populated with retirees and young families.'

Go. Leave me so I can will this headache away. Her patience stretched nearly to breaking point. 'Me?' She needed to sit and have a cup of tea and maybe a couple of headache tablets. 'Our centre is just as efficient as any other centre of care. What's the difference between here and the city? Are you a "tertiary hospital or nothing" snob?'

'No.' He looked at her. '"Tertiary hospital" snob?'

'Size isn't everything, you know.'

He raised his brows at her. 'I'm very aware of that. Sorry. I was just wondering when you were going to be one of these women coming in to have your perfect little family.'

That stung because she knew it wasn't a part of any future waiting for her on the horizon. Though it should have been. 'There is no perfect little family.'

She looked at him coldly, because abruptly the anger bubbled and flared and her head hurt too much to pretend it wasn't there. 'Where's your perfect little family? Where are your children?'

Lordy, that had sounded terrible. She felt like clapping her hand over her mouth but something about his probing was getting right up her nose.

He winced but his voice was calm. 'Not everyone is lucky enough to have children. I probably won't have any, much to my father's disgust. You're a midwife with empathy pouring out of every inch of you, just watching other women become mothers.'

Easily said. She closed her eyes wearily. 'There's no difference between you and me.'

He didn't say anything and when she opened her eyes he shook his head slowly. 'I saw the way you looked at Renee's baby. And Josie's. As if each one is a miracle that still amazes you.'

'And you?' She waved a listless hand. 'There's nothing there that spells "misogynist and loner".'

He physically stepped back. 'I really shouldn't have started this conversation, should I?'

'No.' She stood up and advanced on him. She even felt the temptation to poke him in the chest. She didn't. She never poked anyone in the chest. But the pressure in her head combined with the emotion, stresses, and fear from the last few days—fear for Marni's baby, her horrible fear of frogs and this man who was disrupting her little world—and she knew she had a reason to be running scared. Add lack of sleep and it wasn't surprising she had a migraine coming on like a fist behind her eyes.

Stop it, she told herself. She closed her eyes again and then looked down. She said with weary resignation, because she knew she was being unreasonable, 'Sorry. Can you just go?'

She didn't know how she could tell he was looking at her despite the fact she was considering his shoes. His voice floated to her. 'I'm sorry. My fault for being personal.'

That made her look up. He actually did look apologetic when it was she who was pouring abuse like a shrew and had lost it. Her head pounded. She felt like she was going to burst into tears. Actually, she felt sick.

She bolted for the nearest ladies' room and hoped like hell there wasn't a frog in the sink.

Afterwards, when she'd washed her face and didn't feel much better, she dragged herself to the door, hoping he had gone. Of course, he hadn't; he had waited for her outside in the corridor.

'You okay?'

'Fine.' The lights behind her eyes flickered and then disappeared into a pinpoint of light. She swayed and everything went dim and then black.

Sam saw the colour drain from Ellie's face, the skin tone leeching from pink to white in seconds. His brain noted the drama of the phenomenon while his hands automatically reached out and caught her.

'Whoa there,' he muttered, and scooped her up. She was lighter than he expected, like a child in his arms, though she wasn't a tiny woman with her long arms and neck that looked almost broken, like a swan's, as she lay limp in his embrace.

Unfortunately there was no denying the surge of protective instinct that flooded him as he rested her gently on the immaculate cover of the nearest bed. He'd really have to watch that. He was already thinking about her too much when he wasn't here, when in fact it was unusual for him to feel anything for anybody at all.

Her damn collar was buttoned to the neck again—how on earth did she stand it?—and he undid the first and second buttons and placed his finger gently against her warm skin to feel the beating of her carotid artery.

Her skin was like silk and warmer than he expected. She must be brewing something. Sudden onset, pallor, faint... He didn't know her but she hadn't struck him as the fainting type... Before he could decide what to do she groaned and her eyelids fluttered. Then she was staring up at him. Her blue eyes were almost violet. Quite beautiful.

'Where am I?'

He glanced at the sign on the door. 'Room one.'

She drew her dark brows together impatiently. 'How did I get here?'

'You fainted.'

The brows went up. 'You carried me?' He quite liked her brows. Amusing little blighters. Her words penetrated and he realised he was going mad again. She was the only one who did that to him.

He repeated. 'You fainted. I caught you. Can't have you hitting your head.' She struggled to sit up and he helped her. 'Slowly does it.'

'I never faint.'

He bit back the smile. 'I'm afraid you can't say that any more.'

She actually sagged a little at that and he bit back another smile. Behind her now not-so-tightly buttoned collar, which she hadn't noticed he'd unbuttoned, she wasn't the tough matron she pretended to be. She was cute, though he'd die rather than tell her that. He could just imagine the explosion. 'Stay there. I'll get you some water.' He paused at the door. 'Did you eat breakfast this morning?'

She passed a hand over her face. 'I can't remember.'

'I'll get you water and then I'll get you something to eat.' He could already tell she was going to protest. 'You made me coffee on Monday. I can do this for you. It'd be too embarrassing to fall into my arms again, right?'

She subsided. The fact she stayed put actually gave him a sense of wicked satisfaction that made his lips curve. *Tough luck. My rules this time.*

With a stab of painful guilt that washed away any amusement, he remembered he hadn't looked after Bree enough, hadn't been able to save her, or his own premature children. But maybe he could look after Ellie—at least for the month he was here.

He heard her talking to herself as he left. 'I'll have to get a relief midwife to come in.'

He walked out for the water but didn't know where to get the glass from. He'd have to ask her, so was back a few seconds later.

She was still mumbling. 'I'll be out for at least twelve hours.'

He stopped beside the bed. 'Does your head hurt?'

She glared at him. 'Like the blazes. I thought you were getting water.'

'Cups?'

'Oh. Paper ones on the wall beside the tap.'

Ellie closed her eyes as Sam left the room. How embarrassing! She hadn't fainted in her life and now she'd done it in front of a man she'd particularly wanted to maintain professional barriers with. She'd never fainted with a migraine before. Oh, goody, something new to add to the repertoire.

Where was Myra when she needed her? She wished Sam would just leave. Though when he returned with the water she gulped it thirstily.

'Go easy. I don't have a bowl or know where they live.'

Ellie pulled the paper cup away from her lips. He was right. She was still feeling sensitive but her throat was dry and raw. She sank back against the pillows. She'd have to strip this bed because she'd crumpled it.

Maybe the weekend midwife could come early. This afternoon. She'd meant to go shopping for food and now she knew she didn't have the energy. She'd just hole up until tomorrow, when she'd be fine. The thoughts rolled around in her head, darting from one half-considered worry to another.

'Stop it.'

She blinked. 'Stop what?'

'Trying to solve all the logistical problems you can see because you do everything around here.'

'How do you know I'm thinking that?' It came out more plaintively than she'd expected. How did he know she did do most things?

He looked disgustingly pleased with himself. 'Because the expressions on your face mirror your every thought. Like reading a book.'

Great. Not! 'Well, stop reading my book.'

'Yes, ma'am.' But his eyes said, *I quite like it*.

She reached down into her fast fading resources. 'If you would like to help, could you please ask Myra to come around from the coffee shop?'

'Myra has left for the weekend. Going away somewhere. There's a young woman holding the fort, if you would like a sandwich.'

Her heart sank. Clarise... Clarise could make toast, which might help, but she'd have to do everything else herself. 'Already? Damn.'

'Can I do something for you?' He spread his hands. 'I've done all my homework.'

Ellie looked at him. Tall, too handsome, and relaxed with one hand in his pocket. Leaning on the door jamb as if he had all the time in the world. She had a sudden picture of him in his usual habitat surrounded by a deferential crowd of students, the man with all the answers, dealing with medical emergencies with swift decision and effectiveness. She had no right to give this man a hard time. Her head throbbed and the light was hurting her eyes. Now she felt like crying again. Stupid weakness.

His voice intruded on her thoughts and there was understanding in his eyes, almost as if he knew how much she hated this. 'You look sad. Is it so bad to have to ask me for help?'

My word, it is. 'Yes.'

Of course he smiled at that. 'Pretend I'm someone you hired.'

'I don't have to pretend. I did hire you.'

He laughed at that. 'Technically the administration officer hired me.'

'That would be me.'

'So what would you like me to do?'

She sat up carefully and swung her legs over the bed. He came in closer as if to catch her if she fell. It was lucky, because her head swam and she didn't want to smack the linoleum with her face.

'Just make sure I make it to the desk and the phone and the rest I can manage. Maybe you could stay in case anyone else comes in while we wait for my replacement. Even I can see there's no use me being here if I can't be trusted not to fall on my face.'

'Especially when it's far too pretty a face to fall on.'

She looked at him. Narrowed her eyes. 'Don't even go there.'

He held up his hands but she suspected he was laughing at her again. Together they made their way over to the desk and with relief she sank into her usual chair. She reached into her handbag, pulled out her sunglasses and put them on. The pain from the glare eased.

It only took an hour for her replacement to arrive but it felt like six. She just wanted to lie down. In fact her replacement's arrival had been arranged faster than expected, and was only possible because the midwife had decided to spend an extra day at Lighthouse Beach, on the bay, before work.

Ellie had sipped half a cup of tea. She'd taken two strong headache tablets and really wanted to sink into her bed. Standing at the door with her bag over her arm, she wasn't sure how she was going to get up the hill to her croft.

'I'll drive you.'

He was back. And he'd read her mind again. She wished he'd stop doing that. He'd left for an outpatient in the other part of the hospital after Ellie had assured him she'd be fine until the relief midwife arrived and she had been hoping to sneak away.

She'd have loved to say no. 'If you don't mind, I'll have to take you up on that offer.'

'So graciously accepted,' he gently mocked.

He was right. But she didn't care. All she could think about was getting her head down and sinking into a deep sleep.

He ushered her to his car, and made sure she was safely tucked in before he shut the door.

'Do you always walk to work?'

'It's only at the top of the hill.' She rested her head back against the soft leather headrests and breathed in the aroma of money. Not something she'd sniffed a lot of in her time. 'I always walk except in the rain. It's a little slippery on the road when it's wet.'

'Did you come down in the dark, last night?'

She didn't bother opening her eyes. 'I have a torch.'

'You should drive down at night.'

Spare me. 'It's two hundred and fifty metres.'

He put the car into gear, turned up the steep hill and then turned a sharp left away from the lighthouse, onto the road with three cottages spaced privately along the headland. 'Who owns the other ones?'

'I'm in the first, Myra is the end one and the middle one is Trina, so try not to rev your engine because she's probably sleeping.'

'I'll try not to.' Irony lay thick in his voice. He parked outside the first cottage and turned the car off. She'd hoped she could just slip out and he'd drive away.

They sat for a moment with the engine ticking down. Ellie's headache had reached the stage where she didn't want to move and she could feel his glance on her. She didn't check to see if she was imagining it. Then she heard his door open and the car shifted as he got out.

When her door opened the cool salt air and the crash from the waves on the cliffs below rushed in and she revived a little.

Sam spoke slowly and quietly as if to a frightened child. 'If you give me the key, I could open the door for you?'

'It's not locked.'

'You're kidding me?' The words hung in disbelief above her. Apparently that concept wasn't greeted with approval. He said in a flat voice, 'Tonight it should be.'

She held her head stiffly, trying not to jar it, and turned in the seat. She locked it at night but the daytime was a test for herself. She would not let her life be run by fear. 'Thank you for the lift.'

He put out his hand and Ellie wearily decided it was easier just to take it and use his strength to achieve a vertical position. Her legs wobbled a bit. He hissed out a breath and picked her up.

'Hey.'

'Hey, what?' A tinge of impatience shone through.

'You'll fall down if you try to walk by yourself.'

And then she was cradled tight against his solid warm chest and carried carefully towards her door. He leant her against the solid wood and turned the handle, then they were both inside.

Sam had expected the inside to be made up of smaller compartments but it was a big room that held everything. There was a tiny kitchen at the back with a chimney over the big, old wood-burner stove. A shiny gas stove and refrigerator stood next to it and a scrubbed wooden table and four chairs.

A faded but beautiful Turkish rug drew the sections of the home together in the middle where it held a soft cushioned sofa with a coffee table in front that faced the full-length glass doors out to sea. Bookshelves lined the rear walls and a couple of dark lighthouse paintings were discernible in the corners. There was a fireplace. A big red-and-white Malibu surfboard leant against the wall. His father's. He looked at it for a moment then away.

A patchwork-quilted wooden bed sat half-hidden behind a floral screen, pastel sheets and towels were stacked neatly in open shelves and across the room was a closed door which he presumed was the bathroom. Nothing like the sterile apartment he'd moved into after Bree's death and where he'd never unpacked properly.

The bed, he decided, and carried her across and placed her gently on the high bed's quilt.

'Come in,' she said with an exhausted edge to her voice as he put her down. Talk about ungrateful.

He stepped back and looked at her. She looked limp, with flushed spots in her pale face. Still so pale. Pale and interesting. She was too interesting and she was sick. He told himself she was a big girl. But that didn't mean he liked leaving her. 'Can I make you a cup of tea before I go?'

'No, thank you.'

He sighed and glanced at the room behind him again, as if seeking inspiration. He saw his dad's surfboard again. He'd said the midwife was minding it for him and that Sam should try it out. Maybe he would one day. But not today. It would be a good reason to come back.

He glanced through the double-glazed doors facing the ocean and he could imagine it would be a fabulous sight on wild weather days. But it was also too high up and exposed for him to feel totally comfortable. And she lived here alone.

He thought about the other two crofts and their occupants. It was a shame Myra was away.

'How about I leave a note for Trina and ask her if she'll check on you later?' *Before she goes to work for the night and leaves you up here all alone,* he added silently.

'No, thank you.' Her eyes were shut and he knew she was wishing him gone.

She was so stubborn. Why did he care? But he did. 'It's that or I'll come back.'

She opened her eyes. 'Fine. Leave a note for Trina. Ask if she'll drop in just before dark. I'll probably be fine by then.'

Sounded reasonable. Then she could lock the door.

That was all he could do. He saw her fight to raise her head and tilt it meaningfully at the door and he couldn't think of any other reason to stay.

He walked to the sink. Took a rinsed glass from the dish rack and filled it with water. Carried it back without a word and put it beside her. Then he felt in his pocket, retrieved his wallet and took out a business card. 'That's my mobile number. Ring me if you become seriously ill. Or if you need medication. I'll come. No problem.'

Then he tore himself away and shut the door carefully behind him, grimacing to himself that he couldn't lock it. Anybody could come up here and just waltz in while she was sleeping. Surely she locked it at night?

When he went next door and wrote on another of his business cards, he decided he should at least see if he could hear if Trina was awake. He walked all the way around the little house. Because he could. It was just like Ellie's, though there was a hedge separating them from each other and the cliff path that ran in front of the houses.

Anybody could walk all the way around these houses. The view was impressively dramatic, except he didn't enjoy it. The little crofts clung to the edge of the cliff like fat turtles and the narrow walkway against the cliff made his mouth dry.

At least the dwellings looked like they wouldn't blow off into the sea. They were thick-walled, with shutters tied back until needed for the really wild weather. Daring the ocean winds to try and shift them.

He was back at the front door again. No sounds from Trina's. She could sleep right through until tonight. He'd have to come back himself. Before dark, like Ellie had said.

Sam drove back down the hill to his guesthouse. He let himself in the quaint side entrance with his key and up the stairs to his balcony room. He threw the keys from his pocket onto the dresser, opened the little fridge, took out a bottle of orange juice and sipped it thoughtfully as he walked towards the windows.

She'd sleep for a while. He wished she'd let him stay but of course she'd sleep better without him prowling around. He knew it was selfish because if he'd been there he wouldn't have had to worry about her. Being away from her like this, he couldn't settle.

He felt a sudden tinge of remorse that made him grimace, an admission of unfaithfulness to Bree's memory. It hung like a mist damning him, because he was so fixated on Ellie, but also underneath was a little touch of relief that he was still capable of finally feeling something other than guilt and devastation.

His father would be pleased. He'd say it was time to let go of the millstone of his guilt over Bree, that it was holding him back and not doing the memory of their relationship justice. Was it time finally to allow himself the freedom to feel something for someone else?

His heartbeat accelerated at the thought but he told himself it would all be fine. He was only here for another few weeks, after all, and he'd be heading home after that. Strangely, the time limit helped to make him feel more comfortable with his strange urge to look after Ellie.

The sun shone and turned the blue of the ocean to a brilliant sapphire and he decided he'd go for another swim. No wonder his dad had raved about this place. Then he'd go back and check on Ellie after he'd showered.

CHAPTER FIVE

ELLIE HEARD SAM close the door when he left. She pulled the blanket up higher to calm the shudders that wracked her body. He'd been very good, and she should have said thank you, but the headache had built steadily again. It was easier to breathe in and out deeply, to make it go away and wait for sleep to claim her, and then maybe she'd wake up and all this would just have been a bad dream. Her hair was heavy on her forehead and she brushed it away. She was too disinclined to move to take a sip of the water he'd put there. Mercifully, everything faded.

When she fell asleep she had the nightmare.

She moaned because her head hurt as well.

Slowly the afternoon passed. As evening closed in the nightmares swirled around her, mixed themselves with imagined and remembered events.

But while she slept her troubled sleep there were moments when she felt safe. Moments when she felt a damp, refreshing washcloth on her brow. She dreamt she sipped fluid and it was cool and soothing on her throat. Even swallowed some tablets.

The bad dream returned. Incidents from her time with Wayne mixed in with it. Incidents from their spiral downhill flashed through her mind: cameos of her hurt and bewilderment when he'd barely spoken to her, mocked and ridiculed her...her phobia, her need for nurturing. Screaming he never wanted a family that time she'd thought she was pregnant. *All* she wanted was a family.

The dream flashed to the afternoon at the swimming pool again and she moaned in the bed. Twisted the sheets in her hand.

She fought the change room door. Ran into the boys outside...

She sobbed. She sobbed and sobbed.

'It's okay, sweetheart. Stop. My God. It's okay.'

The words were seeping through the horror and the mists of sweat and anguish. Sam's voice. His arms were around her. Her head was tucked into his chest, her hair was being stroked.

'Ellie. Wake up. It's a dream. Wake up!'

Ellie opened her eyes and a shirt button was pressing into her nose. A man's shirt.

'It's okay.' It was Sam's voice, Sam's big hands rubbing her back. A man's scent. So it must be Sam's shirt. Sam?

She was still foggy but clearing fast. What was he doing here? She pushed him away.

His hands moved back and his body shifted to the edge of the bed from where he'd reached for her. 'That's some nightmare.'

She brushed her damp hair out of her face, muttered, 'Why are you here?'

'Because Trina is at work, Myra's away and I wasn't sure you wouldn't get worse.'

He raised his brows and shook his head. 'You did get worse. It's almost midnight and you've been mumbling and tossing most of the evening. If you didn't get better soon I was going to admit you and put up a drip.'

Dimly she realised her head didn't hurt any more but it felt dense like a bowling ball, and just as heavy. It would clear soon, she knew that, but she couldn't just lie here crumpled and teary. The tendrils of the nightmare retreated and she wiped her face and shifted herself back up the bed away from him, pushing the last disquieting memories back into their dark place in her brain at the same time.

As she wriggled, he reached and flipped the pillows over and rearranged them so she could sit up.

Then he rose. She wasn't sure if that was better because now he towered over her, and it must have shown on her face, because he moved back and then turned away to walk to the kitchen alcove.

He switched on the jug, turned his head towards her and said quietly, 'Would you like a drink? Something hot?'

Her mouth tasted like some dusty desert cavern. She'd kill for a cup of tea. Maybe it wasn't so bad he was here. 'Yes, please. Tea?' She sounded like a scared kitten. She cleared her throat, mumbled, 'Thank you,' in a slightly stronger voice. She glanced down at her crumpled uniform but it was gone and she was in her bra and pants. Her face flushed as she yanked the covers up to her neck.

'You took off my shirt and trousers?'

'You were tangled in them. Sweating. I asked you and you said yes.'

She narrowed her eyes at him. 'I don't remember that.'

He came back with the mug of tea. 'I'm not surprised. You've been barely coherent. If that's a migraine, I hope I don't get one. Nasty.'

'I can't believe you undressed me.'

He waggled his brows. 'I left the essentials on.'

Her face grew even hotter. *Cheeky blighter.*

He put the tea down beside her. 'Do you have a dressing gown or something I can get you?'

'In the bathroom, hanging behind the door.' She took a sip and it tasted wonderful. Black. Not too hot. He must have put cold water in it so she didn't burn her tongue. That was thoughtful. While she sipped he poked his head into the little bathroom and returned with her gown.

Speaking of the bathroom… She needed to go, and imagined taking a shower. Oh, yes…that wouldn't go astray either if she could stay standing long enough to have it. The idea of feeling fresh and clean again grew overpoweringly attractive.

'Um... If you turn around, I'd like to get up.'

He considered her and must have decided she had more stamina than she thought she had because he nodded.

'Sure.' He crossed his arms and turned around, presenting his broad back to her. She shifted herself to the edge of the bed and swung her legs out. For a moment the room tilted and then it righted.

'You okay?' His voice came but he didn't turn. At least he played fair.

'Fine.' She took another breath, reached down and snatched clean underwear and a nightgown from the drawer beside her bed and stood up on wobbly legs. By the time she shut the door behind her in the bathroom, she was feeling better than she expected. *Good tea.*

By the time she showered and donned her nightdress and dressing gown again, she was feeling almost human.

When she opened the door the steam billowed into the room and for a moment she thought the cottage was empty. But he was sitting on the sofa with his head resting back and she remembered he'd been here all evening.

Guilt swamped her and she padded silently towards him to see if he'd fallen asleep. His eyes were definitely open as she tipped her head down to peer at him. There was a black cat at his feet. She'd forgotten Myra's cat.

'Did you feed Millicent?'

He patted the sofa seat beside him. 'Yes. She had sardines. You look better. I'll go soon, but first tell me about your dream.'

Instinctively she shook her head but she saw there were two cups and her teapot on the low table in front of him. She could do another civilised cup of tea after he'd been so good.

She remembered his arms, comforting her, making her feel safe, as though she were finding refuge from the mental storm she'd created from her past, and her cheeks heated.

She pulled her dressing gown neckline closer and sat gingerly a safe distance along the sofa from him. 'Thank you for looking after me,' she said, and even to her own ears it sounded prim and stilted.

'You. Are. Very. Welcome.' He enunciated slowly as if to a child, and she glanced at him to see if he was making fun of her. There was a twinkle, but mostly there was genuine kindness without any dramatics.

She glanced back at the bed. It was suspiciously tidy. And a different colour. 'Did you change the sheets?'

'I did. The damp ones are on the kitchen chair. Where is your laundry in your little hobbit house?'

She had to smile at that. 'Does that make me a hobbit?'

'If so, you're a pretty little hobbit.'

'That's a bit personal between a doctor and a patient, isn't it?'

He waggled his finger, making the point. 'You are my friend. Definitely not my patient. I'm glad I didn't have to admit you.'

She wasn't quite sure how to take that and then he said very quietly, 'But listening to you suffer through those dreams was pretty personal. You nearly broke my heart.'

She moved to rise but he touched her arm. 'As your non-doctor friend, can I say I think now is a really good time for you to share your nightmares. Stop the power they have over you.'

She shivered but she subsided and glanced around the room. Anywhere but at him. The dish rack was empty. No dirty dishes. Distractions would be good. 'Have you eaten?'

He patted his flat belly. 'I ate early, before I came. In case I needed to stay. But I've helped myself to your tea.'

His arm came out and quite naturally he slid it around her waist. Bizarrely her body remembered that feeling, although her memory didn't, as he pulled her snug up against his firm hip. 'Tell me. Was it frogs?'

She shuddered. 'It's a long story.'

She felt him shrug under her. 'We have many hours until morning.'

She looked at him. 'It's not that long a story.'

He chuckled quietly, and it was an 'everything is normal even though we are sitting like this in the dark' sound, and despite the unconventional situation she felt herself relax against him.

'I'm all ears,' he said.

She turned her head and looked at him. 'They're big but I wouldn't say you are *all* ears.'

'Stop procrastinating.'

So she told him about the frog in the change room at school and the boys and, hearing it out loud for the second time since the therapist, she felt some of the power of it drain away. It was a little girl's story. Dramatic at the time but so long ago it shouldn't affect her now. In the cool quiet of the morning, with waves crashing distantly, she could accept that the frog was long dead and the little boys were all probably daddies with their own children now. That quite possibly Sam's idea of repeating it now could have merit because it seemed to have muted its power.

He said thoughtfully, 'If you could go back in time, to the morning before that, if you could prepare that little girl in some way, how could you help that young Ellie? What would you tell her?'

She thought about that. Wondered about what the misty memory of her mother might have said to her as a little girl if she had known it was going to happen.

'The frog is more frightened than you are?' The words came from some distant place she couldn't recognise but with them came a gentle wave of comfort. Relief, even. She thought of the child that she had been all those years ago. Sad eyes under the pony tail, freckles, scuffed knees from climbing tress to get away from teasing boys.

'If I had the chance. That might help her,' she said, and looked at Sam.

Sam nodded and squeezed her shoulder. 'So it was the same dream. Over and over?'

She looked at the floor. 'The other one's an even longer story and I don't think I'm up to that tonight.'

He looked at her and she shifted under his scrutiny. 'Okay. So, will you invite me back?'

Why on earth would he want to come back after these last exhausting hours? 'For frog stories?'

He shrugged again. 'There doesn't have to be stories. Can't I come back because I'd like to come back?'

She felt the shift in herself. Felt the weight of his arm, suddenly unbearable. Could almost imagine the bricks all slamming together between them, creating a wall like a scene in a fantasy movie.

Her voice was flat. Different from what it had sounded like only minutes ago. There was no way he could miss the change. 'You live in Brisbane. Your world is different to mine. We'll never be friends.' She tried to shrug off his arm and after a moment he let it fall. He shifted his body away to give her space and she appreciated his acceptance.

He looked at her and suddenly she felt the wall go up from him as well. Contrarily, she immediately wanted the openness that had been there before. Served her right.

But his voice was calm. It hadn't changed like hers had. 'I disagree. Friends can be made on short acquaintance. I'd like to come back later today and just check you're okay.'

Was he thick? Or just stubborn? How did she say no after he'd sat up here and minded her? Made her tea? After all, he would be gone in a few weeks. 'Did you give me water and wipe my face?'

He nodded. 'I didn't think you'd remember that. You weren't awake.'

'There were parts of the dream that weren't all bad.' She looked at him. 'It gets cool here in the night. Were you warm enough?'

He gestured to the throw folded at the end of the sofa. 'If somebody had visited, they would have found a very strange man wearing a blanket.'

She digested that and said simply, 'Thank you.' She shook her head because she couldn't understand the mystery of his actions. 'Why did you stay?'

He shrugged. As if it was nothing special. No mystery for him. Lucky him. 'Because I didn't know if you would actually ring me if you needed help. You might have needed someone and I couldn't see anyone else coming.'

He'd stayed out of pity. The thought sat like dirty oil in the bottom of her stomach. She shouldn't have been surprised, because she was alone. No family. No husband. 'So you felt sorry for me.'

Sam compressed his lips as if being very careful about what came out of his mouth. She could live with the truth as long as it *was* the truth.

'I had sympathy for you, yes. You were unwell. I hope you would have done it for me if the roles had been reversed.'

She thought about that. Narrowed her eyes. 'Maybe. That's a sneaky way of wriggling out of the "pity" accusation.'

He sighed. Stood up. 'I'm tired. And I might yet get called out. I'm going home. I'll drop back before lunch and see how you are.'

'You could just call me on the phone to check on me.'

He studied her. 'I'll drop back after I do a round at the hospital.'

She stood up, careful to keep distance between them. 'You don't have to do rounds on the weekend. Only if they call you.'

He shrugged. 'Patients are still there. I'll do a round every day unless I can't.' He gestured to the corner of the room. 'You should go back to bed. I think you'll sleep better now.' Then he walked to the door, opened it and quietly closed it after himself. She heard the lock click.

* * *

Sam walked away but his thoughts remained focussed on the little cabin on top of the hill. There was something about Ellie, and this place, that connected so strongly with his emotions. He didn't know what it was about her that made him feel so anxious to help. Shame he hadn't been able to break through the barriers to Bree the way he seemed to be able to with Ellie, especially as for the last few years he hadn't really connected to anyone. He glanced out over the bay as he walked down the hill to the hospital. The lighthouse seemed to look down on him with benevolence.

CHAPTER SIX

ELLIE WENT BACK to the bed. Climbed into the clean sheets that a man she'd only known for less than a week had changed for her. She saw the hospital corners and wondered who'd taught him to make a bed like that. It certainly wouldn't have been med school. She looked at the half-full glass of water he'd left her in a fresh glass.

Then she thought of the fact she'd been in her underwear when she'd woken properly, and wondered with pink cheeks when he'd undressed her. Had she helped him, or fought him, or been a limp lump he'd had to struggle with? Had she missed the opportunity of a lifetime?

She frowned at the random and totally inappropriate thought. How on earth would she face him? Then stopped herself. *It's done. You're not eight years old now.*

She considered the result of holding in the swimming pool incident for all those years and even now the tragedy was fading. When Sam returned to Brisbane she'd be able to thank him for that, too.

Her eyes closed and it didn't happen immediately but eventually she drifted off and, strangely, she didn't dream at all.

The next morning was Saturday. Ellie woke after the sun was well and truly up and lay with her eyes open for several minutes as she went over the recent events, both hazy and clear, and how a man who was almost a stranger had taken control of her world, if only for a few hours.

Even a few days ago the idea of that happening would have been ludicrous but in the cold light of day she could be grateful if a little wary. He'd been circumspect, really. Except for taking off her uniform but then she would have done the same if she'd been nursing someone in the throes of sweaty delirium. She tried not to think of stripping off Sam's shirt and trousers if he was sick—but the option to expand her imagination was tantalising her. *No!*

She glanced at the clock. Almost ten. He said he'd drop in after his weekend round.

When she put her feet on the ground her head didn't hurt. The headache had gone. It had disabled her but now her step was steady as she made her way into the bathroom with an armful of clothes.

By the time she came out, hair piled into a towel, teeth cleaned and mouth washed, she was starting to feel the emptiness in her belly and a hankering for fresh air.

As she opened the door to let the world in, Sam was standing outside with his phone in his hand.

That would be Sam who had seen her frogs and all. Sam who looked ridiculously handsome. Sam who'd carried her into her bed. 'Oh. Hello. Have you been here long?'

'Just a few minutes. I knocked and when you didn't answer I was going to ring you.'

She opened her eyes wide. 'Do you have my number?'

'The relief midwife gave it to me when I said I might check on you again.'

Confidentiality clauses and all that obviously didn't hold much water when it was Sam asking. Nice of her, she thought sourly. But sensible too. 'I'm much better, thank you.'

She examined him in the bright morning light. Tall. Smiling like he was glad to see her. She shied away from that thought.

Not too many shadows under his eyes, considering his onerous midnight duties. 'How are you after spending the evening with a raving woman?'

'Starving.' He gestured to the plastic shopping bag that hung from his hand. 'Any chance of a table and chairs where I can lay this out?'

'Food?' Her stomach grumbled and heat ran up her cheeks. She peeked at him from under her eyelashes to see if he'd heard and saw he was biting his lip. She could see the dimple at the side where he was holding it in.

He'd heard her stomach. Not much mystery left about her for this guy. 'Okay. I'm hungry. So in that case you are very welcome.' Although as she said it she remembered she hadn't made her bed yet, then mentally shrugged.

He'd changed the blinking sheets. He'd survive an unmade bed. 'We'll take it through to the front deck. We can open the doors from the inside.'

Sam followed her and she was very conscious that the collar on her long-sleeved top wasn't as high as normal and there was some cleavage showing. Maybe she should put on a scarf? Again she reminded herself that he'd seen her in her bra and pants so any more than that was not a concern.

She sighed. He had the advantage of more knowledge of her than she had of him and she didn't like it. In fact she wasn't sure how she'd ended up with a guy who knew so much stuff about her and was walking around in her house like he owned it.

Before he followed her out onto the little veranda, he paused. 'Can I put my milk and cold things in your fridge? I came straight here from the supermarket, but have a few supplies for my flat as well.'

'Sure. There's plenty of room in the fridge.' Ellie winced a little at the hollow emptiness of the food supplies in her kitchen. She needed to shop and restock the cupboards herself.

When he'd done that he followed her to the balcony that overlooked the ocean. She noticed he hesitated at the door.

As he stood there he said quietly, 'Who built these cottages? The view is incredible.'

She stopped and looked in the direction he was looking, sweeping her gaze over the little cliff top that held the three tiny homes, the expanse of the sea out in front of them with the wheeling gulls and fluffy white clouds, the majesty of the tall, white lighthouse on the opposite ridge, which drew visitors on Sundays for lighthouse tours, its tiny top deck enclosed by a white handrail for the visitors as they examined the internal workings of the light through the windows.

'The cottages were built for three spinster sisters in the middle of the last century. They were all nurses at the hospital down the hill.'

She laughed. 'Myra said that the three of us who live here now are modern day reincarnations. Their father ran the lighthouse and when they were in their mid-twenties the eldest came into some money and had the cottages built. There's only one of them alive now. I visit her sometimes in the nursing home. She's ninety and sharp as a tack. Just frail and happy to have other people make her meals now.'

'So they lived here, unmarried, until they were too old and then they moved out?'

'Yep. Fabulous, isn't it?' There were privacy hedges between the three dwellings. In the past the sisters had kept the hedge levels down below waist height but since she'd moved in they'd grown and it was their own little private promontory over the ocean. She loved it. She moved to the edge and peered out at a ship that was far away on the horizon.

When she turned back she could see that Sam was looking uncomfortable and she glanced around to see why. 'You okay?'

'Not a fan of being at the edge of heights.'

'Oh.' The last thing she'd do was make someone with a phobia uncomfortable. 'We'll go back inside, then.'

'No. Just sit me on this side of the table and I'll be fine.' He lifted the bags up and placed them on the little outdoor table. 'It's perfect here.'

She smiled at him. 'As we dwell in Phobia Central.'

For some silly reason she felt closer to him because he'd admitted to having a weakness for heights. It made her feel not so stupid with her phobia of frogs. She had a sudden horrid thought that perhaps he'd made that up, just to get into her good graces, and then pushed the thought away.

Wayne had done that.

But Sam was not like Wayne. She pushed harder on the thought and it bobbed around in her mind like a cork in a bathtub. She couldn't make it stay down. Sam was not like Wayne, she repeated to herself. Sam told the truth. She hoped.

As if he could read her thoughts, Sam said, 'My aversion to heights is not quite a phobia but I might not be particularly keen to fix the aerial on the roof.'

Somehow, that helped. 'And I'll never be a plumber because of the frogs. You're a good doctor. That's enough.'

'I'm a doctor but not your doctor.' He grinned at her. 'That said, I'm pretty impressed with your recovery mechanism.'

She shrugged. 'I don't get many migraines but when I do get one it's bad.' She didn't add that they usually came after she had the nightmare, or had forced contact with Wayne, and that she'd had fewer nightmares and migraines since she'd shaken him off her trail.

'I can see they wipe you out. If it happens again, you could call me.'

Yeah, right. 'All the way from Brisbane?' She raised her brows at him. At least she knew he was joking. 'Good to know.'

She began laying out the fresh rolls and ham as she reminded herself he'd be gone in a few weeks. Maybe she could just enjoy his company while she had it. It was the first time she'd had a man in her house to share lunch since she'd moved in. Not that she could take any credit for him being here. The only reason it had happened was because he'd invited himself.

It was strange but pleasant. Mostly because she knew it was just a window of opportunity that would close soon when he went back to where he'd come from. Back to his busy trendy life with its 'double shot espresso and milk on the side' lifestyle.

Sam paused as if to say something but didn't. Instead he opened a tray of strawberries and blueberries and produced a tub of Greek yoghurt. 'I'll grab the plates and spoons.' He headed back inside and Ellie looked after him.

'I guess you know where they are,' she murmured more to herself. Then she lifted her voice. 'And grab the butter out of the fridge, please.'

This was all very domestic. Apparently there was nothing like being undressed when semi-delirious for breaking down barriers. But what was she supposed to say? *No. That's my kitchen! Stay out!*

Sam was back while she was still staring after him and mulling over the phenomenon of his intrusion into her world.

He looked so at ease. 'You're very domesticated. Why aren't you married?'

His face stilled. 'My wife died four years ago. It's unlikely I'll marry again.' Then he looked down at the food in his hands.

Oh, heck. 'I'm sorry.' Then added almost to herself, 'Don't you hate that?' The last words fell out as if she hadn't already put her foot in her mouth enough.

He looked up. 'Hate what? When wives die?' He was looking at her quizzically, when really she deserved disapproval. But underneath the lightness of tone was another wall. She could see it as plain as the sun on the ocean below. She knew about walls.

She'd done it again. Talk about lacking tact. She'd said what she thought without thinking. She wasn't usually so socially inept but there was something about this fledgling relationship… She paused at that thought and shied away, slightly horrified.

Anyway… 'I'm making it worse. Of course it's terrible your wife died, but I meant when you ask a question and the worst possible scenario comes back at you and you wished you'd never opened your mouth.'

'I know what you mean. Forget it. A *Monty Python* moment.'

His eyes were shadowed and she hesitated. His wife must have been young. She couldn't help herself.

'How did your wife die?'

He looked up, studied her and then glanced away. 'I'll tell you some time.' Then without looking at her, 'Why do people ask that?'

Now she felt even more inept. Crass. He had answered her and deserved an answer himself. 'I don't know. Curiosity. Because they're afraid of their own mortality?'

That made him look up. 'Are you afraid of your own mortality?'

She shrugged. 'That's a heavy question for eleven in the morning.'

'Heavy question any time of the day,' he said quietly.

The silence lay thick between them. He straightened and looked like he'd wait all day until she answered.

So she did. 'No. I'm not afraid to die. I'm not that special that the world will weep when I'm gone.'

A flash of what looked like pain crossed his face. 'Don't say that. Don't ever say that. Everyone is special and the world will always weep when someone leaves it.'

A breeze tickled her neck from the ocean and she shivered. This conversation was the pits. 'Can we just talk about the weather?'

He stopped. He looked at her and then slowly he smiled, mocking them both. 'Sure. There's a very nice ocean breeze sitting out here.'

She smiled at him primly. Relief rolled over her like one of those swells away down below running in towards the cliffs. A hump. They'd managed to get over a hump. One that she'd caused. 'I like the way the clouds make shadow patterns on the ocean.'

He glanced at the blue expanse a long way below, then away. 'Yes, very nice.'

She looked at the food spread out. Okay. Now it was awkward. 'Eat.'

So they ate. Conversation was minimal and that kept them away from such topics as death and dying, which was fine by Ellie, and gradually their rapport returned and desultory conversation became easy again.

Sam said, 'Josie went home.'

She looked up. 'Did you do the new-born check?'

'Of course.' A pained look. 'Very efficiently.'

That made her smile. 'I have no doubt.' She took a bite of her roll and chewed thoughtfully. She swallowed, then said, 'When you return to your real world in your hospital will you make sure all of your registrars are proficient at checking new-born babies prior to discharge?'

He shrugged. 'There's a little less time for leisurely learning than there is here but I will be asking the question.' He pretended to growl, 'And they'd better be able to answer it.'

Which made her remember that he was a very distinguished and learned man, one many people looked up to, and she was eating rolls with him and treating him like a barely tolerated servant. *Oops.*

She put her roll down. 'Speaking of questions I've been meaning to ask... Do you know anything about midwifery-led birthing units? Do you think it would work here?'

He paused eating his own meal. 'I don't know. Work how?'

She shrugged, looking around for inspiration, how to explain her dream. 'It would be wonderful if we could provide a publicly funded service for pregnant women that didn't need locums.'

'Gee, thanks.' He pretended to be offended.

'Nothing personal. But cover isn't consistent.' She grinned at him. 'I'd like to see a proper centre for planned low-risk births here without having to rely on locum doctors to ensure we can have babies here.' She was gabbling. But she half-expected him to mock her and tell her she was dreaming, that big centres were more financially viable—although she already knew that. But he didn't mock her. She should have had more faith.

'There are models like that springing up all over New South Wales and Victoria.' He said it slowly, as if he was searching around in his mind for what he knew. Ellie could feel herself relax. He wasn't going to tell her she was mad.

He went on. 'Not so many in Queensland yet, but I'm hearing that mothers and midwives are keen. But you'd need more staff.' He gestured to the isolation around them. 'You're a bit of a one-man band here.'

She'd get help. She'd already had two nibbles from the weekend midwives to work here permanently. And why not? A fulfilling job right on the ocean and the chance to become a respected part of a smaller community wasn't to be sniffed at. Trina and Faith were also in.

'We may be a small band at the moment. Or possibly five women, anyway—Trina, Faith, and I and the weekend midwives from the base. If we changed our model of care we could attract more midwives. We would certainly attract more women to birth here if we offered caseload. Most women would love to have the option to have their own midwife throughout the whole pregnancy and birth. Then get followed by them for the next six weeks after the baby is born. It's a wonderful service.'

He studied her for a moment as if weighing up what he was going to say. 'It would be a great service.'

She sagged with relief.

Then he went on, 'Though it does sound demanding for the midwives, seeing as babies come when they want and pregnant women have issues on and off for most of the forty weeks. If one person was responsible for all that—and I imagine you'd have a caseload of about twenty women a year—it seems a huge commitment and would almost certainly affect your private life. Are you prepared for that?'

Private life? What private life. She was a Monday-to-Friday, love-my-job romantic. Not the other sort. But she didn't say any of that.

Instead she said, 'We are. And, paperwork wise, I have a friend who has just set up a service like that on the south coast. She said she'd come up and help me in the early stages. And Myra was a legal secretary before she bought her restaurant. She said she'd give me one day a week.'

'So you have gone into it a bit.' He nodded. Paused. 'And how are you going to deal with emergencies?'

'The same way we deal with them now—stabilise and transfer if needed. But the women will be healthy and the care will be excellent.'

'I have no doubt about that,' he said, and the genuine smile that accompanied the statement warmed her with his faith when he barely knew her.

This wasn't about her as a woman. This was about her as a midwife and she could take compliments about that. 'It's women's choice to decide how and where they want to meet their baby, and women here have been asking for that choice.'

It was so satisfying to have this conversation with somebody who at least understood the questions and the reasons behind them. So she didn't expect the turn when it came.

'Very ideological. So you're going to submerge yourself even deeper in these new families—be available for more times when you're needed—because in my experience babies tend to come in waves. Slow and then all at once. You'll be working sixty hours a week. Be the auntie to hundreds of new babies over the next thirty years.'

What was he getting at?'

Her smile faltered. 'I hope so.'

His brows were up. She didn't like the expression on his face.

'And wake up at sixty and say "Where has my life gone?"?'

'No.' She shook her head vehemently. 'I'll wake up at sixty and feel like I'm having a life that enriches others.'

The mood plunged with her disappointment. She'd thought

he'd seen the vision but now he was looking at her like she needed psychiatric help. Like Wayne used to look at her. That was sad and it was stupid of her to have thought he would be different.

Ooh... Ellie could feel the rage build. Somewhere inside she knew it was out of proportion to what he'd said. That if she chose that path it didn't mean she'd never have a family of her own. But him saying that seemed to ignite her anger.

She leaned towards him. 'How is that different from your life? You said yourself you're probably not going to marry again or have children. Will you spend the next thirty years working? How is that different to me?'

He shrugged. 'I'm a man. It's my job to work till I'm sixty-five or seventy, so it should be rewarding.'

'You're a chauvinist. My working life deserves reward too. How about you stay barefoot and pregnant and make my dinner while I go to work? Is that okay?'

Sam had no idea how the conversation had become so heated. One minute it had been warm and friendly—she'd been gradually relaxing with him—and then she'd waxed on about giving the rest of her life to strangers like some first world saint and he'd found himself getting angry.

He needed to remind himself that he was a man who respected women's choices, and of course he respected her choice. She was right. He should recognise that what she wanted to do was parallel to his own ambition of single-minded dedication. And look how useless that had been for getting over Bree's death. Maybe it was because he did recognise himself in what she said that he'd reacted so stupidly to seeing it through her eyes.

He took one look at her face and concluded he needed to redeem himself fast or he'd be out on his ear with his blueberries in his lap.

He held up both hands in surrender. 'I'm sorry. I have no

right to judge your life decisions. You should choose your path and do whatever fulfils you. Truce.'

Her open mouth shut with a click and he knew he'd just averted Armageddon. Wow.

She was a feisty little thing when she didn't like what he said. And, come to think of it, what the heck had come over him? If she wanted to grow old in this eyrie of a house, alone every night just living for her work, then that was her choice. A small voice asked if that wasn't his choice too. He might not live on top of a cliff, but it wasn't so different from his trendy city flat overlooking the Brisbane River that he barely saw and the twenty-four-seven availability he gave his own hospital.

He'd known her for less than a week and already he was sticking his nose in. Normally he didn't even see other people and what they were doing with their lives but the idea of Ellie's future life made him go cold. It sounded very like his and he wanted more for her. He shivered.

She sat stonily staring out over the ocean and he could discern the slow breaths she was taking to calm down. Typical midwife—deep breathing experts. His mouth twitched and he struggled to keep it under control. Imagine if she saw him laughing at her.

They were both being silly. Fighting about the next thirty years when they should be enjoying the present moment. He was here with a gorgeously interesting woman. He wasn't sure when she'd changed from pretty to gorgeous, but the word definitely fit her better. The sun was drying her dark hair, bringing out red highlights, and the ocean stretched away behind her. He liked the way her hair fell heavily on her neck when she didn't have it in the pony tail. He could remember the weighty silkiness of it in his hand as he'd held it off her face as he'd soothed her during her nightmare.

He remembered unbuttoning her shirt when she'd lifted her hand to her buttons as if the neckline and collar were choking her. He'd slipped the whole shirt off her shoulders, and she'd pushed at her buttoned work trousers, so he'd helped her with those too. She'd relaxed back into the cool sheets with relief and he'd covered her up, trying to blot out the delectable picture of her golden skin in lacy bra and briefs. Feeling a little apprehensive about what she'd say to him when she woke.

'You.' She turned towards him and his little flight of fantasy crashed and burned. Apparently the deep breathing hadn't worked.

'Tell me how your wife died!' There was nothing warm and fuzzy about the request.

That snapped him out of his rosy fantasies and the guilt he mostly kept at bay from his failure to save Bree swamped him. He didn't know why he answered her.

'She killed herself.'

CHAPTER SEVEN

'IT LOOKED LIKE a parachute accident. Except she left a note.' He kept staring at his clenched fingers. Didn't look at her. He couldn't believe he'd said that to a stranger and opened himself up to the inevitable questions.

Ellie's voice was a whisper. 'Oh, heck.' Closer than before. 'Why would she do that?'

He figured he might as well get the rest out. Be done with it. 'Because we lost our third baby at twenty weeks' gestation and she said she couldn't go on.' His voice was flat because if he let the emotion in it would demolish him. His inability to help his own family had destroyed Bree. 'I was next to useless, and using work to bury my own grief, and she refused to talk about it together. We drifted apart. Each suffering in our own way but unable to connect. Then it was too late.'

Her voice was different now. Compassionate. 'Is that why you were so determined Marni be transferred?'

He jerked back to the present with the question. Her thought processes were way different to his. He took a deep breath of his own. Was that the only satisfaction he'd had in the last four years?

Sam thought about what she'd asked. It had kept him sane, having a mission. 'Probably. Since Bree died I've been work-

ing on a regime for women who have repeat extreme premature labours, and the results have been promising with the new
treatments.'

When he looked up from his hands he saw she was beside
him. Her voice was soft. 'Your way of managing the grief?'

'Or the guilt.' Why was he talking about this? He never spoke
about Bree. Her hand touched his shoulder as she bent over him.
It was feather-light but he felt the pressure as if it was burning
into him like a hot coal through ice. Melting him.

'What was she like? What did she do? Your dad must have
been upset as well.'

'Before the babies Bree was happy. A great paediatrician,
wonderful with kids. Afterwards...' he paused and shook his
head, speaking so quietly it was as if he'd forgotten she was
there. 'She hid her depression using work too. We both did. She
said she wanted more space. When she died my dad felt almost
as bad as I did that we hadn't seen it coming. So it was tough
for him as well.'

She leant her head down and put her face against his hair.
'I'm sorry for your loss.' Her lemony freshness surrounded him
like angel dust as she reached down and hugged him.

Nobody had hugged him since Bree had died. His dad was
more of handshake kind of guy and he didn't have any women
friends. Then she slid her hands around his shoulders, pulled his
head onto her chest and stroked his hair. Her hands were warm
whispers of comfort, infused with empathy. 'I'm so sorry. But
it's not your fault.'

He twisted his head and looked at her, saying very slowly
and deliberately, his voice harsh and thick, 'You've got as much
right to say that as I had to say you can't waste your life the way
you're planning to.'

He thought she'd draw away at that. He hoped she would because the scent was fogging his brain and the emotions of the
last few minutes were far too volatile for bodily contact. All
those fantasies he'd been battling with since he'd arrived in this

damn place were rising like mist off the ocean. She was holding him close. Pulling him in like a siren on a rock. Drowning him.

She pressed her face against his. 'I should never have asked. We're both too nosy.' She kissed his cheek as if she couldn't help herself. 'I'm sorry.'

If he'd thought her enticing while he watched her from a distance, up close she was irresistible. The scent of her, the feel of her, the warmth of her, was intoxicating, and when she leaned in to say something else he lifted his mouth and captured hers as it passed. She stilled—she tasted like the first day of spring.

She'd made it happen. The kiss had been an apology. A dangerous one. Kissing Sam was a mistake because when he kissed her back driving him away was the last thing on her mind.

Somehow she was on his lap, both her arms were around his hard shoulders, and he was holding her mouth against him with a firm palm to the back of her head.

Inhaling his scent, his taste, his maleness was glorious. The kiss seemed to go on and on even though it was only a minute. His mouth was a whole subterranean world of wonder. In heated waves he kissed her and she kissed him back in time to the crash of the ocean below—rising and falling, sometimes peaking in a crest and then drawing Ellie down into a swirling world she was lost in...one she hadn't visited before. Until the phone rang.

It took a few moments for the sound to penetrate and then she felt his hand ease back.

He pulled away but his eyes were dark and hot as he watched her blink. She raised her trembling fingers to her lips.

His voice was deep, too damn sexy, and he smiled at her in a way that made her blush. 'Your phone is ringing.'

She blinked. Scrambled off his lap. 'Right.' She blinked again and then bolted for the phone while all the time her mind was screaming, *what the heck made you start that?*

It was the weekend midwife, Roz. 'Can you come, Ellie? One of the holidaymakers from the caravan park is in labour. Just walked in. Thirty-five weeks. Twins. Feeling pushy. I'll ring the doctor next.'

'Twins! Sam's here. I'll bring him. We'll be there in three minutes. Get help from the hospital to make some calls. Get them to ring the ambulance to come ASAP.'

Ellie strode to the door where Sam was collecting dishes away from the edge from his side of the table. 'Let's go, Sam. Thirty-five-week twins. Second stage.' Ellie was pulling on her sneakers. She could put a surgical gown over her clothes.

Sam matched Ellie's calm professional face. 'My car's outside.'

They were there in less than two minutes. Just before they arrived, Sam said, 'Ellie?'

She looked at him. She was still off-balance but immensely glad her mind could be on a hundred things other than what position she'd been in and where that could have led only five minutes ago.

This was an emergency. She'd had two sets of twins when she'd been working with a midwife in the centre of Australia. She'd need to watch out for so many things in the coming hour. They had very little equipment for prems. They'd either have a birth of two premature babies here or a harrowing trip to the base hospital. Twin births could be tricky.

'Ellie?'

'What?'

Sam's voice was so calm. 'This is what I do. Thirty-five-week twins are fine. Not like pre-viable twins. Everything will be fine.'

Ellie felt the tension ease to a more useful alertness. He was asking for a little faith in the team. She smiled at him. 'Okay. You're right.'

A dusty campervan with flowers and a slogan painted on it sat haphazardly in the car park. There was no sign of anyone as they hurried through the doors to the maternity unit but sounds coming from the birthing rooms indicated action.

'We'll just use the one neo-natal resuscitation trolley. The other's too slow to heat up and warmth will be the issue.' Ellie was thinking of the babies. The twins could stay together if they needed help. They'd been closer than that inside their mum and might even comfort each other if kept together.

The obstetric part, Sam could handle. Thank goodness. The mother might not feel lucky at the moment but she was.

They entered the room one after the other and the relief on Roz's face would have been comical if the situation hadn't been so serious. 'Her waters just broke. Nine centimetres. At least it's clear and not meconium-stained.'

Then Roz collected herself. Glancing apologetically at the mother and father, she explained, 'Dr Southwell's an obstetrician from Brisbane Mothers and Babies, and this is the midwife in charge here, Ellie. This is Annette and Paul Keen.'

Everyone tried hard to smile at each other. Sam succeeded and Ellie gave them a wave on her way to sort out the required equipment in case they needed to resuscitate either baby or, heaven forbid, both.

Roz was reciting, 'Annette's twins were due in five weeks. They were packing up from the park to go home today. Labour started an hour ago but she thought she had a tummy bug because Paul had one a few days ago.'

Annette opened her mouth to say hello and changed it to a groan as the next wave of contraction hit her. She ground out, 'I feel like pushing.'

Sam stepped closer to the bed. He looked into the terrified woman's face as she sat high in the bed with lines of strain creasing her face and touched her arm. 'I'm Sam. It's okay, Annette, we've got this. You just listen to your body and your babies, let go of the fear and we'll do the rest. It's their birthday.'

Ellie's hands paused on the suction as she heard his voice and in that moment realised what she was missing in her life. A safe harbour. It would never be Sam, but just maybe someone somewhere might be out there for her, someone like this man who could invest so much comfort in words and took the time to offer them. Such a man would be worth coming home to. She wondered if he had always been such a calming influence. Whether he'd grown to understand a parent's fears since his own loss.

'It's my fault,' Paul mumbled from the corner of the room as he twisted his hands. 'I should never have pushed for this holiday before the babies were born. It's my fault.' Ellie glanced his way but it looked like nobody else had heard him.

Roz bent down and placed the little Doppler on Annette's stomach. First one and then, after she shifted to the other side of Annette's magnificent belly, another heartbeat echoed around the room.

Sam nodded, patted Annette's arm, turned, walked to the sink and washed his hands.

Ellie checked the oxygen and air cylinders were full and then moved to Paul's side. She spoke very quietly so no one else could hear. 'You heard the doctor, Paul. The time for worrying is gone. Now is the time to be the rock Annette needs you to be. Hold her hand. Share the moment. You're about to be a father.'

Paul's eyes locked on hers and he nodded jerkily. 'Right. Rock.' He looked at his hand and scurried over to his wife. He took up her fingers and kissed them. 'Sorry. Lost it for a minute.'

Annette squeezed his hand and Ellie saw the man's fingers go white. Saw Paul wince as the pressure increased and with a smile her eyes were drawn to Sam as he stood quietly at the side of the bed with his gloved fingers intertwined, waiting. As if they had all the time in the world and this was a normal day. She felt the calm settle in the room and smiled quietly to herself.

Roz folded back the sheets to above Annette's thighs.

The first twin came quickly, a fine scattering of hair on her head, a thick coating of white vernix covering her back, and then she slipped into Sam's waiting hands. Not as small as they'd feared, probably over two thousand, five hundred grams, which was good for a twin.

The little girl feebly protested at the brush of air on her skin until Ellie wiped her quickly with a towel and settled her against her mother with a warmed bunny rug over her back. Annette's hands came down to greet her as she shifted the sticky little body so she could see her. The mother's face was round with wonder.

'Oh, my. Hello, little Rosebud.'

Ellie smiled to herself at the name, actually appropriate for the pink pursed mouth, and positioned the tiny girl strategically to make room for the next baby, making sure her chin was angled to breathe easily.

Ellie slipped a pink knitted beanie on the downy head. The soft cap was too big but would do the job of keeping her little head warm and slow the loss of heat. When she glanced at Paul, tears were sliding down his cheeks as he gazed in awe at his wife and new daughter.

Annette's brows drew together but this time she was confident. 'I need to push again.'

Paul started, and Ellie grabbed another towel and blanket from the stack Roz had collected under the warmer. They all waited.

'This one's breech,' Sam said quietly.

The contraction passed and they all waited for the next.

Annette breathed out heavily and Ellie looked down and saw the little bottom and scrotum inching out, the cord falling down as the belly and back eased up in a long sweep. First one leg sprang free and then, finally, the other leg. It was happening so fast. The contraction finished and they all waited.

'Going beautifully,' Sam murmured two minutes later as the pale shoulders rotated and birthed one by one, followed by the arms, in a slow dance of angles and rotations that magically happened the way nature intended thanks to the curves of his mother's pelvis.

Ellie stood awed at how quickly the baby was delivering by himself.

Sam hadn't touched the torso. His gloved fingers hovered

just above in case baby took a wrong turn as it went through the normal mechanisms and she remembered the mantra 'hands off the breech'. He was certainly doing that.

Then, unexpectedly, the rapid progress stopped. Annette pushed again. Just the head to come, Ellie thought. *Come on.* Annette was still pushing.

'Deflexed head,' Sam muttered and glanced at Ellie. He slipped his arm under the baby's body to support it and gently felt for the face with his lower hand. With the hand she could see he placed his second and fourth fingers on each side of the baby's nape at the back.

'Annette. We need to flex the baby's head for birth. I'm going to get Ellie to push on your tummy just above the pelvic bone.'

Annette hissed an assent as she concentrated.

Sam went on. 'Ellie, palpate just above the pelvic brim. You'll feel the head. Lean on that ball firmly while I tip baby's chin down from here.' He glanced at Annette. 'Don't be surprised if baby needs to go to the resus trolley for a bit to wake up, okay?'

Paul's eyes widened. Annette nodded as she concentrated. Ellie could feel the solid trust in the room and marvelled how Sam had achieved that in so short a time. It was worth its weight in gold when full co-operation was needed.

Sam's firm voice. 'Okay, push, Annette. Lean, Ellie.'

Ellie did as she was asked and suddenly the head released. Baby's chin must have shifted towards his chest, allowing the smaller diameters of the head under the pubic arch and through the pelvis, and in a steady progression the whole head was born. Sam expelled a breath and Ellie began to breathe again too.

The little boy was limp in Sam's hands.

Paul swayed and Roz pushed the chair under him. 'Sit.' The dad collapsed back into the chair with his hand over his mouth.

Sam quickly clamped and cut the cord and Ellie reached in, wiped the new-born with the warm towel and bundled him up to transfer to the resuscitation trolley. 'Come over when you're up to it, Paul,' she said over her shoulder as she went.

Sam spoke to Roz. 'Can you take over here, Roz? Call out if you need me.' He followed Ellie.

Ellie hit the timer on to measure how long since birth, and dried the new-born with another warm towel to stimulate him, but he remained limp.

Sam positioned the baby's head in a sniffing position and applied the tiny mask over his chin and nose. The little chest rose and fell with Sam's inflation of the lungs through the mask.

Ellie listened to the baby's chest. 'Heart rate eighty.' She applied the little pulse oximeter to the baby's wrist which would allow them to see how much oxygen from their lung inflations was circulating in the baby's body.

'Thirty seconds since birth,' Ellie said, and leant down to listen to his heart rate again, even though the oximeter had picked it up now. 'Seventy.' If the rate fell below sixty they would have to do cardiac massage.

'Okay,' Sam said and continued watching the steady rise and fall of the small chest. They both knew it wasn't great but it also wasn't dire yet. Babies were designed to breathe. Unlike adults, new-born babies needed inflation of their lungs to start, were respiratory driven, and even more important than cardiac massage was the initiation of breathing and the expulsion of the fluid from the untried lungs.

Ellie reminded herself she had great faith in the way babies had recovered from much more dramatic births than this one.

Sam continued with his inflations for another thirty seconds, Ellie wrote down the observations and finally the baby wriggled a tiny bit. Ellie felt the tension ease. 'Come on, junior.'

'His name is Thorn.' Paul was there and he wasn't swaying. He seemed to have pulled himself together. 'Come on, Thorn,' he said sternly, staring down at his son. 'This is your dad speaking. Wake up.'

Ellie decided it was just coincidence but Thorn's blue eyes opened at the command. The baby blinked and struggled and began to cry. The pulse oximeter rate flew from eighty to a hundred and thirty in the blink of an eye and Sam eased back on the mask.

'Well, that worked,' she said and smiled at Paul. A sudden exuberance was bubbling inside her and she looked across at Sam, who grinned back at her. She guessed he was feeling it too.

'Good work, Thorn,' Roz's relieved voice called across and Ellie heard Annette's shaky relief as she laughed.

Thorn was roaring now and, after a glance at Sam and catching his nod, Ellie scooped the baby up and carried him back to his mother. He was soon nestled in beside his sister on his mother's chest.

There was a knock on the door and one of the young ambulance officers poked her head in. 'Did you guys call us?'

Sam said, 'Thanks for coming. Transfer to the base hospital, thirty-five-week twins, but we'd like to wait half an hour—check the bleeding is settled and babies stable—if you want to come back.'

'We'll have coffee. Haven't had lunch. Ring us when you're ready.' She looked to the bed. 'Congratulations.' Then she disappeared.

Ellie decided that was eminently sensible. The impact of an urgent emergency transfer of all concerned would have ruined the moment when everyone was settled. More brownie points for Sam.

She wouldn't have taken the responsibility for delaying transfer but having an obstetrician on site made all the difference. It was fabulous for Annette and Paul to have a chance to collect themselves before they had to leave.

Roz was standing beside Annette, helping her sort the babies, and Sam and Ellie went over to the sink to strip off their gloves and apply new ones.

'Rosebud and Thorn,' Sam said in an undertone, and his eyes were alight with humour.

The names clicked. 'Cute,' she whispered back, grinning, and realised this was a moment she wasn't used to—savouring the feeling of camaraderie and a sudden urge to throw her arms around Sam and dance a little.

She whispered, 'That was very exciting and dramatic. Thank goodness everything is great.'

'Ditto.' Sam grinned at her.

Normally the nurse from the hospital disappeared as soon as the birth was safely complete, and most of the locums were burnt out and uninterested, so as soon as the excitement was over Ellie didn't usually have a third person to talk over the birth with. 'I'll remember that hint with the after-coming head if I have another unexpected breech delivery,' she said now, thinking back over Thorn's birth. The two breeches she'd been present at before had progressed to birth easily.

Sam nodded sagely. 'He was star-gazing. Silly boy. You have to keep your chin tucked in if you want your head to pop out.'

Ellie bit her lip to stop the laugh. Stargazing... A funny way to say it, but clear as a bell to her. She smiled up at him as the last of the tension inside her released.

She stayed with Roz in birthing until the ambulance officers returned. Thorn and Rosebud were positioned twin style at each breast and did an excellent job with their first breastfeeding lesson in life. Besotted parents marvelled, wept and kept thanking the three staff, so much so that Sam escaped from the room to write up the transfer papers.

Just under an hour after the twins were born, Ellie and Sam stood watching as they were loaded into the back of the ambulance.

'Come back and visit us next year when you come on your holiday. We'd love to see you all.' Ellie said.

She'd offered to go in the ambulance but Roz had laughed and said she should take the easy job and stay with the empty ward. Hopefully nobody would come in. Surely they'd had their quota for the week?

Which left Ellie and Sam standing at the door, waving off the ambulance.

As the vehicle turned out of the driveway Ellie told herself to keep her mind on what needed to be done but she could feel Sam's gaze. She kept her own on the spot where the ambulance disappeared and then suddenly turned away. Over her shoulder she said, 'Thank you. You were great. I'll be fine now.'

Sam didn't move. 'So I should go?' His voice was quiet, neutral, so she had to stop or it would have been rude. But her feet itched to scoot away as fast as she could because this man was the one she had kissed. On whose lap she had squirmed and wanted more. *Oh, my*—where was she supposed to look?

She didn't decide on flight quickly enough.

Still quietly, he said, 'You don't need me any more—that right? And we both pretend this morning didn't happen? Is that what you want, Ellie?' She didn't say anything so he added, 'Just checking.' There was definite sardonic tinge to that last statement.

She forced herself to look at him. Maybe she could tell him the truth about Wayne. Because she wasn't going to pursue any crumbs of attention he wanted to give her for the next three weeks and it was all her fault this morning had got out of hand. Maybe she owed him that—telling him how she'd been made a fool of. Lied to. Ridiculed. Abused. She shuddered at the thought. Or perhaps she owed him an apology. She could do that at least.

'I'm sorry, Sam. I don't know what happened. It's all my fault, and I apologise. Can't we just blame the aftermath of my migraine for the strange behaviour on my part and forget it?'

He was studying her thoughtfully, and for so long that Ellie felt like an insect under a magnifying glass. Finally he said, 'What if I don't want to forget it? What if I want to hear the rest of your stories?'

Why would he want to do that? She couldn't do that. Should never have started it. 'You'll have to do without. Because there'll be no repeat.' She heard the finality in her voice and hoped he did too. 'I'd like you to go now, please.'

* * *

Sam looked at the woman in front of him and felt the frustration of the impenetrable wall between them yet again. The really disturbing thing was an inexplicable certainty that Ellie Swift wasn't supposed to be like this. It made no sense. He could very clearly see that underneath the prickly exterior and gazetted loner lay a warm and passionate woman he wanted to know more about. Wanted to lose himself in kissing again. And more.

That she'd had a disastrous relationship was of course the most likely reason she was like this. Underneath her armour lay something or someone who had scarred her and she wasn't risking that kind of pain again. He got that. Boy, did he get that. But it wasn't all about the frog phobia. There had to be something else.

But whether or not he'd get the opportunity to explore that conundrum and the tantalising glimpses of the woman who had reached down and kissed him with such sweetness was a very moot point.

Maybe he should just cut and run. Do what he always did when he felt things were getting too personal or emotional. But, for the first time since Bree had died, he wanted to explore the way he was feeling. Wanted to find out if this glimpse he'd had of a better life was real, or if he was just suffering from some unexpected aberration he'd forget about when he went back to the real world.

Maybe he'd better research his own reasons for pursuing Ellie first before he caused any more damage to this vulnerable woman in front of him, and it was only that overriding consideration which finally made him agree to leave. Since Bree's death he'd lost his confidence in his own emotional stability.

CHAPTER EIGHT

ELLIE WATCHED HIM go and, after having asked him to leave, now, conversely, wanted him to stay. It was the kiss that stopped her asking him to come back. Ellie had never tried to hurt anyone in her life before—so why had she hurt Sam by asking him so baldly about his wife? He was already punishing himself and didn't need her input. He'd been mortally wounded by his love—she knew how that felt—and she'd broken open his unhealed wound with her harsh request. He'd deserved none of it.

So she'd kissed him better—and to make herself feel better. Although 'better' wasn't really the right word for what she'd felt.

Ellie had an epiphany. She'd wanted to hurt him because that way she'd drive him away for her own safety—she'd had no kind thought for him.

And then they'd kissed and everything had changed. And she was running scared. It had all been pushed back by the birth of the twins but the reality was—things had changed.

Ellie sighed. It would have been good to talk more about the birth. He could have stayed for that. And that was the only reason, she told herself.

She looked around the empty ward, disorientated for a moment. Then she busied herself pushing books across the desk.

It was Sunday tomorrow and she probably needed the space

from this man. He was taking up too much room in her head. Luckily she had a whole day to get her head sorted by Monday.

She slowly turned towards the birthing unit and walked in to strip the bed. What a morning. Premature twins. That was a first for her since she'd arrived last year. Thank goodness everything had progressed smoothly.

She thought about Sam's expertise with Thorn's birth in the breech position. Sam's calmness. She wanted to cry, which was stupid. It was Sam's quiet confidence that had made them all seamless in their care and his rock-solid capability that made it so positive and not fraught as it could have been for Paul and Annette with a less experienced practitioner. How lucky they'd been that it had been Sam. She dragged her mind away from where it wanted to go.

She had to stay away from Sam's hands holding her, his lips on hers, their breaths mingled. No. If she let Sam in and he let her down like Wayne had, she suspected she'd never, ever recover.

She took herself into the small staff change room and opened her locker where she kept a spare clean uniform. She'd been stuck here before out of uniform and didn't like it.

She told herself that was the reason she needed more armour. She took off her loose trousers and blouse and pulled on the fitted blue work trousers and her white-collared shirt and buttoned it to the top. Funny how she felt protected by the uniform. Professional and capable. Not an emotional idiot throwing out accusations and making stupid moves on men who were just being kind.

What an emotional roller coaster the last few days had been. And action packed on the ward.

By rights they should have no babies for a week or more because the ward had been too crazy since Sam had arrived. Maybe he drew the excitement to him like a magnet. She grimaced. He certainly did that in more ways than one and she needed to put that demon to sleep.

By the time Roz returned Ellie had the ward returned to its pristine orderliness, and the paper work sorted and filed. Ellie stood up to leave but Roz put her hand on her arm.

Looking a little worse for wear, Roz said, 'Please stay for a bit. Have a cup of tea with me. I'm bursting to talk about it. Not often you get to see twins born without any intervention. Wasn't Dr Sam awesome?' Roz's eyes were shining and she was obviously still on a high from the birth.

Ellie didn't have the heart to leave. She put the plastic bag with her bundled civilian clothes down.

'Sure. Of course. The jug's just boiled. I'll make a pot while you freshen up if you want?'

Roz nodded and Ellie had to smile at the bouncy excitement that exuded from her.

Roz was right. This was an opportunity to think about how they'd handled the situation, what they'd done well and what they could possibly have done better. All future planning for a unit she wanted to see become one of the best of its kind.

She couldn't believe Sam had driven all her normal thought processes into such confusion. *See?* She needed to stay on track and not be diverted by good-looking doctors who had the capacity to derail all her plans.

As Ellie made a pot of tea and brought two cups to the desk she knew with a pang of discomfort that a week ago Roz wouldn't have been able to drag her away from talking about the birth and the outcomes. Maybe it was just that she'd been sick. Maybe it had nothing to do with the fact that she was running scared because a certain man had disturbed her force field and anything to do with talking about him made her want to run a mile.

'I can't get over the breech birth.' Roz was back. Her hair was brushed, lipstick reapplied and she looked as animated as Ellie had ever seen her. She could feel the energy and excitement and welcomed the uncomplicated joy Roz exuded, because joy was dearly bought.

Yes. They should be celebrating. Every midwife loved the un-expected birth that progressed fast and complication-free with a great outcome. And when it was twins it was twice as exciting.

'I just feel so lucky I was here.' Roz's eyes were glowing and Ellie felt the tension slipping away. She was glad Roz asked her to stay.

Roz went on. 'But I was super-glad when you two walked in together. Especially since, the last time I saw you, you looked like death warmed up.'

Roz stopped and thought about that. 'Did you say on the phone you were together when I called?'

Ellie fought to keep the colour out of her cheeks. 'Dr South-well had dropped in to ask if I needed anything. But I'm usually good when the migraine goes. It just takes about twelve hours. I'm feeling normal now.' Or as normal as she could, consider-ing the emotional upheavals of the last few days.

Roz studied her. 'You're still a bit pale. And I shouldn't be keeping you here on your day off. Sorry.'

'No. It's good to talk about it. You're right. You did really well getting us here, and everything was ready. You must have got a shock when they walked in and you realised you were ac-tually going to have the babies.'

Roz nodded enthusiastically, totally diverted from the how Ellie and Sam had walked in together. Thank goodness. Ellie returned her attention to Roz, cross with herself, as her brain kept wandering off topic.

'Paul was almost incoherent, Annette was still in the car and I didn't get that it was twins until she was in here and I saw how big she was. Then he said they were premature and she was booked in to have them at the tertiary hospital and I nearly had a heart attack. All I could think about was ringing you, and I was hoping like heck you'd be able to come.'

'I'm fine. But I guess we need to plan that a bit better for the future too. Maybe make a list to work down if one of the call-ins can't make it, rather than ringing around at the time when you have much better things to do than make phone calls.'

Roz nodded agreement. She said thoughtfully, 'I did get the nurse over from the main hospital, and she could have phoned around if needed.'

How it should be. 'That's great. And the babies came out well, which is always a relief.'

Roz frowned as she remembered. 'The boy was a bit stunned. Annette and Paul weren't the only ones worried.'

Ellie thought about Thorn as he'd lain unmoving under their hands, of Sam's presence beside her as they'd worked in unison, both wordlessly supporting the other as they'd efficiently managed the resuscitation. Her stomach clenched as she remembered. At the time it had been all action with no time to be emotionally involved. It was afterwards they thanked their lucky stars everything had worked out well.

That was why debriefing became important, because clearing stark pictures by talking about them and explaining the reasons let her release mental stresses.

Ellie said, 'He wasn't responding for a bit. We gave him an Apgar of three at one minute but by five minutes he was an eight out of ten. I've only been at a few breech births and they often do seem to take a little longer than cephalic births to get going.'

Roz nodded as she thought about it. 'I guess it could be that the cord is out and it has to be compressed against the body coming through. Or the rapid descent of the head afterwards might stun them too. But he came good by two minutes.'

The door opened and they both looked up. Sam was back. Ellie felt her heart give a little leap but it was followed by a frown as all her indecision and tangled emotions flooded back with full force. Damn. She'd been engrossed in this discussion and should have made her escape.

Her face must have shown her displeasure because he raised his brows. 'Sorry for interrupting.'

'No. Come in. Welcome!' Roz jumped up. 'Have a cup of

tea with us. It's great you're here.' She turned to Ellie. 'Isn't it, Ellie? We were just talking about the birth.'

Sam looked at her. 'I'll come back.' Then he turned to Roz. 'I thought Ellie had gone and I wondered if you had any questions, Roz. It was a big morning.'

Ellie heard his words and felt ashamed. She reached down inside and retrieved the normal Ellie from the layers of confusion. Found her equilibrium. There she was—the one who'd greeted him, had it been only six days ago?

She smiled almost naturally. 'Please stay. I was going but you're both right. It's really good to talk over things while they are fresh in our minds. We were talking about breech babies that take a while to respond after birth.'

The conversation that followed was all Ellie hoped it would be. Sam shared his fierce intellect and grasp of the intricacies of breech birth from a consultant's perspective—they even covered a spirited discussion on the pros and cons of breech birth for first-time mums—and by the time she was ready to leave Ellie was comfortable again in Sam's company.

Or perhaps it would be fairer to say in Dr Southwell's company, because she was every inch the woman behind the uniform in charge of the ward and her feet were very firmly planted in the real world of the hospital that she loved.

'I'll leave you two to talk more. I'm going home.'

Sam stood up. 'I'll come with you. I need to grab the milk I left in your fridge.'

They both stood and as Ellie walked to the door with him she heard Roz murmur after them, 'Better than checking out her collection of stamps.' Ellie winced and pretended she didn't hear.

'The breech was great,' Ellie said to change the subject. They went out into the sunlight and Ellie was thankfully aware of the cool ocean breeze brushing her face—helping calm the blush that heated her cheeks.

'So, was it easy to find the hard baby's head through the ab-

domen when you leant down on it?' Sam asked her with a smile
on his face. They had shared something special.

Ellie thought back to the moment when little Thorn's birth
progress had stalled. The sudden increase in tension in the room.
The mother pushing and nothing happening. The clock ticking. The baby's body turning pale. Then the calm voice of Sam
instructing her to help with downward pressure just above the
mother's pubic bone.

'Yes. A solid little ball that just pushed away, and then he
was born.' She pictured the baby's position in her mind. 'So his
chin must have lifted and changed the diameters of the presenting part which made him jam up. It certainly made a difference
to re-tuck his chin in, and then he was born. All great learning
experiences that make sense when you think about it.'

'Something simple like that can change the outcome so dramatically. The days of pulling down on a breech baby, which of
course made the chin obstruct further, thankfully have gone.'

'I've seen two other normal breech births, the rest have been
caesareans, so it was a great learning experience for me.'

'You have good instincts. Listen to them and you'll be fine.'

It was a nice thing to say, but she didn't know what to do
with the compliment because it was midwifery-orientated but
also personal. So she changed the subject. The crashing of the
waves from beyond the headland seemed louder than normal.
Instead of turning up the hill to her house Ellie turned her head
towards the ocean. 'The sea's rough today! I'm up for a walk out
to the lighthouse before I go home. If you'd like to have a look,
you could come. I need to lose some excess energy.'

'So, excitement makes you energetic?'

She shrugged. 'I'm energetic most of the time.' Except when
she had nightmares, but she was well over that now. Luckily
they didn't leave her listless for long. 'So what have you been
doing on your time off? Have you looked around the bay? Met
anybody interesting?'

Sam nodded mock-solemnly. 'My friend with the ingrown toenail is my new best bud. He dropped off a dozen prawns yesterday at lunchtime and offered me a trip on his trawler but I said I needed to be on call.'

She'd never been interested in offshore fishing but she was happy to hop on board a small tin dinghy and putt-putt around the creek.

'Would you like to go out on a prawn trawler?'

'It'd be interesting. Different way of spending your life than in a hospital seven days a week.'

She threw a look at him. 'Seven days a week is not healthy.'

He raised his brows. His long stride shortened to match her shorter one. 'I thought we'd agreed to disagree on how the other person spends their life.'

Oops. 'That's true. Let's talk about lighthouses. Lighthouse keepers worked seven days a week and only had one holiday a year.'

There was a pause while he digested that. 'Lighthouses. Yes. Let's talk about lighthouses.' The smile he gave her was so sweet she had a sudden vision of Sam as a very young boy with the innate kindness she could see in him now. She couldn't say why, but she knew without a doubt he would never tease a heartbroken little girl who missed her mummy. He would more likely scold anyone who did. She really liked that little boy.

She blinked away the silly fantasy and brought herself back to the hillside path they were on now. The grassy path wound along the edge of the cliff edge, a pristine white fence separated them from the drop and tufts of grass hid the crumbly edge. It was maintained by the present custodian of the lighthouse who lived off site. Glancing at Sam she manoeuvred herself to the side of the path nearest the cliff.

'The lighthouse was built in the eighteen hundreds and is part of a network that was built right along the eastern seaboard after ships were floundering on the underwater rocks.'

He was smiling at something then paused, turned and looked at her.

'Are you listening to me being your guide?'

He grinned. 'Sorry. I was thinking I could see you as a lighthouse keeper.'

She thought about that. Yes, she could have been a lighthouse keeper. 'Except the position was only open to men—though they did prefer married men with families.'

He smiled at that. 'I imagine they would have big families if stuck in a lighthouse together.'

She grinned at him. 'The first couple who lived here had eleven children. He'd been a widower and he fell in love with a local girl—said the bay and the woman he found here healed him. They ended up with a big family. All natural births and all survived.'

'What an amazing woman. And did they live here happily-ever-after?'

'They moved to a lighthouse with bigger family quarters. Once in the lighthouse business, you tended to stay in the lighthouse business.'

'She should have been a midwife.' He laughed at that. 'The children would have had a wonderful childhood.'

'Some families were very isolated but at least here, at the bay, the children went to school and played with other children.'

They arrived at the top of the hill. The base of the lighthouse and the tall tower were painted pristine white with concrete walls that were a third of a metre thick, which gave a hint at how solid the lighthouse was. They both looked up to the wrought-iron rail away at the top where the windows and the light were.

'They have a tour tomorrow. You can go up the stairs inside and come out onto the walkway. It's a great view.'

Sam patted the solid walls. 'Is this how thick the walls of your cottage are?'

'Yep. It wasn't usual for lighthouses to be built of concrete but there's a couple on the north coast like that. I think the sisters liked it and that's why they copied it.'

Sam watched her glance across the bay in the direction of the three cliff-top dwellings.

She went on. 'I love knowing my cottage is strong. I know the big bad wolf can't blow my house down.'

He'd suspected that was a reason she was holed away here in her house with thick walls. 'Do you want to tell me about your big bad wolf?'

'Nope.' She glanced his way but her eyes skidded past his without meeting them. 'Why spoil the afternoon?'

She pushed past the lighthouse into the little forecourt that looked over the ocean. The thick walls bounded the scrubby cliff face and they could see right out to where the blue ocean met the horizon. An oil tanker was away in the distance and closer to the shore two small sailboats were ballooning across the waves. The wind blew her hair across her face and he wanted to lean in and move it, maybe trace her cheek.

'I'm glad you're enjoying present company.'

She stared out over the ocean. He could feel the wall between them again. She was very good at erecting it. An absolute expert. Darn it.

She said, 'I enjoy the company of most people.'

That showed him. 'I won't get over myself, then.' He smiled down at his hands as he stroked the round concrete cap on top of the wall. She was good for his ego. He wouldn't have one at all by the time he left here.

The stone was warm from the sun, like Ellie had been warm. Sam remembered big hands cupping her firmly, stroking. Enjoying the feel of her under his fingers too.

He could feel his body stir. She had him on the ropes just by being there. He tried to distract himself with the structure of the building. 'It's been designed well.'

'What?' She looked startled for a minute and he guessed it

was too much to hope that she'd been thinking the same thing he'd been thinking. She worried at her lip and he wanted to reach out and tell her not to. He felt his fingers itch to touch that soft skin of her mouth. Gentle it. But he didn't. He kept his hands where they were because of the damn wall. Not the wall under his hands. He patted that one. He guessed he had a few walls himself.

'Yes.' She turned away from him, sent him a distracted smile still without meeting his eyes. 'I've had enough. It's getting cool. Think I'll go home and catch up on my Saturday chores. Maybe even light a fire for tonight.'

Those were his marching orders. Get your milk and go. And he was learning that, when she said enough, it meant enough. He'd love to know what the guy in her past had done to her. And maybe take him out into a dark alley and make him regret it.

Sam didn't see Ellie at all on Sunday. He thought about going up and asking for his dad's surfboard as an excuse but that was lame.

Monday and Tuesday there were no inpatients in Maternity and no births, so apart from a sociable few minutes he didn't see Ellie, who was busy with antenatal women. He was called in to a birth Trina had overnight but the woman went home as soon as the four hours were up.

By Friday he was going stir crazy. Maybe it was the wind. There were storm warnings and the ocean had been too rough to swim in this morning. He thought of her up there, with the wind howling, all by herself. Tomorrow he wouldn't even have the excuse of work to see her.

At the end of Friday's work day, late that afternoon before he left as they stood outside in the warm sunshine, he searched his brain for ideas to meet up with Ellie. She had her bag and he was jingling his keys in his pocket even though he hadn't brought his car.

He needed inspiration for an invite. 'That cyclone far north is staying nearer the coast than they thought it would.'

'So it'll be a windy night up in my cottage.' She looked higher towards her house. Clouds were building. 'I love nights when the wind creaks against the windows and you can hear the ocean smashing against the rocks below.'

'It could turn nasty.'

She looked at him as if he were crazy. Maybe he should have suggested picking up the board. He tried again. Time was running out. 'This one might be more wind than you bargain for.'

She shrugged and began walking out to the road. The intersection loomed where she'd head up to her house and he'd head down to his guesthouse. It had been a forlorn hope she'd invite him up.

Obviously that wasn't on Ellie's mind. 'The warnings come all the time. Cyclones usually veer away at the last minute. Either way, I'll be fine.'

Sam wasn't sure what had gone wrong. He'd thought they were getting along well, not too many pitfalls, but it seemed there always were pitfalls with Ellie Swift. And he kept falling into them. But there was nothing he could do except wave her goodbye. There was something about the set of her chin that warned him this wasn't a good time to ask what she was doing tomorrow. He doubted he'd be lucky enough for another set of twins to call her out.

CHAPTER NINE

OVER THE NEXT few hours the wind blew more forcefully, the trees bent and swayed under it, and branches and twigs were flying down the street in front of the hospital. Sam dropped in to see if there were any medical needs but the wards remained quiet. Maternity sat empty. Empty without Ellie.

As he battled his way back to his guesthouse he glared up towards Ellie's house. Trina had gone away for the weekend and Myra had left as well. Again. Ellie was up there completely alone.

He kept telling himself to stop it. She'd managed perfectly well without him worrying about her before. Her house was built to withstand anything the cliff tops could throw at it, and most likely she'd be offended if he asked if she wanted company. He wasn't silly enough to think she'd want to move anywhere else to take refuge.

He kept checking to see when the cyclone would veer out to the ocean and take the wind with it, but it hadn't died down at all. If anything it blew even stronger.

He drove down to the boat shed to chat to his friend, the prawn-trawler captain, and the seafarer shook his head sagely and said they were in for a 'right good blow'.

On the way back to the guesthouse, the weather warning over the radio finally clinched it.

'Cyclone Athena will hit land just north of Lighthouse Bay in less than an hour.'

That did it.

He turned the car around, drove slowly up the cliff road to Ellie's house and parked outside. He sat for a minute and looked at the other two houses, dark and deserted. He stared at Ellie's. The light behind Ellie's blinds bled into the late-afternoon gloom and the little flowering shrubs outside her door were bending in the wind.

When he opened his car door it was a struggle to climb out. The wind pushed hard and he manhandled his door open and almost lost his grip when the wind slammed into him in a gust that would have broken his arm if he'd been caught between the car and the door.

Now that would be embarrassing—coming up to help and having to be saved by Ellie. The wind pushed him towards Ellie's door like a big hand in the small of his back and he realised that it really was too dangerous to be outside in this.

Ellie only heard the knock at the door because it fell just as there was a pause in the commercial break.

Funny how she knew who it was. When she opened the door, Sam would have loomed over her in his big coat if he wasn't down one decent-sized step from her. As it was their noses were level. 'Didn't you see the weather warning?'

Nice greeting. She had no idea how but she had the feeling he'd been stewing over something. 'No. I'm watching a movie. It's very peaceful inside!'

'The cyclone is heading this way. You can't sleep up here tonight.'

Was he for real? As he finished speaking, a sudden gust buffeted the little house and the windows creaked.

Ellie glared at Sam and narrowed her eyes. Just then a squall of rain swept sideways into Sam's back and Ellie instinctively stepped aside. 'Quickly. You'll get drenched. Come in.'

Sam bent down to take off his shoes and she dragged his arm impatiently. 'Do that in here.' As soon as he was across the threshold, she closed the door on the splattering raindrops that were making their way around his large body and onto the floor.

Sam stood on one leg and pulled his loafers off. She caught the smell of damp leather, the expensive suede mottled in places, with grass stuck to the edges from where she'd furiously cut the lawn even shorter as she'd tried to exorcise her demons earlier this afternoon.

'You've probably wrecked your shoes coming up here in them.'

His face was strangely impassive. 'Normal people don't live on cliff tops.'

What was his problem? 'Normal people leave other people alone when they've been asked to.' They were both speaking in the polite tones of people with patience tried by another's stupidity.

At that moment a fist of wind slammed solidly against the glass double doors facing the sea. The panes rattled. Then the wind sucked back fiercely before it slammed into the window again.

Ellie stopped and stared. The windows creaked and Sam placed his second loafer onto the little tray of seashells Ellie used for lining up inside shoes off the floor and he wiped the water droplets from his hair with a handkerchief.

'That's strong,' she said lamely in a normal voice.

'Really?' She could hear the exasperation in his voice. 'I couldn't leave you up here by yourself.' Sam was still speaking quietly.

'I wasn't by myself.' She indicated Myra's cat. Millicent appeared absorbed in the television and the antics of a well-dressed woman feeding cat food to a white Persian feline.

'Perfect reasoning,' he said mildly. It was infuriating he had regained equilibrium faster than she had. She'd just have to try harder.

'Would you like a cup of tea?' Politeness was good. The wind slammed against the windows again. No doubt it was slamming against her solid thick walls as well but nobody could tell that. 'My croft won't blow down, you know.'

Sam looked at the walls thoughtfully. 'I can imagine that you are correct. But it has weaknesses.' His voice lowered to an almost undistinguishable mumble. 'And obviously so do I.'

She heard him sigh as he straightened. 'I just want to make sure you...' He glanced at Millicent and corrected himself. 'You're both okay.'

He pointed to the windows. 'I seem to remember there are shutters that close from the outside—is that right?'

Ellie had forgotten the shutters. Too late. Next time. She didn't fancy the idea of going out in that maelstrom to shut them. 'Yes, but it might be too windy to shut them now.'

Sam looked at her as if she'd grown two heads. What was his problem? 'A woman's logic.'

'Excuse me?'

As if to a child, he said, 'The shutters are there to use during extreme wind.' He spoke as if she was slow to understand. She was getting sick of his 'silly little Ellie' attitude. 'So the glass doesn't blow in?'

'The glass won't blow in.' She said it confidently. At least, the words came out confidently. Ellie had a sudden vision of glass flying all over the room. Of Millicent splattered with dangerous fragments and the wind and rain belting into the little room. Her calmness wavered. Millicent had to be safe. 'You're sure it's going to be that strong?'

Just then Ellie's feline friend disappeared and the serious voice of the weather forecaster broke into the room.

'This is an SES announcement. Severe wind warning for the north coast of New South Wales has been posted. The tail of Cyclone Athena, which had previously been expected to head

out to sea, has swung back into the coast with two-hundred-kilometre winds expected right along the eastern seaboard. Residents are recommended to stay in their homes and cancel all unnecessary travel on the roads until further notice. Flash flooding and wind damage is expected. The State Emergency Service can be reached on this number...'

A six-digit number flashed onto the screen just before the power went out.

The windows rattled menacingly in the sudden silence. Ellie stared at Sam.

He said quietly, 'Now can we close the shutters?'

'Might be a good idea.' The wind slammed again.

Sam was staring at the rain spotting the windows. 'Maybe it is too late for that. I think coming down to the hospital and staying there might be a better idea.'

As if. 'I'm not dragging Millicent through this wind. We'll be fine. But you're right. You should go before the wind gets stronger and you can't make it down the hill.'

He rolled his eyes. 'I'll do the shutters.'

No way! 'I'll do the shutters, because this is my house and I know how they fasten. And you're afraid of heights.'

He sighed, this time with exasperation. 'I'm wary of heights and more afraid that you'll blow off the cliff.'

Her eyes flew to his and the certainty in his face made her stop. He really was worried about her, to the extent he was willing to do something he normally wouldn't consider. Wayne would never have done that. The little voice inside her whispered, *Sam isn't like Wayne.* From the set chin to the determined gaze, he wasn't going to be swayed.

He lowered his voice. 'You need to stay here with Millicent.' He smiled down at the black cat who had crept across and was rubbing against Ellie's leg. He spoke to the animal. 'Can you mind Aunty Ellie while I go out and close the shutters against the wind, please?'

Millicent miaowed and Sam laughed. 'The cat wins.'

Ellie looked around. It was dark without the television.

'Fine. I'll light the lamps that I keep in the cupboard for when the silly old lights and TV go off.' She added breezily, 'It happens all the time when the wind blows strongly.'

'Do you have candles?'

She thought about Sam and her in her house, cut off from the world, with candles. 'I might.'

Ellie's face heated and she hoped he couldn't see. It was pretty dim in here. She couldn't read his eyes but she suspected they'd darkened.

Instead she went to the cupboard beside the door and took out a huge pair of black gumboots and a man's raincoat. 'These came with the house. You might still be able to salvage your loafers if you leave them to dry.'

Sam stood outside the hastily closed door, the wind buffeting him. He was mad. Obviously he still needed to feel as though he was protecting Ellie. Leftover from not protecting Bree, maybe? The wind tore at the belted raincoat and the splatter of needled rain hit his nose, and he turned his face to protect his eyes. This was dumb. Maybe they should have just let the windows blow in.

A picture of Ellie in her rain-damaged room if that did happen made his feet move and he chose to start with the worst of them first—the windows that backed onto the cliff edge. Here the force of the gale was building and he moved into it out of the lee of the building, where the full force struck him and he staggered against the wall of the building on the little porch overlooking the ocean. Ellie was looking at him from the inside with absolute horror on her face. *Great. Thanks. Very reassuring.* He managed to keep his face calm.

'Continue blowing me against the house,' he muttered. 'Happy with that.' And he kept that picture of Ellie watching him through the window in his mind to keep out the one of him being sucked off the porch and over the cliff to his death.

How had he got here? Right on the edge of a cliff in a cyclone, to be exact. Risking his life for a woman who wouldn't let him close to her. Did he hope being the hero might work when everything else hadn't?

Not that she'd wanted him to be there, and it served him right, because now he was clinging for his life, shutting oil-bereft hinges on shutters that should have been closed hours ago.

When he'd said he was more worried she would do it herself, he'd been one hundred percent telling the truth. It was that thought that drove him like a machine, unclipping, man-handling and latching each shutter closed until he was back at the side door.

He couldn't quite believe he'd been all the way around the house. It had been a real struggle, and by the end, when the wind had built to almost twice the strength from when he started, he knew Ellie would not have been able to do it.

When he fell into the room and the door was shut, he stopped. He was dripping, gasping for breath, his face stinging from the lash of the rain, back on secure footing and out of the wind into the calm of another world. Now he felt as if...he'd come home.

CHAPTER TEN

THE ROOM WAS lit rosily. The fire Ellie kept mostly for decoration was burning merrily and Millicent was lying in front of it washing her paws. The cat barely glanced at him, she was so intent on her ablutions. *It's okay. I saved you, cat.*

But Ellie stared. Her worried face was pale, deathly pale, and he remembered the time she'd fainted, but then she flew across the room and smashed into him. She was pulling at his coat, helping him get out of his boots and then hugging him. And she buried her beautiful head in his chest. Okay. This was nice.

'That was…was dangerous. Don't do that again. I had no idea it would blow up that strong. I should never have let…' She was whispering and gabbling, Sam couldn't help thinking to himself it had all been very worth it, then, and the only way to stop her seemed perfectly reasonable to him.

He kissed her.

Sam kissed her. It was a short, cold, hard kiss, then another slower one, as if he needed to do it again, in case she'd missed the first one. She hadn't missed it. Then he hugged her. 'It's okay. I'm fine.' He spoke quietly into her hair as if she needed comfort. Darn right she needed comfort.

He tasted like the storm. It was different from the kiss they'd shared at lunch that day. Ellie hugged the wet coldness of his skin close to her. He buried her face in his damp chest, inhaling the strong scent of the sea, his aftershave and the briny tang of a man who had struggled against nature and won. For her.

He could have been blown off the cliff and she wouldn't have been able to do anything to help him. She should have gone with him, watched him, held a rope or something... It hadn't sunk into her how dangerous it was until she'd seen Sam battling to stay upright through the balcony's glass doors. She'd been so frightened for him. She'd never experienced wind like that before and even now her heart thumped at the memory.

In fact, she'd never seen someone so close to death before and that it was lovely Sam, who'd only wanted to help her, seemed ironically tragic. And she was so hard on him.

When he'd safely traversed the more dangerous face of the building she'd run around lighting candles and lighting the old fuel stove that always sat with kindling waiting in the corner of the kitchen alcove in case of blackouts. She'd set the old kettle on to heat water.

He put her away from him. 'You'll get wet. Wait until I dry and then you can cuddle me.'

She half laughed, half sobbed. 'Sorry. I got a bit emotional.' She scurried away, grabbed a towel and handed it to him. 'That was terrifying, watching you out there.'

'Tell me about it,' he said and rubbed his hair. 'It was a lot worse from where I was.' He dabbed around his neck and handed back the towel. Smiled at her. 'All good. Done now.' He glanced around and she saw the approval. 'This looks nice. Can I stay till the storm blows out?'

She looked at him. Tall. Tousled. Ridiculously handsome, yet reassuring too. The full package. Obviously he cared about her, and she wasn't stupid...she knew he fancied her. Well, heck, she fancied him too, if she was honest with herself, despite all her kicking and screaming. And he was only here for another two weeks so it wouldn't be a long-term commitment.

The wind howled and continued to build outside. 'I suppose I can't throw you out now,' she agreed a little breathlessly, happy to play down the tension of the last few minutes while he'd been outside. That had been horrible.

She remembered his car. 'Though I'm not sure how happy your lovely car will be out there with all the debris flying round.'

'There are probably less branches up here than down in the town. I'm not worried. Plus, it's there if I get called out.'

Despite the fact every birth helped her numbers and the overall viability of her plans for the hospital, she actually preferred the idea that he would not be called out. *Please.*

Ellie looked across at the stove and saw the kettle wasn't even steaming yet. 'Are you cold? I've got the kettle on. The good news is I have pasta already cooked, and can just transfer it to an earthen dish and pop it in the fuel stove to reheat.'

He frowned. 'I've landed myself on you for dinner. I should have brought something.'

'You brought lunch the other day.' *And yourself tonight.* Her turn to look around the softly lit room. At the fire crackling. The candles. She'd pretended to herself she'd only set them because Sam had suggested them. But there was no denying the soft light added to the ambience. 'Even if the power comes on, now that I'm sorted, I like the power off.'

She suddenly felt quite calm that Sam was here. Felt strangely peaceful now she'd accepted she was attracted to him, but somehow because of the wind and the fact they were battened down here like a ship at sea in a storm it was bizarrely safe to allow herself the luxury, because it was done. He was here. She even walked across and turned off the television so it didn't blare at them in a surge when they were reconnected. She remembered the light switch and did the same to that.

It was as if some other Ellie had morphed from her body and evicted the prickly one. 'The refrigerator will make a noise when the power comes back on. That's enough to wake the dead.' The other Ellie sat down on the sofa and patted the seat beside her.

'Sit down. Rest after your efforts. Relax.' Then she thought of something. 'I've got a question.' It was a silly question but it had been bugging her.

He sat down next to her, right next to her, his hip touching hers, and the sofa creaked with his weight. He was warm, so the coat must have worked well or he had a really good reheating system. Her mind took a little wander and she imagined what it would feel like to have a lot more of Sam's skin against hers. She wondered how much heat they could generate together. How his skin would feel? She knew from the solid impact they'd just shared, when she'd thrown herself at him like a maniac when he'd come in, that his body would be rock-solid under her hands. Her face heated and she hurriedly diverted her mad mind. The question. Yes.

After a sideways glance, Ellie decided he looked a little wary and, considering some of the questions she'd asked him, she wasn't surprised.

'I just wanted to know who taught you to make a bed with hospital corners.'

He laughed. His look said, *Is that all?* 'My mother. She was a matron, like you,' he teased. 'Met and married my dad late in life and brought us up to be "useful", as well as doctors. My sister and I were the only ones at med school who made their beds with hospital corners. We had a great childhood.'

Ellie knew his dad was a widower. 'Where is your sister now?'

His answer was easy and affectionate. 'In Italy. Doing a term of obstetrics in Rome.' Ellie could see they were still close. 'She's a workaholic.'

'Imagine. Another person striving for further knowledge.' She thought of his father. 'And your dad doesn't think of retirement? Don't you people have holidays?'

He shrugged. 'Every year when we were kids. My parents always loved the sea, so we spent summer holidays there. Christmas at whatever beach house they'd rented for the New Year.

But we always had to make our own beds.' He smiled at the memories. 'Mum and Dad adored each other until she passed away ten years ago.'

The sadness was tinged with wonderful memories. Ellie wished she had more memories of her mother. 'I'm sorry for your loss. I knew your dad was a widower.'

He smiled gently at her. 'Dad's been surfing ever since. Says it's when he feels happiest.'

Sam's smile wasn't melancholy, so she shouldn't be. 'That makes sense. He always had a smile on his face when he came in after being in the ocean.'

'So, that's my story.' He turned fully to face her. 'You owe me a little about your life, don't you think?'

'Mine's boringly tragic. As you know from my nightmares, Mum died when I was six. My dad brought me up. He never married again, though I had a nice auntie.'

She smiled at him. 'A real auntie—Dad's sister. I'd go for holidays with my Aunty Dell. She was an Outback nurse and I visited her in whatever little hospital she was working at. That was when I was happiest. I admired her so much that nursing and midwifery were the natural way for me to go. We've done a few emergency births together. She can do everything.'

He was watching her and she suddenly felt a little shy at being under such scrutiny. Wayne had asked questions about her early in their relationship, but once he'd established nobody was going to rescue her he'd stopped hearing her answers. It was something she'd missed early on and should have realised it was a danger sign.

Sam's voice brought her back and she wanted to shake off the sudden darkness that had come with thoughts of Wayne. Sam wasn't pretending interest. He *was* interested. 'So, no brothers or sisters?'

She shook her head. 'Nope.'

'And where's Aunty Dell now?'

Aunty Dell. For her, Ellie could smile. 'Kununurra. She's

slowly moving around the top of Western Australia in her mobile home.'

His voice had softened. 'So no rowdy family Christmases for you?' Wayne had played on her need for 'jolly family time', and she knew it with a bitterness that stung.

Sam's face was sympathetic but she couldn't help her reaction. It erupted like a little volcano of hurt. 'Don't pity me. I've had lots of lovely Christmases at work. Making it special for people who find themselves away from home.'

Sam's expression didn't change and she took a quick breath to calm herself—remind herself this was Sam, not Wayne— and felt a little ashamed of her outburst.

He said, 'That was empathy, not pity. I can see you have a thing about pity. There's a difference. What I'd really like to know about is the relationship that's made you so bitter and prickly. It obviously didn't work out.'

Wayne hadn't been a relationship. He'd been a debilitating illness that had almost become terminal. The kettle began to sing and she heard it with relief. 'No. My relationship didn't work out.' The old Ellie was back and she stood up. 'I'll make a hot drink. Would you like tea, coffee or hot chocolate?'

He put his hand on her arm. 'Do you know what I'd really like? More than a hot drink?'

The kettle sang louder. 'What?'

Sam seemed oblivious to the noise. 'To hear about that time in your life that still affects you so much now.'

She looked down at him. Nope. She couldn't do that. She knew what would happen. Talking about Wayne and the loss of her innocence, the tearing down of her dreams, the descent into abuse she'd suffered, would spoil what she had here with Sam. Tonight couldn't be the start of a long-term thing but it was special. She wouldn't infect this moment with the past.

This thing with Sam, this fledgling, careful awareness that she was only just allowing into her world along with Sam, was too precious. Too easily damaged. 'How about you talk about your marriage first?'

'Touché.' He grimaced. She read it in his face. He knew analysing his past would harm what they had as well. 'Let's have hot chocolate instead.'

Sam sipped his hot chocolate. The fire flickered, the woman who had attracted him crazily for the first time in years sat beside him, while a big black cat purred against his side. A hell of a lot different from work, work, work. It was probably the most peaceful evening he'd spent since well before Bree's death, which was crazy, considering the tempest outside. But since he'd closed the shutters they were locked in an impervious cave, immune to the elements. There was just the rattle of rain on the roof and the background thrum of the ocean crashing on the cliffs below joining with it to make a symphony rather than a discordant refrain.

The candles flickered and as far as he was concerned Ellie looked like an angel, her cheeks slightly pink as she laughed about the time when Jeff, the lifesaver and prawn-trawler captain, the meanest, toughest guy in town, had fainted at his wife giving birth.

She turned to look at him. 'You must have had funny things happen in your work?'

'Not often.' Or maybe he'd lost his sense of humour so long ago that he'd missed the occasions. He hadn't smiled as much as he had since he'd arrived here. He wondered if it was the place or the woman beside him. He suspected it was the latter and marvelled that one person could turn his thoughts around so swiftly.

It was almost as if, the first time he'd seen her, she'd magically switched on his party lights.

She nudged him with her shoulder. 'Come on. Something funny must have happened at your work!'

He pretended to sigh. 'Very recently I was called into a birth centre and the husband was stark, staring naked in the shower with his wife and two sons while she pushed the baby out. They were from a nudist colony.'

He could tell she was trying not to laugh but he suspected it was more at his horror than the picture he painted.

She pursed her lips in mock shock. 'What about the midwife?'

He looked sternly at her. 'She was dressed. Thank goodness.'

She let go and laughed. 'You're a prude. I'm guessing if they'd had a home birth the midwife from their colony would have been naked. Birth is such an important event that, if your belief system celebrates the naked body, I can see why they would want to be naked for it.'

He'd started the story to make her smile but she made him think more about the people, not the events. It was something he'd had trouble doing at the time and now he felt slightly ashamed. 'I'm not really complaining. The mother had had a previous caesarean, which ruled out a home birth, and they were "reclaiming her birthing ability".'

She tilted her head and looked at him. 'It's pretty cool you get that.'

He grimaced. 'I didn't get it.' He shook his head. He couldn't take credit when it wasn't due. 'I'm repeating what the midwife told me when she saw my face.'

Her gaze softened. 'But you get it now. I can see that.'

More than that had shifted since he'd come here. 'I think so.'

He tried to explain. 'I've been living a very narrow existence since Bree died. Concentrating on the end goal, which is my research on extreme premature labour. And, although it's too late to save Bree or our babies, maybe I could save other babies and somehow she'd know I was still trying.' He shook his head. 'I don't know. I've been avoiding where possible the more emotive and connecting aspects of my work. My father saw how distanced from people I was becoming so it's not surprising he saw this place as a change of scene for me.' He glanced at her ruefully. 'A chance to try to jolt me out of it.'

'And have we jolted you out of it?'

You have, he thought, but he didn't say it. He let his gaze drift around the candlelit room. Somehow it was easier to talk about it here, now, in the quiet, with just the two of them. 'I feel different. Even that first fast birth in the first half-hour here, with Josie and John. I felt connected. Involved. Not a separate watcher who only stepped in as needed.' He grimaced. 'I even recall their names.' To his shame he hadn't been able to do that for far too long.

He could see she remembered the moment. He wasn't surprised she smiled at the memory. 'You were needed.'

He shook his head. 'Not really. You had it under control. And you loved it all so much. Lived it. It slapped me in the face that I'd lost that in my work.'

She winced at his choice of words. 'Slapped? I'm definitely not a violent person.'

He smiled. 'It was a gentle, metaphorical slap. But I can change that to "nudged me into realising", if you prefer.'

He bumped her shoulder gently with his own. 'Like you nudged me to remember something funny a minute ago.'

'I'm glad you've seen the light.' She said it simply.

'And since then it's been a roller coaster. Lighthouse Bay doesn't win the birth number-count but every patient has had a story, an emotional tag I'm seeing now. That's a good thing. I think.'

She touched his arm. 'It's definitely a good thing.'

That wasn't all he was seeing. He was seeing a beautiful woman, just out of reach. He really wanted to reach. He just hoped she was also feeling the magic that had snared him.

'Come here.' He lifted his arm and to his immense relief she snuggled in under the weight of it. Then it was easy to tilt her chin with his other hand and brush her lips with his. He could feel the tingle of connection all the way down to his toes. He sighed and suddenly felt ten years younger. Now he was alive.

Ellie had known they were going to kiss. Eventually. And surprisingly she was quite calm about it. It wasn't as if they hadn't before and he was very good at it. That other Ellie was stretching inside her and saying, *Yes, please*, as Sam pulled her close. *Hurry up and kiss me some more*, that other Ellie was saying. She was such a hussy.

His mouth touched hers. Mmm… Kissing Sam tasted crazy good. Strangely their bodies were communing like two old lovers—not new ones—and inexplicably she once again found herself in his lap. She kept her eyes closed dreamily as she slid her arms around his strong neck and savoured the virile hardness and warmth of him. The slowness and languorous progression of his mouth from gentle to intense, hard to soft, and back again. It felt so powerful with him holding her face, her cheeks, cradled between his palms as if he held delicate china in his hands. Tasting her and letting her taste him. As though she was precious and special. Breathing in each other's breath as they shared the most intimate connection with their mouths.

Distantly she heard the rain beat on the roof and the spiral of delight just went on, deeper and more poignantly, until she wanted to cry with the beauty of his mouth against hers, his tongue curled around hers, until her whole body seemed to glow from the inside out. Kissing and more kissing. She hadn't realised she could love kissing this much. That kissing was actually the be all and end all. That it could be a whole play and not just an act of the play. She'd never been kissed like this—as if he couldn't get enough of her mouth. His hands roamed, as if gathering her even closer, but always they came back to her face, gently holding her mouth to his as if he couldn't get enough. Yes. She couldn't get enough, either.

Sam was staying the night. Tomorrow was Saturday. They had all night—or even all weekend, if they wanted.

* * *

He stayed all weekend. Sunday morning, she woke to the warmth of Sam's big naked body snug up against her and her cheek on Sam's skin. The blond hairs on his body tickled her nose and her hand closed over the wedge-shaped muscle of his chest as her face grew steadily pinker. Oh, my. What they had done since Friday night?

As if he'd heard her thoughts, his voice announced he was awake too. 'I'm wondering if perhaps we could do some of that again...'

Sam's voice was a seductive rumble and she could feel the smile curve across her face. No doubt she looked like Millicent after scoring a treat. She knew now what Trina was missing and why the young widow had chosen to work most nights. Waking to someone warm and loving beside her. A man spoiling her until she begged him to stop. Being held until she fell asleep.

Cheeks still red, she tried to not jump on him. 'Aren't you hungry?'

'Oh, yeah, I'm starving.' He pulled her on top of him and kissed her thoroughly.

An hour later Ellie watched the steam follow Sam out of the bathroom and ran her hands slowly over her tingling body. She'd had no idea such a sensuous world existed, though how on earth she was going to face Sam at work and not think lurid thoughts defied her imagination. Sam had told her to stay and enjoy the shower while he made breakfast but what she really wanted to do was drag the gorgeous person back to bed. She'd had no idea she was a nymphomaniac. Must be. Surely other people didn't do it so much as they had in the last thirty-six hours?

She didn't know how it could work between them. If it even could work. He was based in Brisbane. She was here. But they were fabulous together so surely that meant something? Maybe she could learn to trust a relationship with a man. A long-distance relationship. If that man was Sam. No. She wasn't in love with him. Was she? She wasn't going there, but she sure as heck was in lust with him.

And if it didn't work long-distance, that was okay, because he would only be here for another two weeks and she deserved great sex at least once in her life. More than once. She grimaced over the word. They hadn't had sex—Sam had made love to her. Gloriously tender love that healed and nurtured and told her he thought she was the sexiest woman in the world. Who would have known? Her cheeks glowed again.

CHAPTER ELEVEN

MONDAY MORNING DAWNED, blustery, and Ellie tweaked her collar tighter to her throat as she closed her front door. She'd slept deeply after Sam had left on Sunday evening. They'd walked for hours hand in hand along Nine Mile Beach, splashing through the waves, coming back after lunch ravenous again. Ellie was convinced that the sun, the exercise and—she grinned to herself—the loving meant she'd slept the best she'd slept for years.

This morning the air felt damp and exhilarating as she trod lightly down the road to work just before seven a.m. She'd skipped her beach walk this morning—strangely, her hips were tender. Must be all the exercise. She blushed sheepishly.

The sea remained wild, white caps out to the horizon, booming swells smashing against the cliff below, and Ellie breathed in the fresh salt with a sigh of pleasure. She loved the coast. Loved the isolation of her croft, though isolation wasn't something she'd savoured over the weekend. She saw Myra's car was back and smiled to herself. She didn't know. *Tee-hee.*

She laughed out loud and conversely had a sudden desire to share the amusing thought with Sam. There was a little wonky logic in that thought and it was not very loyal to her friend.

On her arrival she saw that Trina had had a slow night. The ward remained empty. Her friend had been bored, hence she had reorganised the whole sterile stockroom—a job Ellie had been putting off until a quiet day—and there was a small pile of out-of-date stock that she needed to reorder from the base hospital. At least she had a chore to start her day with.

Later, if no birthing women came in or needed transfer, Ellie would do the same for the medication cupboard. Spring cleaning suited the feeling of determined efficiency she'd decided she needed to ground herself in. Get her head out of the clouds that her thoughts kept drifting up towards.

The expected arrival of Dr Southwell would not faze her, though seriously she wouldn't be able to look at him without blushing, and she wasn't sure how she was going to manage it.

Maybe, as they had no patients, he could go straight through to the clinic in the main hospital to give her a chance to think of what to say.

Except it wasn't Sam who arrived.

Wayne Donnelly was an undeniable presence. Like everyone's favourite young uncle. You could just imagine him dangling babies on his knees, which was what Ellie had thought when he'd begun to pursue her. Whenever Ellie was around he'd made such a fuss of any child and everyone had smiled at him. He'd made her think of families. Dream families. Christmases, Easter egg hunts. All the things Ellie had ever wanted, and she'd fallen headlong in love with the fantasy.

In truth, he hated kids, and was a narcissist and a sociopath. He had no guilt, no shame, no feeling for other people, and could only see the world through eyes that saw himself first.

But he was like a seasoned politician versed in the art of crowd pleasing. Crinkled laughter lines jumped up at the edges of blue eyes framed by thick, black lashes and high cheekbones. Nothing in his looks gave him away. Except maybe the confident, beaming, too-white smile. He had a small cleft in his strong chin and women instinctively gave him another look.

Later she'd found out there was a pattern. He serenaded his victims, pretended to marry them, created joint bank accounts and then sauntered off after skilfully denigrating the woman so she felt it was all her fault everything had failed. A master of psychological abuse.

When Ellie saw him her stomach lurched with bile. Out of the corner of her eye she saw Trina, about to head home to bed, instinctively pat her hair. Yep. He'd already sucked in Trina.

'What are you doing here?' Ellie watched his smile broaden, the fake smile he used like oil to smooth his way in so he could use someone. She'd been incredibly blind. She wasn't any more.

'Too early in the morning for manners, El? Introduce me to your beautiful friend before we find ourselves bickering.'

'No.' Ellie turned from him to Trina. 'He's a cad and a slime, Trina. I'd leave if I was you.'

Wayne laughed. Trina looked at Ellie and shut her gaping mouth with a click. She blinked a few times as her tired brain tried to work it out. Then she stepped closer to Ellie. 'If you say so, I believe you.'

Ironic choice of words from her friend. One of the people in the room was a huge liar.

Trina frowned. 'But...' She wrinkled her brow. 'If he's a cad shouldn't I stay?'

Ellie shook her head. 'I'd prefer you didn't. He won't be here long. You could ring the security man, though. Ask him to come over and sit at my desk. That would be good in case he won't leave.'

Trina didn't look again at Ellie's acquaintance, just crossed to the desk and picked up the phone. She spoke quietly into it and then picked up her bag. 'If you're sure.'

Ellie nodded again. 'Please. And thanks.'

Trina nodded. 'See you tomorrow morning.'

'Sure.' Ellie Looked back at Wayne. Raised her brows. 'Yes?'

'I need money.'

'Really.' He had taken a great deal of that from her already. Along with her naivety. She looked at the impeccable clothes. 'I've seen people far worse off than you.'

'Thank you.' As if she'd given him a wonderful compliment. 'Nice little caravan park you have here. Think I might stay around for a while. Reacquaint myself with my kin.'

'You have no kin. But I can't stop you. Luckily, it's high season and will cost you an arm and a leg. So you will have to move on eventually.' She wasn't moving on. Not this time.

He spread his hands. 'Gambling debts.'

Nothing new. 'Gamblers tend to get those.'

'This time they threatened to harm my family.'

He'd had three 'wives' that she knew of. 'Which family?'

'All of them. You included. I thought I'd better warn you.'

He didn't give a damn. 'You don't care about anyone but yourself. You'd do better going to the police.'

'I don't think that the police station is a safe place for me to go. Would you look forward to identifying my body?'

'Go away, Wayne. Your disasters have nothing to do with me.' And she could feel the shakes coming on. He'd tried to rape her once. After she'd said she was leaving him. And he'd denied it. Said she'd been playing hard to get.

She'd escaped that night and had begun to plan carefully to get away, because he'd taken all her resources. Her wallet, her licence, her bank accounts… Everything had been unavailable when she'd needed it. She'd stumbled into Myra's coffee shop, distraught, and made a friend for life. Myra had helped her create the wall of protection she needed to be free.

'You've turned all bitter and twisted. Not the sweet Ellie I used to know.'

That wasn't even worth answering. Ellie heard the door from the main hospital open and was glad the security guard was here. She needed to end this. She pretended she didn't know help had arrived. She couldn't keep running.

'Leave the ward, please, Mr Donnelly.'

'You didn't call me "Mr Donnelly" when we were married.'

'We were never married.' Ellie turned away from him to the security guard and her stomach dropped. It wasn't security, it was Sam. No. No. *No*. Her face flushed and she felt dreadfully, horribly sick. She didn't want Sam to know about this. But then maybe it was best. Then he could see she could never truly give a man power over her ever again.

'Good morning, matron,' Sam said.

Ellie saw him glance at Wayne and give him an inscrutable nod. 'We need to discuss the patients.' Sam's voice was surprisingly crisp. Authoritative. No hint of friendliness.

Ellie raised her brows. He knew there were no patients. 'Certainly, Dr Southwell.'

'Fine. When you're ready, please.'

'She's busy. Talking to me.' Wayne squared his shoulders but he was at a disadvantage in both height and muscle. They all knew it. An adolescent part of Ellie secretly revelled in it.

Still politely, Sam said, 'You're a doctor?'

'No. I'm her...'

Before Wayne could complete his sentence, Sam spoke coldly right over the top of him. There was no doubting his authority. 'This is a hospital. If you are not a medical practitioner, matron's attention is mine. There is a waiting room, though, in the main hospital where you can sit, but this could take some time.'

Ellie added helpfully, 'He's leaving.'

'Excellent. Come with me, matron.' Sam indicated with his hand that he expected Ellie to head down the corridor to the empty rooms in front of him.

She looked at Wayne and made the decision to enforce her freedom from dreaded drop-in visits like this. She didn't know why she hadn't done it before but knew it was a fault she needed to remedy immediately. 'If you don't leave town, I'll lodge a restraining order with the police this afternoon. I've kept evidence of our fake marriage certificate. This won't happen again.'

Then she turned to Sam. 'This way, doctor.'

Sam ignored Wayne and followed Ellie. She could feel his large body blocking Wayne's view of her as they turned into an empty room and stood silently in the centre of it out of sight.

Ellie clasped her hands together to stop them shaking, unable to look at Sam. They both heard footsteps retreating, and the automatic doors open and close, and Ellie sagged against a wall. Sam watched her but he didn't come any closer, as if he knew she needed space at this moment.

'Your ex-husband, I assume?'

'He was a bigamist. Or trigamist, if there is such a word. So never legally my husband.'

Sam whistled. 'Ouch.'

She said very quietly, 'There were worse things about him than that.'

Sam studied her. 'Would you like me to follow and punch him out?'

He was deadly serious. She could see that.

She could almost smile at that except her heart was broken. Yes, she was beginning to love Sam. That was so dangerous to her peace of mind. It frightened the stuffing out of her. And she loved him even more for the offer, but Wayne had made her see how impossible it all was. She couldn't do this—start again with Sam. She didn't have the trust in her to build a strong relationship and Sam needed a woman to love him wholeheartedly.

Not one who'd locked him out like Bree had. Bree, who had almost destroyed him while she'd destroyed herself. He deserved that trust. She could give him love. She was more than halfway to falling in love with him already. But she couldn't give him trust. She'd thought she could but she couldn't. Trust had died in her for ever. Killed by the man who had just left.

'Thank you for the thought but I wouldn't like to ask you to sink to his level.' She straightened off the wall.

'Now you can see, Sam, why I'm so wary of men. Why I know I'll never let myself get that close to someone again. I'm sorry if I gave you the wrong idea this weekend. It was lovely, what we shared, but it's finished. You'll leave soon and that's good.' She took a step towards the door and it was the hardest step she'd ever taken. 'Let's go back to the desk.'

His fingers lifted to touch her arm, then dropped. 'Ellie.'

'Yes?' She looked at his caring eyes. His beautiful mouth. The kindness that shone on his face. It broke her heart.

'I'm sorry you've been wounded by a pathetic man. We're not all like that.'

She heard him. Saw that he meant it. But that didn't help. She wished she could believe it as deeply as she needed to be fair to Sam. 'I know. I really don't think you are that sort of man, but I don't have the capacity in me to risk a relationship again. A relationship needs to be good for both of us and I wouldn't be good for you.'

'But—'

She cut him off. 'Thank you. I don't want to talk about it any more.'

Sam sighed impatiently. 'I can understand that here. But later, I think we should.'

'No, Sam. We won't.' Then she turned and walked away.

Sam left Ellie soon after. He went out the front door to make sure her ex-bigamist had departed but there was no sign of him. He actually would have liked to slam the sleazy little mongrel up against a wall and warn him never to approach Ellie again, but he might find a place in himself that would do more than that, and he'd taken an oath to not harm.

His fingers clenched by his sides. No wonder she had trust issues and didn't want to ask any man for help. Even himself. He wasn't a violent man but after what they'd shared the last two days the idea of someone abusing Ellie's trust to that extent devastated him. And made him furious. But in the end it wasn't any of his business unless he was looking for something long-term—which wasn't his intention. Or was it? Hell, he didn't know. Did he even have a choice?

Ellie spent the next five days rearranging antenatal schedules and managed to book a different pregnant woman for antenatal appointments for every morning during the time Sam would be around.

They had two normal births, one on Faith's shift and one on Trina's, so Ellie was spared having to call Sam in. She could only be glad the babies were being kind to her. But every afternoon when she went home the house was empty, where before it had been welcoming.

Sam came on Wednesday afternoon for his father's surfboard and she gave it to him, refused to talk and didn't invite him in.

On Thursday Myra cornered her and told her Sam had asked her to see if Ellie would change her mind. Spend some time with him. They had their first ever disagreement when both women were so determined to change the other's mind about what was right.

By Friday Ellie knew she needed to get away or she would make herself sick, so as soon as she finished work she took herself off availability for call-backs and loaded her car.

Ellie felt the need to abandon her cottage and head to a different world. It had everything to do with avoiding a certain visitor who just might drop in again.

She didn't know where to go, so she drove north to the Gold Coast, where she could find a cheap hotel and just hibernate for two nights in a place that nobody knew her.

She stayed in her room all day Saturday and drove back Sunday via the base hospital where two of her patients were still inpatients.

She did her own visiting, with a quiet chat in the big antenatal ward with Marni, who was going home tomorrow. Bob arrived not long after she did, and she was pleased to hear that the young mum's contractions had settled down, and Bob had painted inside their house while Marni was in hospital so she didn't have to be exposed to the smell of new paint.

She showed Ellie the quilt she was making the baby, and there was something about Marni's determined optimism that made her feel ashamed. Marni had explained that when she was bored she sewed another little animal onto the patchwork cot-blanket, pouring love and calmness into it, determined to do everything asked of her to keep her pregnancy on track.

After Marni, Ellie visited the postnatal ward area, where Annette sat happily with her twins, who were being star patients and were almost ready to go home.

'Still perfect?' Ellie grinned at the two sleeping bundles and the relaxed mum sitting with a magazine in her lap.

'They have their moments. Rosebud is the impatient one, so has to be fed first, while Thorn needs a bit of encouragement to keep at it.'

'So they are still how they started out, then.'

'Exactly.' Both women laughed.

'How is that gorgeous Dr Sam?'

'Fine.' Ellie felt her face freeze, as if all the muscles had suddenly stopped working. 'He's here for another week and then he's gone.' Her voice was bright. 'Then I guess we'll have another new locum. Did you know his father was here first? He was a surfer, though I'm not sure how good his surfing will be for a while, because he broke his arm. That's why his son came.'

'So Dr Sam's not coming back?'

'No.' It would be better if Sam never came back. She suspected every time he came it would hurt more to keep saying goodbye to him. 'He has a high-flying job in Brisbane. He was only doing everyone a favour.' Including her.

On the drive home she thought about her dilemma. She'd had sex with a man she'd known for only two weeks by that point, and who was just passing through. Maybe she even understood her friend Faith, who had never said she regretted the man who'd come, disappeared and left her with a baby. She'd never been close to understanding before.

Sex. She grimaced and reminded herself that that was all it was. Then her sensible voice returned. That was okay. She was a grown-up. Afterwards she could go back to how it had been before and concentrate on work.

* * *

On Monday morning when Sam walked in to the maternity ward the Ellie he found was the woman from three weeks ago. White shirt buttoned to the neck, grey eyes serene and cool, her manner very businesslike.

'Good morning, doctor.'

His temper was less than sunny after being frustrated all weekend. He'd thought if he just waited until Saturday morning they could sort it all out. He'd taken croissants and blueberry yoghurt, as she'd liked that last time, and then had stood there like an idiot until he'd realised she'd left. He'd rung Myra each morning and afternoon all weekend to check in case she'd returned.

Now he stared with narrowed eyes as she stood officiously in front of him. 'Good morning, Ellie.' He stressed her first name, disappointed but not surprised this ice maiden didn't resemble the woman he had held in his arms all weekend just over a week ago. He was back to square one, and despite his best efforts there was no breaking through her barriers. Maybe he should just give up.

They had five days to go. Then he'd be gone. He could lose himself in his work again. Treat it as an interlude that had shown him he could finally care for another woman. But he wasn't so sure he could care for one as much as he'd grown to care for Ellie.

On Friday morning, Sam's last day there, Ellie went back to the beach. She'd been avoiding it all week in case Sam was there in the mornings surfing but she missed the peace she gained from her daily walk. Peace was at a premium at the moment and she needed it before facing today.

It had rained last night, and the ocean was too rough for surfers out there. As she trod down the path even the frogs weren't penetrating the gloom she was wrapped in. At least she had Sam to thank for losing the majority of her phobia. She wasn't going to touch one but the croaking barely bothered her now—there were worse things that could happen than frogs. Such as Sam going and never seeing him again.

She reached the sand, slipped off her footwear and stood for a moment. Gazing out. A new weather pattern was coming in. More high winds and rough seas. She breathed in deeply and let the crash of the waves on the cliffs across the bay penetrate, feeling the cool white sand between her toes, the turbulent, curving waves tumbling onto themselves and running up the sand to kiss her better. The biggest waves made a cracking noise as they slid all the way up to her to foam around her toes then crackle into the sand as it drank in the water and the cries of the gulls overhead. This was why she lived here. Because it made her strong.

Yes, it was sad that Sam was going, more than sad, but it was good as well. It would never have worked and what he'd given her in the two days they'd been together was something she could hold to her heart in the years to come. She wished him happiness with a woman who deserved him. She just wished she could have been that woman.

Ellie lifted her head and breathed in another gulp of sea air past the stinging in her throat and then she set off along the beach. She would get through today, kiss Sam's cheek and say goodbye.

Sam knew she was going to kiss his cheek. He didn't want her platonic guilt. If she wasn't going to kiss him properly then he didn't want her to kiss him at all. He stepped back as she moved forward to say goodbye and saw her blink in confusion as he avoided her.

That's right, Ellie. Feels bad, doesn't it, to be knocked back? He didn't say it but he knew it was there in his eyes. He was still pretty darn angry with her for not fighting for what they might have had.

'Goodbye, Ellie Swift. I wish you a great life with your midwifery centre.' He turned away quickly because if he didn't he'd grab her and kiss her until she begged him to stay. But that wouldn't happen.

He'd driven an hour towards Brisbane when the radio alert of another storm warning jerked him back to sense. Ellie was on the seaboard. Right on the edge of a cliff, to be exact. Her little house would bear the brunt of the storm and he wouldn't be there to make sure she was all right.

Not that she'd want him to be there, but suddenly he asked himself why would he drive away from a woman who'd finally made him want to look at the future again? One he wanted to wake up next to for the rest of his life? He loved Ellie. How many times did real love actually come to a man?

After he'd stepped back from her he'd seen the look of hurt on her face and it came back to haunt him now. What if she was feeling the same pain he was? Wasn't he as bad as she was for not fighting for what they could have?

He'd loved Bree, and it had destroyed him when she'd died. But Ellie was right. It hadn't been his fault. He didn't know she'd been so unstable that she would take her own life. And he'd lost himself in work.

If it wasn't for Lighthouse Bay and Ellie he might be still lost. He could have woken up in thirty years and realised he'd been a shell for decades. He didn't want to be a shell. He wanted to be the man who held Ellie every night. The man who held the babies she was destined to have with him, and might never have if he kept driving away. He loved her. He wanted her. And he would fight for her.

He pulled over and turned around. The storm up ahead was flashing lightning across the hills. Great sheets of white light. Ellie was over there somewhere. Alone.

The thunder crashed outside. The scent of ozone filled the air, lighting up the sky all the way out to sea. This storm was more electrical than the other one. She shied away from those memories of the night Sam came, like Millicent had skidded away from the window.

Myra was gone again and Ellie suspected she had a male friend she was visiting. She even suspected it might be the 'elder' Dr Southwell. Good for her.

But Ellie knew the man she should have fought for was gone. Sam was gone. In her head he was gone. In her heart he was buried under protection so thick she felt like she was walking around inside a big, white cotton-wool ball, adding more layers all week, so that by the time Sam had left this afternoon she could barely hear, she was so distanced from everyone. He'd turned away from her coldly in the end and she deserved that. She'd been a coward and deserved his scorn.

She wished she'd never ever started this painful process of letting someone else in. Because for the first time in a long time she wondered if, if she'd tried a little bit harder to let go of the past, she just might have had a future. With Sam. Was it too late? Could she contact him through his father? Myra would be all over her like a rash if she asked for Sam's phone number. Or his flat address. Maybe she could turn up at his flat. Her heart began to pound and she looked down at Millicent. 'Am I mad to think of it or mad not to do it, cat?'

She had a sudden memory of Marni, determined to fight for her baby. Shoring herself up with positive actions. Stitching her quilt of love so that she would be ready when the good things happened. Ellie had done the opposite, undermined her own confidence with the past every time Sam broke through her barriers.

Stop it. Too late, it's over. She stroked the soft fur between Millicent's pointy ears.

She sat up straight. 'You know what, Milly? It's not over till the fat lady sings. I'll find him tomorrow and see if we can at least spend some time together.' She would try and, if it didn't work out, then she might just have to get a cat of her own. Maybe a kitten so she could have the full experience of being a mother. Yeah, right. Full experience.

The knock came in between two claps of thunder and she frowned at the improbability of visitors.

Then, there was Sam. Standing on the bottom step, his nose level with hers, his dark eyes staring into hers. 'Can I come in?' A flash of lighting illuminated them both and a nearby tree exploded into sparks. The explosion made her ears ring and she put out her hand to drag him in.

'Damn it, Sam. You could get killed standing out in that. You're mad.' Her heart was thumping at the closeness of the strike and the concept that again she could have got Sam killed by keeping him outside her house.

Then he was inside, the door was shut and they both stood there, panting, a few inches of air and a huge chasm between them.

He didn't seem perturbed about what had almost happened. He just said softly, 'You haven't closed the shutters again.'

She couldn't believe he was here. As if she'd conjured him. 'I know. It's not that windy. And you can't do it because it's too dangerous to go out in case the lightning gets you.' She licked her dry lips. 'Why are you here, Sam?'

He was staring down at her. She couldn't read the expression in his eyes but it was nothing like the one he'd left with today. It was warm, gentle and determined. 'Can I share the storm with you?'

Her cheeks were heating. He looked so good. Smelt so good. She knew he would feel so good. 'That would be nice,' she said carefully.

His brows rode up. 'Nice?' He put down his coat. 'It could be more than nice. Because I've decided to fight for you.'

This was all happening way too fast for her to erect the barriers she needed. Hang on—she didn't need barriers. Her brain was fogging. Softening. Revelling in the fact that Sam was here.

Sam said, 'I'm going to wear you down until you say yes.'

He wasn't gone. She hadn't ruined everything. Yet! Then his words sank in. 'Yes to what?'

'Will you marry me, Ellie? Be my wife. We'll work out the logistics—our work, your fears, my baggage. But driving away from you today and knowing I wasn't coming back was the loneliest thing I've ever done in my life, and I don't want to do it again. I love you.'

He loved her. 'Oh, Sam.' She loved him. Lord, she loved him so much. She lifted her head. She loved him too much to push him away for a second time. She would just have to break free from the past and be everything Sam needed. For the sake of both their futures. 'I love you too.'

He closed his eyes. 'It was too close, Ellie. We were too close to losing this.' Then he stepped in and picked her up. Hugged her to him and swung her around. And she laughed out loud. Sam's arms had her. They both were laughing and then he kissed her, and Ellie knew, at last, that she had found her 'for ever' family.

CHAPTER TWELVE

SAM STOOD WAITING, his heart pounding as he watched for the first signs of the bridal car to descend the gravel road to the beach, and he appreciated the grounding effect of the cool sand under his bare feet as he waited for the warmth of the sun. But, more impatiently, he waited for the glowing warmth of the woman he would spend the rest of his life with. Where was Ellie?

The light touch of a hand on his arm broke into his thoughts and he turned with a smile to his father. He saw the old man's eyes were damp and shadowed with that memory of past sadness, yet glowing with pride too. Happy and sad at the same moment. Sam knew all about that. They both glanced at Sam's sister as she stood with her Italian friends, back on sabbatical to her old hospital while she attended her only brother's wedding.

His dad cleared his throat and said quietly, 'Your mother would have been so proud of you, son. So happy for you.'

Sam patted his shoulder. Felt the sinewy strength under his hand and was glad his dad was healed again. 'She'd be happy for you too. We've both been blessed twice with wonderful women.'

'I can see you love your Ellie, Sam.'

Sam felt his face relax, felt his mind expand with just thinking about her. Felt the joy surge up into his chest. Such elation.

'She's turned the world on for me, Dad. Ellie, this place, the future.' He shook his head, still unable to believe his grey life had been hit by a sunburst called Ellie Swift. Soon to be Mrs Southwell. 'I just wish she'd hurry up and arrive.'

The first rays of the sunrise struck the cliff in front of them at the exact moment an old-fashioned black saloon descended the steep slope and finally drew up at the place reserved for the bride in the crowded car park.

The whole town had come out in the dark to wait for the sunrise and for Ellie. The dapper chauffer, not resembling a prawn-trawler captain at all, opened the door onto a long blue roll of carpet that reached all the way across the sand to Sam.

He helped the two golden bridesmaids in their beautiful sheath dresses, Trina and Faith, and the stately Matron of Honour in a vintage gold dress, his dad's fiancée, Myra, and then Sam heard the hushed gasp from a town full of supporters as Ellie stepped out in a vision of white with her father's hand in hers.

Ellie had been shy about a veil, a white dress, the fact that she'd thought she was a bride before and had been mistaken, but Sam had taken her in his arms and told her his dream...of Ellie on the beach dressed as a bride. Sam had spoken quietly of the pureness of their love, the freshness of their commitment and his desire for her to feel the bride of her dreams—because their life together would be that dream.

And there she was, drifting towards him, the veil dancing at the sides of her face in the morning breeze, walking a little too quickly in her bare feet as she always did, her eyes on his, her smile wide and excited as she closed the gap between them. She came first, not after the bridesmaids, almost dragging her dad, and Sam was glad, because he could watch her close the gap between them all the way, and he barely saw the three smiling women behind her. He'd told them he wasn't talking to them anyway—they'd kept his Ellie at Myra's house last night sequestered away from him. They and her Aunty Dell, back from Western Australia for her only niece's wedding.

When Ellie stopped in front of him her eyes were glowing behind the fine material of the veil and he took her hand in his and felt the tension drain from his shoulders like an eddy rushing from a freshly filled rock pool. Ellie's dad released his daughter's hand, smiled wistfully and waved them on.

The sun chose that moment to break free of the ocean and bathed the whole wedding party in golden-pink rays as they rearranged themselves in front of the minister. The crowd drew closer, the waves pounded on the rocks by the cliff, Sam's hand tightened on Ellie's and the ceremony began, accompanied by the sound of the gulls overhead.

Afterwards the wedding breakfast was set out on white-cloth-covered tables on the long veranda of the surf club restaurant that looked out over the bay. The local Country Women's Association ladies had whipped up a magnificent repast and Ellie's new husband kept catching her eye with such love, such devotion and pride, she constantly fought back happy tears which she refused to let free. Not now. Not today. She had never thought she could be this happy.

She touched the sleeve of his white tuxedo coat. 'Sam, let's take a minute to ourselves. Walk with me on the beach.' She watched his face soften, saw it glow with love and pride, and those blinking tears that had stung her eyes threatened again. She willed them away.

So they turned down the steps of the surf club, away from the revelries, and people parted smilingly and nudged each other. 'Let them go. Young lovers.'

Finally it was just Ellie and Sam walking along the beach, barefoot in the morning sunlight, Ellie's dress hitched over her arm, toes making fresh footprints in virgin sand, and every now and then the froth of the chuckling waves tickled their ankles.

'I love you, Sam.'

'I love you too, my wife.'

She hugged the words to herself and used them to make her brave. She had news and she wanted to share it but they hadn't had a moment together alone all morning.

'This morning...' she began, and felt the nerves well. Hoped desperately he would be glad. 'This morning, I did a test.'

His big, dark brows, those brows she loved and traced at night with her fingers, drew together. He didn't get it. 'And did you pass your test?'

'It was positive.'

She let the words hang suspended with the sound of the sea between them. Squeezed his hand in hers and waited. Felt his fingers still beneath hers.

'Pregnant?' His voice was almost a whisper.

Her heart squeezed and she nodded. 'Our baby. Just weeks in time, but it feels good. The feeling is right. Everything will be fine, Sam.' She stopped and turned to him, took his face in hers instead of the other way around. Felt the skin of his cheeks tense as he realised what she'd been trying to tell him 'My darling, everything will be perfect.'

His face stilled and then slowly, ever so slowly, he smiled. It rose from somewhere so deep inside him that she was blinded by the joy she had been so afraid would be missing, consumed instead by fear that what had happened to Bree would happen to her too.

He smiled, then he grinned, picked her up and swung her around as if she were a feather, and then he hugged her. Fiercely. Put her down. Glanced around and then picked her up again. Laughed out loud. Ellie was giddy with relief, giddy with swinging, giddy with Sam.

The only minor glitch would be the time she spent on maternity leave.

But Lighthouse Bay Mothers and Babies would be fine. Sam had taken the post of Director of Obstetrics at the base hospital an hour away and his father had become the permanent GP for Lighthouse Bay. Soon Ellie would have the midwifery service she dreamed of, because now she had a straight pathway of referral to a higher level of service if needed. She knew the obstetrician in charge—her new husband—very well, and he was extremely supportive. And in the wings was Trina, ready to come off night duty and take over when Ellie stepped down. And after her there was Faith, and then Roz, and other midwives waiting to be a part of the journey travelled by the midwives of Lighthouse Bay.

* * * * *

Healed By The
Midwife's Kiss

Dear Reader,

Welcome back to The Midwives of Lighthouse Bay. Lighthouse Bay is a small seaside town on the eastern coast of Australia, with pastel houses, crofts on the cliffs, a soaring lighthouse and a bevy of dedicated midwives who love their work.

A year on from Ellie and Sam's journey to happiness, we find Trina, or Catrina, as Finn calls her, our night-duty midwife, spotlighted in her own love story.

Two years ago, Catrina lost her darling husband, Ed, and has spent her nights since then catching babies to avoid waking to the cold, empty space beside her in bed. But her boss, Ellie, is expecting a baby, and Catrina is offered daytime in-charge, so it's time to face the world.

Finlay Foley is a single dad with his own heartbreak and loss, but at least he has his daughter, a one-year-old little ray of sunshine called Piper. I loved Finn as Catrina's hero, and Piper is an absolute doll who brings out the beautiful dad that Finn is.

I hope you enjoy Finn and Catrina's story as they tentatively hold hands and move into the golden light and sands of Lighthouse Bay and their future together.

I wish you a delightful holiday in your mind as you read *Healed by the Midwife's Kiss*.

With warmest regards,

xx Fi

Dedicated to Finn, author Kelly Hunter's legend of a four-legged friend who went to doggy heaven while I was writing this book. It just seemed right to say there are heroes named Finn everywhere. Vale Finn.

PROLOGUE

AT SIX A.M. on a Thursday, Lighthouse Bay's maternity ward held its breath. Midwife Catrina Thomas leaned forward and rubbed the newborn firmly with a warmed towel. The limp infant flexed and wriggled his purple limbs and finally took a gasping indignant lungful.

The baby curled his hands into fists as his now tense body suffused with pink. 'Yours now, Craig. Take him.' She gestured to the nervous dad beside her and mimed what to do as she encouraged Craig's big callused hands to gently lift the precious bundle. One huge splashing silver tear dropped to the sheet from his stubbled cheek as he placed his new son on his wife's warm bare stomach.

Craig released a strangled sob and his wife, leaning back on the bed in relief, half laughed in triumph, then closed her hands over her child and her husband's hands and pulled both upwards to lie between her breasts.

For Catrina, it was this moment. This snapshot in time she identified as her driver, the reason she felt she could be a midwife for ever—this and every other birth moment that had come before. It gave her piercing joy when she'd thought she'd lost all gladness, and it gave her bittersweet regret for the dreams she'd lost. But mostly, definitely, it gave her joy.

An hour later Catrina hugged her boss awkwardly, because Ellie's big pregnant belly bulged in the way as they came together, but no less enthusiastically because she would miss seeing her friend in the morning before she finished her shift. 'I can't believe it's your last day.' She rolled her eyes. 'Or my last night shift tomorrow.'

'Neither can I.' Ellie's brilliant smile lit the room even more than the sunlight streaming in through the maternity ward windows.

Trina marvelled at the pure happiness that radiated from a woman who had blossomed, and not just in belly size but in every way in just one year of marriage. Another reason Trina needed to change her life and move on. She wanted what Ellie had.

A family and a life outside work. She would have the latter next week when she took on Ellie's job as Midwifery Unit Manager for Ellie's year of maternity leave.

She'd have daylight hours to see the world and evenings to think about going out for dinner with the not infrequent men who had asked her. The excuse of night shift would be taken out of her grasp. Which was a good thing. She'd hidden for two years and the time to be brave had arrived.

She stepped back from Ellie, picked up her bag and blew her a kiss. 'Happy last day. I'll see you at your lunch tomorrow.' Then she lifted her chin and stepped out of the door into the cool morning.

The tangy morning breeze promised a shower later, and pattering rain on the roof on a cool day made diving into bed in the daylight hours oh, so much more attractive than the usual sunny weather of Lighthouse Bay. Summer turning to autumn was her favourite time of year. Trina turned her face into the salty spray from the sea as she walked down towards the beach.

She slept better if she walked before going up the hill to her croft cottage, even if just a quick dash along the breakwall path that ran at right angles to the beach.

Especially after a birth. Her teeth clenched as she sucked in the salty air and tried not to dwell on the resting mother lying snug and content in the ward with her brand-new pink-faced baby.

Trina looked ahead to the curved crescent of the beach as she swung down the path from the hospital. The sapphire blue of the ocean stretching out to the horizon where the water met the sky, her favourite contemplation, and, closer, the rolling waves crashing and turning into fur-like foam edges that raced across the footprint-free sand to sink in and disappear.

Every day the small creek flowing into the ocean changed, the sandbars shifting and melding with the tides. The granite boulders like big seals set into the creek bed, lying lazily and oblivious to the shifting sand around them. Like life, Trina thought whimsically. You could fight against life until you realised that the past was gone and you needed to wait to see what the next tide brought. If only you could let go.

Ahead she saw that solitary dad. The one with his little girl in the backpack, striding along the beach with those long powerful strides as he covered the distance from headland to headland. Just like he had every morning she'd walked for the last four weeks. A tall, broad-shouldered, dark-haired man with a swift stride.

Sometimes the two were draped in raincoats, sometimes his daughter wore a cheery little hat with pom-poms. Sometimes, like today, they both wore beanies and a scarf.

Trina shivered. She could have done with a scarf. When she was tired it was easy to feel the cold. It would be good to move to day shifts after almost two bleak years on nights, but falling into bed exhausted in the daytime had been preferable to the dread of lying lonely and alone in the small dark hours.

She focused on the couple coming towards her. The little girl must have been around twelve months old, and seemed to be always gurgling with laughter, her crinkled eyes, waving fists and gap-toothed smile a delight to start the day with. The father, on the other hand, smiled with his mouth only when he barely lifted his hand but his storm-blue eyes glittered distant and broken beneath the dark brows. Trina didn't need to soak in anyone else's grief.

They all guessed about his story because, for once, nobody had gleaned any information and shared it with the inhabitants of Lighthouse Bay.

They drew closer and passed. 'Morning.' Trina inclined her head and waved at the little girl who, delightfully, waved back with a toothy chuckle.

'Morning,' the father said and lifted the corner of his lips before he passed.

And that was that for another day. Trina guessed she knew exactly how he felt. But she was changing.

CHAPTER ONE

Finn

AT SEVEN-THIRTY A.M. on the golden sands of Lighthouse Bay Beach Finlay Foley grimaced at the girl as she went past. Always in the purple scrubs so he knew she was one of the midwives from the hospital. A midwife. Last person he wanted to talk to.

It had been a midwife, one who put her face close to his and stared at him suspiciously, who told him his wife had left their baby and him behind, and ran away.

But the dark-haired girl with golden glints in her hair never invaded his space. She exuded a gentle warmth and empathy that had begun to brush over him lightly like a consistent warm beam of sunlight through leaves. Or like that soft shaft of light that reached into a corner of his cottage from the lighthouse on the cliff by some bizarre refraction. And always that feather-stroke of compassion without pity in her brown-eyed glance that thawed his frozen soul a little more each day when they passed.

She always smiled and so did he. But neither of them stopped. Thank goodness.

Piper gurgled behind his ear and he tilted his head to catch her words. 'Did you say something, Piper?'

'Mum, Mum, Mum, Mum.'

Finn felt the tightness crunch his sternum as if someone had grabbed his shirt and dug their nails into his chest. Guilt. Because he hadn't found her. He closed his eyes for a second. Nothing should be this hard. 'Try Dad, Dad, Dad, Dad,' he said past the tightness in his throat.

Obediently Piper chanted in her musical little voice, 'Dad, Dad, Dad, Dad.'

'Clever girl.' His mouth lifted this time and he felt a brief piercing of warmth from another beam of light in his cave-like existence.

Which was why he'd moved here. To make himself shift into the light. For Piper. And it did seem to be working. Something about this place, this haven of ocean and sand and cliffs and smiling people like the morning midwife soothed his ragged nerves and restored his faith in finding a way into the future.

A future he needed to create for Piper. Always the jolliest baby, now giggling toddler and all-round ray of puppy-like delight, Piper had kept him sane mainly because he had to greet each day to meet her needs.

His sister had said Piper had begun to look sad. Suspected she wasn't happy in the busy day care. Didn't see enough of her dad when he worked long hours. And he'd lifted his head and seen what his sister had seen.

Piper had been clingy. Harder to leave when he dropped her off at the busy centre. Drooping as he dressed her for 'school' in the morning. Quiet when he picked her up ten hours later.

Of course he needed to get a life and smile for his daughter. So he'd listened when his sister suggested he take a break from the paediatric practice where he'd continued as if on autopilot. Maybe escape to a place one of her friends had visited recently, where he knew no one, and heal for a week or two, or even a month for his daughter's sake. Maybe go back part-time for a while and spend more time with Piper. So he'd come. Here. To Lighthouse Bay.

Even on the first day it had felt right, just a glimmer of a breakthrough in the darkness, and he'd known it had been a good move.

The first morning in the guesthouse, when he'd walked the beach with Piper on his back, he'd felt a stirring of the peace he had found so elusive in his empty, echoing, accusing house. Saw the girl with the smile. Said, 'Good morning.'

After a few days he'd rented a cottage just above the beach for a week to avoid the other boisterous guests—happy families and young lovers he didn't need to talk to at breakfast—and moved to a place more private and offering solitude, but the inactivity of a rented house had been the exact opposite to what he needed.

Serendipitously, the cottage next door to that had come up for sale—*Would suit handyman*—which he'd never been. He was not even close to handy. Impulsively, after he'd discussed it with Piper, who had smiled and nodded and gurgled away his lack of handyman skills with great enthusiasm, he'd bought it. Then and there. The bonus of vacant possession meant an immediate move in even before the papers were signed.

He had a holiday house at the very least and a home if he never moved back to his old life. Radical stuff for a single parent, escaped paediatrician, failed husband, and one who had been used to the conveniences of a large town.

The first part of the one big room he'd clumsily beautified was Piper's corner and she didn't mind the smudges here and there and the chaos of spackle and paint tins and drip sheets and brushes.

Finally, he'd stood back with his daughter in his arms and considered he might survive the next week and maybe even the one after that. The first truly positive achievement he'd accomplished since Clancy left.

Clancy left.

How many times had he tried to grasp that fact? His wife of less than a year had walked away. Run, really. Left him, left her day-old daughter, and disappeared. With another man, if the private investigator had been correct. But still a missing person. Someone who in almost twelve months had never turned up in a hospital, or a morgue, or on her credit card. He had even had the PI check if she was working somewhere but that answer had come back as a no. And his sister, who had introduced them, couldn't find her either.

Because of the note she'd given the midwives, the police had only been mildly interested. Hence the PI.

Look after Piper. She's yours. Don't try to find me. I'm never coming back.

That was what the note had said. The gossip had been less direct. He suspected what the questions had been. Imagined what the midwives had thought. *Why did his wife leave him? What did he do to her? It must have been bad if she left her baby behind...*

The ones who knew him well shook their heads and said, *She'd liked her freedom too much, that one.*

At first he'd been in deep shock. Then denial. She'd come back. A moment's madness. She'd done it before. Left for days. With the reality of a demanding newborn and his worry making it hard for him to sleep at all, his work had suffered. But his largest concern had been the spectre of Clancy with an un-diagnosed postnatal depression. Or, worse, the peril of a post-natal psychosis. What other reason could she have for leaving so suddenly so soon after the birth?

Hence he'd paid the private investigator, because there were no forensic leads—the police were inundated with more impor-tant affairs than flighty wives. But still no word. All he could do was pray she was safe, at least.

So life had gone on. One painful questioning new morn-ing after another. Day after day with no relief. He hadn't been able to do his job as well as he should have and he'd needed a break from it all.

Buying the cottage had been a good move. Piper stood and cheered him on in her cot when he was doing something tricky, something that didn't need to have a lively little octopus climb all over him while he did it, and she waved her fists and gurgled and encouraged him as he learnt to be a painter. Or a carpenter. Or a tiler.

Or a cook. Or a cleaner. Or a dad.

He was doing okay.

He threw a last look out over the beach towards the grey sea and turned for home. 'That's our walk done for this morning, chicken. Let's go in and have breakfast. Then you can have a sleep and Daddy will grout those tiles in the shower so we can stop having bird baths in the sink.'

Piper loved the shower. Finn did too. When he held her soft, squirming satin baby skin against his chest, the water making her belly laugh as she ducked her head in and out of the stream always made him smile. Sometimes even made him laugh.

So he'd spent extra time on the shower. Adding tiles with animals, starfish, moon shapes and flowers, things they could talk about and keep it a happy place for Piper. And he'd made a square-tiled base with a plug. Soon she could have a little bath. One she could splash in even though it was only the size of the shower.

Doing things for Piper kept him sane. He didn't need the psychologist his sister said he did, or the medication his brother-in-law recommended. Just until he'd climbed out of the hole he'd dug himself to hide in, he would stay here. In Lighthouse Bay. Where nobody pointed or pitied him and every corner didn't hold a memory that scraped like fingernails on the chalkboard of his heavy heart.

Except that around the next corner his heart froze for a millisecond to see the morning midwife crouched on the path in front of him.

He quickened his pace. 'Are you okay?'

She turned to look up at him, cradling something brightly coloured against her chest, and with the shift of her shoulders he saw the bird cupped in her hands. 'She flew into that window and knocked herself out.'

The lorikeet, blue-headed with a red and yellow chest, lay limp with lime-green wings folded back in her hands. A most flaccid bird.

Still, the red beak and chest shuddered gently so it wasn't dead. 'How do you know it's a girl?' He couldn't believe he'd just said that. But he'd actually thought it was her that had been hurt and relief had made him stupid.

She must have thought he was stupid too. 'I didn't actually lift her legs and look. Not really of major importance, is it?'

Just a little bit of impatience and, surprisingly, it was good to be at the receiving end of a bit of healthy sarcasm. So much better than unending sympathy.

He held up his hands in surrender and Piper's voice floated over both of them from his back. 'Dad, Dad, Dad!'

The girl sucked in her breath and he could see her swan-like neck was tinged with pink. 'Sorry. Night duty ill temper.'

'My bad. All mine. Stupid thing to say. Can you stand up? It's tricky to crouch down with Piper on my back. Let's have a look at her.'

The morning midwife rose fluidly, calves of steel obviously; even he was impressed with her grace—must be all those uphill walks she did. 'She's not fluttering her wings,' she said, empathy lacing a voice that, had it not been agitated, would have soothed the bird. He shook himself. She was just being a typical midwife. That was how most of them had spoken to him when Clancy had disappeared.

'Still breathing.' He stroked the soft feathers as the bird lay in her small hands. 'She's limp, but I think if you put her in a box for a couple of hours in the dark, she'll rouse when she's had a sleep to get over the shock.'

'Do you think so?'

'I do. She's not bleeding. Just cover the box with a light cloth so she can let you know she can fly away when she's ready.'

'Do I have to put food or water in there?'

'Not food. A little water as long as she doesn't fall into it and drown.' He grimaced at another stupid comment.

She grinned at him and suddenly the day was much brighter than it had been. 'Are you a vet?'

'No.'

'Just a bird wrangler?'

She was a stunner. He stepped back. 'One of my many talents. I'll leave you to it.'

'Thank you.'

'Bye.'

She looked at him oddly. Not surprising. He was odd. He walked on up the hill.

Her voice followed him. 'Bye, Piper.' He heard Piper chuckle.

CHAPTER TWO

Trina

TRINA FINISHED HER night shift at seven a.m. on Friday and picked up her mini-tote to sling it on her shoulder. Her last night done, except for emergencies, and she did a little skip as she came out of the door. At first, she'd been reluctant to take the night shift to day shift change that Ellie had offered her because change could be scary, but it had started the whole paradigm inversion that her life had needed. Look out daylight. Here she comes.

Yes. She'd come a long way in almost two years since Ed had died.

Not just because on Monday morning she'd return as acting Midwifery Unit Manager, an unexpected positive career move for Trina at Lighthouse Bay Maternity.

But things had changed.

Her grief stayed internal, or only rarely escaped under her pillow when she was alone in her croft on the cliff.

And since Ellie's wedding last year she'd begun to think that maybe, some time in the future, she too could look at being friends with a man. If the right one came along.

Not a relationship yet. That idea had been so terrifying, almost like PTSD—the fear of imagining what if history repeated itself; what if that immense pain of loss and grief hit her again? What then?

She'd been catatonic with that thought and to divert herself she'd begun to think of all the other things that terrified her. She'd decided to strengthen her Be Brave muscle.

Last week she'd had her first scuba lesson. Something that had fascinated but petrified her since she'd watched the movie *Finding Nemo* with the daughter of a friend. And in the sparkling cove around the corner from Lighthouse Bay the kindly instructor had been so reassuring, so patient, well... Maybe she'd go back on Saturday for another lesson.

And when she'd mastered that she was going out on a day of deep-sea fishing. The captain's wife had not long delivered a late-in-life baby and Trina had been the midwife. Even though he'd fainted again, he'd promised her a day of deep-sea fishing when he felt better. She'd bought seasickness bands and stored them in her drawer just in case.

She wasn't sure about the parachuting. The girls at work had all joined the idea factory and brochures and social media tags of extreme sports and adventure holidays appeared like magic in her pigeonhole and on her private page. Parachuting? She didn't think so but she'd worry about that later.

Her aim to do one challenge a month seemed possible to allay the fear that she was relying on work to be her whole world. Though not too adventurous—she didn't want to kill herself. Not now.

Her friends were cheering. Thinking of the midwives of Lighthouse Bay...well, that made her whole world warm into a rosy glow. A fiercely loyal flotsam of women tossed here by the fickle cruelty of life, forging into a circle of hands supporting birthing women and each other. All acutely aware of how fortunate they were to have found the magic of the bay.

There was something healing about that crescent of sand that led to the cliffs.

A mystical benevolence about the soaring white lighthouse on the tallest point that looked benignly over the tiny hamlet of coloured houses and shone reassuring light.

And the pretty pastel abodes like a quaint European seaside town were a delight, a new trend that had taken off with the gentle crayon façades dipping in colour like playful toes into the sea.

Crazy coloured houses, and if she could do all those crazy-coloured feats of bravery then just maybe she could be brave enough to begin a real conversation with a man. Like yesterday. She'd almost forgotten the handsome dad was a man when she'd snapped at him. They'd almost had a whole conversation. She wouldn't mind another one so he didn't think she was a short-tempered shrew but she had been concerned about the bird. The one that had flown away two hours later, just like he said it would.

If she could talk to a man she could try again to go out with one. At least once. She'd been turning them down for six months now. None of them had been Ed.

Now there were more midwives around to lessen the on-call restrictions. Four new midwives had come on board to swell their ranks with the shift to a midwife-led unit. They still had old Dr Southwell in the hospital for non-maternity patients and maternity emergencies, but all the midwives had moved to four days of ten-hour shifts and caring for a caseload of women, so suddenly there was more time for life with an extra day free and people to cover you if needed. And she'd scored the admin side Monday to Thursday, daylight hours, for a year. Starting Monday. Imagine.

So she'd better get out there and grab that exciting life before it drifted past in a haze of regrets. She lifted her head and sucked in a pure lungful of gorgeous sea air.

Without realising it her feet had followed the well-beaten path down to the beach and just as she turned to start her morning breakwall walk she saw the dad and his little girl come up off the beach.

He looked happier today. Nice. It made her smile warmer. 'Beautiful morning.'

He looked startled for a minute. 'Yes, it is.' Almost as if he was surprised. 'Good morning—how is your bird?'

'Flew away two hours later. Didn't look any worse for wear.'

He gave her the first real smile she'd seen. 'That's good.'

Then he was past. Trina turned her head to glance back and the little fair-haired girl waved.

Trina smiled and yawned. She should go to bed and get a couple of hours' sleep before Ellie's farewell lunch. Just a quick walk.

CHAPTER THREE

Finn

THE EARLY-MORNING BREEZE off the ocean seemed cooler. The water had taken till now to shine like a jewel. She'd been late this morning. Finn had waited a minute, hoping she wouldn't see him do it, and strangely the minute seemed to take for ever, then he'd looked back. He'd been thinking of her last night. Wondering if she were sad about a dead bird or happy when it flew away.

He thought back to her response. Now that was a smile. He could see it in his retina like a glance at the sun. Warm and glowing. Saw her walking quite a way in the distance—she'd moved fast. He'd noticed that before, that her pace ran to brisk rather than dawdling. Nurses often did walk briskly. Couldn't seem to slow themselves enough to meander even on a seaside walk. He tore his eyes away.

He'd done the breakwall walk she did a couple of times when he'd first come here but he liked the effort of walking through the sand with Piper on his back. If nothing else he'd become fit and tanned and physically healthier here in a month. And Piper too had sun-kissed limbs and sparkling eyes that exuded health.

His sister would be pleased when she came today. His first

visitor. He shied away from that intrusion into his safe world and thought again of the young midwife. Maybe not so young because he'd seen the signs of loss and life in her big coffee eyes—even in those brief glances they'd shot at each other. For the first time he wondered if other people had suffered as much as he had? Well, that at least seemed a positive sign that he could reconnect with his inherent compassion that he'd seemed to have lost.

The thought made him wonder what it would be like to talk to someone who could actually begin to understand his hell, and then called himself crazy for making up a past about someone he didn't know. Poor woman probably had never had a sad day in her life. But something told him otherwise.

Just before one p.m. his sister stepped out of her red convertible and through his front gate. 'It's beautiful, Finn. I can't believe you've done all this yourself!' Her perfectly pencilled brows were raised as she gazed at the pale pink external walls of the house and the rose-red door.

He'd been a little surprised himself. And the front path bordered by pansies and baby's breath looked as if it belonged to some older lady with a green thumb—not a guilt-deranged paediatrician running from life.

She rocked her head slowly. He'd expected disbelief but not this patent incredulity. He felt strangely offended. 'I didn't even know you like to garden!'

He shrugged, urging her towards the door. 'Neither did I. But Piper loves being outside and we needed to do something while we're out here.'

Frances rubbernecked her way up the path, nice and slow for the neighbours, he thought dryly, and sighed while she gushed. She gushed when she didn't know what to say, though what the problem was he had no idea.

'And the house. Freshly painted? You actually painted?' She

glanced around. 'Pastel like the others in the street. It's gorgeous.'

Finn looked at the stucco walls. They'd been a pain to paint. 'Piper chose the colour. I would have preferred a blue but, given the choice, she went for pink every time. Never thought I'd have a stereotypical daughter.'

Frances laughed and waved her hand dismissively. 'Piper's too young to choose.'

'No, she's not,' he said mildly. 'How can you say it's not her choice if I give her four colours and she keeps choosing pink?'

Frances looked at him as if he needed a big dose of sympathy for his feeble brain. 'You didn't pretend she was choosing?'

'Who else was I going to ask?' He heard the edge in his voice. And his sister shut up. So then he felt mean.

It was always like this. On and on until he shut her down. She meant well, but for heaven's sake. He wanted her gone already.

They finally made it to the front door.

In an attempt to lighten the mood he stopped to show her something else. 'Piper helped everywhere.' He kissed the top of his daughter's head as she perched on his hip. Quiet for a change because she hadn't quite found her ease with her aunt. Or maybe she was picking up Finn's nervous vibes. Either way she leaned into him, unusually subdued.

He pointed to a handprint on the front step that he'd finished with instant cement. Using a layer of cling wrap over the wet surface, he'd pressed her starfish hand into the step on each side while holding her clamped to his side. The little palm prints made him smile every time he opened the door.

'Come in.' He heard the pride in his voice and mocked himself. Finn the decorator. 'There's still the kitchen and laundry, but I've finished Piper's corner, the bathroom and the floating boards on the floor because she'll need a solid surface to learn to walk on.'

Frances rotated her neck, as if stuck to the step and that was the only part of her body she could move. 'It's tiny.'

He frowned. 'Yes. It's a beach cottage. Not a mansion.'

She blinked. Shifted uneasily. 'Oh, yes. Of course. But your other beautiful house...'

'Is on the market.'

Now the shock was real. Frances had approved mightily of his imposing residence on top of the hill. Two hills over from her imposing residence. He'd only liked it because Clancy, his missing wife, had loved it.

Frances spluttered, 'You're buying a new house?'

'I've bought a new house.' He put out one hand and gestured. 'This house. I'm staying here.'

'I... I thought you'd done this for the owners. That you rented?'

'I am the owner.' *A little too fierce, Finn*, he chided himself.

Frances leaned towards him pleadingly. 'But your work?'

'Will be here too when I'm ready. One of the GPs here has offered me a place in his practice when I'm ready. I'll specialise in children but do all the GP stuff I've almost forgotten. It'll be good.' He wasn't sure who he was convincing, Frances or himself. 'It won't be yet because I'm in no hurry.'

'But...'

'But what?'

His sister turned worried eyes on his. 'You were only supposed to come here for a few weeks and then come back. Come home.'

'Home to where, Frances? To what? To an empty castle on a hill full of ghosts and pain. To a clinic with not enough hours in the day so I had to keep my daughter in long day care?'

Frances looked stricken and he leaned in and shared a hug with her, Piper still a limpet on his other hip. Frances meant well and she truly loved him. And now that Mum was gone she was all the family he had. Of course she'd never understood him with the ten-year age difference. Frances hadn't understood Mum either, if they were being honest. 'It's okay. This is a magic place to live and for Piper and me this is the right place at the right time. We're staying.'

Frances almost wrung her hands. 'You won't meet any eligible women here.'

He could feel his mood slip further. His irritation rise. His disappointment deepen. His sister didn't understand his guilt couldn't be fixed by an eligible woman. 'Eligible for what, Frances? I'm no good for any woman at the moment and won't be...' he didn't say *ever* '...for a very long time.'

He decided not to demonstrate the shower. Or point anything else out. Ditched the plans to take a picnic to the beach.

Instead he took Frances to the most expensive restaurant in town, where Piper slept in her stroller beside the table despite the noise of conversations and laughter all around, and listened to her stories of droll people and dire events in her husband's practice.

In the corner of the restaurant he noticed a very attractive brunette. She nodded at him and he realised it was his morning midwife, elegantly dressed—*sans* scrubs—and made-up like a model, her brown hair blow-dried and shining, the glints catching the sun. Looking like a million bucks. Other men were looking at her. He preferred the windblown version.

She sat, a little isolated, in a lively group of people, all chinking champagne flutes to celebrate. Frances would approve of the clientele, he thought dryly, but recognised the older doctor he'd mentioned to his sister, and noted the stylish older woman next to him who leant into his shoulder, probably his wife. Another young woman he hadn't seen around was chatting to the vibrantly glowing woman in the latter stages of pregnancy who drank water, and next to her a man hovered protectively, obviously the doting father-to-be.

He wished him better luck than he'd had. Finn felt his heart twist in self-disgust. He'd tried that. A lot of good that had done him.

'Finn?'

His sister's voice called him back to the present and he jerked his face away from them. 'Sorry. You were telling me about Gerry's partner?'

Frances hovered over being cross for a moment and thankfully decided to forgive graciously. 'I was saying she has no idea how a doctor's wife should dress.'

The lunch dragged on until finally Piper woke up and gave him an excuse to pay the bill.

They waved Frances goodbye after lunch with much relief. 'Seriously, Piper. Your aunt is getting worse. We're lucky to be so far away.'

They took the sand buckets and spade back down to the beach in the afternoon because Piper's routine had been disrupted and she needed to get some play time in and wear herself out before bedtime.

To his surprise, and with a seagull-like swoop of uplifting spirits, the morning midwife sat there on the breakwall, back in beach clothes and mussed by the wind. He smiled at her like a long-lost friend. After the visit from his sister he felt as if he needed a pal.

CHAPTER FOUR

Trina

TRINA SAT SWINGING her legs on the breakwall down on the beach and breathed in the salt. The sea air blew strands into her eyes but it felt too good to worry about that. She saw him before he saw her and a deep, slashing frown marred his forehead. Different to this morning. Then his expression changed as he saw her, the etched lines disappeared and an unexpected, ridiculously sexy, warmly welcoming smile curved in a big sweep. *Goodness.* What had she done to deserve that?

'Lovely afternoon,' he said and the little girl waved.

Trina's mouth twitched as she waved back. 'Beautiful. I saw you at lunch. That's three times in a day.'

'A new world record,' he agreed and she blushed. No idea why.

He paused beside her, another world record, and looked down from far too high. Up close and stationary, told herself again, he would be a very good-looking man—to other women. She studied him almost dispassionately. Long lashes framed those brilliant blue eyes and his dark brown wavy hair curled a tad too long over his ears. His chin was set firm and his cheekbones bordered on harsh in the bright light. She could see his effort to be social cost him. She knew the feeling.

'I'm Catrina Thomas.' She didn't enlarge. He could ask if he was interested, but something told her he wasn't so much interested as in need of a friend. Which suited her perfectly.

'Finlay Foley. And you've met Piper. My daughter.' The little girl bounced in the backpack.

You could do nothing but smile at Piper. 'Piper looks like she wants to get down amongst the sand.'

'Piper is happiest when she's caked in sand.' His hand lifted to stroke the wiggling little leg at his chest. Strong brown fingers tickling a plump golden baby ankle. 'We're going to build sandcastles. Piper is going to play hard and long and get extremely tired so she will sleep all night.' Trina wasn't sure if he was telling her or telling Piper. She suspected the latter.

'Nice theory,' Trina agreed judiciously. 'I see you have it all worked out.'

He began to fiddle with the straps as he extricated his daughter from the backpack and clinically she watched the muscle play as man power pulled his loose white shirt tight. His thick dark hair tousled in the wind and drew her eyes until she was distracted again by the wriggling child. Finlay popped her down in the sand on her bottom and put a spade and bucket beside her.

'There, miss.' He glanced up at Trina. 'Her aunt came today and she's ruined our sleep routine.' He paused at that. 'Speaking of routines, this is late in the day for you to be on the beach.'

'Nice of you to notice.' She wasn't sure if it was. There had been a suspicious lift of her spirits when she'd realised the woman he'd shared lunch with was his sister. What was that? She didn't have expectations and he wouldn't either—not that she supposed he would have. She wasn't ready for that. 'Don't get ideas or I'll have to leave.' Almost a joke. But she explained.

'Today is my first official Friday off for a long time. I'm off nights and on day shifts for the next year. Monday to Thursday.' She looked around at the little groups and families on the beach and under the trees at the park. Pulled a mock frowning face. 'I'll have to talk to people and socialise, I guess.'

'I know. Sucks, doesn't it.' The underlying truth made them both stop and consider. And smile a little sheepishly at each other.

Another urge to be truthful came out of nowhere. 'I'm a widow and not that keen on pretending to be a social butterfly. Hence the last two years on night duty.'

He said more slowly, as if he wasn't sure why he was following suit either, 'My wife left us when Piper was born. A day later. I've morphed into antisocial and now I'm hiding here.'

Died? Or left? How could his wife leave when their daughter was born? She closed her mouth with a snap. Not normal. Something told her Piper's mum hadn't died, though she didn't know why. Postnatal depression then? A chilling thought. Not domestic violence?

As if he read her thoughts, he added, 'I think she left with another man.' He seemed to take a perverse pleasure in her disbelief. 'I need to start thinking about going back to work soon. Learn to stop trying to guess what happened. To have adult conversations.'

He shrugged those impressive shoulders. Glanced around at the white sand and waves. 'I'm talking to Piper's dolls now.'

Still bemused by the first statement, the second took a second to sink in. Surprisingly, Trina giggled. She couldn't remember the last time she'd giggled like a schoolgirl.

He smiled and then sobered. 'Which means Piper and her dolls must go into day care if I go back to work.'

'That's hard,' Trina agreed but wondered what sort of work he could 'start thinking about going back to'. Not that there were screeds of choices around here. 'Maybe part-time?'

'I think so.'

'Are you a builder? The house looks good.'

He laughed at that. 'No. Far from it. Piper's taught me everything I know.'

Trina giggled again. *Stop it.* She sounded like a twit. But he was funny. 'I didn't have you pegged as a comedian.'

His half-laugh held a hint of derision at himself. 'Not usually. Remember? Antisocial.'

She nodded with solemn agreement. 'You're safe with me. If you need a protected space to tell your latest doll story you can find me.' She waited until his eyes met hers. 'But that's all.'

'Handy to know. Where do I find you? You know where I live.' Then he turned away as if he regretted asking.

'Of course I know where you live. It's a small town and single men with babies are rare.' Trina looked at him. 'I meant... find me here. But I'll think about it. I'm happy to have a male friend but not a stalker.'

She felt like an idiot saying that but thankfully he just looked relieved. 'Hallelujah. And I promise I will never, ever turn up uninvited.'

'We have that sorted.' She glanced at Piper, who sat on the sand licking white granules off her fingers, and bit back a grin. 'It's good when children will eat anything.'

Finn focused instantly on his daughter and scooped her up. Trina could see him mentally chastising himself. She imagined something like, *See what happens when you don't concentrate on your daughter*, and she knew he'd forgotten her. Was happy for the breathing space because, speaking of breathing, she was having a little trouble.

She heard his voice from a long way away. 'Sand is for playing—not eating, missy.' He scooped the grains from her mouth and brushed her lips. His quick glance brushed over Trina as well as he began to move away. 'Better go wash her mouth out and concentrate. Nice to meet you, Catrina.'

'You too,' she said, suddenly needing to bolt home and shut her door.

Ten minutes later the lock clunked home solidly and she leant back against the wood. Another scary challenge achieved.

Not that she'd been in danger—just a little more challenged than she'd been ready for. And she had been remarkably loose with her tongue. Told him she was a widow. About her job. The hours she worked. What had got into her? That was a worry. So much so that it did feel incredibly comforting to be home. Though, now that she looked around, it seemed dark inside. She frowned. Didn't just *seem* dark.

Her home was dark.

And just a little dismal. She frowned and then hurried to re-assure herself. Not tragically so, more efficiently gloomy for a person who slept through a lot of the daylight hours. She pulled the cord on the kitchen blind and it rolled up obediently and light flooded in from the front, where the little dead-end road finished next door.

She moved to the side windows and thinned the bunching of the white curtains so she could see through them. Maybe she could open those curtains too. Now that she'd be awake in the daytime. Moving out of the dark, physically and figuratively.

So, she'd better see to lightening it up. Maybe a few bright cushions on her grey lounge suite; even a bright rug on the floor would be nice. She stared down at the grey and black swirled rug she'd bought in a monotone furnishing package when she moved in. Decided she didn't like the lack of colour.

She crossed the room and threw open the heavy curtains that blocked the view. Unlocking the double glass doors and pushing them slowly open, she stepped out onto her patio to look out over the glittering expanse of ocean that lay before her like a big blue shot-thread quilt as far as the eye could see. She didn't look down to the beach, though she wanted too. Better not see if there was the figure of a man and a little girl play-ing in the waves.

Instead she glanced at the little croft to her right where Ellie and Sam lived while Sam built the big house on the headland for their growing family. She wondered if they would keep the croft, as they said they would. It would be strange to have new neighbours on top of everything else.

The three crofts sat like seabirds perched on a branch of the headland, the thick walls painted white like the lighthouse across the bay and from the same solid stone blocks. Trina's veranda had a little awning over the deck the others lacked. A thick green evergreen hedge separated the buildings to shoulder height.

On the other side of her house lay Myra's croft. Originally from Paddington in Sydney, stylish Myra ran the coffee shop at the hospital and had recently married the older Dr Southwell—her boss Ellie's father-in-law.

Two brides in two months, living each side of her, and maybe that had jolted her out of her apathy as much as anything else. Surrounded by people jumping bravely into new relationships and new lives had to make a woman think.

She stepped out and crossed to the two-person swing seat she'd tussled with for hours to assemble. Her last purchase as a flat-pack. Last *ever*, she promised herself.

She'd never seen so many screws and bolts and instructions in one flat-pack. Then she'd been left with a contraption that had to be dragged inside when it got too windy here on top of the cliffs because it banged and rattled and made her nervous that it would fly into the ocean on a gust. It wasn't really that she thought about the fact it needed a second person. Not at all.

She stepped back inside, glanced around then picked up the sewing basket and dug in it for the ribbons she'd put away. Went back to the double doors and tied back the curtains so they were right off the windows. Not that she was getting visitors—her mind shied away from the mental picture of a man and his baby daughter.

No. She'd lighten it because now she didn't need to exclude the light to help her sleep. She was a day-shift person. She was brave. And tomorrow she'd scuba again, and maybe talk to Finlay and Piper if she saw them because she was resurrecting her social skills and stepping forward. Carefully.

CHAPTER FIVE

Finn

FINN GLANCED BACK to the rocky breakwall once, to the spot where Catrina—nice name—had disappeared, as he crouched with Piper at the edge of the water to rinse her mouth of sand. It seemed other people did hurt like he did. And were left with scars that impacted hugely on how they lived their lives.

Two years working on night duty. He shuddered but could see the logic. Side-stepping the cold space beside you in the bed at night and avoiding that feeling of loss being the first thing you noticed in the day. Maybe he should have given that a go.

But the way she'd said she hadn't pegged him as a comedian surprised him out of his usual lethargy. He'd made her laugh twice—that was pretty stellar. Apart from his daughter, whose sense of humour ran to very simple slapstick, he hadn't made anyone giggle for a long time. He could almost hear her again. Such a delicious giggle. More of a gurgle really.

So—a widow? Lost like him, for a different reason. He wondered how her husband had died but in the end it didn't really change her pain. He was gone. For ever. Unlike the uncertainty he lived with.

Would Clancy ever come back? In a year. In ten years? Was

she even alive? But, most of all, what would he tell Piper when she grew up? How could he say her mother loved her when she'd walked away and never asked about her again? The pain for Piper's future angst had grown larger than his own loss and he had no desire to rush the explanations.

Milestones with Piper never passed without him singeing himself with bitterness that Clancy wasn't there to see them. First tooth. First word. First step last week—though she still spent most of her time on her bottom. And on Sunday—first birthday. He felt his jaw stiffen. That would be the day he said *enough*. Enough holding his breath, expecting Clancy to walk through the door.

A milestone he'd never thought he'd get to. He hadn't decided whether to stay in Lighthouse Bay for the day with their usual routine; he was leaning towards taking Piper shopping, something he loathed, so that the logistics of strollers and car parking and crowd managing with a toddler drowned out the reminders of the best day of his life twelve months ago that had changed so soon after.

He wondered suddenly if he could ask Catrina to come. As a diversion, a pseudo-mother for the day, and then found himself swamped by such intense anger at Clancy for leaving their daughter he almost moaned. Piper clutched his hand and he looked down to see his daughter's eyes staring up at him as if she could sense his pain.

He scooped her up and hugged her, felt the lump in his chest and willed it away. Whatever they did, he needed to remember it was a celebration of this angel in his arms, not of the woman who'd left them.

'I'll always love you, darling.' The words came out thickly. 'What would you like to do on Sunday, Piper?'

'Mum, Mum, Mum, Mum.'

He groaned and buried his face in her shimmering golden cloud of hair. Fine mist-like hair that floated in the breeze and tangled if he didn't tie it back but he couldn't bring himself to get it cut. His gorgeous little buttercup with her fine-spun headache of hair.

'Mum, Mum, Mum,' Piper chirped.

The last thing he needed to hear at this moment. 'Oh, baby, don't. Please.'

She squirmed and the baby voice drifted up to him. Uncertain. 'Dad, Dad, Dad, Dad?'

Pull yourself together. He lifted his head and looked into the soft dimpled face so close to his. 'Yes. Dad, Dad, Dad, Dad.' He carried her into the waves to dangle her feet and she wriggled happily. He concentrated on his fingers holding her as he swept her ankles through the waves and the foam ran up her knees as she squealed in delight. Guilt swamped him all over again. 'You can say *Mum, Mum, Mum* any time, my darling. Of course you can. Daddy's being silly.' *Stupid!*

Piper gurgled with laughter. 'Dad, Dad, Dad, Dad.' Finn could feel his heart shattering into a million pieces again and any lingering thoughts of Catrina the midwife washed into the sea with the grains of sand stuck to Piper's feet.

CHAPTER SIX

Trina

THE EARLY-MORNING SUNBEAM poked Trina in the eye with an unfamiliar exuberance and she groaned and threw her hand up to cover her face. *Who left the curtains open?* Only one answer to that. The twinge of morning memory and loss made her breath hitch and she forced herself to breathe calmly.

Saturday morning. Scuba lesson. She groaned again and all the doubts and fears from last week came rushing back to twist her stomach. Why had she said she wanted to do this again? Why the need to push herself to extremes she didn't feel comfortable with?

She flung the bedclothes back and swung her legs. The floor was warmed a little under her feet from the sun. That too seemed different.

Okay. Why was she fighting this? This was a new chapter in her life. Same book. She wasn't removing any of the pages—just going forward.

She squinted at the morning beams painting the inside of her one-room croft in golden stripes and decided they were quite lovely. Not worth groaning about at all.

She padded across to the uncurtained double doors looking

out over the ocean and decided the light streaming in shone still a little too bright until she'd made an Earl Grey to start the day and turned her back.

As she busied herself in the tiny kitchen nook, she pondered on yesterday and the advances she'd made towards holding a sensible conversation with an eligible male. Though technically she guessed he wasn't eligible. But probably safe to practise on, as long as he was okay with it.

Not that she had any long-term intentions but she'd done all right. Beaten the bogeyman, and so had he. That made it a little easier. And no doubt different for him, as his wife had chosen to go. How on earth could a woman leave her baby? And why would she leave Finlay? That too was a teensy worry.

Trina thought back to where she'd been a year ago. Still in a black fog with a bright shiny mask on her face for work.

She didn't believe that time healed all wounds, but maybe it scabbed over some of the deeper lacerations. The problem with losing your true love was they were never really gone, always hovering, a comfort, and an ache that flared into pain that burned right through you.

Boy, did she recognise the symptoms of reluctantly dipping a toe into the real world after the misty haze of deep grief. There were some aspects of her loss of Ed that would never disappear but in other ways she could, and would, live a happy life. She didn't think that Finlay Foley had reached that stage yet. Which was a tiny shame.

But she'd better get on and prepare for her scuba lesson. She'd eat when she came back.

By the time Trina left her croft on the cliff she knew she'd be late if she didn't hurry and her steps skipped as she descended to the beach with her towel and specially fitted snorkelling mask. That was one good thing about living right on the beach—she didn't need to carry much because home was always a few steps away.

The path stopped at the sand and Trina began walking

quickly around the headland. She'd glanced once towards the curve of the bay but no Finlay and Piper there, no sign of him, so tall and broad and unmistakable, so no golden-haired Piper on his back either, and fancifully it felt strange to be hurrying away without seeing them.

She forced herself to look forward again and concentrated on the scuba lessons she'd learnt last week from old Tom, running through the procedures.

'Nice even breathing through the mouthpiece; no holding your breath. This is how to replace a regulator in your mouth if it gets knocked out. This is how to control the speed of your ascent and descent by letting air in and out via the buoyancy control, so your ears don't hurt. Nothing to be nervous about. We'll go as slow as you need.'

Two hours later as she walked home in a much more desultory fashion a glow of pride warmed her as she remembered old Tom's quiet pleasure in her. 'You're a natural,' he'd told her.

A natural scuba diver? Who would have known? But today he'd taken her to the little island just off the beach and they'd dived slowly around the tiny inlets and rocks and seen colourful fish, delicate submarine plant life that swayed with the rhythm of the ocean, once a small stingray and one slightly larger shark, and it had all been Technicolor brilliant. Exciting. And, to her absolute delight, she'd loved it.

Her mind danced with snapshots of the morning and she didn't see the man and little girl sitting in a shallow rock pool under the cliff until she was almost upon them.

'Oh. You. Hello,' she stammered as she was jerked out of her happy reveries.

'Good morning, Catrina,' Finlay said. Though how on earth he could remain nonchalant while sitting in a sandy-bottom indent in the rock where the water barely covered his outstretched legs, she had no idea. 'You look very pleased with yourself.'

She regarded them. She liked the way they looked—so calm and happy, Piper dressed in her frilly pink swimsuit that covered her arms and legs. And she liked the way he called her Catrina. Ed had always called her Trina and she wasn't ready for another man to shorten her name. 'Good morning to you, Finlay.'

'Finn. Please. I'm usually Finn. Don't know why I was so formal yesterday.'

'Finn.' She nodded and smiled down at Piper. 'Hello, Piper. What can you see in the rock pool?'

The little girl turned her big green eyes back to the water. Pointed one plump finger. 'Fiss,' Piper said and Finn's eyes widened.

His mouth opened and closed just like the word his daughter had almost mouthed.

'She said fish!' His eyes were alight with wonder and the huge smile on his face made Trina want to hug him to celebrate the moment of pure joy untinged by bitterness. 'I can't believe she said fish.'

'Clever girl,' Trina said and battled not to laugh out loud. She'd thought it had been more like a mumbled *fiss*. But she was sure her father knew better. Her mouth struggled to remain serious. In the end she giggled. Giggled? Again? *What the heck?*

She'd never been a giggler but this guy made her smiles turn into noises she cringed at.

To hide her idiotic response she said, 'I've seen fish too, Piper.'

Finn glanced at her mask. 'You've been snorkelling?'

Trina spread her arms and said with solemn pride, almost dramatically, 'I have been scuba diving.'

'Have you? Go you. I used to love to scuba.' He glanced around. 'Would you like to join us in our pool? There's no lifeguard except me but if you promise not to run or dive we'll let you share.'

Trina scanned the area too. Nobody she knew. She'd look ridiculous, though a voice inside her head said he looked anything but ridiculous in his skin-tight blue rash shirt and board shorts that left not one gorgeous muscle top or bottom unaccounted for.

She put down her mask and the sandals she carried, folded her towel to sit on, hiked up her sundress so it didn't drag in the water and eased herself down at the edge of the pool and put her feet in. The water felt deliciously cool against her suddenly warmer skin.

Finn watched her and she tried not to be aware of that. Then Piper splashed him and the mood broke into something more relaxed. 'So where did you go to scuba?'

She glanced the way she'd come. 'Have you been around the headland?'

He nodded. 'Around the next two until Piper started to feel like a bag of cement on my back.'

Trina laughed. She could so imagine that. She smiled at him. 'The next bay is called Island Bay and the little rocky island that's about four hundred metres out is called Bay Island.'

He laughed. 'Creative people around here.'

She pretended to frown at him. 'I like to think of it as being whimsical.'

'Whimsical. Right.'

She nodded at him. 'Thank you. So, Bay Island is where I did this morning's lesson. Old Tom takes beginners out.'

Piper sat between Finn's legs and he had his big brown long-fingered hands around her tiny waist so she couldn't slip. She was splashing with her starfish hands and silver droplets of water dripped in chasing drops down her father's chest. An unexpected melancholy overwhelmed Trina because the picture made her ache for lost opportunities she should have had with Ed. Opportunities Finn should have had with his wife. She wondered when these thoughts would stop colouring her every experience.

Finn smiled. 'Let me guess. His business is called Old Tom's Dive Shop.'

She jerked back to the present. Her brows crinkled in mock disbelief and she drew the sentence out slowly. 'How did you know that?'

'I'm psychic.' His expression remained serious.

'Really?' She tried for serious too but he was doing it again and her mouth twitched.

'Mmm-hmm. True story.'

'Wow.' She noted the little girl had found a treasure. 'So you can see your daughter is about to put a shell in her mouth?'

Without taking his eyes off Trina's face, his hand came up gently and directed Piper's hand away from her lips. Brushed her fingers open until she dropped the shell and bent down and kissed the little fingers. 'Absolutely.'

'That's fascinating.' And it was. Watching this big bronzed man being so gentle and connected to this tiny girl-child. The bond between them made tears sting Trina's eyes and she pretended she'd splashed water in them. Until she felt, and heard, her tummy rumble with sullen emptiness and seized on the excuse.

'Well, as lovely as your private ocean pool is, I need to have food. I missed breakfast and I'm starving.'

'Ah. So that's what the noise was,' he teased. 'I thought it was an outboard motor.'

She flicked tiny droplets from her damp fingers at him. 'Too rude.'

He rolled his eyes at her, then shifted Piper from between his legs to sit in the shallow pool and stood up easily. He leant down to offer her his hand. 'Piper's hungry. I should feed her too.'

She barely heard him. His so casually offered fingers were a stumbling block and she hesitated. Piper splashed and she knew she was holding them up. Reluctantly she put out her hand to his and his strong brown fingers closed over hers to lift her smoothly. Way too easily. But the touch of his fingers on hers created such a vibration between them that their eyes met. One pair as startled as the other.

When she was standing he let go quickly and bent down to hoist his daughter into his arms. His face stayed hidden as he tickled her and Trina straightened her own shocked features into a mask of politeness as Piper giggled.

'Well,' she said awkwardly, still rocked by the frisson of awareness that had warmed her whole hand. Her whole arm really. 'Thanks for the swim.'

'Can we walk back with you?'

No, she thought. 'Of course,' she said. And resisted the urge to hold her tingling hand in the other. She bent down and picked up her sandals and mask, slung her towel over her shoulder and resolutely faced the bay until they began walking beside her.

'Would you like to have lunch with us?'

No, she thought. *I can't. I don't know what I'm feeling and it's making me more nervous than scuba diving ever did.* But that was the idea of these new challenges. To challenge things that seemed daunting. And Finn was safe. It took her a long time to answer but strangely she didn't feel pressured to make that snap decision. So she thought about it some more. It was just an impromptu lunch. And Piper made it much easier than if there were just the two of them. 'Okay. Where?'

'How about the beach shop? They have a closed-in play area that Piper loves to crawl around. It's shady and the breeze is always good there.'

'Sounds easy. But how about I meet you there? I didn't bring my purse. I can just run up to the croft and get it.'

He looked a little crestfallen. 'Piper may not last that long. She's nearly ready for her sleep. I could shout you. You could pay for ice creams or something next time?'

Next time? They hadn't tried this time yet. This was all happening way too fast. And wasn't he having as much trouble as she was, putting a toe in the water of opposite sex conversation? Panic built like a wave rising from the ocean to her left. She tried to ride it and not be dumped.

He must have seen the indecision on her face because his features softened in understanding. 'It's okay. We can do a rain-check for another day.'

Disappointment dipped in her stomach. Did she want that? Why was everything so hard? 'No. Let's not. Thank you. I'll just buy the next one, if that's okay. A quick bite would be nice with company.'

They sat under the umbrellas and watched Piper play with a stand of coloured balls, then crawl importantly to steer a pretend ship with a bright blue Captain's wheel. Every time the conversation flagged, Piper sparked a new discussion with some cute little parody of life in her determination to experience all that the colourful play area offered.

Trina could do with her enthusiasm. Considered that fact. 'Babies should be compulsory on all outings. You could watch her all day.'

Finn laughed. Then, more seriously, said, 'I do. She keeps me sane. Makes me get out of bed in the morning.'

Trina knew that feeling. 'Well, you've certainly been busy since you got here. Your cottage is pretty in pink.'

'Piper chose the colour,' he said and then looked at her as if expecting her to laugh.

'So she's a pink girl. I can believe that. It looks good on her.' Trina rested her cheek on her hand to watch his face, trying to understand why he should be so wary. 'How did you get her to choose?'

'I gave her swatches. I was hoping for blue but she took the pink every time.'

Too funny. Trina laughed. 'Great idea. I can see that too.' She looked at his face and his beautiful smile. She shook her head. 'Her decision. You were stuck with it. Nothing you can do about that, then.'

He shrugged, his expression light and relaxed. It made her warm that he could be that way around her. 'I'm used to it now. I've been learning to be a handyman. And quite enjoying the challenge.'

Handyman. Or woman. The bane of her life. She rolled her eyes. 'Boy, have I had some repair challenges in the last two years? I've had to learn that too. Maybe I should paint my croft. Just yesterday I was thinking it looks very dark inside.' She shut her mouth. Now, why did she say that? Almost an invitation for help.

Finn's voice was light—lighter than her thoughts. 'I can send Piper up if you like. To talk colours with you.'

Trina felt herself relax. He got it. Her expression had probably telegraphed the message that she'd regretted being so open. 'I might take you up on that one day.' She could hear the relief in her voice. Hoped he couldn't.

They'd finished their roast beef sandwiches and iced coffee and Trina desperately needed some distance to think about the morning with Finn but the moment passed.

A commotion at the next table made them both turn. A woman had overturned her chair and the crash turned every head her way. She shook a small child hysterically. 'Spit it out. Come on.' She glanced around wildly. 'He swallowed a button.'

The child gasped weakly, tried to cry and couldn't find enough air to do so as he gulped and coughed. His face was tinged an alarming shade of blue as his mouth quivered.

Finn rose from their table and crossed the space in two strides. 'May I? I'm a doctor.' He didn't wait long.

The woman sagged, nodded and, sobbing in panic, watched as Finn took the child from her. Trina had followed him and righted the woman's chair and urged her back into it. Finn was a doctor. *Wow.* He'd said he wasn't a vet.

Finn sank into the nearest seat and lay the little boy, head down, across his knees and patted his mid back firmly in slow pats.

Trina leaned towards him. 'Can I help?'

Finn shook his head and concentrated on the boy. He patted again, then tipped him further. 'Come on now, mate. Everything is fine. Cough it up.'

To Trina's relief a sudden plop heralded the arrival of the

button as it flew out onto the floor, initiating a collective sigh of relief from the entire café. And her. *Wow. Calmness is us.*

Finn righted the little boy and gave him a reassuring squeeze. Then he stood up with the exhausted child in his arms and passed him to his mother as if nothing had happened.

'He'll be fine. Just needs a minute to get his breath back.' He rested his hand on her shoulder and spoke quietly into her ear. Trina couldn't hear what he said but the woman nodded. Once. Twice. Glanced at the boy in her arms and squeezed him tighter. Then looked back at Finn with a vehement nod. 'Thank you.' The words were heartfelt.

Trina felt her eyes sting. Her heart still thudded from the spectre of a child choking to death in front of them all. She had no doubt everyone there had felt for the fear of the mother, though Trina would have liked to have given her a few pointers about first aid manoeuvres.

She glanced to where Piper played contentedly, oblivious to the drama she'd missed, and oblivious to the fact her daddy had quite possibly just saved a little boy's life. Trina wanted to go home. She felt too emotional to be out in public. Though she suspected she would still be thinking about Finn even if she was away from him.

When Finn sat back down and the conversations around them had begun again she nodded towards the woman, who was paying her bill and leaving with her little boy hugging her leg as he waited.

'Good job. What did you say to her?' She didn't mention he'd said he was a doctor. It didn't matter what he was.

'I asked if she'd seen what I did and, if there was a next time, to try that instead. That shaking didn't help and was actually dangerous. That calm speaking would relax the oesophagus as well.'

'I'm impressed. Discreet and direct.' The guy did everything right. But she still needed to get away from the emotionally charged atmosphere. She collected her mask and towel from the ground beside her and pushed her chair back. 'Before all the excitement I was about to leave. So thank you for lunch.' She glanced at his daughter, who had apparently wrung every conceivable amusement out of the play area and looked to be ready to depart as well.

'Maybe next weekend I could repay the favour.' Piper wailed. 'As long as Piper is free?'

Finn stood up to rescue his daughter. 'I'll look in her calendar and let you know.'

Their eyes connected for a moment, both a little bemused by the ease of their conversation. 'That would be lovely. Thank you, Finn.'

'Thank you, Catrina.' He watched her again and she knew he didn't want her to go. His approval circled her like a whisper of flame crackling and warming her around the base of her lost confidence. But the lure of time away from this new and challenging situation beckoned enticingly.

She stood and waved to the tiny girl. 'Bye, Piper.'

CHAPTER SEVEN

Finn

FINN WATCHED HER walk swiftly across the car park to the path. Almost hurrying away from him. Was it the incident with the little boy? That had turned out okay. Poor terrified little kid and mum—but all right now.

His eyes followed Catrina as Piper leaned into his neck. Maybe she'd left because she felt he was pushing for her company? He was. Why was he pressuring her? If someone had pushed him like he was pushing her he'd have run for the hills. Or a croft. Which she did.

Maybe he was sabotaging himself and hoping she'd stop it before he did? But there was no getting over the fact he'd been a little desperate for Catrina to stay.

And then there had been that jolt when he'd helped her stand at the rock pool. Unconsciously his hands came together to replicate the action, as if to see if he could still feel that vibration that had taken them both by surprise. It had been bizarre, and he'd seen the shock in her face—apparently he hadn't been the only one to feel it—before he'd picked up Piper to give himself a moment to recover.

He wished he'd told her it was Piper's birthday tomorrow.

Because at lunch, after an initial stiffness, conversation had felt so easy. It had been strangely healing to have her sitting opposite him as they both watched his baby playing. When Catrina was there it was easier not to think about where Piper's mother would be tomorrow.

The guilt hit him like a fist in the chest and he sucked in his breath. What was he doing? How could he think that? He was a coward and tomorrow he'd celebrate Piper—he needed to be man enough not to cower in a corner feeling sorry for himself. He paid the bill and gathered Piper up in his arms.

Tomorrow he'd survive and Monday he'd see about getting a job.

Sunday morning Finn woke with a headache. Unusually, Piper had been unsettled most of the night and he wondered if they were both coming down with a cold. Or if the emotion of the coming anniversary of Clancy's desertion was rubbing off him and onto Piper.

He took two paracetamol and a vitamin tablet, and hand-squeezed an orange to give Piper with her breakfast. Because she was still asleep, he decided they wouldn't go out for the day if they were both unwell. He looked at the two wrapped presents he had for Piper. One was a tiny gardening set in a flower-decorated garden basket and the other a push-along block set for inside or out.

The cupboard above the sink drew his eyes and he crossed the room and searched for the packet cake mix he'd thrown in there a month ago in case he needed to make Piper's birthday cake. The packet mix came with little blue cupcake wrappers, pink frosting and fairy princess stickers to press into the icing after they'd been cooked.

The instructions seemed basic and he set it all out, with the candle, for later when he could make some noise. He glanced across at Piper but she snored gently and he wandered to the front of the beach house and stared out at the waves across the bay.

He could see Catrina walking along the breakwall and watched her brisk walk as she strode further away, the wind whipping her hair across her face. He wanted to wave and call her and share the burden and the blessing of this day with her, but knew he wouldn't.

'Last thing she needs,' he told himself out loud, keeping his voice quiet.

'Boo,' said a little voice from behind him and he turned to see Piper standing in her cot with her bunny cuddle blanket over her face.

Despite his aching heart, he smiled. 'Where's Piper?'

Piper pulled the blanket off her head and appeared like magic. Her eyes crinkled with delight at her own cleverness. 'Boo.'

'There she is.' He crossed the room to her but before he arrived he put his hands over his face and then pulled them away. 'Boo to you too, missy. Happy birthday, Piper!' He lifted her up out of her cot and hugged her. She gurgled with squirming delight and he had to force himself not to squeeze her too tight.

He began to sing 'Happy birthday' but faltered halfway through when he thought of Clancy and all she was missing. Forcing himself to finish the song, he carried Piper over to the window. 'It's a breezy sunny day for your birthday. What would you like to do?'

Piper put her head on his shoulder and snuggled in.

Suddenly it was okay again. They could do this. 'You feeling a little fragile today, poppet? Me too. But I'm making you a cake this morning. You can help by pushing on the stickers. It will be our first cake but your daddy is a doctor and supposed to be very smart. I'm sure we can manage little pink cakes for our birthday girl.' She bounced with a little more enthusiasm in his arms.

'Then we can sit outside and let the sunshine and fresh air kill all the germs, if there are any. No work today. Lazy day.'

He put Piper down on the floor and she crawled away from him to her box of toys in the corner with just a little less than her usual surprising speed.

He watched her go and thought about looking for childcare tomorrow. If he couldn't find anything then they'd leave it all for a while longer. That thought brought comfort. Surely it would be hard to find someone in a small town like this at such short notice.

He glanced out of the window again down to the beach and saw Catrina was on her way back. She didn't pass his house, or hadn't in the past or he would have noticed, and he leaned towards the window and saw her moving up the hill towards the cliff opposite the lighthouse. She'd said 'croft' yesterday. Maybe she was in one of those three little cottages on the cliffs that matched the lighthouse. All white stone.

He'd liked the look of them but the real estate agent had said they weren't for sale. He'd never actually gone up that way towards the hospital along the cliff path. Maybe it would be a nice place to go for a change when he went walking with Piper. Just in case he was missing out on a good walk, he reassured himself. But not today. He had promised he'd never drop in uninvited and had no intention of doing so.

Except the morning dragged. They went to the beach but the wind was a little cool to get wet and if Piper was coming down with a cold he didn't want to make it worse. Before long they went home and played inside. But he felt closed in staying indoors. Piper seemed to have recovered and before lunch she'd become unusually bored.

So after lunch, full from eating little pink cakes and with a sealed bag holding an extra one, he hefted Piper onto his back and went for a walk up the hill.

Yes, he nodded to himself dryly, towards the cliff path, not totally directed to one of the crofts that he wondered might belong to Catrina, but certainly it felt good to be outside, with a fresh breeze blowing the cobwebs and fingers of darkness from his lowered mood.

'Dad, Dad, Dad,' Piper burbled from behind his ear—so Piper liked being outside too, and it was her birthday. He was supposed to be doing what she wanted. Each of his steps up the hill lightened his mood and the hill path was well maintained and solid under his feet. He could feel the exertion and decided Catrina could probably run up this hill if she did it a couple of times a day. He wasn't quite up to that yet.

The path forked towards the cottages one way and down onto a cliff edge path on the other and he realised the crofts had hedges around them for privacy from below.

That was good. He wouldn't want anybody to be able to peek into Catrina's house just by walking along the path, but it was a tiny bit disappointing that he couldn't see any of the buildings up close. Then he rounded a bend and the path snaked up again and as he trekked up the hill he realised they'd come out past the cottages.

Quite ingenious really. At the top they came out onto a little open area with a bench and an ancient telescope that had been cemented into the footpath to look out to sea.

He paused and bent down to peer through it, which was hard with Piper suddenly excited and bouncing on his back, when a voice spoke behind him.

'I bet Piper is heavier going uphill.'

He could feel the smile on his face as he turned— he hadn't imagined her.

'Hello there, Catrina.'

'Hello, you two, and what are you doing up here in the clouds?'

'We've never been here before. And it's Piper's birthday.'

Her face broke into a shining sunbeam of a smile and she stepped closer to drop a kiss on Piper's cheek. 'Happy birthday, sweetheart. I hope Daddy made you a cake.'

Piper bounced and crowed.

'Of course. Though really we made cupcakes with pink princess stickers.'

This time the smile was for him. 'I wish I could have seen them.'

It felt good to know he'd thought ahead. 'By a stroke of luck, we do have a spare one in our bag which I'm sure Piper would love to share with you?' He looked around and considered the logistics of Piper and a cliff edge. Maybe not.

It seemed that Catrina got it in one. 'It's too tricky here for a birthday girl. Come back and I'll show you the croft. We can sit on the balcony; it's well fenced and safe.'

CHAPTER EIGHT

Trina

TRINA TURNED ON the path and directed them along the other fork back towards her house, beckoning them to follow. Thankfully, facing the other way, Finn couldn't see the expression on her face. She still couldn't believe she'd invited them into her home. So blithely. Since when had her bravery suddenly known no bounds?

Well, she could hear Finn's springing footsteps behind her as she led the way around the loop that led to the cottages again and within seconds they'd popped out onto the road outside the last croft, where Myra and Dr Southwell lived. As they passed the door opened and the older gentleman stepped out.

He smiled when he saw her, and then his face lit up further when he saw who followed her. 'Trina. And Finn. And Piper. Hello. Delightful. So, you've met.'

Trina could feel herself blush. 'Hello. Yes. At the beach.' Glancing around for inspiration to change the subject, she added, 'Lovely day.' Not only had she invited a man back to her house but she'd been caught in the act. Everyone would know. Dr Southwell wasn't a gossip but, seriously, Ellie's father-in-law? *Small blinkin' towns.*

Trina blushed again under Dr Southwell's pleased smile.

'The weather is super. Love to stay and chat but I'm off to the hospital.' He waved and strode off.

Trina shrugged off the awkwardness with determination. 'So that's who lives next door on this side and my boss, Ellie, and her husband, who happens to be an obstetrician, Dr Southwell's son, live on the other side.'

He looked around at the three crofts as they came to hers, and paused. 'You're well covered for medical help then.' He smiled a little awkwardly.

'Never too many in an emergency.' She smiled back, too concerned with whether she'd left the house tidy before he arrived to worry about trying to read his reaction to her neighbours. She indicated her own front path. 'Come in. It's small but compact, much like yours is, I imagine.'

'Yes. Tiny, but I like it. You'll have to come and see my renovations.'

Not your etchings? She thought it and smiled to herself. Didn't risk saying anything in case he heard the amusement in her voice. At least she could be amused by something that she would have run a mile from a month ago. In fact, she could have rubbed her knuckles on her chest. Darn proud of herself, really.

She pushed open the door and was glad she'd opened all the blinds this morning. With everything open the sea seemed to be a part of the room, with all eyes being drawn to the open French windows out onto the little terrace. She gestured him to walk that way.

'Great view,' Finn said after a low whistle. 'That's really magic.' He walked slowly to the French windows and absently began to undo Piper's straps.

Trina came up behind him and undid the other one. 'Here, let me help.' She lifted Piper out of the straps and set her down. 'There's nothing to climb on. I only keep the swing chair out there and it's against the house wall. It has to come in when it's windy.'

Piper crawled straight for the rails and her little hands grabbed on as she pulled herself up. She bounced on the balls of her feet. Finn followed her out and Trina stood back a little and admired them both.

A bouncy, healthy little girl and her gorgeous dad. She wasn't sure when he'd graduated from attractive to other women to gorgeous for her, but she had to admit he made an admirable picture with his big shoulders and strong back silhouetted against the ocean. His long fingers rested lightly and then the curved muscles in his arms bunched as he gripped the rail for a minute. She wondered what he was thinking about as he stood guard over his daughter, his powerful thighs either side of her as one hand left the rail and brushed her small head.

Then the penny dropped. Piper's birthday. And his wife had left soon after Piper's birth. That made this time of year a distressing anniversary as well as a day for celebration for Piper. Tough call. She hadn't even crawled out of bed on the anniversary of losing Ed.

Why hadn't he said something yesterday? Then she chastised herself. Why would he share that with a stranger?

She swallowed past the lump that had suddenly formed in her throat. 'Would you two like a cold drink?' She managed to even her voice. 'I have a spill-proof cup I use for one of my friend's daughters.'

'Piper has her water here, thanks.' He came back in and bent down to Piper's pack. Pulled out a little pink pop-top bottle. 'She'll use hers.' Then he pulled out a Ziploc bag. 'Aha! Here's your part of Piper's birthday cake.'

He glanced back at his daughter. 'Probably best she doesn't see it as I had no idea she could gobble as many as she did and she'll be sick if she eats any more.'

Trina nodded and swiped the bag, turning her back to the veranda and opening the seal. She lifted out the little blue-papered cake and admired the rough pink icing and slightly off-centre sticker. 'It's magnificent.'

'Piper put the stickers on herself.'

'Clever girl.' She looked at him. 'Clever Daddy for the rest.'

He looked at her. Maybe saw the lingering distress in her eyes and he closed his own for a minute and then looked at her again. Nodded. 'So you've guessed it's a tough day?'

'You have a different set of triggers but I was just thinking I didn't even get out of bed when mine went past.' They needed to get out and fill the day with something. 'How about we go for a walk along the cliffs further? There's a really cool cave overlooking the ocean about a kilometre north I could show you. And there's a sweet little dip of green grass Piper would love.' She smiled at the thought. 'She could probably log roll down the tiny hill. I watched some kids do that one day and it looked fun.'

She saw relief lift the creases from his brow. 'That does sound good. Is there somewhere you'd prefer me to change Piper before we go? I have a change mat.'

'You have everything!' And wasn't that true. 'Change mats are great. You can use my bed and save you bending down. I'll make a little snack for the meadow.' She turned away. Excited for the first time in a long while with a task she couldn't wait to play with.

She slipped in two small cans of mixer cordial that she'd bought on a whim. A packet of dates and apricots for Piper. She even had arrowroot biscuits, perfect for a little girl to make a mess with. Threw in some crisps, two apples and a banana. It all fitted in her little cool bag she carried to work each day, along with the tiny checked throw she had never had the opportunity to use for a picnic.

They set off ten minutes later, Piper bouncing on her daddy's back and Trina swinging along beside them as if she was a part of the little family. She winced at her instinctive comparison. No. Like a party of friends. Looking out for each other.

The sun shone clear and warm on their backs as they strode along the path. The sea breeze blew Piper's bright golden mist of hair around her chubby face as she chattered away. Trina decided Finn looked so much more relaxed out in the open. It made her feel good that she'd helped.

A cruise ship hugged the horizon and she pointed it out to Finn. Piper saw a seabird dive into the water far below and they had to stop and watch for a minute until it came out again with a fish in its beak.

Trina admired the skill of the surfers, bobbing and swooping like brilliant supple-bodied flying fish on the curling waves.

When she commented, Finn shared, 'I love surfing.'

'I've never tried.' Maybe she could add that to her adventure list.

Finn said, 'When Piper is old enough I'll teach her to surf. This looks a great place to do that.'

'Dr Southwell used to surf every morning before he was married. Though I have to admit he did come a cropper when he was washed off the shelf last year.'

He looked back the way they'd come. 'Really? Ouch. Which shelf?'

She pointed. 'The ones under the cliffs, with the rock pools we were in yesterday.'

Finn frowned. 'It doesn't look dangerous there.'

'It is on a king tide. And his timing was off if you ask him. They lifted him out with a chopper but the good news was his son met Ellie, my boss, when he came to locum while his father was away, and they married and are having a baby. That's why I'm doing Ellie's job for the next year—hence the change from night duty.'

'Happy ending.' His voice held only a trace of bitterness. She got that. But she'd moved on herself, thankfully.

She wondered if he'd heard his own subtext because his voice came out warmer than before. 'So were they all the people in the restaurant on Friday?'

She'd forgotten. 'Yes, that's right—you were there. With

Piper and your sister.' She thought back over those present. 'They were celebrating Ellie's leave and my promotion.'

'Congratulations.'

She laughed. 'Thanks. First day tomorrow. We'll see.'

She thought back to Friday and the pleasant lunch. Her own surprise to see Finn there. With another woman. Felt just a little embarrassed now she knew it was his sister. Hurried on in case it showed on her face. 'The other older lady at the table is the one who makes the most divine cakes—Dr Southwell's wife, Myra.'

'I guess I'll get to know them all. Dr Southwell's offered me a place in his practice. I'll start as soon as I can find day care for Piper.'

She raised her brows. 'Do you have a specialty?'

'I started in general practice. Then I went on and studied paediatrics. I thought everyone knew?' Then he shook his head. 'I guess I haven't really spoken to many people. I have my Diploma of Obstetrics from my GP days, but no real experience in that. Just the antenatal side of it. Not the delivery part.'

He didn't look old enough to have done all that. Catrina smiled at him, decided she wouldn't share that thought and shook her head mockingly. 'We don't say delivery any more. Especially in Lighthouse Bay. We're Midwifery Group Practice.'

He put his hands up. 'Midwifery Group Practice. And I said *delivery*. My bad.'

'Very.' She smiled at him. 'Everything is midwifery-led and woman-centred. The antenatal clinic is drop-in and popular. When the mother births, we support her choice to stay or go, and she's visited at home within the day after if that's what she wants or she can stay for a few days in the hospital. Either way, we don't call a doctor unless someone is sick.'

He put out his hands helplessly and pretended to sigh. 'I'm defunct and I haven't even started.'

She laughed. 'You'll get used to it. You should meet Ellie and her husband. Sam's the Director of Obstetrics at the base hospital and fell in love with Lighthouse Bay too. And Ellie, of course.' She smiled at the thought. 'Sam moved here from a big Brisbane Hospital so we're lucky to have him as an unofficial back-up in real emergencies when he's not on-call at the base hospital.'

She looked at him thoughtfully. 'I've thought of someone who could mind Piper, if you're interested.'

His face went blank and she hesitated. Maybe he wasn't ready yet.

'I'll need to find someone eventually,' he managed but she could see it cost him. She wished she hadn't mentioned it now.

Then he said more firmly, 'Sure. That would be great. I need to start looking.'

Trina thought about Marni. She didn't regret mentioning her, though. 'She's a doll. A natural mother. Her twins are six months old and she's just registered for day care status.'

CHAPTER NINE

Finn

FINN FELT HIS stomach drop. He wasn't seeing the path or the ocean or the sky overhead. He shouldn't have asked about day care. But something inside had dared him to. Something that wanted him to move on, as if he'd known he'd be catapulted into a decision if he put it out there. All his instincts wanted to draw back. Stop her telling him. Say he'd ask if he decided it was time. She'd understand. Not sure how he knew that but he believed in the truth of it.

Instead he said, 'Would you recommend her?'

She looked at him thoughtfully. Kindly. 'That's tough because it's not about me,' she said gently, as if she could read his distress. Then she looked at Piper. 'Marni could mind my child, if I had one.' The tone was almost joking. He saw something that looked like pain flit across her face and remembered again there were people out there who did suffer as much as he did. People like Catrina. Left alone by the love of their life— without choice and unintentionally. Loss of love and no baby to hold like he did. Imagine life without Piper.

Catrina's voice wasn't quite steady but he could hear the struggle to make it so. It had been a very brave thing to say and he wanted to tell her that. Wanted to tell her that he understood. But still the coward inside him shied away from so much emotion.

Catrina said, 'Maybe you could see if Piper likes her before you commit to work and see how she goes? Just an hour or two?'

'That's a good idea. Tell me about her.'

He saw her gaze into the distance, a soft smile on her face and a glimmer of distress, though this time he didn't think it was for herself. 'She's a younger mum. Early twenties. She and her husband own the dry-cleaners in town but she's a stay-at-home mum. Marni's Mother Earth and the boys are six months old. Bundles of energy, healthy as all get-out, which is great because she nearly lost them at twenty-three weeks, and she spent a lot of time in hospital. As far as the midwives of Lighthouse Bay think, she's a hero to us.'

He had to smile at that. *'The Midwives of Lighthouse Bay.* Sounds like a serial on TV.'

She laughed a little self-consciously and he regretted making light of the one stable thing she had in her life, hadn't meant to embarrass her. 'Don't get me wrong. It's another good ending to a story.'

Catrina seemed to relax. 'It really was. Ellie's husband, Sam, had been involved in research into preventing extreme premature birth in Brisbane, and thankfully he was here when she went into labour. Marni and Bob are a lovely couple who'd already lost an extremely premature baby daughter.'

Finn wasn't so sure. She already had twins and he wanted someone who could concentrate on Piper. 'How could she care for Piper as well?' Finn was more uncertain now. 'Sounds a bit hectic. She has twins and she's doing day care?'

He caught Trina's encouraging smile and suddenly saw how she could be a good midwife. Her empathy shone warm—he felt she understood and was reassuring him that he would conquer his fear of letting Piper out of his sight. All without putting on pressure. Encouraging him to test his own strength without expectations. Treating him like a woman in labour battling her own fear. *Wow*. She had it down pat.

Then she said, 'She loves minding babies. And babies love her. Usually she's minding them for free. We keep telling her she should become a midwife and I wouldn't be surprised when the boys go to school if she'll look at it. But, for now, she's just starting up official day care.'

Absently he bent and stroked Piper's leg at his side. 'Maybe I could meet her before I talk to Dr Southwell? It's a good idea to see if Piper likes her before I commit to work, though. You'll have to give me her number.'

'Or we could visit her. Meet her and her husband. See their house. They're a lovely couple and live only a few doors up from you. In the blue pastel cottage.'

It was all happening too quickly. He could feel the panic build and squashed it down again. He could do this. Just not today.

Catrina touched his arm—the first time she had physically connected with him of her own volition—and again that frisson of awareness hummed where they touched. He glanced at her but her expression still showed only compassionate support. 'It's something to think about. Marni is just the one I know. There will be others when you're ready.'

His relief made his shoulders sag. She must have seen it on his face. Was he that transparent? He'd have to work on his game face before he went back to work or his patients' parents would run a mile.

He tried to make light of it. 'I imagine every parent must feel like this when they have to go back to work. Torn.'

'Absolutely. We see mums that can't stay in hospital for one night after birth because they hate leaving the other child or children too much.' She looked towards Piper and smiled. 'I'd find it hard to leave Piper if she were mine.'

His face tightened. He could feel it. Some women could. Piper's mother had no problem. And he'd be the one who had to break his daughter's heart when the time came to tell the truth.

Catrina opened her mouth—he didn't want to talk about Clancy—but all she said was, 'The cave's just around this next headland.' He was glad she'd changed the subject.

The cave, when they arrived, curved back into the cliff and created an overhang half the size of his house. A few round boulders acted as seats for looking out over the ocean out of the sun. Or rain. Plenty of evidence suggested people had camped and made campfires there but on the whole it had stayed clean and cool, and dim towards the back. The sort of place young boys would love to go with their mates.

He could stand up in the cave easily and they stomped around in it for a few minutes before Catrina suggested they go the small distance further to the glade so Piper could be released from the backpack.

The glade, when they arrived, had a park bench and table at the edge of the slope down into the bowl-shaped dip of grass. The bright sunshine made the grass lime cordial-coloured and the thick bed of kikuyu and daisies felt softer and springier than he expected when he put Piper down to crawl. Because of the sloping sides of the bowl Piper tended to end up back in the lowest point in the middle even when she climbed the sides and he could feel his mouth twitching as she furrowed her brows and tried to work out what was happening.

He pulled a bright saucer-sized ball from her backpack and tossed it in the centre of the glade while Catrina set their picnic bag on the table and spread the cloth. Piper crawled to the ball and batted it. Of course it rolled back down the side to her again. She pushed it again and crowed when it rolled back again.

'Clever girl,' he said to his daughter, and 'Clever girl,' to Catrina, who grinned at him as she finished laying out their treats and came to sit next to him on the side of the grass hill. 'I can't remember when I last had a picnic,' he said as he passed an arrowroot biscuit to Piper and took one of the apples for himself.

'I know. Me either.' She handed him the can of drink and took a sip of her own. Then he heard her sigh blissfully.

'We couldn't have had more beautiful weather this afternoon.'

'A bit different to this morning.'

'That's the beauty of Lighthouse Bay. We're temperate. Not too hot for long or too cold for long. Always leaning towards perfect weather.'

'Always?'

Catrina laughed. 'Well, no. We do have wild storms sometimes. That's why I have shutters on my windows and doors. But not often.'

The afternoon passed in a desultory fashion and once, when Piper dozed off in his arms, he and Catrina lay side by side watching the clouds pass overhead in companionable silence. He'd never met anyone as restful as she was. It would have been so simple to slide closer and take her hand but the man who could have done that had broken a year ago.

An hour later, on the way home from their walk, he asked again about the exact location of the day care mum.

'I could come with you to knock on the door? Maybe meeting the family would help?'

'Just drop in?' Despite his initial reluctance, he could see that an impromptu visit could be less orchestrated than one when they expected him. And he had Catrina to come with him to break the ice.

It made sense. Not fair perhaps, but this was his baby he was considering leaving in their care, and he wanted a true representation of the feeling of the household.

When the door opened to answer his knock, a smiling red-haired man answered. Past him they could hear the sound of a child squealing and the smell of a roast dinner drifted out to tantalise his nose. He hadn't had an old-fashioned roast for years. His mouth watered.

'Can I help you?' Then the man saw Catrina and smiled beatifically. 'Trina!'

'Hello, Bob. How are you?' The man stepped forward and hugged her and Finn was surprised.

When they stepped back from each other she said, 'Something smells divine. Lucky you—Sunday roast.'

'You're welcome any time, Trina.' He grinned and looked at her companion.

'This is Finn Foley. He's a friend and I told him about Marni offering childcare and—' she indicated Piper '—he and Piper have just started looking.' Finn glanced at Catrina. Took a second to savour that she'd claimed friendship. She really was his only friend here.

She still spoke to Bob. 'I wondered if he could have a chat with Marni?'

'Absolutely. Any friend of yours and all that.' Bob grinned at Finn. 'Come in. Marni? There's a dad here looking for information about childcare.'

Finn liked the way he said that. To his wife, with deference, and that he wasn't committing to anything. Just asking. His nerves settled a fraction as he followed Catrina, with Piper on his back, in the door.

The room had been divided into two, with a kitchen and lounge on one side and a wall with doors on the other. Bedrooms, he guessed, unlike his one-room cottage. An extension had been built out the back with a big play room that overlooked the tiny fenced garden. Everything sparkled; even the toys strewn on the floor in the play room caught the sunlight and looked new and well cared for. The family warmth in the little abode made the tension drop from his shoulders and his eyes met Trina's in acknowledgement.

A young woman crossed to them, drying her hands on a tea towel. She too hugged Catrina, and her shy smile eased the tension in Finn's stomach like magic. 'Trina. Great to see you.'

'This is Finn, Marni.' She turned to help Finn extricate Piper from the backpack—which he was pretty darn good at, but he had to admit it was quicker with help. And he liked her touching him.

'Nice to meet you, Finn. You live a few doors down, don't you?' she said as she held out her hand. They shook briefly and he liked that her fingers were cool and dry, her grip confident.

'Welcome.' She smiled at Piper, who now sat on his hip, then turned around and pointed to two boys as if introducing her to them not Finn. 'The one on the left is Olly, and the cheekier one is Mikey.' She looked at Piper. 'And what is your name, beautiful?'

Previously fascinated by the smaller humans, Piper looked back at the lady's face, realised everyone was looking at her and then she clutched at his neck and buried her face.

Finn rubbed her back. 'Piper can be shy.'

'Of course she can.' Marni indicated the rear of the cottage. 'Come and sit out on the deck at the back and we'll show you the play area and I can answer your questions.

'So Catrina told you I've started doing childcare?' The smile Marni gave Catrina lit up her face. 'The midwives are my cheer squad. They're all champions up there. If it wasn't for them and the younger Dr Southwell, we wouldn't have our gorgeous boys.'

Finn looked at the two chubby-faced little boys, one sitting in a blue tub of a chair kicking his feet and the other lying on his back on the patterned play carpet with a red spiral rattle. The little boy—Finn thought it was Olly—began to screw his face up, dropped the rattle and began to rock until he rolled over and lay on his stomach. The mischievous chortle he let out at the feat made Finn smile.

'Clever boy, Mikey,' his dad said. So he'd got that wrong, Finn thought. And then Bob gestured to his wife. 'I'll finish the potatoes. You take our guests and Piper out and have a chat.'

Finn liked that too. He could see they were a team and, despite having two babies, the air of serenity as Marni smiled made his trepidations settle. This sort of calm atmosphere looked perfect for Piper to learn about other babies and new adults.

A heck of a lot different to the busy, efficient childcare he'd had her in before. But Piper still clung to him like one of the stripy shells on the side of a rock pool and he remembered the hard times at the big kindergarten when he'd tried to leave.

Marni pointed to a scrubbed wooden table and four sturdy chairs. Two highchairs took up the other spaces. They all sat down and Marni put a soft-sided squeaky farm book on the table in front of Piper without making a fuss of it.

'I am looking for two more toddlers. That will give me enough to cover the wage of the girl working with my husband at the dry-cleaners and then there's no rush for me to go back to work. I'm hoping to stay home for the next year at least. In a perfect world, I won't go back to work until the boys go to school.'

She smiled calmly at Finn. 'But we'll see what happens.'

So a stable place, Finn was thinking, and he wondered, if he offered to pay twice the rate, would Marni consider having Piper by herself, at least at the beginning so the young mum wasn't pushed by the demands of four children? Piper would benefit and money wasn't a problem. Finding someone caring and kind for Piper would be priceless.

He tried to think of a question. 'Catrina said you've just been registered. Having two babies seems intense to me. Piper can keep me busy and there's only one of her.'

She glanced lovingly towards the two gurgling on the floor and then across at her husband. 'I mind lots of children. Have always loved them and thought for a while we'd never be able to have any. But then the boys came along, though I spent a couple of months in hospital hanging onto them, so they are beyond precious.'

She shrugged ruefully. 'I'm worried I might spoil them and want them to learn to share, not just with each other but with other children. Some extra income would help and my husband

and I are both the eldest from big families. Our families are in Western Australia so we miss having lots of kids around.'

'I guess childminding makes sense in that case.'

Piper reached out and picked up the book. Scrunched it with her inquisitive fingers. Barely audible squeaks erupted when she squeezed and a crooked smile tipped her mouth as she battled between shyness and delight.

All the adults looked at her fondly. 'So, information-wise, what sort of minding were you looking for?'

'I've been offered a position three days a week, Monday, Tuesday and Wednesday.'

Marni nodded. 'Three is better than five for Piper. Especially in the beginning. Has she been in care before?'

'Yes, poor baby, most of her life, when I worked. About fifty hours a week. But not for the last six weeks and she was becoming unhappy before that. I was thinking to start a half-day, as a trial, just until Piper gets used to it. If she gets too upset I'd probably not go back to work for a while.' He shrugged his apology.

Apparently she didn't need it. That serene smile drifted across her face. 'Being adaptable is good around kids. One of the secrets. She'll miss you if she's had you to herself for six weeks.' A quirked brow made that question.

'I'm not even sure it's what I'm ready to do.'

'That's fine. You're fact-finding, which is very sensible.'

Well, he'd better glean some facts. This was harder than he'd thought it would be. He glanced at Catrina and she sat tranquilly beside him, lending moral support, not interrupting. Just there. It felt good not to be on his own through this. 'What hours do you have available?'

Marni laughed. 'As I haven't started yet it's hard to say. Big picture—Monday to Friday, no more than forty hours, but the hours are flexible. And I get to keep the weekends for the boys and Bob.'

'Where would she sleep in the daytime?'

'We've a little room next to the boys' room. Bob put two new folding cots in there and I think it'll work well. And I'll supply all the food. No hardship to make for one more and that way nobody wants what others have.'

It all sounded too good to be true. Plus they lived a few doors away from his own house. Even in this short time Piper seemed relaxed here. He gently swung her off his lap, book still in her hands, and rested her bottom on the floor. Just to see if she'd go.

As soon as she hit the floor she dropped the book and crawled curiously towards the two little boys. Stopped about a body's length away and sat up. The three tiny people all looked at each other.

The adults smiled and Finn felt the tension leave his shoulders. The gods, or Catrina, had saved him again.

'What about if I go and talk to my prospective employer tomorrow? Perhaps leave Piper here just for an hour and see how she goes while I negotiate? Then we'll all know more.'

'Why don't you make it two hours? That will be a quarter of the time of her next visit, if you decide to go ahead. Just to give her time to settle. And take the rush out of your appointment. She'll be fine. It will give us all a chance to trial the fit.'

'I think that sounds like a plan. Yes, please.' Finn stood up. Blew out a breath. 'Phew. Thank you. I do feel better for asking and talking to you. That would be great.' He glanced at Catrina, who stood as well. She smiled at him as if he'd just done an excellent job. It felt good. Reassuring.

Marni went across to the dresser and picked up a business card. 'Here's our phone number, and it's got my mobile on it as well. You can ring or drop in when you know your time. The sheet has information about my business.' She handed him a sheet of paper with her numbers and the payment rates. Easy.

'That's great.' He picked up Piper, who had crawled over to him as soon as he stood up. She didn't cling, more curious than panicked he'd leave her. 'I'll leave one of my own cards when I bring Piper. Then you can contact me any time.'

'Give yourself ten extra minutes before you leave her tomorrow. To help her settle.'

He nodded. Then Bob came and shook his hand. Then they were outside and the door closed.

He felt like sagging against it. He'd done it. Another step towards a new life.

'You didn't say much.'

Catrina laughed. 'I didn't have to. You're all made for each other.'

CHAPTER TEN

Trina

TRINA'S FIRST MORNING as Midwifery Unit Manager, and her first day shift for a long time, proved too busy to worry about a man she'd met on the beach and declared her friend. Though she had spent a fair time mulling over all the things she'd learnt about Finn the night before.

This morning, in her new world, the midwife coming off shift had celebrated a birth at five a.m., so still lots of settling of mother and baby for Trina to help with before mother left at lunchtime to go home. Another mother who preferred to rest at home, not separated from her toddler, and it made her think of her conversation with Finn yesterday. Finn again. She pushed those thoughts away and concentrated on the new tasks.

There were Monday pharmacy orders and sterile stock orders, and a hospital meeting and a visit from Myra, her neighbour, which lightened a busy time with a quick break.

'Hello there, new midwife in charge.' Myra's serene face peered around the corner of the nurses' station, where Trina typed efficiently into the discharged mother's electronic medical records.

'Hello, Mrs Southwell, what have you got there?' Myra had

a steaming cup and a white paper bag tucked under her arm. Ellie had said that Myra always brought something when the place got busy.

'A long black with extra water, the way you like it.' She smiled mischievously. 'And a savoury tart with spring onion in case you haven't had lunch.'

Trina glanced at the clock, the hour hand resting on the two. 'An angel. That's what you are.' Though she would pack lunch tomorrow to make sure she had something. She hadn't realised how hard it could be to get away from the ward to the cafeteria. She'd expected that on night duty but not through the day.

Myra tilted her head to scrutinise her. 'Have you had time to stop for a few minutes?'

Trina sat back and gestured to the chair beside her. 'Not yet. But I do now. And I will.' She took the china mug Myra carried and took a sip before she put it down on the desk beside her. 'Ah!' She smiled at the older lady. 'I seriously needed that.' She looked at the mug again and picked it up. Took another sip and closed her eyes. 'The world won't stop turning if I don't achieve everything today.'

Myra laughed. 'Something I've learnt since I came here. So how is it going? Is it strange to be on the ward in the daytime?'

Trina glanced around the sunlit reception area. The windows that showed the gardens. The sunlight slanting across the polished wooden floors. 'It is. And there are so many people I need to talk to.' She pretended to shudder. 'Business requirements have given me interaction overload. Present company excluded, of course.'

'I won't be offended.' Myra looked at her with concern. 'Are you sure you wouldn't prefer sitting in the tea room and I could answer the phone for you while you finish your tart?'

Trina laughed. 'No. This is a social conversation. Much more fun. Besides, I haven't seen you for days. How are you? How is married life? Any adventurous plans?'

'I'm well. Ridiculously content, and I'm trying to talk Reg

into coming away with me on a cruising holiday. There's a last-minute deal that's breaking my heart not to take.'

Trina could see Myra at a Captain's Cocktail Party, dressed to the nines in those stunning vintage outfits she seemed to source at will. Trina could never find anything when she looked in the pre-loved section. Or if she did she looked ridiculous. But Myra looked soft and elegant and stunningly stylish. She sighed and let the envy go. She hadn't really thought much of clothes since Ed. 'That sounds fun. Does he like the idea?'

'More than I thought he would. But it all depends if he finds locum relief for the practice. I'm a little keen for him to scale right back but he's become immersed in the bay and the hospital.'

Trina could see why Myra wanted to play. 'I haven't seen him out on his surfboard lately.'

'He still goes out every Sunday with his son. It's lovely to see. Says he doesn't have the need to get out of bed at the crack of dawn now—especially with me in it.' Myra smiled with just a hint of pink in her cheeks and Trina smiled back.

'Understandable.' She thought of Finn. Her own cheeks heated and she dipped her head and took a sip from her mug to hide it. Of course he was the locum Myra hoped for, and of course she wasn't blushing just because of Myra's mention of mornings in bed. 'Is he hopeful of the locum situation?'

Myra sighed. 'There's a young doctor in town he's had a chat with. Some family issue that's keeping him from starting, but hopefully that will sort soon. If not, I think he should advertise.'

'I met the one I think he's talking about. Finlay Foley. He's a single dad. Has a delightful little one-year-old.'

Myra unwrapped the tart from its white paper bag and pushed it towards Trina. 'That's the one. That's right—Reg said he had a daughter. What's he like?'

'He's an amazing dad. Anyone can see that. It's a wonder you haven't seen him walking along the beach with his little girl on his back.'

Myra's eyes brightened. She lifted her head in delight and glanced towards the general direction of the beach way below, though she wouldn't be able to see it. 'Oh. I have seen him. Younger than I expected. I didn't think of him as a doctor. Looks too young.' She lowered her voice and said suggestively, 'And handsome.'

Trina laughed. 'I used to see them in the mornings after work when I walked. Been here for a month but I've only really talked to him this weekend.' Funny how it felt as if she'd known Finn for ages. What was that? 'His little girl turned one yesterday. And I did mention Marni as a suggestion for child-minding. He's thinking about it.'

'Oh, that's marvellous news. And a really good idea. Marni is the perfect mother to those tiny boys. I might get Reg to give him a nudge—not a big nudger is my Reg. But I would like to catch that sailing if possible.'

Trina laughed. 'You might have a surprise when you get home, then.' She picked up the tart and bit into the buttery pastry with slow enjoyment. The tang of Parmesan cheese, fresh spring onions and cream made her eyes roll. She took another bite and savoured. Before she knew, the tart was gone. 'Goodness, Myra. I should have a standing order for those.'

Myra laughed. 'My man is a bit pleased with my cooking.'

Trina picked up her coffee and then paused as a thought intruded. If Finn took over Dr Southwell's practice while he was away, he'd be working in the hospital. And he'd probably walk through Maternity. Might even seek her out as a friendly face. Not that everyone wasn't friendly at Lighthouse Bay. Maybe he'd even come over if they needed a third for a tricky birth. Their own personal paediatrician.

Her belly seemed to warm and it had nothing to do with food and hot coffee, though they had been good. She finished the last of the coffee not quite in the present moment. It was all positive because he was a paediatrician. Good for those babies that didn't breathe as well as you expected them to. *Oh, my.*

'You look much better for stopping and eating,' Myra said with some satisfaction. She stood up. 'I won't bother you any longer and let you get on before your afternoon midwives come on.'

'You're never a bother. More of a life-saver. Thank you.' She glanced down at the empty crumpled white bag. 'You've made my day.' In more ways than one.

Trina finished work at five-thirty that evening and decided to walk quickly down the breakwall and blow the stress of the day away. The administration side of the maternity unit would take a little time to get used to but she'd mastered most of the things that had slowed her up. The joy of finishing work and not having to worry about sleep until it was dark felt like a sweet novelty. Especially when, on her way back, she saw that Finn and Piper, wrapped in scarves, were walking too. Finn swung along effortlessly, the bundle on his back wriggling when she saw Catrina.

Finn raised his hand and changed direction and she sat on the breakwall and waited for him to reach her. As they approached she couldn't help watching his stride as his strong thighs closed the distance between them. His broad shoulders were silhouetted against the ocean and his eyes crinkled with delight as he came up to her.

The smile he gave her made the waiting even more worth it. She realised she'd been staring and spoke first. 'Hello. How did Piper go today?'

He patted Piper's leg. 'She didn't want to leave when I went to pick her up.'

Trina tried to hide her smile behind a sympathetic look but it didn't stick.

He pretended to scowl at her. 'You think that's amusing?'

She straightened her face. 'I'm pretty sure you were relieved too.'

He dropped his mock-injured façade. 'Absolutely. It felt good to see her so comfortable in another setting. And I owe that to you.' A genuine heartfelt smile which she might just snapshot and pull out later when she got home. 'Thank you, Catrina.'

She'd done nothing. He seemed so serious. And he seemed to expect some comment. 'For the little I did you're very welcome, Finn.'

'I'm serious.' Had he read her mind? 'In fact, Piper and I would like to invite you to our house to share dinner on Thursday night. In celebration of her finding childcare and me starting work next Monday. If you don't have a previous engagement?' There was a tiny hesitation at the last comment and she wondered why he thought she would.

'No previous engagement.'

Was that relief on his face? 'Just our usual slap-up meal. So you don't have to cook when you get home.' He hurried on. 'It will be early and if you needed to you could still be home by dark.'

She laughed. It would certainly be an early dinner as night fell about seven. 'I finish at five-thirty so can be there by six. Though sometimes the wheels fall off at work and that could slow me down or make me cancel.'

He shrugged. 'Been there. We'll take that as we have to.'

Trina smiled. Of course. A paed would know that. 'In that case, lovely. Thank you.' She tweaked the baby toes at Finn's chest. 'Thank you for the invitation, Piper.' The little girl gurgled and said, 'Mum, Mum, Mum.'

Trina pretended she didn't see Finn's wince. 'I bet she was saying that all the time at Marni's house. The boys will come ahead on their speaking with her there.'

He still looked subdued so she went on. 'Soon they'll be able to say *fiss*.'

Finn seemed to shake himself. She saw him cast his mind back and his smile grew. Could see when he remembered the rock pool. Saw the relief for the change of focus.

His smile dipped to rueful. 'You're right.' Then he straightened and gave her his full attention again. 'How was your first day as the boss?'

'Administrative. Hats off to Ellie for never complaining about all the paperwork and ordering. But it's well worth it to have finished work at this time and still get a full night's sleep. It will be amazing when Daylight Saving comes back in and it doesn't get dark till after eight at night.'

CHAPTER ELEVEN

Finn

FINN SHIFTED ON the hard boardwalk, listened, but inside he thought, *Yes, she's coming on Thursday.* He felt like dancing a jig. Didn't want to think about why. The tension that had been building slowly released. She made him feel like a teenager which, though disconcerting, made a good change from feeling like an old man most of the time.

He'd considered the invitation from every angle because it had become increasingly important he didn't scare Catrina away and he still remembered her warnings when they'd first met. Enjoying her company had lifted his life from survival to anticipation. And he anticipated that Catrina could be great company for the foreseeable future if he stayed careful.

But she'd said she didn't want a relationship. It suited him fine, he kept telling himself that, and it had nothing to do with the fact that every time he saw her he noticed something new about her.

Like that especially golden strand of hair that fell across her forehead and made him want to move it out of her eyes. Or the way the soft skin on the curve of her long neck made him want to stroke that vulnerable spot with one finger. Just to assess if it felt like the velvet it resembled.

Of course it was all about Piper—she needed to have a female figure in her life who didn't demand anything—but Catrina gave so much warmth he could feel himself thawing more each day. Or maybe it was the fact he'd told himself he'd change now that Piper's first birthday had passed.

He tamped down the suspicion it could be selfish to blow so persistently on the flame of their friendship when he didn't have much to offer, was still married in fact, but he could feel the restoration of his soul and sensibilities. And the better he was in himself the better he was for Piper.

So he'd considered all the barriers she might have had to agreeing to a first dinner date and had methodically worked on arranging for them to disappear. To make it easy for both of them.

It would be a celebration—Piper's care with Marni and his new job.

She started work early the first four days of the week—so he'd invited her on Thursday—she had to eat, so no reason not to grab a free meal from him on the way home.

Plus he was hoping to set up some connections with her over the coming weekend and that would seem more impromptu if he mentioned those on Thursday.

And the big card—Catrina had to be curious to see his house. It had all paid off.

'Did you like the Southwells' surgery?' Her voice startled him back into the present moment. He thought back to earlier in the day. To the white cottage that held Dr Southwell's medical rooms.

'It's quaint. Not as strange as it could have been. A small practice, one receptionist, and I'd have my own room to settle into, which is always better than using someone else's. I'll have all my equipment sent ASAP.' Or he could drive back and get it, but the idea made him shudder.

Catrina's voice grounded him. 'That's good. Did you see any patients?'

'You mean behave like a real doctor?' He smiled at her. 'Not yet. But I will start with those with urgent needs and Reg seems to think I could concentrate on children, which would suit me very well, and meet a need for the community.'

Catrina nodded slowly as she thought about it. 'I know at the base hospital it takes a few weeks for the paediatrician to see new patients. Perhaps you would even have some of those mums driving their children over this way, like the Lighthouse Bay mums go to the base for the service. Certainly easier for people like Marni to take the boys for their premmie check-ups.'

'Plus I'd be available for general patients when it was busy, but it seemed pretty sleepy today. Perfect hours of work for a dad with a little girl to consider.'

'Did he talk about you covering the general patients in the hospital when he goes away?'

'He did say that. Which is fine with me. It's not a big hospital and I can read up on who's in there when the time comes.'

Catrina stifled a laugh and he glanced at her. 'Dr Southwell's wife is keen on a cruise that leaves soon. Don't be surprised if it happens faster than you think.'

He raised his brows in question. 'Inside information?'

'I saw Myra today and she did mention she hoped Reg would find someone soon and that she had a boat she didn't want to miss.'

'Thanks for the heads-up. I'm sure I'd manage. That's what locums do, after all.' But everything seemed to be happening very fast. 'Do they get called out at night much?'

'Rarely. And it's shared call. So no more than three nights a week as a twenty-four-hour cover.' He watched her expression change as she realised that leaving Piper could be a problem on those nights.

'Hmm.' He could tell they were both thinking of Marni's flexibility as a day care mum.

'Something to think about,' Catrina said with massive understatement. 'And it won't be a problem unless Dr Southwell
takes Myra away.'

'Which apparently might be sooner rather than later.' Had he
started work too soon? Would his boss have an idea? Was it too
much to ask the babysitter for Piper to sleep over those nights?
As long as he didn't go over the forty hours, maybe it would be
okay? His feeling that everything had fallen into place shifted
again and he sighed. He wondered, not for the first time, how
single parents managed to work at all.

Thursday arrived and Finn had been cooking, creating and carv-
ing in the kitchen. Something his mother had tried to instil in
his sister but she'd found more fertile ground with Finn. He'd
loved the times he and his mother had spent cooking, and in his
short marriage the kitchen had been his domain at the weekend. It felt good to make something apart from nutritious finger food for Piper.

So, tonight a roast dinner. Something his wife had scoffed
at but something he loved and missed—possibly because when
they'd called at Marni's house the smell had reminded him how
much he'd enjoyed a roast dinner as a child. And when Catrina
had shared their lunch that first weekend they'd started talking—was it only a week ago?—she'd chosen a roast beef sandwich so she must like meat.

He'd slow roasted the beef and it lay, carved and foil-cov-
ered, in the oven with a veggie dish of potatoes, sweet potato,
pumpkin and whole small onions. A side of fresh beans, car-
rots and broccoli would have Piper in seventh heaven. His jug
of gravy was reheating and fresh bread rolls were on the table
with real butter waiting.

He glanced around. The house remained a little spartan in his
areas and cluttered in Piper's. She lay on her side in the playpen talking to her bunny. She'd had her bath and was dressed

in her pyjamas, now looking a little sleepy, and he wondered if he should give her dinner early in case Catrina was late.

But it would be hard to dish up Piper's and not pick for himself. His belly rumbled. Just then a knock sounded on the door and he put the oven mitt back on the bench. He felt an unaccustomed eagerness as he crossed the room and tried to damp it down. They were just friends.

Then he opened the door and there she stood, the afternoon sunlight a glow around her and an almost shy smile on her beautiful lips. Her eyes were clear and bright and her lovely dark auburn hair swung loose in the sea breeze with glints of gold dancing like ribbons.

She'd changed out of her work clothes. Stood calmly clad in a pretty sundress and a cream cardigan, her bare legs brown and long with painted toes peeping out of coral-coloured sandals. Finn admonished himself not to feel too special because she'd taken the time to change for him.

He couldn't believe how good she looked. Needed to remind himself he barely knew this woman, but it was as if he'd been waiting a long time for this moment. Found himself saying softly, 'You truly are a picture.'

Catrina blushed but lifted her head. He liked the way she did that. No false modesty that she hadn't put in any effort. 'Thank you.' She lifted her chin higher and sniffed slowly. 'And you have a divine aroma floating out of your house.'

He laughed. 'I'll be glad when we can eat. It's been teasing me for hours now.' Not the only sensation that had been teasing him but he was trying not to think about Catrina's mouth.

She laughed then, her lips curving enticingly, but, unlike another woman, this one held no expectations to use her beauty and the tension stayed behind in the swirl of salt and sunshine outside as he invited her in and shut the door.

CHAPTER TWELVE

Trina

TRINA STEPPED INTO Finn's house, still feeling a little mentally fragile at the tiny handprints she'd seen on the step. There was something so heart-wrenchingly adorable about a dad doing cement prints with his baby daughter. If she wasn't careful she'd end up falling for this guy so hard she'd be vulnerable again to loss.

It was a sobering thought.

Then, to make matters more serious, when Finn had opened the door her heart had lifted at the sight of him. Two steps up, he'd towered over her, but his quick movement sideways as if he couldn't wait for her to come in had softened the impression of feeling small into a feeling of being very much appreciated.

She couldn't miss the approval and delight on his face as his gaze had run over her. So, yes, she was glad she'd spent the extra fifteen minutes changing and refreshing her make-up. Brushing her hair loose—not something she did often but it did feel freeing, and apparently it met with Finn's approval.

She felt the warmth of his body as she squeezed past him into the bright and airy room, and more warmth when she saw the way Piper pulled herself up and smiled at her. She bent down and blew a kiss at the little girl, who clutched her bunny and smiled back. Then to be enveloped in the warmth of expectation with a table set and meal prepared for her—well, it did seem a little too good to be true.

She turned back to look at Finn—Dr Finn—lounging against the closed door as if savouring the sight of her. His strong arms were crossed against his chest as if taking the time to watch her reaction. She was getting a little heady here. She licked unexpectedly dry lips. 'I'm feeling special.'

'Good. You are special. Piper and I can thank you for the help you've given us.'

She hadn't done much. But her grandmother had said, *Always answer a compliment with gratitude and don't correct the giver.* 'Thank you.' But she could change the subject. 'It looks great in here. So light and airy and fresh. I love the wood grain in the floor.'

He crossed said floorboards towards her and pulled out her chair. 'Silky oak. It was under the carpet. Feels nice underfoot and I can hear Piper coming up behind me when I'm not looking. Though I had a polisher come and help me rub it back and polish it by hand. Hardest day's work I'd done all year.' He grinned at her and she could see he'd enjoyed the challenge.

'And what did Miss Piper do while you were playing around on the floor?'

'Luckily it was a typical Lighthouse Bay day—sunny—and we put up a little pergola. She stayed just outside the door in her playpen and kept us hard at it.'

Lucky her. To watch two men rubbing polish into wood for a few hours. Something very nice about that thought, Trina mused as she took the seat he held out for her.

Finn crossed to pick up Piper and poked her toes into her high chair and she snaked her way in like a little otter. Then he clipped a pink rubber bib around her neck. Piper did look excited at the thought of food.

'Can I help?' Trina asked, feeling a tad useless.

'It's a tiny kitchen nook, so you girls sit here while I produce my masterpiece and wait on you.' Then he glanced at his fidgety daughter. 'But you could hand Piper that crust on the plastic plate. She can chew on that while she waits for her veggies to cool.' He cast a sideways glance at Trina. 'I learnt it's better to give her something to chew on when she's in the chair or she starts to climb around when I'm not looking.'

'Ah—' Trina hurriedly passed the crust to Piper '—there you go, madam. Diversion tactics.'

Piper held out her hand and gleefully accepted the morsel and Finn strode the few steps to the kitchen bench and back across with the first plate and a jug of gravy.

'Roast veggies. Gravy.' He deposited his load and spun away, then was back in moments with a heaped plate of carved roast beef, the barest hint of pink at the centre of each slice. 'If you don't like it rare the more well-done pieces are at the edge.'

Trina's mouth had begun watering as the food began to arrive. 'I think I'm in heaven. It was busy today and I missed lunch. Plus I haven't had a roast for two years.' Not since before Ed's illness. Guilt and regret swamped her and she tried to keep it from her face.

Finn took a swift glance at her and said smoothly, 'It's all Marni's fault. That first day we visited. The way her house smelled of roast dinner did me in.' She decided he was very determined that they would enjoy the meal. Good thing too.

Trina pulled herself together and asked, 'So is this Piper's first roast dinner?'

'Indeed. More cause for celebration.' He leaned and poured them both a glass of cold water from the carafe on the table. The water glasses looked like crystal to Trina. 'Let's drink to that.' Then he raised his hand to hers and they touched glasses with a tell-tale perfect *ching* and her melancholy fell away as they sipped. Life was pretty darn good.

He indicated the food. 'You serve yours and I'll fix Piper.'

Finn dished some veggies and meat onto Piper's cartoon-illustrated plastic plate and swiftly cut them into bite-sized pieces.

This was all done so efficiently that Trina found herself smiling. Such a maternal thing to do but this dad had it covered.

She arranged her own plate, finishing with a generous serve of gravy, and sat back to wait for Finn.

He wasn't far behind. He topped his meal off with his gravy and then looked up to meet her eyes. *'Bon appétit.'*

They didn't talk much as they ate, neither did they rush, and Trina glanced around as she savoured the subtle and not so subtle flavours of a well-cooked roast dinner. Marvelled at the decorating touches that showed this man's love for his daughter. A mobile of seashells over the cot, a run of circus animals in a wallpaper panel behind her bed. An alphabet mat on the floor with a Piper-sized chair on it. A row of small dolls in bright dresses.

She indicated the dolls with her fork. 'So these are the ladies you talk to?'

'All the time. Especially the brunette on the end. Remarkable conversationalist, really.'

'I can imagine.' She smiled at the dark-haired doll which, at a stretch, could look a little like Trina herself.

'Do you like our home?' Needy? Keen for her approval? But there was something endearing about that.

She nodded sagely. 'I think Piper will be a famous decorator one day.'

She was teasing him but it must have been the right thing to say because his pleasure was almost palpable. 'Remind me to show you the shower. We have very nice tiles.'

'I'll make sure I do that.' And she allowed herself to consider the possibility of a future here. With this man and his daughter. At the very least as friends and with a potential for more…but she wouldn't rush. Couldn't rush. And neither could he.

The thought crashed in. Who knew where his wife was? The thought brought a deluge of dampness to her sunny spirits and she looked down at her food, which suddenly didn't taste as good as it had.

'So tell me about the rest of your week. Did Piper still want to stay at Marni's when you went to pick her up after a full day or did she miss you?'

'Both. Marni is wonderful with her. And your Myra has booked her drop-and-go cruise. A five-nighter to Tasmania. They leave Sunday. So call and three-day rosters at the hospital. Piper will have to stay over when I'm on call. Though they've managed to give me only the one night call, which I appreciate.'

'Wow. You've dived into work with a vengeance.'

'I should have done it earlier. I'm feeling more connected to humanity every day.' He glanced up at her with definite warmth. 'Though that could have been you.'

Glad he thought she was human. But that wasn't what he meant and she knew it. Her face heated and she looked down at her almost empty plate. 'Thank you, kind sir.' She lifted her head and shook the hair away from her face. It was getting hot in here. 'One night seems like the perfect answer. That's not too bad as a start. When did you say that night was?'

'Next Thursday. We'll see how she goes. Marni's not worried.'

She could have offered for a Thursday night but she was glad he hadn't asked. She wasn't ready for that much commitment. 'Well, good luck.' She lifted her glass of water. 'And here's to your first week at the hospital. I'll look forward to your smiling face.'

'I'll try to remember to smile.'

CHAPTER THIRTEEN

Finn

BY MONDAY MORNING, his first day in the hospital, Catrina continued to seep into Finn's thoughts with alarming regularity and he was feeling just as strange about that as he was about the new work model he'd slipped into. A general GP, admittedly with extra specialist paediatric consults on the side, and a rural hospital generalist as well. With maternity cover? Never thought he'd see the day.

Over the weekend he and Catrina had met a lot, each meeting better than the last, plus they'd talked about the hospital and the patients he'd probably find come Monday. About how the medical input had changed since the new midwifery model had started, even some of the times that Dr Southwell had been called away from the main hospital to provide back-up in Maternity.

He could see Catrina enjoyed their discussions and, to be truthful, he was a little curious to see how it all worked. They'd bumped into each other often. Intentionally on his part and, he suspected glumly, unintentionally on hers.

He'd managed the Friday morning beach bump into when, after his own walk, he'd offered to share the breakwall with

Catrina, Piper on his back, and they'd spent more than an hour together talking non-stop.

Saturday morning, after Catrina's scuba lesson, he and Piper had been back in their rock pool at just the right time for her to walk past them again and fortuitously share an early lunch as Catrina offered to return last week's lunch shout at the beach café.

Saturday night he and Piper had been invited to a barbecue dinner at Ellie and Sam's and, of course, Catrina had been there as she lived next door.

Naturally he'd spoken to other people but they'd spent most of the time standing together. He'd had an excellent conversation with Sam on the strangeness of working in a cottage hospital after coming from a tertiary health facility and Myra had shaken his hand and thanked him for making it possible to drag her husband away on a cruise. But the stand-out moments were those watching Catrina's quiet rapport with the other dinner guests.

His eyes had drifted in her direction way too often.

The best had been on Sunday when Catrina had asked if Piper—and Finn—could come and help her choose colours for her new carpet and cushions and they'd had a hilarious day at the nearest large town choosing colours via a one-year-old in a stroller.

A huge weekend, in fact, but one that had passed without kissing her once. And that also was something he couldn't get out of his mind.

Her mouth. So mobile, always smiling and doing that soft chortling thing when he said something to amuse her—a new skill he seemed to have acquired that did more to heal his soul than anything else.

Or that unconscious, but luscious, lip-pursing she did when she seriously considered something he said. Or just her mouth looking downright kissable when he didn't expect it, and he was having a hard time not drifting off and staring at the lift of a corner or the flash of white teeth.

He didn't remember being this fixated on Piper's mother when he'd met her. There had certainly been attraction, almost a forest fire of heat and lust culminating in a headlong rush into marriage when their contraception had failed. More his idea than hers and he had certainly paid the price for that.

But he was coming to the conclusion that he must have been meant to be Piper's daddy because he couldn't imagine life without his baby girl so he thanked Clancy for that. There was a bit of healing in there somewhere and he wasn't sure he didn't owe Catrina for that thought too.

But Catrina? Well? He needed to slow down and not lose the plot, but Catrina made him want to be better at being himself, a better person, even a better partner since he'd obviously fallen short on that last time.

His attraction to Catrina had been exquisitely stoked by want and need, and he feared—or was that dared to hope?—she might be coming to care for him too.

This morning, as he climbed the hill to the little white hospital sitting on a cliff, he hoped that very much. He glanced at the cottage garden as he approached for his first day as visiting medical officer and could feel his spirits soar as he strode towards a new perspective of Catrina at work.

The ocean glittered a sapphire blue today, brighter and more jewel-like than he could remember seeing. Piper had been as lively as a grig being handed over to Marni and the boys. And he, well, he was back at work, feeling almost comfortable already in Reg's practice, like a normal human being. It had taken a year of shadow. And a week. And Catrina.

Except for the colour of the ocean, Catrina had a lot to do with most of his forward progress. Though maybe all the colours were appearing brighter this week because of her as well.

Reg had suggested he call into Maternity first—'Around eight, my boy!'—to see if any women were in labour—'Just so you can be aware.' And then attend to his hospital round on the other side of the small white building.

He suspected that the midwives didn't need the visit but Reg clearly felt paternal in his concern for them. Finn thought it prudent not to share that insight with Catrina.

But what a gift of an excuse, he thought as he stepped through the automatic front door to Maternity and glanced around for her.

Instead, a nurse he'd met on his orientation round with Reg on Friday came in through the side door from the main hospital at a run and her relief at seeing him alerted his instincts faster than her voice. 'Dr Foley—please follow me through to the birthing suite. Urgently!'

The smile slipped from Finn's face and he nodded and followed.

When he entered, he saw Catrina standing over a neonatal resuscitation trolley, her fingers encircling the little chest with her thumb pressing cardiac massage over the baby's sternum in a rhythmic count.

Another nurse held the tiny face mask over the baby's face, inflating the chest with intermittent positive pressure ventilations after every third compression.

Finn stopped beside them, glanced at the seconds ticking past on the trolley clock that indicated time since birth. It showed ninety seconds.

Catrina looked up and the concentrated expression on her face faltered for the briefest moment and he saw the concern and the relief on her face. Then she looked at the clock as well. Her voice remained calm but crisp.

'Rhiannon's baby was born two minutes ago, short cord snapped during delivery so probable neonatal blood loss. Baby is just not getting the hang of this breathing business.' Her voice came out remarkably steady and he filed that away to tell her later.

'Heart rate less than sixty for the last thirty seconds so we added cardiac compression to the IPPV and it's just come back to eighty.' She loosened her fingers around the baby's chest and turned down the oxygen to keep the levels similar to where a two-minute-old baby would normally be. Too much oxygen held as many risks as not enough oxygen for babies.

'This is the paediatrician, Dr Foley, Rhiannon,' she called across to the mum, who was holding the hand of an older woman, concern etched on their faces.

Finn lifted his hand and smiled reassuringly. Because the fact the baby had picked up his heartbeat was an excellent sign. 'Give us a few minutes and I'll come across and explain.'

He glanced at the pulse oximeter someone had strapped to the flaccid pale wrist. 'You're keeping the oxygen levels perfect. Umbilical catheter then,' Finn said calmly. 'I'll top up the fluids and the rest should stabilise.'

'The set-up is in the second drawer. There's a diagram on the lid because we don't use it often.'

He retrieved the transparent plastic box and put it on the nearby bench, squirted antiseptic on his hands and began to assemble the intravenous line that would be inserted a little way into the baby's umbilical cord stump and give a ready-made large bore venous entry point to replace the fluids lost.

He glanced at Catrina. 'Warmed fluids?'

'Cupboard outside the door.' The nurse he'd arrived with handed Catrina the clipboard she'd taken to jot observations on and slipped out to get the fluids. By the time he had all the syringes and tubing set she was back and they primed the line with the warmed fluids and set it aside.

Finn squirted the antiseptic on his hands again and donned the sterile gloves to wipe the baby's belly around the cord with an antiseptic swab, and wiped the cord stump liberally with the solution.

After placing a towel on the baby's belly to give himself a sterile field he could work from, he tied the soft sterile tape around the base of the finger-thick umbilical cord. The tape was a safety measure, so that when they removed the cord clamp Catrina had fastened at birth, he could pull the tape tight around the umbilical cord to control any further blood loss.

Once the tape was in place and fastened firmly, Catrina looked at Finn, who smiled reassuringly because he doubted it was something she did on a newly cut cord very often, and watched her remove the cord clamp with only a trace of anxiety.

Finn nodded to himself, satisfied—no bleeding—then sliced off the nerveless ragged edge of the snapped cord closer to the baby's belly with a scalpel blade, the white tape preventing any further blood loss. Now he could easily see the vessels inside where he wanted to put the tubing.

Using fine artery forceps, he captured one edge of the cord and then offered the forceps to Catrina to hold to free up his other hand.

With the cord now pulled upright, Finn lifted the catheter and another pair of forceps to insert the end into the gaping vessel of the vein in the umbilical cord. He glimpsed the nurse from the main hospital looking wide-eyed and said quietly, 'It's easy to tell which is the vein, being the largest and softest vessel of the three in the cord. That's the one that leads to the heart.'

Catrina asked, 'Do you have to turn the catheter to insert it? Aren't the vessels spiral?'

'Yes, spiral so when the cord is pulled in utero there's give and spring, the longer the cut cord the more spiral you have to traverse until you get to the bloodstream. That's why I cut this fairly short. Not too short that you don't leave yourself a back-up plan, though.'

The fine clear intravenous tubing disappeared just below the baby's abdominal skin. A sudden swirl of blood mixed with the warmed fluid Finn had primed the tubing with.

'And we're in,' Finn said with satisfaction. He adjusted the three-way tap on the line with one hand and slowly injected the warmed saline fluid with a fat syringe into the baby's bloodstream. 'Ten mils per kilo will do it, and I'd say this little tyke is about three kilos.'

He glanced at Catrina, who watched the monitor to see the baby's heart rate slowly increasing. She nodded. He then glanced at her colleague, still calmly applying intermittent puffs of air into the baby's lungs, and then watched as the tiny flaccid hand slowly clenched as tone returned to the baby's body and he began to flex and twitch.

Finn looked over at the mum. 'Not long now.'

'Get ready to tighten the cord again, Catrina,' he said softly and, once the full amount of fluid had been injected and Catrina was ready, he turned the tap on the infusion and removed the syringe.

'We'll just wait a few minutes before we remove it in case we need to give any drugs, but I think that will do the trick.'

CHAPTER FOURTEEN

Trina

TRINA'S GALLOPING PULSE slowed as the baby's heart rate began to rise above eighty. Her hand loosened on the resuscitation trolley she seemed to have gripped as Finn did his thing. After what had seemed like forever the baby's heart rate hit a hundred and ten and finally the baby blinked and struggled, grimaced against the mask and, in the most beautiful screech in the world, he began to cry. The tension in the room fluttered and fell like a diving bird and she watched Finn slowly withdraw the tubing from the vein. She tightened the cord as it came clear and then snapped on a new umbilical clamp close to the end of the stump. Done.

Baby threw his hands and kicked his feet and they pushed the resuscitation trolley closer to the mum's bed so he could be handed across with the pulse oximeter still strapped to his wrist.

Trina considered removing it as he'd become so vigorous with the replacement of fluid but it would be easier to monitor instead of listening with a stethoscope so, despite the tangle of wires, she left him connected and pressed his bare skin to his mother's naked breasts.

Once baby was settled on his mother, his breathing clear

and unobstructed, she could relax a little more. A blanket covered them both, and she glanced at Finn, standing at the side of the trolley, his beautiful mouth soft as he watched the baby and mother finally together. His eyes shone with pleasure and he gave a little nod just before he saw Trina looking at him.

The smile he gave her, one of warmth and pride and appreciation, made her clutch her throat and heat surged into her cheeks. She'd done nothing.

When she looked back at him he was watching the mum again, his eyes still soft as he spoke to her.

'Hello there. Congratulations. As Trina said, I'm Dr Foley, the paediatrician, and your little boy looks great now. Snapped cords are fairly rare, but if a baby grows in utero with a short umbilical cord...' he smiled that warm and reassuring smile that seemed to seep right down to the soles of Trina's feet and he wasn't even looking at her '...which he is perfectly entitled to do.' He shrugged. 'Not surprisingly, though it *is* always a surprise, they can run out of stretch at birth and the cord can pull too tight.'

Rhiannon nodded and her own mother sat back with relief to see her grandchild safely snuggled into Rhiannon's arms.

Finn went on. 'Babies don't have a lot of blood to spare so some extra fluid through that intravenous line allowed his heart to get back into the faster rhythm it needs. As you saw, it's usually a fairly dramatic improvement. We'll do some blood tests and if we need to we'll talk about a blood transfusion. But he looks good.'

'Too much drama for me,' Rhiannon said, as she cuddled her baby close to her chest. Trina could agree with that. Now that she had time to think about it, she had to admit that Finn's appearance had been a miracle she'd very much needed. But there wasn't time for that yet as she began to attend to all the things that needed doing in the immediate time after a baby had been born.

* * *

Two and a half hours later Trina had settled Rhiannon and baby Jackson into their room, and the myriad of paperwork, forms and data entry had been sorted. The nurse from the hospital had stayed to help Trina tidy the ward because Faith, the midwife from night duty, had already stayed later than normal. Trina glanced at the clock, just ten-thirty, so, on top of the tasks still waiting to be done, she did need a moment to sit back in the chair and consider the excitement of the morning.

It had been a little too exciting but thankfully Finn had appeared at exactly the right moment without needing to be called. An opportune thing.

Like he did at that moment. Striding through the doors from the main hospital as if he owned the place.

She felt a smile stretch her face. 'I was just thinking about you.'

His laughing eyes made her belly flip-flop and caution flooded her. He had a wife. Somewhere.

'Good things, I hope?' he said.

She shook her head. Pretended to think about it. 'How I didn't need you this morning and you just pushed in.' Teasing him.

His face froze for a second and she slid her hand over her mouth in horror, saying quickly, 'Joke. A very mean joke. Especially when you were so good. I'm sorry.' But she could feel the creases in her cheeks as she smiled because his shock had been palpable when the statement had been totally ridiculous. He must have known she'd needed him desperately. She had no idea why she'd said such a crazy thing except to startle him. Or maybe because she'd been trying to hide how absolutely thrilled she was that he'd come back to see her when she'd thought he would have been long gone from the hospital.

This man brought out very strange urges in her. At least she wasn't giggling like a twit. She was saying bizarre things instead.

He laughed a little sheepishly. 'I was worried for a minute there.'

She looked up at him. Seriously? 'Don't be. Sorry. I was never so glad to see anybody in my life. My pulse was about a hundred and sixty.' And it wasn't far from that now with him standing so close, which would not do.

He studied her. That didn't help the galloping heart rate. 'Well, you looked as cool as a cucumber.'

'On the outside. Good to know.' Hopefully she looked that way now as well—especially with her brain telling her to do stupid things in fight and flight mode. 'But, seriously, you were very slick with inserting that umbi line. Most impressive.'

And she had no doubt her eyes were telling him a tad more than she was saying because he smiled back at her with a lot more warmth than she deserved after what she'd just done to him. He sat down beside her at the desk.

To hide the heat in her cheeks she looked past his shoulder towards Rhiannon's room and murmured, 'It would have been very tense to keep resuscitating a baby who didn't improve as we expected. He really needed that fluid in his system to get him circulating properly.'

He didn't say anything so she looked at him. He was studying her intently again and her face grew hotter. 'What?'

'We were lucky. That was all it was. I'm wondering if you could call me for the next couple of births through the day while Piper is in care, just so I can sneak in a refresher course on normal birth. It's a long time since my term in Obstetrics working towards my OB Diploma and I want to be up to speed if an emergency occurs.'

His diffidence surprised her. 'Of course, you're welcome. I call in a nurse from the hospital as my second but I can easily call you instead if we have time. Or as well. I don't mind. And I can run a simulation through the latest changes in post-partum haemorrhage and prem labour if you like.'

'Excellent. I've been doing some reading but things aren't always the same when you get to the different hospital sites.'

'We're a birth centre not a hospital, even though we're joined by an external corridor. So all of our women are low risk.' But things still happened. Not with the regularity you saw in a major hospital but they did deal with first line emergencies until a woman or her baby could be transferred to higher care.

He nodded. 'Is that your first snapped cord?'

'My first here.' She shook her head, still a little shocked. 'We've had them tear and bleed but to actually just break like that was a shock.'

'It's rare. Had probably torn already and when the last stretch happened at birth it broke—but you handled it well, getting the clamp on so quickly. I've seen some much worse situations.'

'I kept expecting him to get better, like nearly all babies do when you give them a puff or two, but by the time you arrived I was getting worried.'

He nodded. 'Hypovolemia will do that. How's Mum?'

'Taken it in her stride. Said her angels were looking after her and baby Jackson.' She thought he'd laugh.

'Useful things, angels.' Then, in an aside, 'My mother was a medium. I should have listened to her.'

He shrugged and Trina tried not to gape. His turn to say something off the wall, maybe, or he could be pulling her leg because he grinned at her surprise.

He changed the subject before she could ask. 'Today Jackson also had the midwives and doctor.' He grinned. 'Shall I go down and see if she has any more questions now she's had a chance to think about it?'

Trina stood up as well. Off balance by his throwaway comment about his mother...and his proximity. Moving to a new location sounded like a great idea, she thought, still mentally shaking her head to clear it. That had been the last thing she'd expected him to say. But she'd ask more later. This moment, here at work, wasn't the time. Angel medium? Seriously, she was dying to find out.

'Great idea. Thank you.' She stood up and followed him. Finn was thoughtful, kind and darn slick as a paediatrician. Lighthouse Bay might just have to count its blessings to have another fabulous doctor in the wings when they needed him. Speaking of wings... Angels? Her head spun as she followed him down the hallway.

Over the next four days while Finn covered the hospital, he shared three births with Trina between breakfast and morning tea. It was almost as if the mothers were on a timetable of morning births to make it easy for him to be able to watch and even catch one.

She could tell he was enjoying himself. Basking in the magic that was birth. But the busyness meant she didn't get a chance to ask about him. About his mother's angels. About his childhood. About his marriage—not that she would! The woman who had given birth to Piper and what had happened to her.

Trina hoped they were at the stage of friendship where she could ask about at least some of those things soon. But then again, she hadn't shared anything of her past either. Maybe they should just leave it all in the past and keep talking about Lighthouse Bay nineteen to the dozen like they had been. Share the past slowly because she was probably reading too much into his interest.

Lighthouse Bay Maternity must have decided to draw in the babies for Dr Finn, because they just kept coming. The overdue ones arrived, the early ones came early, and the more time they spent together with new babies and new families the more her curiosity about Finn's world before he came here grew.

He left soon after each birth to continue his appointments at the surgery but returned at late lunchtime with his sandwiches to talk about the morning's events.

On Thursday, his last hospital shift before Dr Southwell returned, Finn entered the birthing room quietly after the soft knock Trina had trained him in. She'd left a message with his secretary to say they were having a water birth, and even though he'd not long gone he'd been very keen to see the way water and birth 'mixed'.

Trina had given him a scolding glance at his wording, but she had immense faith that once he'd seen the beauty of the way the bath environment welcomed babies into the world he'd be converted. She was glad he could make it.

Sara, the birthing mum, was having her second baby and had come in late in the labour. She'd phoned ahead to ensure the bath had been filled, mentioned she wanted lots of photos of her daughter's birth because she had lots from her son's birth.

They arrived almost ready for second stage and Trina had the bath prepared. At Finn's knock her head lifted and Sara frowned at the sound.

Trina worried. Maybe things had changed. 'Are you still okay if the doctor sits in on your birth, Sara?'

'As long as he stays out of the bath, I'm fine,' Sara said with unexpected humour considering the glare at the door and the contraction that had begun to swell and widen her eyes.

Trina turned to hide her grin and motioned for Finn to enter the room. She liked the way he always waited for permission. Though she might have mentioned it a few times and she had no doubt her eyes betrayed her amusement at his docility. No, not docility—respect. Her amusement faded. As he should.

Finn said a brief thanks to Sara and her husband and settled back into the corner on the porcelain throne, making himself as inconspicuous as a six foot tank could be. Once he was seated Trina tried to forget about him.

She suspected by the way Sara was breathing out deeply and slowly that she'd felt the urge to bear down. Second stage. Time to up the monitoring. When the final louder breath had been released Sara lay back with her eyes closed.

Trina murmured, 'Is baby moving down and through, Sara?'

'Yes.'

'Can I listen to the heartbeat between those outward breaths?'

'Yes.' Bare minimum. She had more important things to concentrate on than answering questions and Trina understood that.

Sara arched her belly up until it broke the surface of the bath water and Trina leaned forward and slid the Doppler low on Sara's belly. The sound of a happy clopping heartbeat filled the room. With her eyes closed, Sara smiled.

After a minute Trina moved the Doppler away and Sara sank back below the water, causing ripples to splash the edge of the bath. She didn't open her eyes when another minute passed and her heavy outward sighs started again.

It took fifteen minutes, and five cycles of breathing, listening, smiling and sinking below the surface of the water and then they could see the baby's head below the surface.

Sara's breathing didn't change, nobody spoke. Below, in the water, the small shoulders appeared. Trina hovered, but Sara reached down, waiting, as an expelled breath larger than the rest released a flurry of movement. The movement heralded the rest of the baby's body had been born. Sara clasped her baby firmly between her hands below the water level and lifted her smoothly to the surface to rest on her belly. The little face rose above the water, blue and gaping, and then the baby's eyes opened and she began to breathe in as the air hit her face.

Everyone else breathed out. The father photographing constantly and the glance the couple shared between clicks made tears sting Trina's eyes. So beautiful.

The birth left Finn sitting thoughtfully at her desk as he replayed the scene.

Finally, he said, 'That was amazing. The mum was so in control, lifting the baby after birth out of the water like that.' He quirked one brow at her. 'How could you stop yourself reaching in to do it for her?'

Trina smiled. 'If she'd hesitated or if she'd needed me to, I would have. But Sara had it covered. That's her second water birth so she knew what she wanted and what would happen.'

He rolled a pen between his fingers thoughtfully. 'I have to admit to scepticism. Why add water to the list of things that could go wrong for a baby at birth?' He tapped the pen on the desk. 'I could see Mum looked super-relaxed—baby just appeared with the breathing, not even pushing, and slowly birthed. Hands off. A very relaxed baby though a little bluer than normal in the first few minutes.'

That was true, Trina thought. 'We find the colour can take a minute or two longer to pink up, mainly because the babies may not cry.'

She shrugged. 'People need to remember no analgesia was needed for Mum because of the thirty-seven-degree heat and relaxation of the bath, so babies aren't affected by drugs for the next twenty-four hours like some are. That helps breastfeeding and bonding. She didn't have an epidural so no drip or urinary catheter either.' And no stitches. Trina always felt relieved when that happened—and it was usually when a mother advanced second stage at her own pace. Something they prided themselves on at Lighthouse Bay—but then they had all the well mums and babies to start with.

It had been a beautiful birth and Trina still glowed from the experience, even after all the tidying up and paperwork had been done.

She glanced at the clock. Finn would go soon. Lunchtime seemed to fly when he came to talk about the births and she could feel their rapport and their friendship, the ease she fell into with their conversations, had all grown this week with his shifts.

Finn stroked the cover of the book Trina had lent him to read on water birth. 'I'm intrigued how you managed to sell the idea here to the board of directors. I know water birth was vetoed at my last hospital.'

It had been easier than expected. One of the board member's daughter had had a water birth at another hospital. But they'd

covered their bases. 'Our statistics are meticulous. Ellie has always been firm on keeping good records and it shows we have
excellent outcomes on land and water birth. I'm doing the same.'
She thought about how smoothly their transition to a midwife-
led unit had been in the end. 'Of course it helped with Sam as
back-up. Ellie's husband has such high standing in the area
now. The local authorities consider us backed by experts even
though Sam's not technically here. So water birth with the midwives at Mum's request is the norm here and proved to be very
safe. Just remember we start with well mums and well babies.'

'Good job. Everyone.' He stood up. Looking down at her with
that crooked smile that seemed to make everything shine so
bright it fuddled her brain. 'Well, you've converted me. Which
is lucky as tonight is my all-night on-call.'

He gathered up his lunch wrap from the kiosk meal he'd
bought. 'I'd better get back to the surgery; my afternoon patients will start to arrive at two. Then my first night without
Piper for a year.'

She knew plenty of mums who would love to have a night
where their babies slept overnight with someone else. 'How
does that make you feel?'

He shrugged. Apparently not overjoyed. 'Very strange, I
have to admit. I think I'm going to be lonely. Don't suppose
you'd like to join me?'

'If you get forlorn give me a call.' As soon as she said it Trina
began to blush. What on earth had got into her? Practically
throwing herself at the man at the first opportunity. But she'd
been thinking he'd looked sad when he'd said it.

She soldiered on. 'What I meant was, unlike Piper, I can go
home if you get called out.' That sounded even worse.

His blue eyes sparkled. Mischievously. Suddenly he looked
less like an assured paediatrician and more like a little boy offered a treat. 'Now that's an offer I'd like to take you up on. We
could get takeaway.'

'Now I feel like I've invited myself.'

He laughed. 'Thank goodness. We could both die of old age before I had the nerve to ask you properly and I've been wanting to since Marni agreed to have Piper overnight.'

He flashed her a smile. 'It's a date. You can't back out now. I'll see you at mine at six p.m.'

She couldn't have him cooking for her after work. 'I finish at five. So why don't you come to my house? I can make us dinner or order in and your mobile will go off anywhere. Do on-call from there.'

'If that's okay, then great. I'll appear at six.' He waved and smiled and...left.

Good grief. He'd been wanting to ask her. Then reason marched in. Wanted what? What could happen if she wasn't careful? It was a small town and she needed her reputation and her just healing, skin-grafted heart needed protection. Was she getting too close to this guy—a guy with a cloud of unresolved questions that even he didn't know the answers to?

Well, yes. She was getting too close.

Did it feel right?

Um, yes. So why couldn't she spend the evening, or the night if that came up, with a man she was very, very attracted to?

Because he was married. His wife was missing, alive or dead, he was still married—and she didn't sleep with married men.

CHAPTER FIFTEEN

Finn

FINN KNOCKED ON Catrina's solid timber door and his heart thumped almost as loudly as his knuckles on the wood. He couldn't believe he was back in the game. Taking risks. Making a play. With his twelve-month-old daughter asleep at a babysitter's and his wife still missing.

He wasn't a villain to do this. He was on-call. Calling on Catrina beat the heck out of sitting at home alone, waiting for his mobile phone to ring for work. And Catrina made his world a more rounded place. A warm and wonderful place.

Different to the walls he normally pulled around himself and Piper. Guilt from the past had become less cloying over the last few weeks, the cloud still there but it had gone from dense and choking to thin and drifting away like ocean mist. Like a new day awakening. Thanks to Catrina.

The door opened and she stood there, with that gorgeous smile of hers that lifted his heart and made him want to reach forward and, quite naturally, kiss her. Which, to the surprise of both of them, he did. As if he'd done it every time she opened the door to him—when in fact it hadn't happened before—and, despite the widening of her eyes in surprise, she kissed him back. *Ah, so good.*

So he moved closer and savoured that her mouth melded soft and tentative against his. Luscious and sweet and...

He stepped right in, pulled the door shut behind him, locking the world away from them, because he needed her in his arms, hidden from prying eyes.

She didn't push him away—far from it, her hands crept up to his neck and encircled him as she leaned into his chest. The kiss deepening into a question from him, an answering need from her that made his heart pound again and he tightened his arms even more around her. Their lips pressed, tongues tangled, hands gripping each other until his head swam with the scent and the taste of her. Time passed but, as in all things, slowly reality returned.

He lifted her briefly off her feet and spun her, suddenly exuberant from all the promise in that kiss, then put her down as their mouths broke apart. Both of them were flushed and laughing. He raised his fingers to draw her hold from his neck and kissed the backs of them. 'Such beautiful hands.' He kissed them again.

In turn, she created some sensible space in the heat between them and turned away.

But not before he saw the glow in her eyes that he had no doubt was reflected in his. They could take their time. The first barrier had passed—they'd kissed, and what a kiss. The first since heartache and they'd both survived. Not just survived—they'd thrived! Finn felt like a drooping plant, desperate for water, and he'd just had the first sip. You could tell a lot from a first kiss, and Catrina had blown his socks off.

Finn slowed to watch her cross the room, mostly because she fascinated him—she walked, brisk and swinging, out through the open door of the veranda overlooking the sea, the backdrop of sapphire blue a perfect foil for her dark hair as distance widened between them.

He tried hard not to look at the bed in the corner of the big room as he passed but his quick glance imprinted cushions and the floral quilt they'd bought on Sunday which she said she'd needed to brighten the place. He pulled his eyes away but he could feel the tightening in his groin he couldn't help and imagined carrying Catrina to that corner.

'Come on,' she called from the little covered porch and he quickened his step. Almost guilty now his body had leapt ahead after one kiss but the cheeky smile she'd flung over her shoulder at him eased that dilemma. She was thinking about the bed too. But not today. He needed to make sure she knew it all. Before he tarnished something beautiful and new with ghosts from the past.

He'd never seen her so bubbly—as if she were glowing from the inside—and he watched her, a little dazed, that he'd done this to her. Lit her up. With a kiss as if she were a sleeping princess. But he was no prince. And it was a long time since he'd lit anyone up like this—just Clancy in the beginning—and look how that ended. He pushed that thought away.

She'd set the table with bright place mats and put out salad and pasta and cheese. Orange juice in a pitcher stood beside glasses and the sunlight bathed it all in golden lights and reflections as the day drew to a jewelled close above the sea.

Like a moth to the light, he closed in on her where she'd paused against the rail overlooking the sea. Her silhouette was willowy yet curved in all the right places, her dark hair, sun-kissed in streaks, blowing in the ocean breeze. He came up behind her and put his hands on the rail each side, capturing her. Leant ever so lightly against her curved back, the length of his body warming against her softness, feeling the give against his thighs.

Then he leant down and kissed the soft pearly skin under her ear and she shivered beneath him; her breath caught as she pushed back, into him. His hands left the rail and encircled her hips from behind, spreading low across her stomach and pelvis.

'You're like a sea sprite up here.' His voice came out low and deeper than normal. 'A siren high on her vantage point overlooking the sea.'

She turned her head and, with a slow wicked smile, tilted her face to look at him. 'Does that make you a pirate?'

He lifted his brows. 'I could be?'

'Not today, me hearty,' she said and pushed him back more firmly with her bottom to suggest he give her space and he let his hands slide down the outer curve of her thighs, savouring the feminine shape of her, and then away.

'Right then,' he said and stepped back. 'Do your hostess thing, sea sprite.'

She spun and pulled out a chair at the table. 'Yes, you should eat in case you get called away. It's Thursday and I know there's a buck's party on tonight before the wedding on Saturday. You might be needed if things get silly.'

She indicated the food in bowls. 'Start now, please. Don't wait for me.' She avoided his eyes and he saw the exuberance had passed. There was no rush and this wasn't just about him—it was about this brave, beautiful widow finding her way to exposing her heart again. He reminded himself he knew how that felt though his circumstances were far different. He wanted to do this right. Right for Catrina. Right for him. And right for Piper. He needed to remember Piper. And try not to forget he had Clancy in the wings.

Though how could he do this right with a missing wife God knew where and this woman bruised from her own past? He forced a smile to his mouth. 'The pasta looks amazing.'

He saw the relief as he changed the subject and knew he'd been right to give her space.

She gestured vaguely to the hedge that separated her house from the one next door. 'Herbs make the difference. We share a herb garden. Myra does the tending and Ellie and I share the eating.'

She smiled with her mouth but not her eyes and he wondered what she was thinking while she was talking trivia about herb gardens. Had he been too full-on? Yes, he had—they both had—but that had been some kiss. Like a steam train carrying them both along at great speed and only just finding the brakes.

'But it works for us.'

What works for us? Then he realised she was still talking about the herb garden. He had it bad. Just wasn't so sure about her. He stuffed some pasta in his mouth. A taste explosion rioted there and he groaned in delight. And she could cook. His gaze strayed to her.

Time. *It all takes time*, he reassured himself. Took another scrumptious bite and prayed the phone wouldn't ring at least until he finished his food. Preferably not at all.

She poured him some juice, then sat opposite him, her hair falling to hide her face, but something about the hesitant way she tilted her face as if she were weighing her words before she spoke. He swallowed more divine food and slowed down. Then asked, 'Question?'

'I'm wondering if it's too early to ask you about your mother. You said something on Monday that's been driving me a little wild with curiosity.'

His head came up. More because the idea of her being driven a little wild stirred his interest rather than any concern about her prying into his past. 'A little wild, eh?' He speared a pasta curl.

She looked at him and shook her head. 'You're a dark horse, Dr Foley. One bit of encouragement and I can see where that leads you.'

He grinned at her. Spread his fork hand innocently. 'I'm just happy.'

She laughed. 'I'm happy too. So, now that I've made you happy, can I ask you about your mother?'

'Go ahead.'

'What did you mean she was a medium? It's the last thing I expected.'

He'd come to terms with it years ago. Funny how women

harped on about it. His sister. And Clancy. Both had hated it. Funny he hadn't thought Catrina would be like that. He'd always thought of his mum's beliefs like a choice. Believe in angels or not. Be a vegetarian or not. Take up ballroom dancing or tarot cards.

'What's to expect? She was a psychologist then became fascinated by the cards and became a medium. I loved her. My sister couldn't have been more horrified if my mother had taken six lovers instead of a sudden attraction to talking to the angels.'

Catrina leaned forward earnestly. 'It doesn't repel me. I'm not sure what fascinates me about it. It's just different. That's all. And a bit out there for a paediatrician to have a medium in his family.'

He'd heard that before. 'That's what my sister said. But it made Mum happy and when she went she went with peace. She died not long after I fell for Clancy.' He shrugged but heard the grief shadowed in his voice. Tried to lighten the tone. 'She said that Clancy had sadness wrapped around her like a cloak and she worried about me.'

Catrina opened her eyes wide.

He sighed. 'I didn't listen.'

CHAPTER SIXTEEN

Trina

TRINA GLANCED OVER the rail to the wide ocean in front of them. Sought the point where the ocean met the sky and sighed too. Of all the things she wanted to ask Finn, she wasn't sure why she'd chosen to ask about his mother. And now that she knew she'd never meet her it made her sad. Another mother gone. It had been a ridiculous question.

Or maybe it was about her because she couldn't remember her own mum, could only remember an ethereal figure tucking her in and singing a lullaby she couldn't remember the words to. But she knew mothers were special. She'd always wanted one and Finn's had sounded magical. Someone who talked to angels.

For Trina there'd been a succession of foster homes in her childhood, the quiet child, the plain one with her hair pulled back tightly, the one people were briskly kind to but nobody became interested in, except the younger children she seemed to gather around her every time she ended back in the home.

Many kids had it a lot worse, and she'd come to a stage where she'd asked not to be fostered, not to raise her hopes that she'd find a mother to love, and she'd stayed and helped in the home until she could leave. Had worked for a scholarship, always determined to do her nursing.

A nice sensible profession followed by her glimpse into midwifery—and that was when she'd seen it.

The families. Starting from the glory of birth, the connection to the child, the true beginning of a mother's love. The journey she'd make one day because she knew in her bones this was her destiny and then she'd be home. She had so much love to give.

'I'm sorry your mother died. I would have liked to meet her.'

He looked at her thoughtfully and then nodded. 'She would have liked you too.'

The thought warmed her melancholy and she appreciated his kindness. 'Thank you.'

He was the one with the questioning look now. Weighing the difference of needing to know and being too forward. 'Where did you meet your husband?'

So they'd reached that stage. She'd started it. Gingerly she began to unpack it a little. 'Edward was a nurse like me. At uni. We both worked at a restaurant waiting on tables and we laughed a lot. Then we both graduated and went to work at the same Sydney hospital. We married just before I started my transition to midwifery year. He was my knight in shining armour, my soulmate, an orphan like me and a man who understood my need for family.'

She had to admit Finn looked less happy. 'He sounds a great guy.'

She breathed in slowly. To control the tickle of sadness in her throat. 'He was.' Gone now. They'd been so full of plans. 'We were saving up for our family that never came. Because Ed died. Killed by a fast brain tumour that robbed him of speech before we could say much, and his life before we could properly say goodbye.'

She saw the empathy for her sudden loss. Not as sudden as his. But worse.

Finn said, 'That must have been devastating.'

'It was. I sold our flat and came here. Watching the sea helped.' She'd been adrift, swamped by the withdrawal of a future again, the loss of her love and her husband. She'd sworn she would not risk broken dreams again. But then she'd stumbled into Lighthouse Bay and the warmth of her midwifery family had helped her begin the long, slow journey to heal.

'But it seems I'm resilient. Maybe all those foster families in the past made me tough. Because now I'm scuba diving and I've even had lunch and dinner with a man and his daughter. It took two years but I'm becoming braver.' She looked at him. 'But I'm still wary.'

'I understand that.' He grimaced. 'I'm a little wary myself.'

One more question then, Trina thought as Finn put the last of the pasta into his mouth. She waited for him to swallow. 'So how did you meet Clancy?'

CHAPTER SEVENTEEN

Finn

FINN GUESSED HE owed Catrina that. He remembered the day vividly. Puffy white clouds. Brilliant blue sky. Painted ponies and unicorns. 'At a fairground, of all places. She was riding the merry-go-round with a little girl my sister had taken there. A distant relative she'd asked my help to mind for the day. We were introduced by a five-year-old. Clancy knocked me sideways. Her hair—' he shook his head '—just like Piper's, a daffodil cloud around her head.'

He saw Catrina's wince and mentally smacked himself upside the head. *Idiot. Don't tell one woman another is beautiful.* He moved on quickly. 'I should never have married her. She wasn't that young but she was a child, not a wife.'

'Do you think Clancy knew what she was doing when she ran away? That she planned to stay hidden?'

'I hope so. That has kept me sane. She ran away for a couple of days twice during the pregnancy. I was frantic. Then she reappeared as if she'd never been away and I told myself to stop making a big deal of it. That nobody owns anybody. But to leave straight after the birth?' He shrugged. 'It was a quick labour, but physically it was still a labour. So why would she leave her recovery time and make life hard on herself?'

'What happened?' He heard the gentleness in her voice, the understanding, and, despite his reluctance to talk about a time he wanted to forget, Catrina was a midwife and understood women, plus—he'd kissed her. Planned on doing more. She needed to know.

'Clancy stayed very focused during the birth. Distant, when I look back on it. As if she'd already pulled back from me. Even when Piper was born Clancy pushed her to me and of course I was over the moon. I scooped her up whenever she wanted. Clancy said no to breastfeeding so I gave Piper her first bottle.'

He remembered those first precious moments with his daughter in his arms. 'I've wondered how long she'd known that she was leaving.' He shook his head. Felt Catrina's eyes on him and was glad she didn't interrupt. He just wanted it out. 'So I changed the first nappy, gave Piper her first bath. And when I came back in on the second day to take them home she'd already gone. She'd left Piper with the nurses.'

He saw Catrina's hand cover her mouth but now he was there—in the past—remembered the incomprehension and disbelief. The beginnings of anger and how he'd expected her to walk back in at any moment.

How could Clancy possibly leave her day-old baby? How could she leave him when they were just starting as a family? And the worst. Selfish really. The innuendo that he had been impossible to live with and for what dark reason had she left?

Finn found himself opening his mouth to let those words out too. Ones he'd never shared with anyone else. 'I could feel the sidelong glances from the midwives—domestic violence must have run through their minds. Why would a new mother leave her baby? Was I the sort of man who looked loving on the outside yet was evil on the inside? What had I done to her to make her do this?'

'I don't think so,' Catrina said softly. 'If that were the case,

I imagine the mother would take the baby and not leave a child at risk. The staff would have seen how you cared for Piper.' She reached out and laid her fingers on his arm. 'I see how you care for Piper.'

He appreciated that. He really did. But maybe he had done something Clancy couldn't live with. He'd rehashed their short marriage but couldn't see anything. If only he knew why she'd left. 'I don't want the guilt if something happened to her. But I'm well over waiting for her to turn up every morning. My biggest regret, and it still rips out my heart thinking about it—is how am I going to explain to Piper that her mother walked away from her? That's what makes me angry. I can survive but how does a young girl understand her mother doesn't care enough to at least ask how she is going?'

'Every child needs a mother. But Piper has you. I guess Clancy knew you would make Piper your world. You're a paediatrician so you must love kids. Could keep her safe.'

'Maybe. But to have no contact? Just disappear?'

'You don't know why?'

He shook his head.

'Then you may never know. And it's no wonder you wanted to hide and start again.'

Start again. The words repeated in his head. Yes. He wanted to start again with Catrina. Instead he said, 'Moving here helped with that. Living in our house was pure hell. She wanted the big house, but it wasn't as much fun as she thought it would be. She didn't want a baby, just wanted to enjoy life without worries. She didn't want to be a doctor's wife or a stay-at-home mum. She wanted to be seen with a man on her arm. And I was busy. I guess I did let her down.'

CHAPTER EIGHTEEN

Trina

TRINA LISTENED TO Finn and tried not to judge Piper's mother. Tried not to hear the reverence in his voice when he spoke of her hair. He was right. Of course people would ask why she had left. Would wonder if he'd been the monster to force her into such a desperate act. Would harbour suspicions that somehow he had harmed her. She wondered if Finn knew how lucky he was she'd left the hospital and not when she'd got home, when the innuendos could have been worse. At least he hadn't been the last person to see her.

She tried to comprehend a mental imbalance, or a strange delusion, or just plain selfishness that had made it possible for a woman to leave her day-old baby. To leave without warning, or explanation except for a brief note, but no assurance of her well-being and expect her husband not to suffer with doubts and worry and loss of the family dream all under a cloud of suspicion. It proved difficult to imagine. Poor Finn.

'You said you tried to find her. The police?'

'The police agreed the note was real, didn't find anything and then other cases took precedence. They didn't have the resources for runaway wives.'

'You said you hired a detective?'

Finn waved his hand. 'The detective finally tracked down her last known contact before I met her, an older man, an uncle, but he'd gone overseas recently. The trail stopped there.'

Trina couldn't imagine how hard that must have been. 'She never wrote? Or phoned you?'

'Her phone went straight to message bank and eventually even message bank disconnected. Her credit cards or bank accounts that I knew she had were never touched. She didn't drive so they couldn't trace her through her driver's licence.'

Poor Finn. 'How can someone just disappear?'

'I've asked myself that question many times.'

'Do you think she went with her uncle? Overseas?'

He grimaced. 'It's possible. Or he set her up somewhere. I never met him. Didn't know of his existence until the detective told me.'

'What about your wedding?'

'She wanted the register office. My mother was in her last month and very ill. Half a dozen people came on my side. None on hers.'

It all sounded very sterile and unromantic. Quite horrible really. Not in keeping with this man who adored his daughter and made cupcakes and sandcastles.

She wanted to ask if Finn still loved Clancy. Started to. 'Can I ask…'

Finn's phone rang and they both looked at it vaguely and then reality hit. He was on call.

Finn dug it from his shirt pocket and said, 'I did not plan that.' Then he stood up to listen. Trina tried not to strain her own ears.

Finn left a minute later. 'One of your buck's night boys has cut himself on oysters.' He kissed her cheek. 'Thanks for dinner. And for listening. My turn next time.'

He said *next time*. So she hadn't scared him away. And, despite that harrowing story of his wife's disappearance, he hadn't scared her away either. And he kissed her before he left. Trina hugged herself briefly and began to clear the dishes away. There were lots of reasons not to rush this.

Friday morning Finn met her on her walk and invited her down to his cottage backyard for a barbecue. Despite her need to pre-pare for the next week of work—washing, sorting, a little shop-ping—the day dragged until it was time to go over, and her stomach was knotted with excitement when she arrived. This was not being wary.

He looked so good when he opened the door.

He bowed her in. Then he kissed her. Twice. Piper was tod-dling across the room stark naked and put her arms up to Trina. *Wow.* She scooped her up and hugged her.

'Well, that's a hello anyone would be happy to get.' She met Finn's eyes over the top of Piper's head and her cheeks warmed at the smile Finn sent her. She hoped he didn't think she wanted him naked to greet her at the door. Her face grew warmer.

'Welcome,' Finn said softly. Then changed the subject away from the charged atmosphere of how fast this was all going. 'It's fresh-caught fish tonight. As soon as I bath Piper.'

'Let me.' Trina laughed as the little girl played peek-a-boo around her neck at her father. 'You go ahead. I'll bath her.'

Piper wriggled to be free and Trina put her down. The little girl toddled towards the bathroom. Finn laughed. 'She's get-ting smarter and faster.' Then he gestured with his hand. 'Her clothes are on my bed.'

So Trina bathed Piper in the little shower tub Finn had made. The enchantment of ceramic tiles with starfish, animals, moon and flowers around the walls of the shower cubicle, a mishmash of words that Piper tried to say when Trina pointed them out.

She loved that Finn had created the novelty for his daughter. Loved the way Piper watched her father with sometimes wise eyes. Loved them both. She sighed.

She was in trouble and she knew it. She'd fallen for him and he was still married. Fallen for the idea of joining their family as pseudo mother and she had no right.

Somewhere there was a woman who did have the right and until that dilemma was sorted she should be spending less time with him, not more—but she couldn't seem to say no. She didn't even want to ask if he still loved Clancy. She didn't want to know.

On Saturday morning she met Piper and Finn at the rock pools on her way back from her scuba lesson. 'What a surprise!'

Finn laughed when she teased him about being predictable and they bickered pleasantly about who was paying for lunch this week after a pleasant half an hour splashing.

After lunch Finn took Piper home for her sleep and Trina went home to make a cheesecake.

She'd been invited to Myra and Reg's for another barbecue; they'd arrived home from their cruise excited about the fun they'd had and eager to talk about the adventure.

Reg was impressed when Trina told him of Finn's assistance during Rhiannon's baby's birth and patted himself on the back for finding such a useful fellow. He rubbed his hands and winked at Myra and then Finn arrived and the story was repeated.

Finn came to stand beside Trina with Piper on his hip. Piper leaned towards Trina so naturally she put her hands out and took her from Finn.

'It's a great unit. I was glad to help,' Finn said as Piper's soft little hands reached up and touched Trina's hair on her cheek. Pulled it experimentally. Absently Trina lifted her fingers to free herself and caught Ellie's raised brows as she adjusted the child on her hip more comfortably. It was clear Piper felt at home with Trina and, judging by Ellie's expression, she was wondering why.

Finn went on, oblivious to the unspoken conversation between the two women. 'Catrina was as calm as a cucumber, as was Faith, of course.' She saw him glance around and was glad he'd mentioned Faith. Faith, Trina and Ellie had been the original three midwives and Faith wasn't there to hear. But it was nice to be mentioned. His gaze settled on Ellie. 'You have great midwives.'

Ellie's questioning gaze finally shifted off Trina, who gave a little sigh of relief. 'I know. Though it's the first time we've actually had to give fluids by a UVC in our unit.'

'Happens a couple of times a year where I worked,' Finn said and took a ginger ale from Ellie's husband. 'What about you, Sam? Seen many babies need IV fluids at birth?'

'Nope. And don't want to. That's one of the benefits of working at the base hospital. Paeds do all that stuff. Give me a nice straightforward obstetric emergency every time and leave babies for the paeds.'

Finn laughed. 'Each to their own. I'm the opposite. Though Catrina's been letting me sit in on births for the week as a refresher and we even had a water birth.' He smiled at her and she felt her cheeks heat. Ellie winked at her and she tried unsuccessfully not to blush.

Quickly she decided she might as well join the conversation and try to look normal. 'He's converted. It was Sara and you know how calm she is.'

Ellie nodded. 'I was there for her last baby. Gorgeous. I'm hoping to have a water birth,' she told Finn. Then glanced at Sam, who pretended to sigh.

'I'm just the father. But, as an obstetrician, I'd like to go to the base hospital and feel like I have every conceivable back-up plan in place—but I've been outvoted.' He didn't look too worried.

'When's your baby due?' Finn asked Sam and, seeing the expression on his face, Trina wondered if he was remembering the feeling of being a father and knowing too much—but not wanting to say it.

'Three weeks.' Sam grimaced. 'I'm more nervous than Ellie.'

His wife took his hand and kissed it. 'You're excited, dear, not nervous, and it could take five weeks if I go overdue.'

Sam looked at her, his face softened and he squeezed her hand back. 'I'm very excited.'

Trina decided he was manfully suppressing the *and nervous* addition to that sentence and she remembered that Sam's first wife had miscarried many times. Everyone had their past and their crosses to bear. She should be thankful that she had good friends, wonderful support around her, and now she had Finn. *Be thankful. And stop worrying.*

The night held lots of laughs, tall stories and excitement from Myra and Reg about their cruise. And a few hints that they'd go again soon if Finn was happy to take Reg's on-call roster.

Myra and Trina had shared a bottle of lovely champagne they'd brought back from Tasmania and Trina glowed with good food, good wine and the joy of having a male dinner partner who fancied her for the first time in two years and didn't mind letting others know.

Finn and Trina left the party at the same time. Trina ignored the arch looks. As they stopped at Trina's gate she pointed to her door. 'You're welcome to come in if you like and have coffee.'

'I'd like that but Piper is drooping and she'll go to sleep soon.'

Trina's previous reservations were muted by the delightful fizz of the pleasant evening and she didn't want the night to end. She could sleep in tomorrow. 'I do have a folding cot in the cupboard. Sometimes Faith's daughter sleeps over if her aunt has to go away. She could sleep in there until you go.'

Finn looked surprised. 'I didn't realise Faith had a daughter.'

'We all have life stories. Her daughter's a real doll. We should introduce her to Piper.'

He looked down at his dozing daughter. Pretended to panic. 'I don't think I'm ready to cope with play dates.'

Trina laughed. 'You're funny.' Then glanced at the door. 'Come in or go?'

'If you have a cot, I'll come in. Thank you.'

Trina led the way, pushed open the door and gestured to her bed in an airy fashion. 'You could change her there and I'll make up the cot.'

Finn nodded and carried his daughter across the room and undid the nappy bag while Trina happily poked around in the cupboard and pulled out the bag with the folding cot in it. She had it out in minutes, grinning a little when it proved difficult to stand upright and kept sagging in the middle.

'I think you're tipsy,' Finn said, laughing. 'Here.' He reached forward with one hand and clicked the last lever into place to make the folding cot stand straight.

'Who, me?' Trina laughed. 'Maybe slightly but this cot is tricky.' She smiled at him a little dreamily. 'It was a lovely night.'

Trina laid the two quilts she'd taken from the bag down on the cot mattress—one as a bottom quilt and one to put over Piper as Finn laid her down in the cot. He put her cuddle bunny beside her head and Piper took it, rolled over and put her thumb in her mouth. She closed her eyes, secure that she was safe, even though the bed was different.

Trina gazed at the little girl for a moment and then sighed softly as she turned away. 'I'll put the kettle on.'

'Wait.' Finn's voice was low, gentle. His hand on her arm stopped her. 'What was that sigh for?'

'Just because.'

'Because what?'

She sighed again. 'Because you're a great dad. Because you have a beautiful daughter who doesn't seem to give you a moment's bother.' She paused, then finished the thought. 'And I want that too.' Trina felt herself sobering fast when she realised that she'd actually said that out loud.

She pulled away. 'Must be tipsy. Sorry.'

'Don't be sorry. I wish Piper had a loving mummy like you would be. But that's for the future.' Then he turned her and drew her into his arms. 'It was a lovely night. You looked beautiful and happy and I'd really like to just sit and talk and maybe canoodle a bit. What do you think?'

'Define canoodle?'

He stroked her cheek. 'I really, really want to kiss you.'

And she melted. He drew her to the sofa and as he sat he pulled her towards his lap. She wasn't fighting him. In fact she did a bit of climbing on herself. They both laughed. 'So beautiful. So sweet,' he said and then his mouth touched hers and she lost herself in the joy of being cherished.

CHAPTER NINETEEN

Finn

FINN WOKE TO moonbeams spilling across the bed and despite
the silver threads of light a feeling of foreboding crept over
him. He didn't like it. Splashes of brightness fell on the gently
rounded form of a naked Catrina in his arms and he could hear
the little snuffles of Piper asleep in the cot they'd moved close
to his side of the bed.

They should have waited. His fault. They should have talked
about worst-case scenarios if Clancy came back. Should have
put in a plan to protect Catrina, but his resistance had been
tempted beyond sense once Catrina had climbed onto his lap.

He thought about waking her. Telling her that he would start
looking again so he could end his marriage. Protect Catrina
from gossip. Gossip that if he stayed would follow her from tomorrow morning when he was seen leaving her croft.

He whispered, 'It might not happen but there's a chance...'
But she was asleep. Sound asleep.

Finn slid his arm out gently from beneath Catrina and paused
to look down at her in the moonlight. How had he been so lucky
to have found this woman—how could he have been so careless to fall in love when he didn't have the right?

He should never have slept with her, should never have let her fall in love with him, with everything still unsettled, and he knew she did love him enough to be vulnerable to hurt, knew she trusted him now, knew he had to fix this if she was ever to forgive him for such carelessness.

He considered waking her then. He'd always intended warning her there was still a chance but the time had never been right to say it again. What they had nurtured between them had seemed so fragile, so new, had happened so fast, he'd feared to destroy it before it began.

Impossible. Fraught with danger. To lose what they'd just found was unthinkable. He needed to work out tonight how they could move forward with Clancy still out there. But for the moment he could prevent some of the gossip. He'd come back tomorrow.

He wrote a quick note on the back of one of his business cards, then gathered up his sleeping baby, felt her snuggle into his shoulder with complete trust. Like Catrina had. He winced. Slung the nappy bag over his other shoulder and let himself out.

The moon was up, full and bright like daylight, which was lucky as he had no hand free for a torch. Suitable really—he'd been baying at the moon like an idiot, following the siren's lure. Impulsive fool, risking Catrina's happiness.

In minutes he was home, had tucked his daughter into her cot and sat on his own empty bed to stare at his feet.

He should never have slept with Catrina with his wife still out there somewhere.

CHAPTER TWENTY

Trina

SUNLIGHT PEEPED AROUND the curtains in Trina's croft as she stretched her toes luxuriously and remembered Finn's arms. She could almost feel the warmth and strength around her that she'd missed so much and couldn't believe she'd found again. Found again but different. Fairy tales did come true.

It was as if she'd turned into someone other than the broken-hearted woman she'd been for the last two years; she even had a new name. She was Finn's Catrina. Not Ed's Trina. Or maybe both.

She squashed down the piercing guilt and sent love to her departed husband. Yes, she would always love him, but now, after these last few weeks, she knew she loved Finn too. Needed to love Finn. In a different way. But in a real way. Not the ethereal way she loved and always would love Ed. And then there was Piper. Sweet, motherless Piper. She loved Piper too. And, my goodness, she loved life!

How had she been so lucky? She stretched again and wondered what Finn was thinking this morning. She'd found his note.

Spare the gossips—we need to get this sorted.
Finn Xx

Her thoughts took a sensuous turn down the hill towards his house and she was tempted to sneak down there and snuggle into his bed. And him. But apparently, until they told people, they should be discreet. For her sake, he said. But he was the new doctor. For his sake as well. She got that. But what a whirlwind these last two weeks had been.

Maybe a six a.m. break and enter wasn't discreet.

She took her time. Showered in a leisurely fashion. Washed and dried her hair. Applied light make-up though—she stared into the glass with a small curve of her mouth—her well-kissed lips needed no colour this morning. The heat surged into her cheeks. Nor did her face need blusher either. She smiled at herself—a cat-that-ate-the-cream smile—and turned away from the blushing woman in the mirror.

She'd never been that uninhibited with Ed. Their lovemaking had been wonderful but there was something about Finn that drove her a little wild. Or a lot wild. Apparently, she did the same to him. She smiled again.

Her chin lifted. Life was too damned fickle not to take advantage of that fact and she wouldn't be ashamed, and she never, ever wanted to be cold in the night again.

She could grow used to being driven wild in bed. She drew the gaily coloured scarf that Finn had said he liked from the drawer and flung it around her neck. She looked like an excited schoolgirl.

She tried to think of an excuse to turn up that wasn't purely, *Let me into your bed.*

Maybe she could make a breakfast picnic and they could take it down to the beach and eat it on the breakwall? Piper would like that. She could just knock on his door like a neighbour and invite him to join her. Her stomach flipped at the thought of the light in his eyes. That special smile he seemed to find when she appeared.

She took off the scarf again and made bacon and egg sandwiches, the delicious scent swirling and teasing and making her belly rumble. She was hungry for everything this morning. Even the coffee smelt divine as she made up the Thermos, and extravagantly tucked in a small bottle of orange juice as well. She packed her checked rug and tucked her little picnic bag under her arm as she closed the door.

Then she stopped. Leaned back against the cool wood and sucked in a breath as if someone had thrown a bucket of cold water over her. Finn would be there for her.

For ever? The words trickled through her brain like rivulets of pain on her mind. Questioning. Prodding scarred memories. Undermining her belief in their future.

What if he couldn't? It hit her. What if he wasn't there? What if she fell more and more and more in love with Finn until it was too late? What if something happened to Finn and she'd given the last half of her heart, all that was left of her own self, to him and it got smashed and broken and buried in a coffin like the half she'd given to Ed? What if the worst happened and Finn died and left her for ever? She had said she'd never allow herself to feel that pain again. Piper would go to her aunt and Trina would be alone again. Smashed to smithereens like the broken shells pounded by the surf on the beach below.

She sucked in a burning breath and clutched the ball of pain in her chest. It was too easy to remember the ripping pain of loss. Too devastating to imagine her empty bed now tainted with Finn's imprint so it would always be there. *No!* Nobody could be that unlucky!

She reached out to lay her hand against the wood of the door. Seeking support. Felt the hard wood as a solid force and drew strength from it. Drew another deep breath as if she were one of her mothers and she needed to be coached through a tough contraction. *Okay then.* Breathed again. That wasn't going to happen.

She sagged against the door. Beat it. She'd beaten it. But the voice inside her mind wasn't finished yet.

So, you don't want to imagine that? The voice in her head tried another tack. What if the almost as bad happened and his wife came back and Finn chose her as Piper's mother over Trina? She'd never asked if he still loved Clancy. Had she?

Of course Piper's needs would outweigh hers, maybe even outweigh Finn's, to be fair to him. Either way, she would lose.

Of course Piper needed her mother. If Finn had Clancy he wouldn't need Trina either.

No! They were going to talk about that. Make plans. She straightened her spine. Thought back to the gentle way Finn had cradled her through the night. The whispered promises. The closeness. Finn was a worthy man and she trusted him. And she needed to trust in the future.

Catrina tweaked her scarf reassuringly, lifted her head and a little less jauntily set off down the hill. Felt the promise of the day fill the void. She stopped and closed her eyes and welcomed the sunshine in. Felt it flooding through her body, healing the fear that had gripped her moments before. Opened her eyes and began walking again. A panic attack. She'd had a panic attack. That was what it was. *Silly girl.* Everything would be fine. She clutched the picnic bag and lifted her face again. Smiled.

The sun seemed to be shining with extra brightness today— what was that? Overhead, gulls soared and swooped and she could feel the rocks scatter and pop with exuberance under her every step. The salty breeze brushed her hair across her cheek and it tickled, making her smile. Like Piper had tickled her cheek with her hair. It began to seep back into her. The joy she'd woken with, the excited thrum of blood in her veins. It had been so long since she'd felt this way—excited, alive and happy, yes, happy. Too long. She'd just been frightened for a moment but she was fine now. One night in Finn's arms and she was a goner. But what a night!

Life had certainly taken a turn for the good. New job, new man friend—she shied away from the word *lover* as she glanced down through the trees to where she could see Finn's front door.

There was an unfamiliar car in the driveway and she slowed her steps. Then she remembered Finn telling her about his sister's new car. A red convertible. That was who it would be. *Darn it*. She couldn't be neighbourly when he had a visitor.

Her footsteps slowed. The door opened and Trina stopped in the lee of a telegraph pole, not wanting to intrude on goodbyes. Three people stepped out. One was Finn with Piper on his hip, clinging like a limpet. Trina smiled fondly.

One was the woman Trina had seen at the restaurant that day that seemed so long ago but was only weeks—Finn's sister. She'd been right. She had a look of Finn.

And the other... Well, the other had a mist of fine flyaway hair the colour of sun-kissed corn, the exact hue of daffodils, just like Piper's. Finn and the woman stood together and only Finn's sister got into the car. Trina felt as if her heart stopped when Finn's sister was the only one who drove away.

Finn and the golden-haired woman turned and went back into the house. The door closed slowly, like the happiness draining from Trina's heart. An icy wind swirled around her shoulders as she stared at the closed door. *Who was that?* But she knew with a cold certainty who it was. Felt the knowledge excising the joy from her day like an assassin's knife. A killing blow. She turned around and climbed the hill like an old woman to her lonely croft.

Once inside she closed the door and locked it. Before she could shut the curtains and climb into bed the phone rang.

It wasn't Finn.

They needed her at work.

CHAPTER TWENTY-ONE

Finn

IN THE MORNING someone knocked on Finn's door. Surely only minutes after he'd fallen asleep just before daybreak. Groggily he sat up, pushed the covers away and automatically glanced at Piper.

Bright inquisitive eyes sparkled at him and she bounced up and down on the balls of her feet, holding onto the top of the cot rail. 'Mum, Mum, Mum,' Piper said gleefully.

'It better not be,' he muttered for the first time but he had to smile. It probably was Catrina. It was good she was here. Though he smiled to himself at her lack of discretion. To think he'd sneaked away to stop the gossips and she'd come at sparrow call anyway. Today he would throw himself on the mercy of the court and find out how to file for divorce. He wanted that new beginning.

Except when he opened the door it wasn't Catrina. It was his sister. Looking shell-shocked and pale. She opened her mouth and closed it again.

'Frances? What's wrong?' Finn reached out to draw her inside but she pulled back. Glanced at her car.

'She's here.'

'Who's here?' He looked at the car. Saw the cloud of floating golden hair and knew. Felt the world slam into him with the
weight of a sledgehammer, driving the breath from his body.
He leant his hand on the door frame to support himself for a
second and then straightened.

Licked his dry lips and managed to say, 'Where did you
find her?'

'She found me. Saw your house was for sale in the paper and
recognised it. The real estate agent rang me.'

Finn's mind had shut down. He couldn't think. Piper was clinging to him and the door was closing his wife and his daughter
inside his house.

One year late.

And—absolute worst—one day late.

Finn shut the front door and turned around to lean against
it, the weight of Piper on his hip grounding him like she had
done so many times before, and he stared unbelievingly at the
woman he'd given up on seeing again.

And, after last night, hadn't wanted to see again. Or not
like this.

She was talking. He could see her lips move, though she was
looking at the ground as she spoke, so that didn't help the com-
prehension. Her hair was that floating cloud of daffodil yellow
that he'd noticed when they'd first met. Beautiful, he thought
clinically, as if he had nothing to do with the scene about to unfold, but too fine; her hair was a golden mist around her head,
like Piper's.

She was still talking but his ears were ringing and seemed to
echo with the weight of his emotion. She wasn't dead. That was
a good thing. That was good for Piper. For the future. Maybe
they would have some connection in the future. Not so good for
him. He was married. And he'd just slept with another woman.
Her timing could not have been worse.

He cut across her long-winded explanations that he hadn't

heard a word of. 'Wait. Sit down. I can't understand you when you talk to the floor like that.'

She glanced around a little wildly, her hair a drift of golden cotton in the breeze of her movement, so fine and light it swayed with her like yellow seaweed under the ocean.

He sat down too. Piper stayed stuck to his hip with her head buried into his shoulder. He wished he could bury his head too. 'Why are you here?'

She spoke softly. Hesitantly. 'To talk to you. Talk to Piper.'

He could feel the scowl on his face. Tried to smooth it out. To listen with empathy as if she were a tiresome patient who refused to take necessary advice. But she wasn't. She was his wife who had abandoned them. Remember his oath to treat the ill to the best of his ability. He'd always known she wasn't one hundred per cent well. It didn't help a lot. 'You're a year late.'

'I'm sorry.'

Well, that didn't cut it, but he hadn't heard the reasons yet. He fought the panic that engulfed him. His brain had seized. His chest felt tight. And he had to keep from squeezing Piper too tightly against him. How could she be here? And—the most frightening of all—was he even glad?

He stood again. Turned his back on his wife and moved across to put Piper down in her playpen, but she clung to him. He kissed the top of her head and reached for the fruit sticks he kept in a jar in the fridge.

'Here you go, sweetheart. A bit cold but you don't mind, do you?' Then he put her in the playpen and she sat quietly with her big eyes watching him as she began to chew the fruity sticks.

He heard Clancy's soft voice. 'You're very good with her.'

He stamped down the anger. 'We are family. Plus...' he looked at her steadily '...someone had to be.'

She flushed. 'I made a mistake.'

Really? he thought. *Just one?* But didn't say it. *And it took a year for you to tell us that?* Instead he tried to make his voice neutral and said, 'I don't understand why you would drop out of nowhere like this. What are you hoping to get out of this?'

'Just to talk. At first.'

He winced at 'at first'.

She went on hesitantly. 'See what happens. If what happens is good then maybe—' she drew a long breath and squared her shoulders for a second '—I'm hoping that we could start again.'

Finn sucked in a breath, stunned she could even contemplate that, but then he was in shock. His thought processes were not good. He needed to be calm.

Her shoulders drooped again. 'I could learn to be a mother.' She looked up at him and her eyes were shiny with tears. 'Maybe even a wife.'

CHAPTER TWENTY-TWO

Trina

TRINA PUSHED OPEN the door to Maternity and from down the hallway she could hear quiet moans from the closed doors of the birthing units. Someone sounded very close to having a baby.

In the other birthing room it sounded as if someone else was also very close to having a baby. It happened sometimes. Not often, but when it did at change of shift a third midwife was needed. Technically she didn't start her Sunday call until after eight a.m. but the other midwife had plans for today and Trina was pathetically grateful to be doing something.

She tucked her bag into her locker and washed her hands. The fine tremor of distress was barely noticeable but still she glared at her quivering digits. *Stop it.* She liked and trusted Finn. She would just have to leave it there, parked, until she finished work.

But, deep inside, a crack of loss began to tear and rip and widen. Too soon for loss. She should have stayed safe from pain for a lot longer. Healed more solidly before ripping at the wound.

The woman down the hall moaned louder and Trina drew a deep breath and shut the world outside the doors far away. This was her world. Inside this unit. This was where she needed to concentrate.

The called-in midwife appeared beside her and spoke very quietly. 'I'm in room one with Bonnie. She won't be long. All going well and I have a nurse with me. Jill has Jemma. It's been a long hard labour and slow second stage. Will you take her?'

Catrina was one hundred per cent there. 'Absolutely.'

She turned and knocked gently and pushed open the door.

Jill, the midwife on night shift, looked up with wordless relief. 'Here's Trina, come in to help,' she said to the woman with a brightness that didn't quite ring true. 'You know Jemma and Pierce, don't you, Trina?'

'Yes, I do. Hello there, Jemma.' She nodded to the usually jolly Pierce as well, but his face had strained into taut lines. Some dynamic wasn't working or there was a problem. 'You both look to be doing an amazing job here.'

Then she looked back to Jill as she reached for the hand-held Doppler to check the baby's heart rate. 'I always like to say good morning to babies too, so is it okay if I have a listen to yours, please, Jemma?'

'Sure,' Jemma sighed as the last of the contraction ebbed away, and Trina put the dome-shaped Doppler on Jemma's large rounded stomach. Instantly the clop-clop of the foetal heart-rate filled the room. The contraction ended and no slowing of beats indicated the baby had become tired or stressed, and the rate sat jauntily around one-forty. There was even a small acceleration of rate as baby shifted under Trina's pressure, which told her that baby still had reserves of energy, despite what she guessed had been a long labour.

She stared at the large shiny belly and guessed the baby's size to be larger than average. Acknowledged that position for birth would be important to optimise pelvic size.

'He/she sounds great,' she said after a minute of staring at the clock. 'Magnificent belly there, Jemma.' The tension in the room eased another fraction.

'Can I check the position, please?' Jemma nodded and Trina ran her hands quickly over Jemma's abdomen. Confirmed the baby was in a good position and head too far down to palpate. That was good. 'So, catch me up on Jemma's progress, Jill?'

Jill glanced at the couple and smiled wearily. 'It's been a long night and they've been amazing. Jemma's due tomorrow; this is her first baby and her waters broke about four p.m. yesterday. The contractions started pretty much straight away and they came in here about five p.m.'

She glanced at the clock that now pointed to almost seven a.m. 'The contractions have been strong and regular since six p.m. so she's been working all night to get to this point. Her observations have stayed normal, and she's been in the shower and the bath, has tried the gas but didn't like it much. We've walked a fair way and at five she felt the urge to push. I checked and she'd reached that stage already.'

Two hours of pushing and head well down. *Good, not great,* Trina thought. 'Wow, that's a hard and long labour,' she said gently and Pierce nodded worriedly.

'So,' Jill went on, 'Jemma's been pushing for just under two hours now; she's tired and we almost have head on view but it hasn't been easy for the last few pushes. We've been in the bathroom for most of that time, but she wanted to lie down so she's just come back to the bed.'

Trina looked at the night midwife and nodded. In bed on her back was the last place any midwife wanted Jemma if she had a big baby on board. Jill wasn't happy with the progress which, on the surface, seemed timely and acceptable so there must be more.

Jemma moaned as the next wave of contraction began to build and Trina tuned to see why Jill would be worried as the team went to work to support Jemma in the expulsive stage.

Tantalisingly close, the baby's head seemed to be hovering but not advancing that last little bit to birth and Trina kept the smile on her face as she suspected Jill's concern.

Trina moved in with the Doppler again to listen to the baby after each contraction. 'How about you give the doctor a ring and he can be here at the birth? Then he can do his round early and leave early. He'll like that. I'll stay with Jemma and Pierce for this last little bit. You can write up your handover notes here in the room, and that way you'll be ready to go as soon as we have this determined little passenger in his mother's arms.'

Gratefully, Jill nodded and they changed places. When Jill had finished the phone call, she settled herself on the stool in the corner at the side desk and they all rested as they waited for the next contraction.

Trina looked into Jemma's tired face. 'After this next one, I'd like you to think about changing position.'

Jemma sighed and Trina smiled. 'I know.'

Jemma grumbled, 'I just want this over.'

Trina nodded and glanced at Pierce. 'I'm thinking Pierce wants to see this baby snuggled up between you both too. Your baby probably has his father's shoulders, so I'm suggesting turning around and kneeling on the bed or even down on the floor, because that position gives you an extra centimetre of room in your pelvis. That tiny amount can make all the difference at this stage when it feels hard to budge.' She smiled at them both. 'It's a good position for making even more room if we need it after baby's head is born.'

'Is there a problem?' Pierce had straightened and looked down at his wife.

'No. But sometimes when second stage slows this much it means there might be less room than expected. We have set body positions a mum can go into that create extra space in her pelvis. I'd rather have Jemma ready to do that, even if we don't need it, than try to awkwardly scramble into position if we have a more urgent need.'

Pierce nodded. 'What do you think, Jem?'

'I think I'd do anything to get this baby here.'

After the next long contraction a weary Jemma rolled over in the bed onto her knees and rested her head on her forearms on the high pillows that had been behind her. Trina settled the thin top sheet over her and gently rubbed the small of her back. Pierce offered her a sip of water from the straw at Trina's silent prompting.

In the new position baby made progress and the first of the head began to appear on view. There was a soft noise at the door and, instead of old Dr Southwell, it was his son, Sam, and Trina could have kissed him.

Reg was good, but there was nothing like an obstetrician when you needed one. 'This is Dr Southwell, Jemma. Pierce, this is Sam.'

The men shook hands quickly as Trina went on. 'We've some second stage progress since Jill spoke to you, after moving to all fours. There's better descent with the last contraction.'

She moved her hand and placed the ultrasound Doppler awkwardly upwards against Jemma's now hanging belly. It wasn't as clear as before in this position but they could hear the steady clopping from the baby on board.

Sam nodded at the sound. 'Baby sounds good. I'm here as extra hands if position changes are needed.' He went to the sink, washed and put gloves on.

Pierce looked at him. He glanced at his wife and seemed to change his mind about asking more. The next contraction rolled over Jemma and she groaned and strained and very slowly the baby's forehead, eyes and nose birthed. But that was all.

'Keep pushing through,' Trina said with a touch of urgency and Sam nodded. But no further descent of baby occurred. Trina found the foetal heart again with the Doppler and it was marginally slower but still okay.

'We'll try putting your head down. Move the pillows, Trina,' Sam said quietly. Jill appeared at their side and Sam said, 'Phone Finn. Tell him I want him up here to stand by.'

Trina looked up as Jill disappeared and her heart sank. Sam must think it was going to be more difficult than expected.

She removed the pillows and encouraged Jemma to put her head on the bed and stretch her knees up towards her chest with her bottom in the air. It would straighten out her sacrum and, hopefully, give them a tiny bit more room in her pelvis.

The head came down another centimetre and the face cleared the birth canal but then the chin seemed to squeeze back inside like a frightened turtle's head against his shell.

Trina listened to the heart rate again and this time they all heard the difference in rate. Much slower. The cord must be squeezed up between the body and the mother's pelvis. That would dramatically reduce the oxygen the baby was getting.

'It looks like your little one has jammed his anterior shoulder against your pubic bone, Jemma. Not letting his body come down, even though his head is out. I'm going to have to try to sweep baby's arm out so the shoulder collapses to make room.'

'Do it,' Jemma panted.

'Try not to push as I slide my hand in.' From where she stood, Trina saw Pierce fall back in his chair and put his hand over his face.

Jemma stared at the ceiling and breathed slowly, striving for the calm that was so important, and Trina felt her eyes prickle with admiration for the mother in crisis as she squeezed her shoulder and spoke reassuring words in Jemma's ear.

She watched Sam's eyes narrow as mentally he followed his hand past the baby's head and reached deeply to slide along the upper arm to the elbow. Trina saw the moment he found the baby's elbow and swept it slowly past the baby's chest and face; she saw the relief and determination and wished Ellie was here to see her amazing husband, saw the muscles on Sam's arm contract and watched the slow easing of the limp arm out of the jammed space and suddenly there was movement.

The arm was out, the head shifted. 'Push, Jemma,' Trina urged, and then the baby's flaccid body slid slowly into Sam's hands.

'I'll take him,' a voice said behind Sam and Trina looked up to see Finn there. The relief that swamped her was so great she didn't care that his wife had arrived. Didn't care her heart was broken. No space for that. She wanted this baby with the best paediatric care and she didn't doubt that was Finn.

Sam cut the cord quickly. Trina saw Jill's worried eyes and knew she'd be better at the resus than Jill without sleep.

'Swap, Jill.'

Jill looked up, relief clear on her face. She nodded and hurried over to change places with Trina beside the mother.

CHAPTER TWENTY-THREE

Finn

FINN HEARD CATRINA say, 'Swap, Jill...' as he carried the silent and limp baby to the resuscitation trolley that Jill had set up. The lights and heater were on and Finn rubbed the wet baby firmly. Catrina handed him the next warmed dry towel and he did it again.

She spun the dial on the air and handed the tiny mask to Finn, who started the intermittent positive pressure breaths while she placed the pulse oximeter lead on the lifeless white wrist.

After thirty seconds, the heart rate was still too slow. 'Cardiac massage.' Finn said briefly.

Catrina circled the baby's chest and Finn wondered if this had happened twice in a fortnight before for her. It was unusual. For a low-risk unit this was too much.

He watched as she began compressing the baby's chest by a third in depth. He intoned, 'One, two, three, breathe. One, two, three, breathe.' For another thirty seconds.

Catrina said, very calmly—too calmly, 'Still heart rate below sixty.'

He glanced at her face and saw the fear she held back. 'Thinking about adrenaline after the next thirty seconds,' Finn said quietly, and then Sam appeared.

'I'll take over the cardiac massage, Trina.' He'd be thinking that, as the midwife, she could find their equipment faster.

Trina nodded and Sam slipped in with barely a pause in the rhythm. She reached down and pulled open the drawer, removed the umbilical catheter set he recognised and pulled out the adrenaline. Once you needed adrenaline things didn't look so good.

Good idea about the umbi catheter. He prayed it wouldn't get to that. Finn hoped this baby would breathe before then. Then the big adrenaline ampoule appeared in his vision; the sound of her snapping off the glass top was reassuring. She was slick and he heard her muttering as she began to draw it up. 'The new guidelines say point five of a mil standard; is that what you want, Finn?'

'Yes, thanks. ARC Guidelines.'

He glanced at the clock. 'Next thirty seconds. Heart rate still fifty. Slightly better. Keep going.' He looked at Catrina and nodded at the box.

Thirty seconds later and Catrina had dashed out for the warmed fluid for the umbilical catheter box.

'Seventy.' He saw her sag with relief. He felt a bit that way himself. *Thank goodness.* No adrenaline needed. No umbi catheter needed. If the heart rate kept going up.

Sam stopped compression and Finn continued on with the breathing. The baby wasn't white any more. Streaks of pinkish blue were coming. The blue on the face stayed but that would be compression of the head causing congestion and that might take hours to go. The body was pink. *Excellent.*

He heard Trina breathe out as the baby's hands flexed, as did his little blue feet. Then the neonate struggled and gasped. And cried. Finn sighed and let the mask lift off his face for a second to see what he did. The baby roared.

He glanced at Trina, saw the tears she was trying to hold back. He didn't blame her. That had been a little too close.

'Good job,' Sam said quietly and Finn looked at him. All in all, it had been an emotional day.

'You too.'

Catrina had gone. Over to the mother to explain her baby was coming over soon. Reassure, like she always did. Being the midwife. To help Jill with settling the woman more comfortably when her baby came across. The baby that was crying vigorously now. Finn felt the muscles in his shoulders release.

Sam said, 'It was in good condition before the cord was occluded by the body. So he had some reserves.'

'They'll have to keep an eye on his blood sugars after that resus.'

'Does he need transfer?'

'See what the glucometer says. Not if his sugars stay good.'

They both knew it wasn't good if a baby had no reserves and got into that kind of bother. Shoulder dystocia was a mongrel. Not common, but fifty per cent of the time there were no risk factors when it happened. At least this baby had been strong enough to come back with a little help.

Sam had lived up to the glowing praise he'd heard. Catrina had been amazing again. They all were. He could grow to be a part of this team.

Then the real world crashed in. If his wife went away and left him to it. And he still hadn't told Catrina that Clancy had arrived.

He stepped back as Catrina lifted the baby to take across to the mum.

Sam was leaving; he'd go too, as soon as he'd spoken to the parents, explained what had happened, that baby had been fine by five-minute Apgar and he didn't expect any sequelae. Then he'd go, but he cast one glance at Catrina. She was busy. Too busy for his drama. It would have to wait. He just hoped he got to her before she found out.

CHAPTER TWENTY-FOUR

Trina

TRINA SAW FINN leave the room after he'd spoken to the parents. *Good.* She didn't have the head space. He'd come to help when he'd been needed. And gone as well. She'd needed him to go.

She didn't think Finn had known his sister would bring his wife. She wasn't that blindly jealous. She even still had faith that he'd come eventually to explain and thanked him mentally for not attempting that now in the midst of the birthing centre drama. But then again, he didn't know that she had seen his visitor. Guest. Whatever.

Her heart cracked a little more and she forced a smile onto her face. 'Let's get you into the shower, Jemma. Then into bed with your little man for a well-earned rest.'

Jemma had physically fared well. Apart from some grazes, she hadn't needed stitches, her bleeding had been normal not excessive, which could happen after a shoulder dystocia, and her baby had recovered to the stage where he'd fed very calmly, had excellent blood sugar readings and gone to sleep in his father's arms after an hour on his mother's skin.

Finn had explained everything very slowly and calmly and both Jemma and Pierce seemed to have come to an understanding of what had happened. And, without being told, what could have happened. They kept thanking everyone. It was after such a harrowing experience that things replayed in a mother's mind—and a father's. So it was very important the information was given and the chance to ask questions was given.

Trina reassured her again. 'It's one of those things that we practice for. Do drills and prepare for because when it happens we need to have a plan.' *We also had two very experienced doctors available*, Trina thought and thanked her lucky stars they hadn't had a tragedy. For a minute she thought how good it would be to talk to Finn about what had happened, then remembered she couldn't. Maybe never would be able to. Pain sliced through her and she hugged it to herself to stop the heartbreak showing on her face. He'd probably leave now and she'd never see him again.

Four hours later the second birthing mother had gone home with her baby and the morning midwife could take over the care of Jemma and baby. Trina could go home. Not that she wanted to but she wasn't needed here now.

She had time to think. Maybe that was for the best. But damned if she was going to regret the fact she had shown Finn she cared. A lot. And he'd cared about her. There was nothing sleazy in their making love last night. Not a lot of sense either. But mostly the fact they hadn't waited showed a whole lot of bad timing.

It would probably be better if she didn't see him again.

Except that when she got home he was leaning against her front door.

Her heart rate thumped into overdrive and suddenly she felt like crying. She forced the words past the thickness in her throat, looking at a spot beyond his left shoulder. 'I didn't expect to see you here.' Understatement of the year.

'I asked the morning midwife to ring me when you left,' he said. His voice came to her low and strained. 'Clancy turned up.'

'I know.' When she glanced at his face she saw his shock. And, if she wasn't mistaken, his distress that she had found out on her own. The thought brought some comfort. At least he cared about that.

'When did you find out?'

She sighed and shrugged. Pushed past him to open her door. 'I saw your sister drive away. Saw a woman with the same hair as Piper go back inside with you. It wasn't hard.' She felt him come in behind her and didn't know if she wanted that or not. Might as well get the whole embarrassing mistake out in the open. But in private. Her face heated a little and she hoped her hair hid it. She'd let it down when she left the ward, needing the screen of it blowing around her face. Even more now. 'I was bringing breakfast.'

His hand touched her shoulder, the barest skim of his fingers, as if he thought she might shy away from him. 'I'm sorry, Catrina. I wouldn't have had you find out like that.'

What was the optimal way to find out your lover's wife had moved back in? She turned to face him. Saw the sincerity in his face, the pain, and spared a moment to think about just how much his world had been turned upside down by the unexpected return of his wife into his house. If she was Superwoman she'd feel sorry for him. Couldn't quite achieve that yet. 'Where's Piper?'

His face twisted. 'With her mother. Who has no idea what to do with her. Thinks she's a doll to play with.'

And that hurt too. And there was the crux of the matter. Trina had grown up without her mother and, even if Clancy was ditzy, like Finn had given her the impression she was, she was still Piper's real mother. Trina would have given anything to have an imperfect mother over no mother. One who was her very own. There was no way she could go anywhere near taking Piper's mother away from her or Piper away from the woman who'd given birth to her.

She forced the words out. 'I'm glad for Piper. Every little girl needs her mother.'

He sighed. Pulled his fingers through his hair as if he wanted to yank it out. 'Surprisingly, so am I. And yes, a little girl does need her mother. But don't get me wrong. Or get Piper's mother wrong. This is why I need to be here now. Tell you now. Clancy doesn't want to be a full-time mother. She has that "deer in the headlights" look in her eyes. I can see that already and I can't even stay here long in case she runs.'

If he was worried about that, despite the fact she needed to hear this, he should go. 'Should you even be here?'

He sighed. 'I phoned my sister. When the hospital rang earlier. She turned around and came straight back. She's with them at the moment. But I had to come. I need to tell you three things.'

She almost laughed. Tried not to let the bitterness out. The loss that she was only just holding back like the little boy with his finger in the dyke. The whole dam was going to swamp her soon and she didn't think she could hold back the disaster from drowning her for much longer. Her voice cracked. 'Only three?'

He stepped closer. His voice softened. 'They're important. Because you are important to me. Just listen. That's all I ask.'

She nodded mutely. She could listen. Just don't ask her to talk. She was totally unable to articulate the words through her closed throat.

He lifted his chin. Stared into her eyes. And his voice rang very firm. 'One, I'm sorry that you've been hurt by this.'

Yes, she'd been hurt, but she knew it was partly her own fault for falling in love with a man she knew wasn't free. She'd known right from the beginning and still she'd sailed along blithely, ignoring the impending disaster that had come just like she deserved.

He put up a second finger. 'Two. The good part of Clancy being here is that I can ask her for a divorce. Start all the paperwork that was impossible while she was missing. That is a huge thing for us. For you and me. And arranging when and how and the logistics of Clancy's access to Piper so that she and Piper can find the bonds that work for them. To create a relationship that is wonderful for both of them too. Piper will have two mothers.' He smiled like a man with a huge load lifted off his shoulders. 'You and I and Piper can look to the future. But that's where it is. In the future. It will take time and I may have to leave for a while as I sort it all out.'

She nodded dumbly, her head spinning.

He stroked her cheek. 'When it's sorted I will come back and ask you to be my wife properly. Romantically. Like you deserve and like I want too. Like I need to because you deserve everything to be perfect.' He shrugged those wonderful shoulders ruefully. 'Perfection can take a little while, with me. I'm sorry you have to wait for that.'

Trina sagged a little, relief bringing the dam closer to cracking. But the words swirled in her head, glimmers of light beginning to penetrate the weight of the wall hanging over her. He still wanted a future with her. Wanted her to be a part of the big picture. Part of his and Piper's future. Was it too good to be true?

'Three.' He paused. Stepped closer to her and tipped her chin up with his finger ever so gently. Wiped the tears that she hadn't realised were running down her face. 'I love you, Catrina Thomas. Fell in love with you weeks ago. And it's real love. Not the infatuation I had for Clancy. This is I-will-die-for-you love.' He sucked in a deep breath as if preparing for battle. 'We will conquer all the obstacles, my love.' He pulled back to see her face. 'Will you accept my apology and wait, dearest beautiful Catrina, while I sort this mess I made? Please.'

Trina drew her breath in with a shudder, trying not to sob with the relief of it all. The incredible wonder of Finn declaring his love when she'd thought it all lost. The unbelievable reprieve from having to rebuild her shattered heart. She moistened dry lips with her tongue and whispered very, very softly, 'Yes, Finn. I'll wait.'

His strong arms closed around her and she buried her face in his beautiful chest and sobbed while Finn leaned into her hair and whispered over and over again that he loved her so much.

EPILOGUE

A FULL YEAR later in a little pink cottage on the foreshore of Lighthouse Bay, Finlay Foley woke with anticipation and wonder at the change in his life. His two-year-old daughter, Piper, bounced in her cot. She'd thrown out all her toys and demanded to be allowed up to start this most special day.

'Cat. Want Cat. Where's Cat?' She bounced and searched with her eyes. Finn had to smile as he picked her up and swung her through the air.

'Try Mum, Mum, Mum, Mum, baby. You can't call your new mummy by her first name. And your other mummy wants to be called Clancy.'

'Mum, Mum, Mum, Cat,' Piper chanted and turned her head this way and that as if Catrina would appear from behind a chair in the tiny house.

'She's not here. It's bad luck for Daddy to see his bride on the day of their wedding.'

Her little face crumpled. 'Want Cat. Now!'

'I know, baby. Daddy wants her too. I can't wait either. But the girls will be here soon to pick you up and take you to Cat. Then you can put on your pretty dress and watch your daddy become the happiest man in the world.' He hugged the small body to him, feeling her warmth, and wondered again how he had been so blessed to have Piper and Catrina in his world.

The village church at Lighthouse Bay stood with the open arms of two white-columned verandas overlooking the sea. The slender throat of the small bell tower and the skirts of soft and springy green grass that surrounded it had begun to fill with milling guests who had arrived before the groom.

The day shone clear and bright, freshly washed by an early morning shower as if the extra sparkle of purity was a gift from the sky to help celebrate their day.

Finn drank in the serenity, the warmth of those who smiled at him as he crossed the iridescent grass with his best man, Sam, and the rightness of Catrina's wish to sanctify their union in front of the townspeople and inside the church. He couldn't wait.

The journey of the last few months had taught him to look forward, and that something good—or, in this case, someone amazing—always came out of struggle. He'd learnt to accept that every day held promise, despite the ups and downs, and now his days with Catrina held an ocean of promise that he couldn't wait to venture into.

The minister moved determinedly to greet them as they reached the porch, his kind eyes and outstretched hand reassuring in appreciation of Finn's nerves.

But Finn's nervousness had left—had departed the day Catrina said yes. Eagerness was more the word he was thinking of.

Ten minutes later he was standing at the front of the wooden church in his morning suit, surrounded by smiling townspeople, with row upon row of well-wishers jammed into the little church. All fidgeting and excited and smiling with enthusiasm for the event about to begin. Finn was pretty certain that, despite their enthusiasm, no one was more impatient than he was.

Sam by his side fidgeted too. Probably waiting to see Ellie. He saw Myra, looking particularly stylish in old lace, with Sam and Ellie's one-year-old daughter, Emily, in her arms. He'd been there when Emily was born. Waited outside the birthing room door just in case, to allay Sam's worries, and his own, and been a part of the joy and celebration of their beautiful birth. He couldn't help thinking of that post-birth hour, how such a magic time was one he wanted to share with Catrina when their time came. And Sam would wait outside the door for them. He'd never seen or been a part of such a place that offered so much solid friendship as Lighthouse Bay. And it had all started with the woman who would walk through that door for him any moment now.

The music soared and finally there was movement at the entrance. His eyes strained to see her. Catrina?

Faith, one of the midwives and Catrina's bridesmaid, appeared with his darling Piper in her arms, framed in the doorway. Faith and Piper's deep frangipani pink dresses matched frangipanis in their hair, and Piper was wriggling to be put down. As soon as she was free she toddled swiftly towards him, drawing gasps of delight from the onlookers as she waved a pink sign on a thin stick that read, *Here comes Mummy, Daddy.*

With Faith sedately bringing up the rear, Piper ran full pelt into his legs and he picked her up and hugged her. His throat was tight, his heart thumped, and then Sam's wife Ellie appeared. He heard Sam's appreciative sigh beside him but Finn was waiting, waiting... And then she was there.

Catrina. His Catrina. Shining in the doorway. Resting her hand on Sam's dad's arm, her beautiful coffee-brown eyes looking straight at him with a world of promise and an ocean of love. Finn wanted her beside him now, but he also wanted everyone to see, admire her, as she stood there in her beautiful ivory gown—looking at him with such joy and wonder. Incredibly beautiful. Incredibly his.

Faith reached across and took Piper from him, and everyone turned to savour the sight of the star, Catrina, his beautiful bride, as she stepped firmly towards him with so much happiness in her face he could feel his eyes sting with the emotion of the moment. How had he been so fortunate to win this woman's love? He didn't know if he deserved her but he would hold her and nurture her and protect their love and his darling wife for the rest of his life.

Catrina walked on a cloud towards Finn.

Her husband-to-be. Tall, incredibly debonair and handsome in his formal suit, his ivory necktie crisp against his strong throat. Emotion swelled but she lifted her chin and savoured it. She loved Finn so much, had been blessed, finding him when she had never thought she could possibly feel this way again. The music swelled to draw her forward. She needed no coaxing, couldn't wait, couldn't smile enough, feel enough, be thankful enough as she walked towards the man gazing at her with so much love her feet barely touched the ground.

'Cat, Cat, Dad,' Piper said. Then she looked at her father. Frowned and then chortled. 'Mum, Mum, Mumcat. Mumcat!' she crowed, as if she'd found the perfect word.

The congregation laughed as her parents touched hands and held on.

Much later, in the cavernous surf club hall, the best party Lighthouse Bay had seen for a year had begun winding down. They'd turned the sand-encrusted, silvered-by-the-sun clubhouse into a flower-filled bower of fragrant frangipanis and greenery. Tables and chairs and a small dais for the bride and groom all glowed under ropes of hanging lanterns and people milled and laughed and slapped Finn on the back as he stood surrounded by friends. Waiting.

In a screened alcove at the back of the hall the midwives of Lighthouse Bay gathered to help the bride change from her beautiful ivory wedding gown into her travel clothes, a trousseau created by her friends. The laughter and smiles filled Catrina's heart to bursting as she looked around and soaked in the affection and happiness that radiated from her friends. Her family.

There was Ellie, with Emily on her hip, taking back the reins of the maternity ward full-time for only as long as Catrina and Finn were away. Then the two friends would share the duties, two mothers who had been blessed with a career they loved, and a workplace that could still leave plenty of time for family. It suited them both.

Ellie held out the gorgeous floral skirt found by Myra that had once belonged to a French princess. It felt like a caress against her skin as she drew it on.

Myra held the hand-embroidered cream blouse made by Faith's aunt especially for the occasion, and Faith clapped her hands as she began to slide it on.

She had two families now in her full life. In the main hall she had her new handsome and adoring husband, Finn, and her gorgeous Piper, soon to be her adopted daughter, and Finn's sister Frances and her husband, and, of course, Clancy—her unexpected almost sister.

Catrina had grown to care for flighty Clancy, saw that she had not a mean bone in her body, just a little foolishness and a wanderer's heart, underscored by an adventurer's gleam in her eye. Clancy would never be happy for too long in one place. But now, because of Piper and the growing relationship that made Catrina's orphan's heart swell with joy, Clancy could come and share family time with Piper, where she could have the best of both worlds without the responsibility that made her run. With Finn's new family she had people who loved her and people who waved goodbye and let her go.

Catrina noted that Faith, kind Faith, stood alone as she watched them all, watching her daughter chasing after a determined to escape Piper, a whimsical half-smile on her pretty face as she dreamed.

Catrina took a moment to suggest to Finn's mother's angels

that Faith should find her own second family and happiness, like she and Ellie had, in the very near future. *Please!*

But then Ellie straightened her collar and she returned to the moment. She was ready and Ellie spun her slowly to ensure she was perfect and the oohs and ahhs of her friends suggested the outfit lived up to expectations. She felt like a princess herself, the beautiful skirt restored to its former glory by Myra, as she floated out from behind the screens to where her husband waited, his eyes lit up.

Finn's eyes found hers, darkened with approval, and she felt a flutter in her stomach at his expression. A look that said she shone like his princess too.

They stepped towards each other and he took her hand and that frisson of awareness ran all the way to her shoulder with the promise of magic to come. Watching her, his beautiful mouth curved and he raised her hand to his lips and pressed his mouth against her palm.

'I've spent too much time away from you today,' he said quietly as the room swelled with excitement at their impending departure.

'Soon.' She leaned up and kissed him and breathed in the wonderful manly scent of him. She loved him and she couldn't wait until they were alone. 'I wonder how Frances and Clancy will manage with Piper tonight?'

He shrugged. 'One night. They'll be fine. She'll be in her own bed and Marni is on call for them and dropping in tomorrow before we come home, just to check. Then we all go on our honeymoon.'

'We could have taken her.'

'One night isn't too much to ask. I've been talking to Marni. She suggested we should go away every month for one night in the future.' He waggled his brows at her. 'I'm thinking that's a wonderful idea.'

Catrina would take as many nights in her husband's arms as he offered and she had no doubt he felt the same about her.

She placed her hand on the crook of his and he captured it there with his other hand.

'Let's go,' he said and, heads high, they walked out into their future.

* * * * *

The Midwife's Secret Child

Dear Reader,

I hope you enjoy the third installment of The Midwives of Lighthouse Bay. It's so wonderful for me to be back with our lovely midwives and the heroes who deserve them.

This is Faith's story, an inspiring single mom who fell in love once, long ago. When Faith discovered she was pregnant and Raimondo didn't answer her letters, she dedicated herself to being the best mom she could be for her baby. Her midwife friends in Lighthouse Bay surrounded her with love and emotional support, along with her amazing aunt, but almost six years later…

Dr. Raimondo Salvanelli fell in love once, in a far-off land, but flew home to Italy to marry for family duty at the deathbed of his grandfather. Almost six years later, he's divorced and buried in his work, and his friend has just attended a wedding in Lighthouse Bay. This friend mentioned the child of the unmarried woman he'd loved.

What if… Five years old? Surely not, or he would have returned!

This is the story of two people and a child whose happiness is the most important thing to both of them, and also a story about finding lost love. I hope you enjoy Faith and Raimondo's story as much in the reading as I did in the writing.

With warmest regards,

xx *Fi*

FionaMcArthurAuthor.com

To Dianne Latham, who won the name in the book competition, and the Lilli Pilli Ladies of the Macleay Valley, who raise money for those being treated for cancer, toward their comfort, and all the wonderful people who support LPL's fab fundraising days. You rock.

CHAPTER ONE

Friday

FAITH FETHERSTONE TAPPED her watch as she stood under the meeting point for the Binimirr Underground Complex. Outside in the car park gravel scattered with a late arrival and the vehicle's throaty rumble deepened then silenced as the newcomer pulled in and stopped. The butcher birds, previously revelling in the bush sunshine, ceased their song as a lone cloud passed over the sun and Faith shivered.

The caves kiosk, which held all the caving equipment as well as promoting the cave-themed mementos of the area, straddled the entrance to the labyrinth which stood tucked into the hill ten kilometres south of Lighthouse Bay.

Faith, today's cave guide, tugged down her 'Ultimate Caving Adventure' T-shirt, which clung too tightly, and thought that perhaps her decision to tumble-dry it on hot when she was running late this morning had been less than wise.

She shrugged. It might stretch later and everyone would be looking at the caves not at her. She tucked away the hair that had escaped her ponytail to surreptitiously study the varied group of adults assembled inside the tourist shop, ready for her tour.

Dianne behind the cash register held up one finger. So, one

still to arrive; hopefully that had been his car outside. So far her only concern seemed the quiet man in his twenties who chewed his nails and glanced towards the entrance to the caves with an intense frown. She'd watch for symptoms of claustrophobia down in the labyrinth.

The most striking group member at the moment had to be the thin, twinkling-eyed older gentleman in an iridescent orange buttoned shirt and matching shoes, an outfit that Faith thought just might glow in the dark once they turned out the lights.

Barney Burrows, proudly seventy years young, had caved in his youth, and chatted to the short, solid woman in her forties, while her two taller teenage sons conversed with a young backpacker couple.

The backpackers had smiling, animated faces and Eastern European accents but their excellent grasp of English reassured Faith they would understand her if she needed to give instructions fast.

Sudden movement at the door made Faith's head turn, her welcome extinguished like a billy of water dumped on a campfire.

A dark-haired, well-muscled man with his haughty Roman nose angled her way loomed in the doorway. A full-lipped sensuous mouth, a mouth she'd never quite been able to forget, unfortunately, held a definite hint of hardness she'd not noticed the last time.

But that had been a long time ago. Those halcyon days had ended after that cryptic phone call from his family back across the world and had removed him from her side.

This man had sworn he could never, ever come back to Lighthouse Bay. Yet here he was. Returned? The prickle on her skin as his glance captured hers was a heated reminder of a limited infatuation of a few intense days, but mammoth proportions. Lordy, she'd been naive, about twenty, and he a worldly twenty-eight.

Almost six years ago.

Raimondo Salvanelli, here?

The man who'd orchestrated her personal Shakespearean tragedy and the guilty party who'd exited stage left to return to Italy and instantly marry another woman.

She might regret her infatuation but never, ever the consequences of the ribbon of time that had changed her life.

She'd even fairly rapidly come to terms with Raimondo's inevitable absence, accepting they'd not been destined for happily ever after. Just an Italian doctor who didn't practise as a doctor and an Australian midwife, passing in the night.

Actually, several nights.

He'd said he wasn't coming back.

Um. So why was he here?

Worse, had he brought his Italian wife for the cave tour and she'd be right in behind him? No. She couldn't see that happening. Besides, her boss had only held up one finger.

The slight hysteria in the last thought resolved and Faith lifted her chin.

She looked again—and accepted that her daughter's father really had arrived and was going to be crawling around behind her in the dark for the next hour or so. Without any premonition on her part or warning on his. Excellent. Not.

To her disgust, she'd never found a man who could hold her attention quite so effortlessly. Apparently, that inevitable fascination was still the same.

An immense man, and harshly handsome, with that mouth she only remembered for its humorous and sexy slant. Now there was grimness—which, unfairly, didn't detract from the picture as much as it should—hence the reason to watch him with the wary fascination she'd have if he were a magnificently coloured red-bellied black snake on a bush path.

Apart from his dark, dark eyes and his way too sexy lips she could see her daughter in him, something she'd always wondered about and a fact that perusal of the newspaper photographs had hidden.

Chloe's dad was here. Holy freakin' cow. And why now?

What did this mean for Chloe? Or Faith?

What made Raimondo present today when he hadn't responded when she'd written of her pregnancy?

He had been equally silent to her brief note after Chloe's birth. No reply by mail or any form of correspondence. Not even to enquire if they were both well, which had shown a coldness she hadn't predicted.

Well, the silence had been unexpected but understood. Sort of. After that phone call from his brother that had ended everything, Raimondo had announced he'd been going home to marry another woman. Hence the never coming back. Or responding to mail either, apparently.

Yet she'd planned to send another note when Chloe started school next year. And perhaps another when her daughter began her senior years.

She'd fought against allowing his disregard to inflame her because she should still pave the way if Chloe wished to pursue meeting her father in the future.

This had never been about Faith—it was about Chloe.

All about Chloe.

But now he was here. Raimondo's dark eyes travelled slowly over her and, surprisingly, they narrowed, as did his mouth. Even as the eternal optimist, Faith could see something was wrong.

Well, whatever it was, she knew it wasn't her fault. She lifted her chin higher.

The possible implications of Raimondo revisiting her life opened like an unexpectedly dark flower in front of her and sent a flutter of maternal panic to quicken her breath.

He had rights.

She'd confirmed his claim in letters.

His name on the birth certificate, something she'd considered long and hard, saw to that as well.

She frowned and looked away in out-of-character confusion

until accidentally glimpsing Dianne, her caving mentor, her caring friend and also her silver-haired boss, at the counter gesturing to Raimondo and the clock. The tour owner's hands were making exuberant waving motions as she encouraged Faith to commence the tour.

Faith glanced guiltily at the time. Five past ten already. The group peered her way expectantly.

All who had paid, including the man at the door, had arrived and it was time to leave. Good grief. It felt like too much to switch brains to tour guide after the shockwave of Raimondo's arrival.

Compartments.

Faith could do compartments.

Faith would have to do emergency situation compartments. Navigating herself and other people through life challenges was her bread and butter in her real profession as a midwife and she'd just have to drag that skill across to caving tours with the man she'd thought she'd never see again.

She could do that.

Mentally she clanked shut doors and boxes in her brain like a theme park gate keeper—clang, bolt, lock until all darting terrors were mostly inside… But Raimondo still loomed across the room. The man who was never coming back. And with a scowl as if he'd been the one left holding the baby.

Faith moistened her suddenly dry lips and cleared her throat.

Later. It would have to be later. 'Good morning. My name is Faith.' She remembered the way his soft vowels had caressed her name and, darn it, she could feel the heat on her cheeks but she pushed on and smiled more determinedly. 'I hope you're all as excited as I am to enjoy the glories of Binimirr Cave this morning.'

Her gaze swept over the others, avoiding the tall, overwhelming presence of the Italian man who'd positioned himself to the back of the group. With a tinge of tour guide unease she hoped his shoulders would fit through one particular narrow opening she could think of in the labyrinth ahead, but reassured herself he'd managed last time. When she'd given him the private tour all those years ago.

Her gaze refocused on the other participants, realised belatedly that the backpackers were in shorts and shook her head. She should have seen that earlier. Every time she crawled through the labyrinth she came home with scratches on her knees and she always wore jeans.

She said gently to everyone, 'This isn't your normal ramble through the paths and steps of a tourist cave. This adventure tour you've signed up for is off the level track and through rough confines. Which means you have to crawl over rough gravel on your knees, squeezing your shoulders and balancing on uneven rocks.'

Faith smiled, admittedly a little blindly, as her brain batted at her like a bat outside a window trying to comprehend why Raimondo would come back when he'd explained very gently five years ago why he never could or would.

Stop it. Clang. Stay locked.

She rubbed her own elbows and knees. 'Unless you're okay with losing your skin I'm very happy to give you a few minutes to pull some jeans on or buy some knee and elbow guards.'

Most of the participants had arrived on the dusty bus parked outside the shop and the scantily clad young couple peeled off from the group and headed for the tour bus at a fast jog. They were very sweet to be so eager. The quiet, nervous man crossed to the inexpensive knee supports and selected a set to purchase.

From the corner of her eyes she could see Raimondo standing to the back like a dark predator, motionless, an ability she suddenly remembered and had admired then, as others shifted and chatted, and against her will she slowly turned her face his way. Their eyes locked, his cocoa irises merging with the pupils, eyes so dark and turbulent with unexpected questions. And hers too, seeking answers and maybe reassurance as well.

Until the flare of connecting heat that she remembered from

their first ever shared glance, all that time ago, hit her like a blast from a furnace. The flush of warmth low in her belly jumped into life and warned that despite her attempts at blocking out the past she 'knew' this man. In the biblical sense. Knew him too many passionate, mind-blowing times in that brief window of craziness.

A hot cascade of visceral memories flashed over her skin the way it had when he'd explored her with his hands. So long ago.

Heat scorched suddenly sensitive skin and molten memories surged with a thrust of explicit detail in her mind until she tore her eyes away, her breathing fast and her mouth dry. Like falling into a hot spring. Good grief.

How was she going to stay sane for the next ninety minutes, having him there, behind her, the whole way around the tour?

She glanced at Dianne but her boss was taking money at the till. Dianne couldn't help. Shouldn't help. It was Faith's problem. No. She'd do it. And when this cave trip was over she'd find out what this was all about because she'd done nothing wrong.

As usual, it only took a couple of brief wardrobe adjustments until the adventurers were ready—shame it had felt like hours—and she was glad Raimondo hadn't chosen this moment of waiting to approach. She told herself she was relieved. Very relieved.

Because she would do this on her terms.

Finally, the party reassembled and she directed everyone to the wall hung with helmets and headlamps, where she picked up a large and small helmet from the wall and two headlamps on elastic headbands. 'Grab a light and find a helmet your size—they're grouped small, medium and large—and I'll check your straps and talk about using your lights before we leave here.'

Then she lifted her head and walked steadily over to Raimondo. Practising the words in her head. *This is unexpected. How unexpected. What a surprise.*

'Raimondo.' She handed him the helmet.

'Faith.' Just his smooth utterance of her name with his delicious Italian accent made the gooseflesh lift on her arms—unfortunately her hands were too full to rub the irritation.

'This is unexpected.' That had sounded too breathless and she reined in her control. 'As you can see—' she gestured with the helmet at the group just out of earshot '—it's my responsibility to return all these people safely to the surface.' That came out much more firmly. 'I can't have distractions so we can talk later, if that's why you are here.'

She waited.

'Certainly.'

She nodded. Get away now. 'I hope you enjoy the tour.'

He inclined his dark head. 'I enjoyed it last time.' The 'with you' remained unsaid. She spun away from him and began to check every other person's chin strap except his—she couldn't quite come at that—until everyone was helmeted, including herself.

After the usual jokes and selfie photos, and some fast Snapchat posting by the teens, they left the tourist shop to cross the dry grass in an enthusiastic crocodile of intrepid cavers.

She chewed her lip, a habit she'd tried to break when she was nervous, though it certainly wasn't the cave Faith was worried about. It was Raimondo and her own lack of concentration caused by the tall brooding man at the rear of the line.

She needed to remain focused on the safety of sometimes unwittingly careless people, and of course the safety of the delicate structures and ecosystem of the caverns, and she prided herself on her safety record. Over two hundred successful tours. Which was why she wanted to stay attentive while doing her job.

One tour nearly every week for the last six years. Except for the months of her pregnancy. She glanced back and wished she could have asked Raimondo *not* to join the tour but it was too late for that now.

They gathered at the entrance to the cave. She plastered her game face on. 'You might enjoy knowing a little of the history as you crawl through so you can imagine the past. We'll stop here just for a minute so I can set the scene for you. And don't forget to ask any questions as we go.'

Raimondo smiled grimly and her gut clenched. She had to concentrate.

'Binimirr Caves. Binimirr is an Aboriginal word, in one particular Indigenous dialect, for long hole, and those clans knew of this cave for perhaps thousands of years.' She smiled blindly at the assembled group and launched into her spiel. 'As far as European settlers' history goes, a lone horseman first discovered this limestone ridge and then the caves in 1899. He thought them so spectacular that he told others and they came to see them, despite the lack of roads to Lighthouse Bay at the time. They became very popular.'

There were some nods.

'These intrepid people climbed down with ropes and candles and discovered a cathedral of stalactites and stalagmites and even though it was before roads came here they still felt they could market the caverns for tourism.' She pointed back towards the bus. 'That's what it's like now so you can imagine how rough it was more than a hundred years ago.'

One of the teenage boys murmured a 'Wow' and Faith smiled at him.

'Thirty years after the caves were discovered, these early day entrepreneurs built a stately manor with huge picture windows overlooking the sea, to use as accommodation and enticement for visitors. You can see the ornate gates and driveway to the left when you first enter the car park. Maybe that was why it was honeymooners of the early nineteen-hundreds who were attracted by the mysterious caves, though others still came to celebrate the majestic setting. Later, that lovely old building closed to the public and became a private residence. We have a few old photos of what it used to be like in the kiosk if you are interested.'

She had a sudden forlorn thought of how she would have

liked a honeymoon in that old mansion and, despite herself, her glance slid to Raimondo.

If it hadn't been for him making the standard so high she might have been married by now!

Faith shook her thoughts away and looked at the eager faces. Best only to look at them. 'Getting inside the cavern and caves is much easier today than it was then.' She gestured to the railed path. 'For them, after days of jolting rides they finally arrived and lowered each other down on ropes tied to the pepper trees, dressed in suits and hats, women in hoops and skirts.'

She waited for the oohs and ahhs to subside as the group imagined the potential wardrobe malfunctions. 'It took those plucky cavers ten hours of clambering, and no doubt countless torn flounces, to crawl through the caves that now take you an hour to circumnavigate when you use the stairs and boardwalks of twentieth century safety.'

She smiled again and it was getting easier to ignore the man at the back. This was her spiel, her forte, sharing this passion. 'In those days there were no pretty electric lights to backdrop the most magnificent of these natural wonders so far below the surface. Just lamps and candles.' She straightened her helmet. 'Okay. We'll enjoy the views you get today when we return to the gentle paths. But first we'll do some rough terrain ourselves and go deeper than the average tourist gets to see.

'Ready?' At their nods she moved forward to the entrance. 'I'll go first and point to where we're exiting the boardwalk. We slip under the rail to seek out the more remote and unusual areas of the cave. When we return you can take your time once you're back on the boardwalk and really savour the lighted areas of the larger caves.'

She looked around for the most nervous faces. 'Anyone who's feeling a little unsure—you should come up here next to me, with the most confident of you at the back.' The quiet man moved diffidently forward and Faith smiled at him. 'It's worth the effort,' she reassured him.

She noted Raimondo had stayed back and she felt the muscles in her shoulders relax a notch. Okay then. He wouldn't be breathing down her neck. Just watching her the whole time. Not great but better.

She went on. 'When you're traversing the cave please remember to use three points of contact to give you balance. Safety is the most important part of stepping off the boardwalk. As you know, we're heading for the dry riverbed which is more than forty metres below the surface and there's no lights down there.'

A few murmurs greeted that. 'If your heart does start to pound—' she slowed so everyone could hear '—if you can feel yourself becoming anxious, take a couple of deep breaths and remember...' They were all listening. She grinned. 'This is fun and there are more of these tours every week and we haven't lost one person yet.'

A ripple of relieved laughter eased the tension. 'Let's go.' Faith ducked her head and stepped down onto the sloping boardwalk. The air temperature cooled as she moved ahead, not too fast, because she could still remember the first time she'd entered the cavern and her open-mouthed awe of the ceilings and floors, but fast enough to encourage people not to stop until she made the point where they left the wooden planks.

A few minutes later she counted eight adults. 'Right then.' She crouched down, slid under the rail and put her weight on the uneven rocks off the main path, the stones like familiar friends under her feet. Then she slid sideways through a crevice, down an incline, and stopped to point out a particularly wobbly rock and let everyone catch up. 'Try to plant your weight on the big rocks—not into the holes.' She heard the crack of a helmet behind her as someone bumped their forehead. Bless the helmets.

'Now sit down on your bottom to slide off this small drop into the darkness below.' A stifled gasp from right behind her suggested someone had sat down too quickly and hit the wet spot on the cavern floor.

She raised her voice a little. 'It might be time to turn that headlamp on. Shine it on your feet, not into the eyes of the person in front, or into their faces behind you when you turn your head.'

This was all the fun stuff but she knew that most of the tourists behind her would be stamping down the claustrophobia of being in a small tunnel space underground with someone in front and someone following them.

It was lucky Raimondo was at the back because the others might forget how much space he took up. Not something Faith could forget, though for a different reason.

She paused at a fork in the path and waited for everyone to catch up, then pointed at a magnificent curtain of rock.

'That veil of rock is where hundreds of years of dripping water have formed a bacon-rind-shaped rim of curved ice that divides the ceiling.' She remembered enthusing about that to Raimondo all those years ago.

She shook the thought off. The beauty truly did make her astonished every time. Lifting her chin, she pulled her imaginary cloak of confidence tightly around her again. 'Ahead are more joined stalactites to reach towards stalagmites and if you look over here there's a magnificent column that stretches from floor to ceiling. What a gift of nature—that took thousands of years.'

The reverence was back in her own voice because, despite the man at the end of the line of tourists, every time she came down here she shook her head in wonder. Which was why she still marvelled that Dianne actually paid her to savour this subterranean cathedral she loved so much.

They'd come to one of the tricky spots. 'This opening's narrow—be careful not to scrape yourself here.' This was the point she had wondered if Raimondo would have difficulty with sliding through.

He seemed even bigger than when she'd met him before. Hard to imagine but true. More wedge-shaped. Toughened and toned. Muscled and honed. Hopefully not so broad that he'd jam in the crevice like a cork in a bottle—but she had a contingency plan for the others if he did. Not so much for him. She stifled an evil grin. Tsk, Faith, she admonished herself.

Still, there was another, less accessible exit for emergencies, and nobody had ever really been stuck.

Yet.

She waited.

Tried not to hold her breath.

Her heart rate picked up as she heard the subtle crunch of rock fragments in a long agonising squeeze, then he pushed through into the small cavern they were all standing in with a slight rush. Close fit.

Her breath puffed out.

He was fine. Bet that made the sweat stand out on his manly brow though. She smiled.

Then frowned at herself.

Another tsk. Not nice, Faith.

This was unlike her and a measure of how much that grim visage of his had affected her equilibrium.

Stop thinking about him.

'We'll edge down this rock face now. The path narrows so please don't touch that glistening rock there,' She shone her headlamp at the shimmering silver wall. 'It has beautiful fragile crystals so you can take photos and admire it, but it will become disfigured if you accidentally touch it.' She watched them and saw with satisfaction how they all leaned the other way to protect the wall.

'Thank you,' she murmured. 'Almost there.' There were a few Hail Marys behind her and she stifled a laugh. The shy quiet man had turned out to be a Catholic comedian. You had to love him.

Finally, after another ten minutes of winding and uneven descent, she stepped into an opening with a sloping floor. It spread out into a wide cavern and she heard the sighs of relief to be able to spread out a little. The distance narrowed between roof and floor and she resisted the urge to duck her head. Enough of that soon enough.

'If you shine your lights down towards your shoes you'll see you're standing on red sandy soil.'

All lights tilted downwards and there were some comments of, 'All the way down here. Wow.'

'So, we're here. You're standing on the bed of a river from thousands of years ago, stretching away in two directions.'

She let that statement sit in the silence as the others thought about that and shone their headlamps around. 'As you can see with your lights…' and that was all they could see with, as no other light could penetrate this far into the cave '…there's a line of white rocks marking off a section of the cave. Also, in front of us, a circle of the same stones to protect an area of new stalactite formation.'

She crouched down and even now she could feel the excitement as her heart rate sped up with the wonder of all this subterranean world so far below the surface. 'See this—' She pointed out the new holes burrowing into the dirt in the centre of the circle.

'Every drop is making the hole larger and eventually it will form a pencil of creation.'

She breathed out and those standing next to her murmured their own awe. This was why she loved these tours. When she felt the connection from others at the opportunity to see something so few people had.

'If you look across from us—' she angled her head and the light shone on the roof '—hanging from the low roof like eyelashes, those are thin tendrils of tree roots that are searching for the water that left eons ago, but the moisture remains and even though the roots don't touch any water the filaments absorb moisture from the air.'

Someone said, 'Amazing.' She smiled in their direction.

'There's no natural light—the creatures who live here are small, without eyes, their bodies are see-through, almost like albino slaters.' She crouched down and drew an example the size of a cat in the red dirt with her finger.

Her comedian said in the darkness, 'That looks too big for comfort,' and laughed nervously. Several other voices murmured.

Faith grinned. 'Not drawn to scale.' She pointed out a tiny white beetle-like creature on a tree root. 'But if you see one of them in front of you when you're crawling, please scoop up a handful of dirt and shift him aside.'

The young woman next to Faith who'd changed into jeans said in a small voice, 'You say we are crawling?'

'Yep, we're sliding under that overhang on our stomachs, using our elbows, for about thirty metres, but it opens into a small cavern after that.'

'Perhaps,' she said in her lilting accent, 'I can stay here and mind the bags?'

Faith looked at her and noted her pinched nostrils and darting eyes. 'Perfectly fine. We'll only be about ten minutes' crawl away, though you mightn't hear us because the riverbed bends a little. Then it opens into another cavern where we can sit up. We'll be gone for about thirty minutes by the time we spend ten minutes there as well as crawling there and back. Will you be fine with that?'

She laughed nervously. 'I find it very peaceful here.'

'I'll stay with her,' one of the teenage boys offered with pretended resignation. It was so obviously what he wanted to do that everyone laughed.

Faith nodded. 'The rest of us can drop all our extra stuff, like cameras and jumpers, here. Too hard to crawl on your belly dragging a drink bottle or camera.'

There was a small wave of tense laughter as people dropped surplus bits and crouched down. The black semi-circular opening above the red sandy floor looked about three feet high and maybe ten feet wide, based with the red sand of the ancient river. A little too much like a mouth that would eat them, Faith had thought the first time, and she guessed a few of the others now thought the same.

'I'll go belly down into the damp dirt first so you know I'm ahead, but I need a volunteer to go last. Someone needs to make sure we all keep going.'

'I will go last.' Raimondo spoke quietly, his thick accent rolling calmly around the tiny space. When the others expelled breaths of relief he said, 'I have been on this tour before and have no concerns.'

Faith knew this last stretch tested the first timers' resolve as they slithered forward in the dark, seeing the backside and feet of the person in front, the circle of light from the person behind washing over them, the roof closing in over their helmeted head. She'd had the occasional talk down of a panicked group member at this part but in the end they all agreed the challenge was worth it.

Faith knelt down until she was lying on the damp sand and glanced at Raimondo, looming above her. He nodded calmly and with a last flashing grin at the rest of the group she propelled herself forward along the riverbed, the circle of her headlamp piercing the darkness ahead with its warm glow.

She heard them behind her and the flicker of the others' lights occasionally shone past until she'd crawled all the way to the cavern.

She sat up and waited, watching the circles of light approach one by one as each crawled out of the hole and into the circle of the cavern.

'You can sit up now. There's a good foot over your head.'

'Gee, thanks,' the first arrival, the other of the solid woman's sons, muttered mock complainingly, and she grinned in his direction.

'Just shimmy around so the next person can sit up and move next to you until we have a circle.' It didn't take long for all of them to arrive and she wasn't sure how Raimondo ended up sitting next to her, but she doubted it was by accident.

Faith cleared her throat. She couldn't change the next bit and he probably knew it. 'We're going to turn out all our lights and just sit here, in the belly of Mother Earth, in the dark, and soak in the wonder of what we are experiencing.'

The same smart alec said, 'Why not?' But everyone laughed. Except Raimondo.

There was a murmur of further surprise and then slowly, as they all began to feel the magic of the space, she could feel the agreement.

She pushed on. 'And we'll sit in silence for a minute or two just to soak it in—where we are, how long this cavern has been here, and how amazing you all are to do this and still be having fun.'

A few murmurs of pride.

'After the silence I'll share an Aboriginal legend I was told about a good spirit from the ocean and a bad spirit from the cave, and how these caves were formed.'

Like good children, one by one they turned out the lights until the darkness fell like a blindfold over them.

Faith closed her eyes. She always found this moment, this silence, incredibly peaceful. The air she breathed felt moist on her nose and throat as she inhaled and she dug her fingers into the damp earth and collected two handfuls of the sleeping riverbed and held them with her eyes shut tight—not that it made any difference, open or shut, in the total dark.

She always felt blessed to have been given this moment in time to embrace the idea of being a part of this river under the earth. Breathing in and out quietly as the silence stretched for several minutes. Nobody fidgeted or spoke until she judged enough time had passed. Then she began to tell the story of the battle of the ancients.

CHAPTER TWO

RAIMONDO BRUNO SALVANELLI closed his eyes as Faith's lilting voice rose from the darkness beside him. He allowed her words to flow over and through him because he'd heard the cave story before, privately, and he wanted to find the peace she'd once told him she found here—for himself.

So, instead of listening to the story, he savoured the cadence of her voice and the reality that she had still been exactly where he'd left her so long ago. Again, he inhaled the oh, so subtle scent of her herbal shampoo and welcomed the warmth in the air from her body so close to his.

The sudden rush of possessiveness he'd felt when he'd first seen her from the tourist shop door had shocked him. An emotion he had no right to, a stranger very briefly in her life almost six years ago, a stranger still, and one who had told her he would never return after he had broken her heart.

That first time had been Sydney Airport where he'd caught her eye, she'd smiled, and he'd instantly invited her to join him when he'd seen her flight had been postponed along with his.

Then, hours later, because still he wasn't ready to lose his new companion, they'd shared dinner in an airport bar, jostled by other stranded passengers yet alone in their own world of discovery, and she had captivated him. He'd watched her mobile face as she'd described her beautiful Lighthouse Bay. Her work as a midwife, her hobby of cave tours and her love of life.

Their flights had been rescheduled again and they'd spent the night stranded, and then, imprudently, tangled together making love in an airport hotel, lost to the wild weather outside that had grounded their aircraft.

The crazy urgency had grown until he'd done something so out of character, so reckless and impulsive, even years later he was still surprised. He'd changed his flight to match her rebooked one, delayed his return to Italy for two days, followed her home to the house on the cliff for the one night and two days he hadn't scheduled and found himself lost in unsophisticated and trusting arms.

This was a world of tenderness he hadn't known since he'd been a child and his parents had been alive.

When she'd taken him the next morning for a personal cave tour before he'd left he'd been captivated again by her passion for the natural wonders she'd shared. Had silently begun to plan to return and see where this craziness between them might lead.

Then the return to sanity from the craziness that had come upon him with Faith. He could have vanished into it for ever if not for that call from his brother—his grandfather lay dying, the man who had raised them since he was seven. The news had been a deluge of cold water that had dashed his dreams and dragged him home to filial duty and deathbed requests. His brother had warned him what lay in store so he had said goodbye to Faith with finality.

Never to return because they were from different worlds. Because of the commitment he'd made to his dying grandfather— one he would never have broken until it had self-destructed—his fault, his ex-wife's fault and also partly this woman's fault because his heart had not been available. His new wife had seen that and hardened her own heart even more. Then his twin brother's tragedy and the need for Raimondo to shoulder the leader's role until Dominico could recover.

At the time, returning to Australia had seemed impossible. His brother had agreed that the woman he'd had so brief a liaison with would have married by now, then the years had slipped by so fast after his marriage had dissolved—his new direction into a general practice for the needy, and the occasional international aid work, placating his feelings of failure and he didn't have the time to fly across the world on a whim.

There had never seemed a future, with Faith settled here and him a son of Italy for ever. Had he been wrong?

He would never have come back except for the news he'd heard.

News he hadn't believed.

News he hadn't been able to risk not investigating.

It had been the mention of a place called Lighthouse Bay in Australia, in a discussion of a wedding one of his colleagues had attended before she'd returned to Florence.

Raimondo had been drawn like a moth to the flame of that conversation.

'So, you have seen Lighthouse Bay?' he'd asked, unable to stop himself.

'Yes, I have been to two weddings there, now. This wedding in the church and one on the beach. Both very beautiful.'

His colleague had appeared mildly curious that he too had seen the place. Again unable to help himself, he had asked about Faith and the answer had stunned him.

'Yes, I met many people. And yes!' There had been an amused glance. 'In fact, I remember Faith, the bridesmaid, and her little girl—so cute.'

He had not known she had a daughter. 'So, she's married then?'

'No, Mr Puritan. She has a daughter without a husband. The child looked about four or five.'

So he'd come.

And on his first sight of Faith, the woman he'd never forgotten but whose charisma had endured as if she were a distant enchanted dream, he'd felt the swell of an emotion he shouldn't have. Here he was, sitting on the sandy bed of an ancient river, forty-five metres below the earth's surface, listening to her so-charming voice as it caressed his ears and wishing he had never left.

That voice was still as restful and as calming. She was as beautiful as he remembered, with her slim but curved body poured into that ridiculous T-shirt and so tight jeans. It proved difficult to resist the urge to slide his fingers through the damp earth and find her hand to take in his, as he had when she'd brought him on a private tour of this place.

His empty hand could even remember the warmth and softness of her small fingers interlaced with his from all that time ago. How could that be? He didn't know. What he did know was that he had not planned well.

A week would not be long enough.

He knew that now from his first sight of her, the way his whole being had come alive from what felt like a deep sleep. And that was without the added possibility that they shared a child.

Faith. He'd lost her and her conviction in the goodness of others and perhaps he would find both again in this place of dark caves and far oceans. He'd forgotten so much about her and he wanted to learn it all over again.

Which would require some negotiation with the life he'd left behind. And his need to encourage his twin brother away from his obsessive focus on the business after losing his family. Raimondo's busy life suddenly seemed far less important than it should, compared to what was happening at Lighthouse Bay.

But that was for later.

He realised the story had finished, the cave silent for those few seconds after a well-told tale, and then soft questions broke out.

Faith answered them quietly then concluded, 'Okay then. Lights on. Those nearest the entrance can start to crawl back and congregate in the next cavern. I'm sure those waiting will be glad to see us. When we make our way back to the main paths and under the rail again, I'll do one more head count then you're free to wander. Just drop your helmets and headlamps back at the shop when you're finished.'

'What if we get lost?' The comedian.

'You'll be on the main path. And they'll switch the spotlights on and off in the cave when it's shutting, so you'll know when we are about to close. In about four hours.' There was a smile in her voice, one he remembered too clearly, and the group laughed.

'I'm used to the dark now,' someone said and the person next to them snorted.

He waited. He knew she would be the last to leave this cavern deep in the earth in case someone became lost or panicked. So he waited with her. As he should have waited before.

Six years! She'd been so young, beautiful, excited and as attracted to him as he'd been to her—the two of them like two silly moths mesmerised by the moment—grounded in an airport cocoon of wild weather and overwhelming fascination increased by the improbability of any future. Once he'd finished his business in Sydney he'd be flying home to Italy, her back to her seaside town and her beloved midwifery. She'd been barely twenty and he eight years senior and should have known better.

But they'd talked until their mouths were dry. Been amazed by the rapport that had sprung between them as if reunited friends from childhood. How could that be? From opposite sides of the world?

From a past life, Faith had said, and he'd hugged her to him for the endearing ridiculousness of that statement.

Though, once she'd laid her head against his chest, it was then that everything had spun out of control. For two full days until his brother had grounded him with familial duty, then he knew their love castles were built on dreams he couldn't follow. Could never follow. A truth he'd left her with. But was that all he'd left her with?

CHAPTER THREE

FAITH WATCHED THE headlamp lights disappear one by one. Damn, she'd missed her chance to send him first.

She tried telepathy.

Go!

She urged the man beside her to move off with the others but he obviously wasn't picking up the vibe. She couldn't go until he had, it was her way, and she broke the silence between them as the last lamp disappeared under the curtain of rock.

'I need you to go now, please.'

He didn't say anything, just moved forward and crawled away from her.

Faith took a moment to breathe deeply and centre herself, and here in the arms of the earth on the soft sand of millennia was a good place to do it.

Okay. She'd get them all back to the safety of the walking path and then they could talk. She didn't have to pick up Chloe until two p.m., just before work, when preschool finished. So she had a couple of hours to discover why Raimondo had returned to rattle her composure and her world.

She wondered what her aunt would say when she told her Chloe's father had arrived, far too many years too late.

* * *

Twenty minutes later she left the group at the boardwalk and her job was done.

Except one of the participants didn't stay behind and she could feel the heat from Raimondo's body as he walked beside her to the exit of the cave. His arm swung beside her arm and she tucked her fingers in close to her body so she didn't accidentally knock his hand.

Out in the bright sunshine Faith stopped on the path and the man beside her stopped too. She lifted her head and met his gaze steadily. 'So why are you here?' She'd done nothing wrong.

His eyes were that deep espresso brown of unfiltered coffee, dark and difficult to see to the bottom of the cup or, more to the point, to the bottom of his heart.

'I have come because I heard you had a child.' His cadence was old-fashioned, she remembered that, formally stiff, but it was a way of speaking she'd found incredibly sexy when she'd been young and silly, in its translated whimsy of sentence structure.

Then his words settled over her like the damp leaves had settled over the forest floor. Thick and stealing the light. He had heard?

She blinked. Pushed back his heaviness. 'I wrote you that. At the beginning and at the end of my pregnancy. Five years ago.'

'No. I did not see this.' He shook his head emphatically, but his face stilled and suddenly expression fled to leave an inscrutable mask of blank shock. 'Madonna.' A quiet explosive hiss.

'Chloe, not Madonna,' she offered with just a little tartness in her voice. She frowned at him. Trying to understand. 'I wrote twice.'

Again he said, 'No.'

He shook his head but he must have seen the truth in her eyes because his face softened slightly as he looked at her. The silence stretched between them until he said softly, 'Then it is as I suspected? You had a child that is mine?'

Unfortunate words if he wanted her to continue this conversation. 'No.' She watched him blink. Good.

He'd relinquished that role by his disinterest. 'You fathered a child who is mine.' She amazed herself with the steadiness and calmness of the answer while her heart bounced in agitation in her chest. 'Her name is Chloe and she is almost five. Chloe Fetherstone.' She needed time to think and her feet moved her forward. He reached out and caught her hand, not tight but with an implacable hold she couldn't shake off without an undignified tug.

She stopped and glanced pointedly at his big fingers on her wrist. 'Let go. I need a minute.' She wasn't the timid junior midwife who'd fallen for him years ago. She was a single mother, a senior midwife, a responsible niece to a woman she admired and who had been the rock this man should have been.

She held his gaze with her eyebrows raised.

His fingers released her.

Faith began to walk again and he fell into step beside her.

He hadn't known?

Had she addressed the envelope correctly?

She'd addressed it so many times until at last she hadn't torn up the letter. He'd told her his home town and she had based her identity search assuming he hadn't lied about that or his true name.

'Where did you send these letters?' His mind must be running along the same lines as hers.

'I looked you up. In the town you'd mentioned. Sent it to your house.' She recited the address. Funny how she could still remember it. She glanced at him. 'Two letters eight months apart. Don't get the wrong idea. I knew where I stood. I wasn't asking for anything. Just giving you information I felt you should have.'

His face had gone back to inscrutable. 'Did you not think it strange when no answer returned?'

'Of course. Though "strange" was not the word I would have

chosen. Thoughtless. Uncaring. Bitterly disappointing.' She shrugged.

It was a long time ago now and she was over it. Over him. 'You said you would never return. I expected little. I did my part and it was not my fault if you defaulted on yours.'

'I did not...' His voice had grown harsher, risen just a little. 'Default.' Then the last word more quietly. He looked at her. 'My apologies. This is...difficult.'

She laughed with little amusement. So was meeting a transient lover from years ago when she'd been young and silly enough to fall pregnant. 'Take your time.'

Faith looked ahead to the tourist shop they'd almost reached. 'Give me your helmet and headlamp. I'll get my things and we can go for a coffee somewhere.'

She surprised herself with the stability in her voice when inside she was panicking and fretting. She wished her heart would settle into a cold calm. What did this mean for the world she had created for Chloe and herself? She hated not being in control—even if it didn't show.

No. He would not cast her into turmoil again. She had this. She had to have it. She was comfortable in her shoes as the one who had done the right thing and as a single mother who loved her child more than life itself. He was the one who had had the shock and would have to change the way he thought.

By the time she returned from the shop the tracks he'd made with his pacing showed dirt underneath the mounds of blue metal road gravel. Worn away with his exasperation. She almost smiled at that but if he hadn't known about Chloe at all then she could feel sympathy for his shock. She could still remember that cold horror from the unforgettable day her pregnancy test had shown a positive reading.

Yes, she had sympathy, but no, she wasn't relaxing. She didn't have the luxury of softness or at least she didn't have the headspace for it just yet. Would Isabel think her mad or prudent to let him into their lives? Then again, her aunt was a sensible woman with few prejudices.

'Which is your car?' Hers was way across the car park under a tree and they'd have to drive to Lighthouse Bay for coffee. She didn't want him following her straight to Chloe. They'd go somewhere first. Talk. She wasn't taking him home. Yet.

He indicated the black Mustang Shelby not far from her vehicle, well splattered with dirt and mud from the road into the caves, and even from a distance it seemed to glower at the assortment of vehicles in the cleared space. Like Raimondo had glowered when he'd first arrived. She wasn't taking attitude from either of them, gave the car a disdainful look then caught herself.

Silly, she chided. It was just a rental car and she was getting fanciful, but the model was unusual for these parts. Still, to him she raised her brows. Why was she not surprised he'd hire the most expensive and flamboyant one possible?

Years ago, when she'd searched on the web for him, she'd seen the terrifying extent of his family's influence and power, their pharmaceutical company, backed by a photo of Raimondo and his brother and an elderly, strong-jawed, massive-shouldered man who had to be his late grandfather—long Roman noses making it clear they were all related—and was almost glad she didn't have to meet that old man, that family, and parade her naïveté.

Though she'd decided when Chloe was older she could make the decision for herself as to whether she would contact her father or not and Faith would support her daughter's decision.

Well, that was moot now. He was here to talk about Chloe. 'That car looks like you.'

'How so?' His brow quirked.

'Expensive. Black. Muscly.' She had to smile. 'Low to the ground doesn't fit though.'

He was looking at her as if he couldn't quite work her out. She guessed she had changed from the agreeable, star-struck twit she'd been when she'd met him all those years ago into a seemingly confident woman. No. Not seemingly. She was confident. She wondered if he was having a problem understanding why she had hadn't fallen into hysterics when he'd appeared.

Time to show that maturity she had spent years acquiring. 'We can have coffee at the little café down on the beach at Lighthouse Bay.'

If he'd found her here he could find the town beach. 'I'll meet you there.'

'I will follow you.' He touched her hand and she looked back at him. 'When will I meet our daughter?'

She let the 'our' go. At least he'd shifted from 'my'. 'Soon. After we talk I'll let you know.'

The hard stare that followed her response made her pulse jump a little. She hadn't seen this side of him and she realised they'd both grown up. She reminded herself how he might be feeling and tempered her response. 'It will happen.' *As long as you're good*, but she didn't say that out loud. Might not be polite.

'Faith!' Dianne's voice called out and Faith spun to answer the urgency she could hear in her boss's call.

She jogged back to the shop and could hear Raimondo behind her, which was a good thing when she saw the lovely older gentleman from the cave tour, his iridescent shoes shining up at them as he lay face up on the floor of the shop with his wrinkled face quickly turning blue. Dianne knelt beside the man, shaking him. She had the box with the bag and resuscitation mask beside her but hadn't had a chance to open it. She was fumbling with the catch.

Her eyes were huge. 'He staggered in and then just sagged to the floor. I rolled him over but he's gone blue.'

'Dianne, you ring the ambulance then come back. We'll start here.' Faith knelt down to tilt the man's head and check his airway. She placed her cheek near his nose and mouth but couldn't feel any movement. 'He's not breathing.'

Raimondo nodded and shifted forward to lean over the man

and begin efficient cardiac massage. Thank goodness she and Dianne weren't alone to manage until the ambulance came. As quickly as she could, Faith assembled the bag and mask Dianne had left and positioned them over the elderly man's face. She squeezed a breath into his lungs after every thirty compressions that Raimondo made.

After four cycles and no visible improvement they swapped places as Dianne came back. She was puffing from the run. 'Ambulance is on the way.'

'Do you have a defibrillator? An AED?' Raimondo's question made Faith's head lift. She felt like slapping her forehead. Why hadn't she thought to ask for that before Dianne went to the phone? She knew they had one. For every minute the patient didn't respond their survival rate dropped by ten per cent. The sooner the defibrillator was attached the better.

Dianne stared at Raimondo for a second as her brain caught up. 'Yes. On the wall.' She spun around and disappeared then reappeared almost instantly, holding the yellow box with the small Automated Emergency Defibrillator.

'Well done.' Raimondo shot her a smile. 'Can you take over the bagging from me after the next two breaths and I'll take over the cardiac massage from Faith? Count to thirty compressions and then two breaths. Faith can position the defibrillator while we continue on.'

Faith looked at him. Nice. It was exhausting work even though she'd made sure she had her shoulders straight over her locked hands. She was slowing already and Raimondo could make a much more efficient compression of the chest walls than she could when tiring.

She heard the two breaths go in, Raimondo put down the bag and mask and slid in beside her to take over with very little interruption to the rhythm.

Very slick, she thought gratefully as she moved quickly to the man's shirt and pulled it open. Luckily his chest had scarce hair so the connection would be good without the shaving they didn't have time to do. Peeling off the backing paper, she slapped the adhesive pads onto his chest wall above the right nipple and the left pad below the heart.

Switching on the machine, the automated voice intoned 'Stop CPR, do not touch patient, analysing.'

'Clear the patient.' Raimondo's firm voice reminded them not to touch the man in case a rescuer's pulse was counted accidentally by the sensors. Everyone sat back. Raimondo's eyes met Faith's. This was the man's best chance but they also knew that a shock would only be useful if the rhythm was one that could be corrected by an electric surge.

'VT or VF,' Faith hoped out loud as she crossed her fingers.

Raimondo said to Dianne, 'If it says shock, stay back and don't touch him. After the shock we will begin CPR again for two minutes. Then the machine will reassess so we will stop again. If it says "no shock required" we will recommence cardiac massage.'

'I never thought I'd see this thing used,' Dianne said shakily.

'Shock advised.' Said the machine.

'Stand clear,' Raimondo said again and it felt surreal to Faith that a man she hadn't seen for so long sat beside her. Not only that, he'd joined her in a resuscitation in a tourist shop near Lighthouse Bay. Not how she'd seen today pan out, but at this moment she couldn't be happier he was here.

The machine began the warning noises until the patient's body jerked with the surge of electricity and, with an odd gurgling noise, the man's chest heaved as he dragged in a shuddering breath. His eyelids flickered but didn't open.

Faith looked at Raimondo. 'Thank God,' she said at the same time as Dianne murmured the same.

Raimondo's lips twitched. *'Sì.'* He lifted his head and listened. 'The ambulance is nearly here as well.' They all listened to the faint wail in the distance.

Faith narrowed her eyes as she thought about the road in. 'It's a few minutes away. Will we roll him onto his side?'

'Yes.' They did so, the man mumbling something, causing Faith to bend down near his ear.

'It's okay. You've been unwell but you're looking better now. The ambulance is coming and they'll take you to hospital.'

He struggled to open his eyes and when he saw her he sagged back and relaxed, though his hand crept up to his chest. Whether from cardiac pain or bruising to his ribs from Raimondo, she couldn't tell. 'Faith. You. Thank you.'

'We all helped. Lie quietly. The ambulance will bring oxygen and pain relief.'

'Okay,' on an outward sigh as he closed his eyes. She had no doubt he would have some significant pain.

Five minutes later the ambulance arrived and everything moved quickly after that.

Faith left Raimondo to assist and explain to the paramedics and took Dianne into the shop for a cup of tea as the older lady looked shaky after the excitement.

Faith was feeling a little shaky herself. Cardiac arrest was not something she'd seen in the maternity ward, thank goodness, though, because it was possible, they all did their yearly competencies in resuscitation. It was reassuring she'd remembered what to do.

'So lucky we had the doctor here.' Dianne was still coming down from the good outcome.

'Yes. Very lucky.' She'd known Raimondo had finished medicine, but had thought he worked at the drug company, but he'd been as slick as an ED doctor. She guessed she'd find out. Six years was time for many things to change.

'And that you know him,' Dianne enthused. 'He was so calm. And you were too, dear. I'm very glad you were both here.' That last was said a little tearfully and Faith gave Dianne's hand a squeeze.

'You were brilliant too, Dianne. Barney is very lucky. Getting the equipment. Ringing the ambulance and then taking over perfectly while I put the chest stickers on. You were a marvel.'

'We were a good team.' Dianne nodded and lifted her chin.

Raimondo had made the difference out of all of them though, Chloe thought. Cardiac massage was hard work and without his arms beside her she would have been scrambling to get it all done and keep the perfusion up for Barney to give him that second chance.

Raimondo's big hands and strong arms. His presence. So many facets that had captured her so long ago, and she could appreciate them now. But she wouldn't be swayed into softening. She couldn't.

They heard the ambulance leave and Raimondo appeared at the door. Faith kissed Dianne's cheek. 'You did really well. I'll go now if you're okay.'

'I'm fine.' Dianne took a deep breath and plastered a smile on her face. 'A day with a difference, that's for sure.'

Faith glanced at the man at the door. 'Absolutely.'

'You were excellent,' Raimondo said to Dianne. 'As was Faith.' He gestured to the AED, which was in Faith's hand.

'I'll replace the sticky pads from the hospital stores and bring it back.'

He nodded. 'All things we needed done were done.' He inclined his head. 'Thank you.' Smiled his killer smile at Dianne, who blinked and smiled back, half-besotted.

'Thank you, Doctor.'

Faith rolled her eyes. She was getting over the benefit side of Raimondo being there now and moving to the worry.

'Raimondo and I have to go,' she said and led the way from the shop to head across the car park.

CHAPTER FOUR

RAIMONDO'S GAZE REMAINED on her as Faith walked across the gravel of the car park, her tall, willowy body weaving between the parked vehicles with a natural grace that held his eye and made his heart pound. He'd been a fool not to return. And doubly so because of Chloe. If only he'd known.

But Faith? Faith made his heart pound even more than working on a cardiac arrest. *Dios.* What a day. Faith had been magnificent. Of course. He had known the young woman he had left behind all those years ago had strength and today he had seen the growth of that inner steel for himself.

With the resuscitation, the elderly man had been fortunate, and he wished him well. In fact, he would telephone the regional hospital he would be taken to. The paramedics had said they would bypass Lighthouse Bay Hospital for the more cardiac-focused regional centre. He knew instinctively Faith would want to know as well. Funny how already he was back to considering what Faith would want and including her in his plans.

But this moment, this second in the deserted car park, he could see her dark hair, halfway down her back now that it was loose from the ponytail she'd worn for the tour. Hair that glistened as it captured the sun in subtle red highlights, cascading in a riot of soft waves. He could almost feel the texture of those thick strands between his fingers and frowned at himself.

This was not why he'd come.

For these feelings to reappear was not reasonable. He'd come here because he'd suspected this woman had purposely excluded him from his daughter's life. And why had that been so incredibly painful that he'd boarded the first plane he could?

Probably because in his heart he could not believe that was like the Faith of his treasured memories. And yes, if letters had been sent, and intercepted, twice, with malice or agenda, then it would be like Maria to have done that. His bitter, conceited, forever dissatisfied ex-wife. It would have amused Maria to have caused that loss.

Yes, he believed it of Maria but not of Faith. The last damaging laugh to Maria. With Faith and her daughter the most injured parties.

Faith turned her head as if she'd caught his thoughts and he saw her brows crease. He waved and forced a smile. He needed to reassure her that he had no plans to do anything she didn't want. She did not trust him. Why should she? He had left her with a child and never answered her letters.

Dios.

As if encouraged by his smile, she waved back and climbed into her car and had him fumbling at the remote to open his own car in his haste to follow before she drove out of his sight.

He mused that this too was like the first moment he'd seen her walk by and felt this same sense of urgency to obey his instinct. What was it about Faith that grabbed him by the throat, shoved him by the shoulder, so he had to follow when he was in her orbit?

He slid into the car and turned on the guttural engine. Yes, he'd been self-indulgent with this hire, and not sensible really when he knew he'd be driving out along this dirt road to the caves, he thought as he shadowed her car down the dusty forest road towards Lighthouse Bay. But it was deeply, primitively satisfying to know she would not be able to speed away if she tried to lose him. He had it bad. But she hadn't tried to run.

Faith was as he'd remembered. With the passing of years she'd grown even more beautiful, more poised and personable, which sat well with her good heart. A heart he hoped he could still believe in because he was afraid he'd been fooling himself that he'd forgotten the woman who had captured his attention so easily.

See what he had done with his recklessness.

She had been left with a child.

He had carelessly altered both their futures and hurt the child he didn't know was his by his irresponsible actions. He shook his head as he drove, shadowing her car, unconsciously ready at any moment to pursue if needed.

Yet, despite his unexpected arrival today, she had not criticised him. Faith had spoken to him with kindness and sense; no rancour or revenge came his way when it should. He knew no other woman who would be so generous and honest. He'd met many who had nowhere near her decency.

Again, here was a growing need to understand what it was about Faith Fetherstone that touched him so much, as well as finding out about the daughter he had yet to meet.

When he'd first suspected about the child he'd done his homework. He'd looked Miss Fetherstone up and seen her address remained the same. Had decided on reintroducing himself at the caves because she couldn't avoid him in a group. Had even booked the tour online after confirming with the owner that the guide—*Faith, who had taken him before*—worked that day. Seemed the best way of making sure she'd be there before he'd booked his flights from Florence.

It had all turned out as he'd planned. And now he was to meet his daughter. Children had been his dream for so long but Maria had turned him from any thought of another arranged marriage.

But a child. Almost five? The thought suddenly filled him with trepidation that he was not worthy.

What if Chloe was afraid of him? He, a big dark-haired Italian man with no skill for children because only one nephew had bounced on his knee—a nephew gone. Coming from a family with everything except the richest prize. The next generation.

He remembered well when his parents had died how it had felt to face the stern grandfather who was to be his and his brother's future. No softness. Just duty. Sadly, he worried his brother was turning into their grandfather.

Imagine if his own daughter saw his grandfather in him.

He shuddered and his hands clenched on the steering wheel until he forced them to relax. He had faith. And Faith. She would help, but first he needed to convince her he meant no harm. He could appreciate the care she took of her daughter and understand the need to confirm his motives before she gave him access.

The problem was—how much access did he really want and how much would be good for his new family?

CHAPTER FIVE

FAITH DROVE STEADILY, trying not to glance too often in the rear-view mirror as she traversed the winding roads to the turn onto Lighthouse Bay Road. The big black car stayed reasonably back but she was constantly aware of the leashed power of the vehicle.

The charismatic power of the stern-visaged driver.

The relentless momentum of being manoeuvred into this meeting by a man she could see expected his own way.

How had he known she was at the caves? How much planning had he done before he'd arrived and how did she make sure she wasn't on the back foot trying to catch up to him?

All thoughts that continued to swirl fifteen minutes later when Raimondo solicitously ushered her into her seat at the beachside café as if she were a flower of extreme fragility.

A tiny pang pierced her composure. She remembered this feeling. This subtle olde-worlde charm of Raimondo. Being the focus of his dark eyes.

Nobody had pulled her chair out for her since, well, since Raimondo, and it did make her feel more feminine than she had for a long time. But then again, maybe someone else might have been equally caring if she'd been interested in looking for an escort. She'd been too busy being a mum and a midwife and ensuring the protection of her family life to risk a relationship.

Or she hadn't found anyone who made her feel as this man did and it wasn't worth the bother.

The reality of how she reacted to Raimondo made her grip the edges of her seat. He looked calm. Calm like she wanted to be, but she'd been working herself up on the drive, she realised.

His ease, and his ability to even glance around approvingly before he sat, suddenly agitated her. With a rising, and possibly irrational, irritation words spilled out as soon as his backside hit the chair. 'So what does your wife think of you coming all the way to Australia on the chance of paternity?' Shut her mouth. At least she'd said it quietly.

Grimaced at herself. Impatience had made her too blunt. To her relief the oblivious waitress arrived and took their coffee orders and when she'd left it wasn't surprising the silence hung between them.

He studied the table a moment longer before looking across at her and she watched his big fingers smooth the pressed shell and sand placemat in front of him without thought. 'My wife and I annulled our marriage after one year.' His tone remained matter-of-fact though there was an emotion which she couldn't identify lacing the dry words. 'Our legal commitments were met with regard to my grandfather's wishes and it was not required to continue.'

'Annulled?' Legal commitments? But the first part remained her focus. She couldn't help the disbelief in her voice. Her memories did not include a celibate Raimondo. Or a cold-blooded legal brain.

The whirlwind that had been their relationship had exploded into mutual, foolish abandon. Embarrassing in retrospect; though she could never regret her beautiful Chloe, she did regret her trust in this man. And he hadn't even made the woman he'd left her for happy?

Maybe she, Faith, had had a lucky escape.

'So does annulled mean something different in Italy?' How could they be married for a year and not sleep together?

He shrugged. 'I have little knowledge of your Australian laws. My grandfather in Italy was set on our marriage to combine the two great houses through our offspring. A pact of long standing. Without children the company would move from Florentine control to a Roman cousin. As this was his dying wish, and my brother and his wife had not yet conceived, I met his demands with little choice and speed before he passed—as I explained when I left.'

He'd left like a shot from a gun. 'At the time you said your life was in Italy and you were marrying because of a previous arrangement.' Might have been nice to know that before she'd invited him home.

Her shiny Italian hero had left without looking back. Her turn to wave away the past. 'That's all in the past. Now you're saying you never slept with your wife?' Really? Not the Raimondo she'd known.

'No.' He raised one brow and she decided he did it with a hint of satirical amusement at her expense. She narrowed her eyes. 'The marriage was annulled for infertility not disclosed—not celibacy. My ex-wife is barren. She did not tell me she had been forced by her father to wed or that she had known with certainty of her infertility. As my late grandfather's wish for our marriage relied on children, that made for reasonable grounds for annulment.'

And boy, did that sound horrible and cold. She rubbed her suddenly chilled arms. And this was her daughter's father? So she'd been lucky he'd been called away then. His unemotional recital made her wonder if his wife had been so dispassionate at being deemed unworthy. She shuddered. Like her mother and the small child Faith had been were deemed unworthy when her own father had left.

Her revulsion must have shown on her face because he said, 'Do not judge me for this. Maria never wanted me. She left with more wealth and has found a new husband. I wish her well.'

'Big of you.'

'Especially as she was unfaithful during our marriage.' Then he waved in the air. 'Pah!' He waved again, obviously annoyed with himself. 'This is not your concern. I find myself baring my soul to a woman I barely knew six years ago and again today. Forgive me.'

He was cross with himself all right. If he hadn't looked so sinfully sexy during his sudden almost-tantrum she would have laughed. But his honesty shone through the big hand that pulled regretfully over his face. Maybe she hadn't been as ridiculously blind as she had thought all that time ago. No, don't go there. Things were very different now.

She lifted her chin. 'My fault for asking. But at least I know a little more of you.' Though she didn't really. Except... 'You really didn't get my letters?'

'No. I am sorry.' His brow furrowed. 'Though I can guess who did.'

She supposed so. 'Your wife?'

He shook his head with more regret. Not helpful to Chloe, though. 'Hard to understand Maria could be so cruel, but she felt the lack of children greatly and resented our marriage even more.' He looked at her. 'I'm sorry I wasn't there when you needed me.'

No, you weren't there, she thought, but she could see why he hadn't been. 'My aunt Isabel was there for me. She's still my rock. Though younger than my mum, she stood as my mother's rock as well. We manage very well together.'

'No need for others?' He asked the question with a bitterness she didn't deserve.

'We manage very well. Thank you,' she agreed with composure that was slipping a little. Sadness for her daughter had tightened her throat.

A comedy of errors, five years of her daughter's life, and he was the loser if he'd wanted to be involved. And maybe it hadn't been all his fault. She'd lost as well because even if they'd not ended up together she suspected this man would have been an attentive dad to her little girl as much as he could, considering the physical distance between their two countries.

As in the past, their thoughts seemed to mesh. 'Tell me about your pregnancy. Her birth. Her infancy.' His eyes softened. 'About Chloe. Your daughter.'

Her daughter. Not his. He was trying to see her side too. But she couldn't soften too much. Couldn't trust that much yet.

Where did she start? 'Chloe was born here at Lighthouse Bay Hospital. A beautiful water birth. It was the most amazing day of my life.' Her eyes misted with the memory. The recollection of those first moments with the weight of her new daughter, pink and wet, heavy between her bare breasts. The scent of her, the downy head and snuffly noises against her skin and the glory that was the wonder of birth.

Her own pride in her achievement. She would never forget that. But that was all too private. Instead she said, 'It will be her birthday soon. She'll be five in two days.'

He leaned forward, his face lighting. 'Two days?'

'Seventeenth of November.'

'May I be there for her birthday?' Nice of him to ask, but she wasn't a fool.

She had no right to bar him, despite her misgivings. She didn't believe he'd cause trouble but to be wrong would be bad. 'That's up to you.' She met his eyes. 'And up to Chloe. And how long you plan on staying might be nice to know as well.' She lifted a hand, palm up, in question.

'A week. I have given myself a week. I fly out next Friday.'

She could do a week. If his family didn't call him back. Ha!

Could protect herself for a week as well.

Protect herself against the chemistry between them that she could still faintly feel, even through the thickest wall she could erect and had become very good at maintaining ever since Chloe's birth.

Then he would be gone and her life would, hopefully could,

return to normal. She wasn't moving to Italy and he wasn't moving to Lighthouse Bay so all would sort in the end.

He sat back. Studied her with that intense expression on his face. 'What is she like? This daughter of ours?' Avoiding discussion on what happened after he flew away again, but she guessed nobody knew the answer to that yet.

Knowing the extent of his stay was solid ground, as was the topic of Chloe. She could talk of her daughter until the sun set. 'She's dark-haired and strong...' *Like you*, the thought flashed through her brain, but a wholly feminine version of Raimondo's darkness.

She went on, '... With green eyes and long lashes.'

'Like you.' She lifted her head at the echo of her thoughts and she heard the smile in his voice as he said it.

Maybe. 'She's a minx who gives us pleasure in her company every single day.' She shook her head at the memories that swirled like bright confetti when she thought of her daughter. 'To hear her funny little cackle of a witch's laugh is to know the joy of being a parent.' She stopped. Could have snatched back the thoughtless cliché. 'I'm sorry. Poor word choice in the circumstances.'

He waved that away, still watching her face with an intensity she found discomfiting. 'You love her dearly.'

'More than life itself.' Twice today she'd had that thought and a cold foreboding washed over her. She shivered and his hand came across the table to touch hers.

'I would never do anything to hurt you or Chloe,' he said softly. Sincerely. His eyes held her gaze like his fingers held her wrist and warmth flooded over her. 'Never.'

She nodded. 'I hope I can believe you.' But still the feeling of foreboding didn't go away.

She changed the subject and eased her hand free. 'Where are you staying?'

He gestured to the hill with the same hand. 'In the guest house down from the hospital.'

She knew it well. 'Our locum doctors stay there.'

'Do they?' He smiled at her. 'And how is your little hospital that you loved so much?' As if again sensing her need to regroup.

A safe topic she could also talk about for hours. 'Grown. We birth over a hundred babies a year here now.'

'Then you must have found more doctors to carry on. There were staffing hardships before.'

'A lot has changed since you were here.' And wasn't that an understatement. Her. Their daughter. She thought about the new families in Lighthouse Bay. Her wonderful circle of friends that grew with each new relationship.

'We are a midwife-led unit now, so doctors come only for the general patients and obstetric emergencies.'

He smiled. 'I would be redundant already.'

'You never planned to work here.' Wouldn't that be a hard thing for her to come to terms with if he was here all the time? Crikey.

He inclined his head. 'As you say. I never planned this. Though I have been doing locum work since my wife and I parted. In poorer suburbs in Italy. A little aid work in Third World countries. My brother has occasionally forgone the pens of the pharmaceutical business and has sometimes joined me in aid work.'

She remembered he had mentioned his work doubts even when they'd met. His new focus helped her to relax a little more when he added, 'The work is much more satisfying and demanding to fill my life. I regret that even your Lighthouse Bay receded into a moment in time.'

Then he could have come back after his divorce, she mused. Come back at least to see if what they'd experienced really had been as special as she'd thought.He'd decided not to, obviously. But things worked out, or didn't, as the case might be, for reasons no one knew, she told herself. Out of sight, out of mind, she supposed a little drearily.

'Tell me what else has changed in this place you love so much over the years.'

She wasn't sure what he was thinking now but she ploughed on, relieved to have a lighter topic to discuss. 'My boss, Ellie, has married, and my friend, Catrina, as well.'

He lifted his head. 'Ah, Catrina.' He smiled and she tilted her head to understand why Trina's name had brought amusement.

He went on, 'It was this Catrina's wedding that brought me here. One of my colleagues at the hospital came to this wedding. She is a friend of Sam's sister and was back visiting—apparently she was at Sam and Ellie's wedding too, and mentioned to me about you and your Chloe.'

Faith stared at him. Trina's wedding? A guest from his town in Italy? 'Mentioned my daughter and me?' There had been some Italian doctors, friends of Sam's sister, but she'd thought them from the city. Surely not. 'Who was your colleague?'

'Francesca Moran. I heard her mention your Lighthouse Bay and I asked after you.' He spread his hands depreciatingly. 'It had been so long since I'd heard of this place so of course the name called to me.' He shrugged and there was a decidedly amused glint in his eyes. 'And, of course, my...' he paused as if searching '...ears prickled?'

'Ears pricked up. Yes.' With a little impatience. 'Why?' She tried to remember if he'd met Trina before. But their intense relationship/liaison had been so short and all-encompassing she didn't think they'd left her cottage except to go to the cave.

As some of those very intimate recollections intruded her face warmed and she looked away. She'd had these memories locked up so long she'd almost forgotten the details. If she let herself relive how it was she might not sleep for a week.

Thankfully, Raimondo seemed to have missed her embarrassment and tutted as if impatient with the subject. 'I asked if she'd seen you and she remembered yes, because your daughter Chloe had been very pretty and had been chasing the tiny flower girl of Trina's husband.'

Faith remembered, though it was more than a year ago. Chloe had been adorable, as had Trina's stepdaughter Piper, and some of her embarrassed confusion seeped away and was replaced with maternal pride. 'She was charged with looking after Piper. And yes, Piper was only two and the flower girl. Chloe can be very responsible for her age.'

He smiled at her obvious pride. 'Of course she is. She will be composed like her mother.'

She didn't know about that—she was feeling anything but composed at this moment and she needed to get this conversation back on steady ground.

'And because of this you came?'

'Because of this I came.'

Nope. She didn't understand. 'I could have been married with many children.' But she wasn't, mostly because of the impact he'd had on her life, not something she'd dwelt on but she thought of it now. And narrowed her eyes at him.

A shadow crossed his face. 'As you say. Though I was told otherwise. My friend knew you had no husband and Chloe's age made me wonder.'

Obviously, it had made him wonder. 'Wonder enough to cross the world and see?'

'Yes.'

She watched his face. 'And did you investigate further?'

'As you say.' His expression remained unreadable. She decided he was being deliberately vague. 'I owe you many apologies,' he added.

Like that would help, she thought, but she'd decided against stewing in bitterness a long time ago. It changed nothing and she refused to colour her own and Chloe's lives with negative thoughts. That philosophy had stood her in good stead and she wasn't being driven by someone else to change now.

He asked quietly, 'Is there a special man in your life?'

She blinked. Guessed she could understand why he would ask as he'd just exploded into their world. She could say yes.

As protection against the tendrils of attraction this man was already curling around her like wisps of smoke. She was fighting it but she had past experience that his illusion of smoke could lead to a sudden flame.

But she wasn't into lying either... 'No.' She lifted her head. 'Not at this time.' Apart from him, there hadn't been a man in her life, really. A few brief ones in uni. Before that, as a child, the father she could barely remember, who had left her mother and her. But she wasn't telling him that. 'Just male friends. And husbands of my friends.'

Her eyes met his and she explained lest he think it was all about him. 'It's better for Chloe that I don't expose her to the whims of a passing relationship.'

She still didn't know what it had been about Raimondo that had penetrated her barriers years ago—why had she, as a young naïve woman, brought this stranger from another land into her home, to all the places that were dear to her and allowed him access to her heart? To her body?

Because of the magic. And that was the torment of it. Spending time with Raimondo had been like sprinkling fairy dust over her world until she'd felt alive and aware, hypersensitive to the beauty all around her. She'd been caught in the bubble of his admiration and returned it to him tenfold. She wouldn't do that this time.

She looked across at the beach in front of her, frowning at it. Even now, the ocean seemed bluer than it had been this morning, the flowers in pots brighter, the sounds of the waves more clear. It was fainter, but she could feel that magic now. Again. Looked back at him as he sat back in his chair and studied her too.

In the past this man had soared into her life like a comet, searing away her reserves, and she knew what had happened the last time with the heat of their collision at the airport. But then he'd rocketed straight out again.

Oh, she was over her feeling of abandonment but she didn't want that for Chloe. No way.

Not really surprising she hadn't rushed into making herself vulnerable to a man again. Not bitter. Just not open to trusting closeness again.

She expanded on her answer, letting him know where her priorities lay. 'I will give Chloe all my time until she starts school before I see if I want to cultivate a man's company on a more permanent basis.'

He raised his brows as if she'd said something vaguely unsettling but he closed his mouth and silence fell between them.

To fill it she said, 'My need for male company has been easily satisfied by social outings with my friends and their husbands or the families of the babies I've welcomed.'

He nodded. 'Then this is good as it is not confusing for Chloe during my visit.'

He was concerned about her daughter's feelings and, against her better judgement, she softened towards him again. A tiny voice whispered plaintively that it was only because of Chloe he was glad there was no another man.

Then she pulled herself up. No. Now she could feel the heat in her cheeks again, damn him. This was how he had managed to get under her guard last time, with solicitude and care and treating her as if she were a princess he needed to guard from the world. Something she'd had no experience of from a man.

And hadn't that changed when his brother had called?

Oh, yes.

She knew where she really stood. Just a phone call and he'd be gone. Not his fault. Oh, no. But family calls…

Her aunt had always said that for the Italian men their family was everything. Well, she had a family, Chloe and Izzy, and she needed to make sure her daughter was safe from the disappointments an unreliable father could bring to her life, so she wasn't falling for his transient solicitude again until he'd proven himself. She would be calm. Careful. Consistent in her barriers.

Who knew what crisis would make him leave next time? She would protect Chloe from the devastation she could suffer when his larger-than-life presence disappeared in a moment. She knew how it felt and Chloe would too in seven days' time. Faith needed to be clear on expectations with Chloe ASAP.

But it was so strange talking like this with a man she'd thought she would never see again.

He'd been watching her silently and she wondered if he could read her thoughts and if they'd crossed her face for him to see. 'What of your friends in your life? Will they be worried that I have come back?'

Did he think it odd she had no man in her life? It could have been tricky if she'd had a boyfriend.

'All my male friends are married to women I care about. Though my aunt has been hinting that when Chloe starts school I should look to building more...adult friendships outside my work.' She looked at him. 'I might look at that then.'

Raimondo glanced around pointedly. 'And no single men have been clamouring at your door? Are they blind not to want to capture you for themselves?' He looked so pleased with her lack of suitors her irritation rose.

She gave him a level stare. 'I've been a fool once. So, of course, I'm reluctant to go there again.'

He winced. 'Of course.'

They'd finished their coffee and she glanced at her watch. It was lunch time. 'I have to go. I need to be at work by two-thirty for the afternoon shift.'

He glanced at his own watch but his face remained difficult to read.

There was a tense pause and finally she said, 'I'm off duty tomorrow.' For Sunday and Monday as well, but she didn't add that. 'If you'd like to come and meet Chloe and my aunt, Isabel, then you could come for breakfast at eight. We could go down to the beach after, as Chloe likes to have a play in the water when she can.'

'Thank you. I would like that. Your aunt cares for Chloe while you work?'

'Yes.' She raised her chin. 'It would have been very difficult without her help.' Again, she noted his grimace of distress, but she'd said it more to show appreciation of her aunt than to make him feel bad. 'Izzy moved in with me just before Chloe was born. She was my mother's youngest sister and only fifteen years older than me and we are our only family. She's put her life on hold for Chloe and me.'

'I imagine there is much closeness between you.'

'There is. Very much. Next year, when Chloe goes to school five days a week, Izzy will be less tied and I'm going to shift to night duty again, which I did in the beginning. There's a young woman from the preschool who has agreed to sleep over with Chloe when I'm at work if Izzy is away. I'll be home to send her off to school and there when she comes back.'

He shook his head. 'I do not like to hear of these hardships inflicted unknowingly on you by my lack of responsibility. I owe you and your aunt a great debt.'

'No. You don't.' No way was he finding a foothold there. 'I love Chloe and there are lots of mothers juggling similar schedules and worse. I get help and wonderful support from my friends as well as Izzy.'

His brow furrowed at being thwarted. A bit too used to getting his own way, she mused, as he said, 'I hope to have some input. But we have time to see.'

She said steadily, 'I've been extremely fortunate and need nothing from you.'

Now his face appeared bland. 'Perhaps this is for another discussion.'

She met his eyes. *Oh, yeah? Let it go, Faith*, she told herself. When she didn't reply he half smiled as if he knew it was her restraint not her change of mind that kept her quiet.

He inclined his head. 'Thank you for your invitation and I will see you at eight tomorrow.'

She did need to get away to think. 'Do you remember where I live?'

He laughed with little amusement. 'Before the cliff. To the left of the crofts. The siren's house above the sea. I remember.'

She laughed. 'I've never been a siren in my life. I'm afraid your memory tricks you.'

One dark brow rose. 'Does it?'

CHAPTER SIX

FAITH DROVE TO the preschool and picked Chloe up way too early. Her daughter didn't see her enter the brightly festooned, noisy room because she sat with her tongue pushed against her teeth as she glued a black felt eye onto a cotton wool ball with fierce concentration.

Her two dark pigtails bounced as she nodded her head to something the little girl beside her said but her attention remained fixed on her task. Chloe was always surrounded by little friends and Faith wondered who she'd inherited her outgoing personality from.

Perhaps Raimondo.

'Chloe, I've come to pick you up.'

'Mummy?' Chloe looked up from her work and her face shone her delight at seeing her mum. She put down the cotton wool ball and jumped up. Threw out her arms. 'My mummy is here. I have to go.' She glanced around the room as if to be sure everyone could see how special the occasion was. Her daughter bounced up and down at the exciting change in routine and happily gathered her new paintings and crafts.

Faith met the amused eyes of the preschool teacher and they both smiled. Chloe ran to the teacher, hugged her, and then back to her mother and caught her hand. 'Let's get my bag.'

Faith savoured the warmth of the little hand in hers, the chatter floating up and the skipping of her daughter's feet as they walked to the car. Her Chloe sunshine.

At least Faith would get home with extra time before work to get her head together. Dashing out to preschool pick-up just before starting shift would have jumbled her thoughts again and she was jumbled enough.

As soon as Faith walked into the little house on the cliff her aunt's dark brows rose and her green eyes widened. Isabel or Aunty Izzy as Chloe called her, didn't miss much. Yup. She knew something had happened.

Izzy took the preschool bag from Faith's slack hand and received her kiss from Chloe. 'Your sliced pear and milk is in the fridge, darling,' she said, pointing the little girl towards the sink and towel waiting for her small hands without taking her eyes off Faith.

As Chloe happily followed routine, Izzy touched Faith's shoulder and concerned eyes searched her face. 'You okay?'

Was she okay? She'd been solid as a rock while she'd been with Raimondo but at this moment she felt weak at the knees.

'Raimondo Salvanelli turned up at the caves this morning.' The words sounded strange even coming from her own mouth. Spreading her hands helplessly, Izzy didn't appear enlightened.

She'd get it. 'He didn't know about Chloe and someone at Trina's wedding mentioned us and he flew in from Florence.'

Izzy's eyes widened. 'The Italian from the airport?' Then she mouthed silently, 'Chloe's father?'

Faith sank onto the sofa, her eyes drawn to her daughter happily setting her own table, playing house with her milk and fruit on her child-size table setting.

'How could he not know? You wrote. Twice.' Izzy manfully tried to catch up.

Faith turned back to her aunt. 'He said he never received the letters, though the address I sent the letters proved correct. And his marriage has been annulled.' She waved her hand impatiently. 'Long story.' She looked at Chloe again. 'He's coming tomorrow morning at eight.' Lowered her voice. 'To meet Chloe.'

'Who's coming to meet me?' a bright voice piped up. Chloe proved she might be quietly doing her thing but she wasn't oblivious to the tension at the other side of the room.

Faith and Izzy exchanged looks. 'One of mummy's friends from a long time ago is coming to visit tomorrow for breakfast. Of course he'd like to meet you too.'

Chloe's bright eyes studied them both. 'Does your friend have a little girl?'

'Not yet.' Another frazzled look at Izzy from Faith. 'But I think he'd like one.'

Izzy made an inarticulate sound and turned away so Chloe couldn't see her expression. She turned back to Faith, her face composed. 'Well, then. Much excitement.' She glanced at the clock on the wall. 'Why don't you go have a nice freshening shower? Chloe and I will make lunch while you get ready for work.' Her aunt looked at her. 'Unless you don't feel up to going?'

That was more of a joke than a question because Faith would have to be dying to not turn up for work.

'I'll be fine. And yes, thanks, a shower would be good. A strategy for dealing with this, so all will become clear.'

She smiled ruefully at her aunt. 'I might bash my head against the wall a few times, so ignore strange sounds.'

Just before two-thirty that afternoon Faith walked through the glass doors of the Lighthouse Bay Mothers and Babies Wing of the tiny hospital and slipped her bag into the cupboard underneath the desk.

When the world was going crazy thank goodness there was work.

The ward seemed quiet and nobody sat at the desk. She let a small sigh of relief escape her. It would be nice to settle into the shift before the ward focused on an impending birth but she knew what to do regardless when she was here. Unlike in her social life at the moment. She could hear a baby crying so at least they had inpatients. She didn't want it so quiet she needed to work elsewhere in the hospital, which they sometimes did between rushes of babies. She didn't have the head space for that today.

Today there had been too many upheavals in her peaceful private world and the question marks for the future unsettled her in a way she hadn't felt for many years.

Raimondo had the knack of that.

'Hey there, Faith.'

Ellie appeared from one of the side rooms on the ward with a grizzling baby tucked under her arm. The manager of the ward, and sometimes the whole hospital, Ellie preferred when she could work as a hands-on midwife, like today.

'Hi, Ellie.' Her boss looked so happy. 'How's your day been?' Not like hers, that was for sure.

'Excellent. Apart from this baby, who seems to have missed the rules on settling after a feed—but I have the technology— new nappy.'

She looked calm and content carrying the little football baby under her arm, the baby's neck securely supported by her cupped hand. She smiled a warm welcome.

Faith tried to smile back but a sudden unexpected fear that she'd never be like Ellie, with a man who worshipped her and a proper family, assailed her. A fear she'd never had before, and shouldn't have now, made her realise how much Raimondo had punctured her serene balloon of existence she'd floated in until now.

Her boss was very, very happily married to an obstetrician. Sam consulted at their regional referral centre and not Lighthouse Bay, but he did emergency calls when needed here. Having Sam in the wings was one of the reasons their birth rate had risen so much.

Faith's mouth opened. 'Chloe's dad turned up this morning

at the caves.' She slapped a hand over her mouth. She had not meant to blurt that out. What was wrong with her?

Except for a slight pucker of her forehead, Ellie's demeanour didn't change. 'I have supreme confidence in your good sense, Faith. Come into the nursery while I change this poo-bottomed boy. Then I'll give you a handover of our one patient and you can tell me all about "him".'

Faith followed her into the nursery, a space with wide sun-filled windows, a soft chair for breastfeeding mothers and tall benches for dressing and bathing babies. Ellie flipped out a fresh bunny rug and gently eased the little boy down until his head was resting on a folded cloth and began to unwrap him. Faith reached for the cleaning wipes to help and then, noting the disaster uncovered, instead wet a cloth nappy and handed it to Ellie, who laughed.

'Yep. I think we need the big guns to fix this mess.'

She smiled down at the baby as she swiftly righted the world. 'So, this is Jonathon, born this morning at seven-thirty to Maurine McKay.'

Faith felt the smile as it stretched her face. 'Little Maurine?' Maurine barely topped a metre and half tall, though her body was all curves and perfectly proportioned. 'How cool.' Faith shared her midwifery case load with Ellie so she knew Maurine well. 'And was it as easy for her as her last one? She was worried.'

'He flew out,' Ellie said. 'She was here about an hour, not saying much, then she did that thing she did with you last time. You know. The stare. And lay down and had him. The woman is a marvel.'

Faith shook her head in awe. 'Some mums are just designed to have babies. Probably helps that her husband is not much bigger than she is.'

'That too, maybe. Maurine's well, no damage, no extra blood loss, and this young man weighed three thousand grams so a nice size for her.'

Faith calculated quickly. 'About six pound six? Her biggest yet, then. Can't wait to congratulate her.' Faith could feel the tensions of the day falling away from her. This was the world she loved and she felt the calming of her lost equilibrium as it settled over her.

'She's looking forward to seeing you.' Ellie rewrapped the now clean baby. 'So. He's fed twice already, his temperature and respirations are normal and he's going to settle for a good sleep now.' This last was said firmly to the baby, who lay quietly with big dark blue eyes gazing steadily at Ellie.

Ellie picked him up. 'I'll take him back to mum and you pop the kettle on. Then you can tell me about your interesting day.'

By the time Ellie had left the ward and Faith had settled Jonathon again with his boisterous siblings and parents in Maurine's room, she was feeling like herself.

Okay. It had been unexpected—she snorted at that and the memory of her first greeting to Raimondo—and decided there was nothing she could do so she would take the benefits provided.

Mentally she ticked them off.

At least her daughter would remember a man called Raimondo when she was asked about her father.

Chloe would have some rapport to build on if she went to meet him one day in Italy when she was grown.

Raimondo could write to Chloe and possibly, though she was still thinking about this, contribute to Chloe's senior school or university in later life if he wished—because education was the best gift to give anyone.

She had to admit Raimondo still seemed the lovely man she'd become briefly infatuated with and, yes, she did feel she could trust him with contact with Chloe from the little she'd seen today. But that didn't mean she would.

She wasn't so sure she could trust herself, so she would be vigilant in guarding her good sense and her heart.

They'd do Christmas cards and maybe phone calls on birthdays—surely he could manage that, though she wasn't sure, and in this initial visit he'd be here for Chloe's birthday at least. Faith would put out the albums of Chloe's childhood for him to see.

She sat back. Yes. All ordered in her head nicely.

Chloe would probably enjoy showing Raimondo her photos over and over again. Faith wasn't so sure she was okay with some of the birth ones but, then again, he had seen her naked before.

Oh, my goodness. Quickly she picked up a pen and began to write out the diet list.

The sound of a car arriving in the driveway outside the ward had her out of her seat. Someone in labour?

Then she saw the sleek black Mustang. What the heck...?

Raimondo's big form climbed out and strode to the passenger seat and now Faith could see the shape of another person through the darkly tinted windows. She proved to be a woman and heavily pregnant. Where had Raimondo found a pregnant woman?

Faith grasped the handles of the wheelchair they left tucked handily behind the corner to the birthing rooms and pushed it towards the now opening door. The woman limped in on an obviously tender right leg and held her stomach.

Yep. In labour. Raimondo had brought her to the right place. His words carried. 'Traffic accident.'

What traffic? Faith thought, but she hurried over. The woman leaned on the door as she waited for Faith to park the chair next to her.

'Can you sit down?' Faith held the chair and Raimondo helped her settle into the chair. 'I'm Faith, the midwife on duty.'

'Cynthia Day. My husband is hurt and going in the ambulance. This man said he was a doctor and thought I should come here. Just until the ambulance is ready to leave and can take me too.' She glanced at Raimondo ruefully. 'I've had a few labour pains.'

'I saw the accident and called the ambulance,' Raimondo said. 'Her husband is stable but there may be a delay before they extricate him and are ready to leave. It seemed better to bring Cynthia to be checked before transfer.'

She looked at him. 'Yes. Good thinking. There's at least an hour's road trip in the ambulance so very sensible.' Then to the woman, 'When is your baby due?'

'Four weeks tomorrow.'

Technically premature, Faith thought, but not perilous. 'We'll check you both out and have the ambulance call here to pick you up. I'll pop you through into the assessment room, which is where we have our babies here. Is that okay?'

'Of course.'

Faith turned the chair and began to push it the other way towards the birthing rooms. Raimondo followed and Faith allowed him for the moment. It wasn't as if he was a stranger to hospitals and she'd keep an extra pair of hands until she could get help.

'Have you been here before?' She spoke from behind the woman as her brain sorted priorities.

She didn't recognise the woman and thought she knew all the ladies booked in to give birth at Lighthouse Bay. So medical or obstetric history might not be available.

'No. We're having the baby in Sydney.'

'That's fine. We can get your notes from there.' She'd have them emailed through once Cynthia had signed the release of information form. Or the supervisor could arrange all that because Faith would be busy on her own.

Cynthia sighed. 'We were going home after visiting relatives when my husband took a funny turn at the wheel. I grabbed the steering wheel but it was too late. We ran into a low wall and the front of the car crumpled in, making it difficult to get him out.'

Unlucky. And scary as a risk for possible hidden pregnancy-related trauma. Risk even from the sudden stop. 'Did you hit your stomach?'

'No. The seat belt jerked me when we hit, but that's all.'

Faith nodded to herself. She would have to watch baby for any signs of distress which could be a shearing bleed from the placenta. 'Was the car going fast when you hit?'

'No. I think John must have known something because he hit the brake just before he went unconscious.' She swivelled her head and looked at Raimondo. 'I'm so worried about him. When can you ring and find out how he is?'

'Dr Salvanelli will be able to do that soon.' She knew there was a good reason she'd subconsciously wanted Raimondo to stay. He'd been helpful already.

'Of course,' he said.

Raimondo and Faith stood on each side of Cynthia, supporting her until she was comfortably sitting upright on the bed, the back raised and one pillow supporting her head.

Faith turned to Raimondo as he stepped back. 'Thank you. I'll make a call and a nurse should be here soon. Will you stay by the desk in case I need you before anyone else arrives?'

'Of course.'

'Thank you. It's a good place to find out about Cynthia's husband. The ambulance control number is in red above the desk. They should be able to give you some information if you explain to them or they'll call you back. Tell them we have Cynthia here and expect her to be transferred as well.'

'*Sì.*'

Faith crossed to the phone in the room and quickly dialled the hospital supervisor. She tucked the phone into her neck to free her hands and twitched the cover off the baby resuscitation trolley, then reached to turn the heater to warm just in case. She'd only checked the equipment half an hour ago, an early in the shift task everyone completed, so she knew everything was ready if they needed it.

'Yes?' the supervisor answered.

'Hi, it's Faith in Maternity. We have an admission, a lady in a car accident. She's stable but contracting and could be in early labour. Can you send over a nurse as my second, please, and phone for Dr Southwell senior? There's an out-of-town doctor here at the moment, so tell the nurse that's who's at the desk when she arrives. Too busy to explain just now.'

She paused. Listened. Said 'Thanks' and put down the phone. 'Right then, Cynthia. Let's have a gentle feel of your tummy and listen to your baby. Raimondo will tell us as soon as he hears any news of your husband.'

Cynthia nodded, her face shining pale against the white pillow, her dark eyes concerned as she held her stomach. 'There's another contraction.'

Faith knitted her forehead. She needed obstetric history soon but the nurse could follow that up when she arrived. Faith crossed to the sink and washed her hands then went back to the bed, drying her fingers on the paper towel. She lowered the bed until Cynthia was lying flat with just the pillow under her head. Palpating a uterus in the upright position wouldn't give the clear picture she needed from an unknown woman.

'Is this your first baby?' They'd have more time if it was, she thought; the contraction had finished as she lifted the pretty blue maternity shirt and gently began to palpate the woman's stomach. Not her first baby, judging by the older silver stretch marks. She laid her fingers each side of the bulge and palpated in Leopold's manoeuvre. 'Nothing painful when I do this?'

'No.'

Good. Less chance of a quiet bleed from the accident then. The height of the uterus was consistent with thirty-six weeks, though the baby didn't shift under her hands, which was a concerning indication of vigour.

'She's not my first baby. This is my fourth. Four in five years.'

'Oh, my. Congratulations.' Faith's brows rose as she looked at the woman again. 'You look too young for four young kids. I have one and look much more careworn.'

Cynthia smiled wanly. 'John and I have just been on a week's holiday together. We were feeling relaxed.' She clutched her stomach again. 'I think this baby is wanting out.'

Faith narrowed her eyes and glanced at the clock. Only two minutes since the last contraction. 'Were there any complications in your previous births? Like a Caesarean or forceps. Or bleeding after the birth?'

'No. Apparently I'm made to have babies.'

Faith smiled. 'Pleased to hear it.' She listened to the clop of the baby's heart rate, which made the mother's mouth tilt up in relief at the comforting sound. Then Cynthia gasped, 'Oops. I think I just had a show or my waters broke a little. Something feels wet.'

By the time Faith had confirmed that there had been a small loss of blood and they'd sorted that development, Cynthia was returned to the sitting position. 'Um.' She fluttered her hands and her eyes darted around the room. 'I need John. I think I want to push.' Cynthia's voice sounded tremulous, alarmed at the speed of change, and Faith frowned and looked at the phone across the room just as the nurse poked her head into the room.

Faith blew out her breath in relief. 'Perfect timing. Can I have a delivery set-up ASAP? And get the supervisor to find out how far away Dr Southwell is. We need him now.' Faith didn't often call the doctor but this was a post-accident baby and it could be born compromised.

There was still that concern about abruption of the placenta from the sudden stop. 'Can you also ask Dr Salvanelli to stand outside the door in case I need to call him in, please, until the doctor arrives?'

The nurse nodded and hurried off after pulling the resus trolley closer to Faith.

Cynthia sighed heavily on the bed and Faith pulled back the sheet she'd lain over her. 'How about we just ditch the whole idea of underwear and check what's going on so we know for sure?'

By the time they'd done that Faith didn't need to check anything more because there was an unmistakable bulge of baby's crown inching into the world.

'I need to move,' Cynthia gasped. Already she was rolling onto her knees. Faith hurriedly stacked pillows so Cynthia could lean over a support. Things were progressing very quickly and the email of pre-birth papers would be moot until after baby's arrival now.

Faith leaned forward and pressed the call bell for the nurse to return. For now she needed an injection for after the birth so they didn't have a haemorrhage. Fourth baby made the risk increased. They could find out the medical history later.

Because the bag of waters was still intact, a large odd-shaped bag of fluid encased in membranes formed in front of the baby's head and through that a dark-haired skull could be seen descending. 'Looks like this baby wants to be born without breaking your waters first.'

'One of my others did that,' Cynthia panted. 'Won't drown, they said.'

Faith did love old wives' tales about midwifery, and even more she loved uncomplicated women like Cynthia who just went ahead and had their babies without any help from anyone.

'Come on, you,' Cynthia muttered as she bore down, because after progressing rapidly, with the birth of more of the head, now the speed of descent seemed to have stopped.

Faith glanced towards the door; it was good knowing she did have backup help if needed, but she refrained from calling in Raimondo.

The nurse came back in carrying an injection tray. Faith smiled at her. 'Brownie points for you.' She nodded at the injection. 'Did you get onto Dr Southwell?' Faith's eyes returned to Cynthia, who had become more distressed.

'They had to find him but he's coming.'

Without looking at the nurse, Faith nodded. 'Great. Thanks.'

'It feels stuck. I need to move.' Faith wasn't surprised. But with a sore ankle, squatting would be hard.

'Would it be okay if I ask Dr Salvanelli to come in? He could take some of your weight as you try to get comfortable while the nurse sets up the rest of the equipment.'

'Do it.' Cynthia didn't have words to waste.

Faith raised her voice. 'Raimondo?'

Within seconds Raimondo stood beside her and between them they lowered the bed closer to the floor, helped Cynthia shift sideways on her knees until she was at the edge of the bed, and waited for the next contraction to ease before they moved further.

A minute later she stretched her left leg down towards the floor, then moaned and they all froze.

Cynthia sucked in a breath. 'That shifted a little. Let's go for a squat, which is how all my other babies were born.' Except this time her right leg wouldn't bear her weight.

Faith and Raimondo's eyes met across the woman's head. 'I always listen to the mother,' Faith said quietly and Raimondo nodded.

'I have you.' Raimondo's hands were under Cynthia's armpits. 'Stand and then you can release the weight.'

Cynthia shuffled sideways with Raimondo taking her full weight, not something Faith or the nurse could have done, and the woman sagged against him and bent her knees. She sighed with relief. 'Better. Much better.'

Faith took the warmed towel the nurse had handed her and wondered philosophically what would happen to Raimondo when the waters broke.

A sudden whoosh delivered the answer as the membranes overextended their elasticity and a wave of amniotic fluid hit the floor and bounced backwards, covering his shoes behind the mother in a hot wave of sticky fluid. Faith bit her lip to stop the smile, safe behind the towel and concentrating on what she hoped would happen next.

As expected, the baby's impacted shoulder that had held up the birth suddenly freed with the extra room in the pelvis from the squatting position, and baby slid into the warm towel Faith caught her with. A slithery cord-wrapped bundle who lay still.

'A girl,' Faith murmured.

The nurse, standing to the side of all the drama, reached over and clicked on the timer to begin recording time passed since birth.

Cynthia swayed and her face paled. 'I need to lie down.' Almost before she'd finished the words Raimondo had scooped her up and put her back against the pillows. The nurse stepped forward with a warm blanket to cover her and Faith juggled the still attached baby onto the edge of the mattress and dried the infant, waiting for the mewling to start.

At the end of the pulsating cord the silent baby didn't cry. Or move.

'Right then,' Faith said quietly as she clamped and cut the cord. 'I'm just going to take her to the trolley and check your baby out, Cynthia. I think she's stunned by the quick trip through the birth canal.'

The nurse took Faith's place beside the bed and patted Cynthia's shoulder. 'I'll take over here. We'll ask if I need any help. Here's a warm blanket as we wait for the afterbirth and your baby to come back. Let's get you comfortable while we wait.'

Raimondo followed Faith as she lifted the little towel-wrapped bundle onto the wheeled resuscitation bench and removed the damp cloth. She began to rub the baby with the new towel waiting under the overhead heater and Raimondo took the stethoscope that hung there and put it in his ears to listen to the baby's chest as soon as Faith finished.

With the lack of response she glanced at the ticking clock and reached for the little mask. 'Positive pressure ventilation at thirty seconds after birth.'

'Heart rate one-ten.' Raimondo stepped back as Faith slid the tiny clear breathing mask over the baby's mouth and nose. They watched the rise of the little chest as she began to puff small breaths of pressured air every second. Raimondo unwound the tiny pulse oximeter lead and strapped the sensor onto the pale baby hand. 'I'll get this running so we can tell how her oxygen levels are.'

'Good. Still think she's just stunned.' Faith turned her head towards the bed. 'Heart rate is good, Cynthia. She's just figuring out this breathing game.'

The nurse called out, 'And we've finished third stage over here and no bleeding after the placenta.'

That was a blessing. 'Thanks, Nurse.'

After thirty seconds of further inflations the tiny limbs began to move. Raimondo had calibrated the pulse oximeter and now the constant read-out of heart rate confirmed baby's heart was chugging along as it should but baby's breathing was still gasping and ineffectual, though Faith's maintenance of air entry stopped deterioration.

'I'll do another thirty seconds of air.' But Faith wasn't happy. Baby should have recovered by now. 'Can you have a look with a laryngoscope? Might be something that blocked the airway.'

Raimondo nodded and the tension in her shoulders increased as he took over the hand-held intermittent positive pressure ventilation for the baby while she assembled the equipment needed. Her hands collected the necessary equipment swiftly as her mind searched for reasons. Simple obstruction was the most likely cause for baby not breathing when the heart rate was so good but she was getting worried.

They didn't have sick babies often but this baby had been in an accident and was slightly premature.

Having Raimondo here beside her while she waited for the other doctor was surreal, wonderful in the circumstances, but probably not legal. Where was their backup?

She took the ventilation mask off Raimondo and he took the laryngoscope gently—angling the curved beak with a light at the end and peering down the baby's throat into the airways. She noted how skilfully he inserted the steel blade and narrowed his eyes at the now open and visible airway. 'A small blood clot obscuring the trachea—it must flop back when you stop forcing the air in.' He held out his hand, still focused on the airway. 'Sucker?'

Faith had the thin clear tubing ready and handed it to him to slide down the curve of the laryngoscope. His finger occluded the mechanism, they heard the gurgling sound of suction, then a dark clot slid up the tube and flashed past towards the vacuum bottle.

Raimondo removed the tube and the laryngoscope from the baby's throat in one smooth movement and Faith felt relief expand inside her. That skill was one she didn't have.

He smoothed the baby's forehead. 'Is this better?' he asked her.

The baby gasped and cried and Faith sagged a little with the rush of success and knew everything would be fine. Her eyes met Raimondo's in a moment of pure relief and satisfaction. 'Thank you,' she mouthed, and when he smiled at her the connection between them flooded all the way down to her toes.

CHAPTER SEVEN

RAIMONDO FELT THE link between them as if it were a physical bond drawing them closer. How was this so? He watched as Faith, after a last glance at him, turned away and carried the now wriggling baby across to the mother, and knew that his life would always hold this so precious memory of working with Faith.

A moment in time.

The beginning of a child's life.

A moment such as this he had missed at his own child's birth.

He jerked himself back to the present. It had been a simple thing to find the airway obstruction, but Faith's adeptness was also a reason for much satisfaction. He'd known she would be efficient and kind in her work but her calmness and competence during the rapid birth and the subsequent neonatal resuscitation made him feel a strange emotion he wasn't familiar with.

Was it pride? Approval that the mother of his daughter was so admirable? He thought about that. No. It was simple pleasure at helping Faith, at sharing a moment of release of tension, of mutual satisfaction and appreciation for the goodness of others. He was glad and thankful to be here for her. That was the emotion he felt. Gratitude.

But standing here now was not needed and impacted on the

privacy of the patient. 'Congratulations, Cynthia. I will go out and try the ambulance control again for an update. Would you like me to pass the news on to your husband?'

The woman looked up. 'Yes. Please. I want to know how he is.'

As Raimondo walked down the hallway an elderly gentleman with a stethoscope around his neck, and a decided limp, hobbled past him towards the birthing unit. The doctor had arrived.

Raimondo didn't slow him with introductions.

By the time he had contacted ambulance control and ascertained the transport for Cynthia would be here soon, the nurse had returned to find out the results of his call. He passed them on and decided he would leave Faith to the no doubt mountain of paperwork she would have after such a rushed birth.

He would see her tomorrow. Today he needed to find himself a base in Lighthouse Bay because already he could tell he would always want to spend time here.

The next morning, just before eight, Raimondo strode up the cliff path towards a small house that sat to the left of the three crofts perched over Lighthouse Bay. He glanced back behind him to the soaring white stone lighthouse silhouetted against the sapphire-blue sky. The white tower seemed to watch him with guarded eyes from the big hill behind the hospital. Willing him to do this right.

So much at stake.

Perhaps even his whole future at stake.

Not just for Chloe, the daughter he had not known he was blessed with, but for Faith. For their future. His and Faith's future as parents together.

A week ago he had only a throwaway comment from a colleague to suggest he had a child.

Twenty-four hours ago he had not known that inside his chest lay a switch that would illuminate the dormant fascination and feelings he still held for Faith. This woman who had borne his child alone yet forgiven his absence so that Chloe would not be soured by a mother's bitterness.

How had he stumbled on this rainbow of hope that could change his life? How did he not destroy his chance here, as he had so many times by taking the wrong path?

Faith had to see he could be trusted and would take as much care not to hurt their daughter as she would.

A stone flew away from the side of his boot and he slowed. He could have driven to Faith's house up the steeply inclined hill from the hospital but he'd preferred to walk to loosen the excited apprehension that had made him toss and turn for most of the night.

He'd run over and over the episode at the hospital and marvelled at the opportunity to see Faith in her work. She'd been as wonderful as he'd expected and the privilege of sharing those moments stayed with him. Comforted him in his anxiety to do everything that was right by Faith.

He shook his head ruefully and smiled at the ancient front gate he approached. The new padlock.

There had been such a high from that shared medical emergency, and perhaps his soaring mood could have been partially responsible for his impulsive purchase of the building he was about to pass.

He turned his head and studied his new acquisition in the morning light: the run-down almost-mansion next door to Faith's home that he'd seen in the real estate window, walking home from the excitement at the hospital.

Still, the technicalities of purchasing something in a foreign country had taken his mind off his nervousness about meeting his daughter today. Perhaps if Chloe knew that her father had actually bought a house in her own town then she would feel more confident he was planning to be a part of her life. Faith would see this too. He hoped that was what she'd see.

But this morning the importance of this meeting with his new daughter had him edgy and unsettled. An unaccustomed apprehension that had not been helped even by rising at dawn and jogging down along the beach to freshen his mind. The cool white Australian sand under his bare feet had reminded him not at all of the hard pebbles of Amalfi beaches, his family holiday destination, and he felt the outsider even more despite his appreciation of the beauty surrounding him.

He'd jogged the sweeping inlet of Lighthouse Bay, the coarse sand curved like a new moon, and passed the rushing of the tide through the fish-filled creek back into the sea.

So few people passed him, strange for a man used to the crowds of Florence! So different to his homeland, but everything was different. His future was different because the occupants of this house he'd stopped outside now held his new world in their hands.

Now the moment had arrived his nerves were taut again and the day felt harshly warm against his skin already.

Or was he hot from nerves?

What if Faith had had a change of heart overnight and decided to exclude him for some reason he could not fight?

What if his daughter cried when she saw him?

Would the father she had never met be a disappointment?

'Calm yourself, Raimondo,' he admonished out loud. His pocket held a small, traditionally dressed Italian doll, a whim he'd scooped up at the airport and had the clerk wrap in tissue paper for protection. The vivid red peasant apron and hat had caught his eye because the figurine had been exclaimed over by a passing young girl of around the same age as Chloe. Such a purchase might give the child he'd come to see a smile.

For that was what he wanted the most.

A smile from a little girl who could be such a shining light in his suddenly empty life—if she'd let him in.

If her mother let him. If he was invited into their world.

The door opened and Faith stood like a Renaissance vision of dark wavy hair and warm tanned skin, framed in the glow of sun that shone across from the windows overlooking the bay. He blinked and, incredibly, forgot for a moment his reason for being here. This woman, how she grabbed his chest and squeezed always.

'You look beautiful.' The words were soft and heartfelt and she stilled while her cheeks pinked.

'Thank you,' said politely like a schoolgirl, which reminded him abruptly about another girl. He had a daughter. *Madonna mia*. So much to take in.

While he still struggled she said, 'Thank you so much for yesterday.' Then she smiled. 'Both times.'

His mind flashed back to the old man and the new infant and the drama that followed the birth. 'You are very welcome.'

'Sorry about your shoes.' They smiled at each other.

'Nothing a shower and clean couldn't fix,' he demurred.

'Come in. I've told Chloe I have a friend from Italy coming this morning.'

Her words sank in and reality slapped him as his fogged brain cleared. The irrational disappointment of not being introduced as Chloe's father redirected his mind from the mother but he schooled his disappointment behind his professional mask.

Of course she would think this was better for the child, less pressure.

Later, he reassured himself, later they could change his title when all went well.

They would. Yes. A definite, not an 'if'.

But his heart sank as he was reminded that his position was precarious still and it wasn't this woman's fault he was the outsider.

His eyes roamed the room as he entered but he couldn't see Chloe.

A tall woman in her forties with Faith's dark hair in a blunt bob stood to one side, a calm expression in her green eyes as she watched him enter. He glimpsed a quickly suppressed smile and his nerves settled a little. No hostility here either, though he wasn't sure he deserved such generosity from the woman he assumed was Faith's aunt.

Faith gestured with her hand. 'Izzy? This is Raimondo. Raimondo, my aunt Isabel.'

'It's a pleasure to meet you, Raimondo.' She stepped forward and took his hand in both of hers. When she squeezed his fingers he felt the friendliness and lack of reserve her niece had projected from the first moment he'd met her.

An amazing family—and one he had let down so badly.

'And you. Thank you for your kindness, Isabel.' Instead of shaking her hand, he leaned forward and gently kissed both soft cheeks.

Then Faith moved from where she'd been blocking his view of Chloe, and finally he could see the child in the room.

His daughter.

There she was.

He could never mistake her for any but his own, though she had Faith's eyes.

'Mia cara bambina...'

The words were low and heartfelt. Except for the green eyes of her mother, she was his own dear *mamma*, a beauty as a young girl, judging from the photo he had in his home.

My darling child. Words failed him and inside his chest it felt as though someone squeezed his heart in warm hands. His Chloe was taller than he'd expected and more curious than he had hoped for as her little face tilted sideways and she examined him with interest.

He looked back at his daughter. She held out her hand as if she were a five-year-old queen. *'Buongiorno,'* she said with an Australian accent and he laughed.

'Buongiorno, piccolo.' He glanced at Faith and for an instant he saw what she had hidden behind her apparent serenity. The clenched hands of trepidation that he would hurt her child, the chewed lip of hope that he would be a good father for Chloe,

and the bowed head of having to share her baby with another parent after all these years.

In a second he saw that and vowed he would protect the mother as well as the child from hurt.

Then Faith smiled, shaking her head at her daughter despite the worry in her eyes. He needed to remember this was so hard for her.

Faith nodded towards her daughter. 'Our one Italian word she practised for you.'

'Spoken perfectly,' he said gravely to Chloe with sincere hope he hadn't embarrassed her by laughing. 'You took me by surprise and I am very impressed. Thank you for learning the greeting.' His heart felt as if it were bursting. She was glorious and intelligent and had humour. And she looked like her beautiful mother. And somehow his. How had he been so blessed?

This was all due to his Faith.

'You're welcome,' she said primly and looked at her mother then back at him. 'Mummy says you're staying for breakfast and then we're going to the beach. We've made coffee in the coffee machine for you. I helped put the froth on top of the cup.'

'This is wonderful. Thank you.' Again his eyes were drawn to Faith, who seemed so remarkably calm, while his heart was pounding and his mouth was dry with excitement. He had a daughter.

He wondered at Faith's serenity then noted the repetitive reach for her necklace when she thought he wasn't looking. Perhaps not so calm.

He owed her so much for this meeting.

Inside he was wanting to shout with unexpected pride and joy and already the idea of leaving in less than a week caused pain that he would have to address and make plans for. Plans that meant his return. But that was for later. Today he would spend time with the daughter he had just found and try to mend bridges with the woman he had so badly disappointed.

Faith's aunt stepped forward. 'Would you like a pastry for

breakfast?' She pointed to the dish of steaming croissants curled on the dish. 'There's butter and jam to go with it. We're having cereal and you can join us as well if you'd prefer.' She glanced around at the girls. 'Then we'll have a croissant to finish with too.'

'Grazie.'

'Before she came to live with us, Izzy travelled a fair bit,' Faith said. 'She says this is the only time of the day to drink cappuccino in Italy without being teased. Is that true?'

Raimondo smiled again. 'True. Milk is for morning *caffè*, and too heavy for the afternoon. And your croissants are perfect, Izzy. Thank you.'

They all stood there for an uncomfortable few seconds until Faith motioned them all to the table.

Again, she had taken control, Raimondo noted. This assertive woman was not how he remembered her, but then years had passed. She intrigued him even more, but then he too had aged. Matured.

He wondered if she noted that. Wondered if she thought of him like that at all. But this was not to be his concern. His concern was the young girl hopping from foot to foot as she tried to understand what was going on. This was about how he could become a part of Chloe's life to her benefit.

'Sit down, everyone. We'll eat then we'll go down to the beach for the morning.' Faith looked at her aunt. 'Have you decided if you're coming to the beach, Izzy?'

'I'll go up and see Myra. She's upset by her husband's fall yesterday.'

Faith turned to Raimondo. 'You would have seen Dr Southwell yesterday, as he came into the hospital limping?'

Raimondo nodded.

'He fell on the path on the way down to our emergency yesterday. He's okay but Myra is upset and worried. It's his second fall. She wants him to retire. They live in one of the crofts up higher.'

'Ah. I'm sorry to hear of his accident. I have seen those crofts. The view must be as good as from here.'

They all glanced towards the windows overlooking the road and the sea. All except his daughter, whose eyes he could feel on him.

'Even better. The ocean seems to go on for ever out of the windows.' He listened to Faith's answer though a part of him remained focused on his daughter. He turned and smiled at the child.

Chloe watched him as the conversation continued and finally she said diffidently, 'Excuse me. Would you like to try your coffee?' Obediently he lifted his cup. Her gaze followed the mug, watching him for his expression, her tiny pink mouth compressed in concentration.

He sipped and, though weak, the flavour tasted very pleasant. *'Perfetto,'* he said.

Her brows creased as she thought about that. 'Perfect?'

Pride expanded in him with an unfamiliar exuberance. 'See. You are a natural.'

CHAPTER EIGHT

A NATURAL? A natural what? A natural linguist?

Her daughter wasn't Italian.

Her daughter was a little Aussie through and through, Faith reassured herself as she remembered the stillness on his face and the blossoming wonder when he first saw Chloe.

And before that the moment when she'd said she'd introduce him as her friend not Chloe's dad. He'd looked gutted and for a moment she wished she could change that and erase his pain. Tell Chloe this man was her father and let Raimondo bask in the moment.

No. It was far too early to trust him not to illuminate their lives and then plunge them back into darkness.

Her brain whirled with each new direction the day was taking. Was it only yesterday Raimondo had reappeared? Her life lay scattered in unexpected directions like the sand down at the beach, covered after a storm with new treasures and new sadness. But they would sort it out. She would sort it out.

She guessed at some stage Chloe would travel to see the land her father came from. Whether or not Faith went along as well would depend on how old her daughter was when this hypothetical trip happened.

Stop. Faith drew a deep breath and sipped her coffee too

fast and had to furtively wipe away the moustache that coated her lip. Cappuccino and croissants for breakfast. Good grief. These logistical issues were all Raimondo's problems, not hers.

She had her own many things to think about and the nebulous future was not as important as today would be.

Raimondo turned his head to answer a question from Izzy. Faith watched her daughter as Chloe gazed at the big Italian, her eyes wide and her attention settled squarely on this stranger at their table. True, it was an unusual sight to see a man in their feminine household. And true, Raimondo was difficult to tear your eyes away from.

Faith had thought that the first time she'd seen him at Sydney Airport—the young excited midwife returning to her little rural hospital after an exciting weekend birthing conference and then tangling gazes with the big handsome Italian man. The overhead announcement of flight delays drawing them together in mutual acceptance of the fickleness of fate.

Then, later, when he'd insisted on buying her dinner when their flights were rescheduled again to an even later flight. The instant, compelling attraction that had leapt between them growing bigger and brighter like a flame the more time they'd spent together. A flame that had taken over all good sense on both sides so that when the flights had been put back again until the next day they'd ended up in her hotel room provided by the airline instead of each to their own room later that night.

The next morning, with stars in their eyes, instead of going their separate ways, he'd followed her home to see this place she loved so much and they'd spent every minute together until the fateful phone call that had torn them apart.

That moment when the magical, marvellous moments had ended abruptly.

With an almost brutal finality.

Raimondo turned back and caught her haunted expression. Yes, I'm shell-shocked, she thought, and wished she could say it out loud. Just like I was years ago, and I don't know why I was destined to meet you like this twice in my lifetime. Not fair, really.

But she would have to deal with the moment and trust that he was trying to right a wrong and not cause more trouble.

What did he expect of her? Of Chloe? And what was the best way to keep her and Chloe safe from falling under his spell again and being hurt? That was what she needed to know. The order of her world seemed to have been snatched from beneath her feet yesterday, but hopefully it would return to how it had been.

Almost six years since she'd been swept along on a wild ride that culminated with the birth of this pretty, dark-haired child who brightened her life with such joy. What would it mean to share her with Raimondo—for that was what she could see coming? Maybe it would be for the best as Chloe did miss having a dad she could at least picture in her mind.

What was not for the best was to risk her own heart falling for the same attraction that had skittled her life last time.

Mentally she checked her defences and they were in place. She would see how the day panned out and make sure she too stayed safe.

An hour later the three of them walked down the hill to the beach.

Chloe was dressed head to foot in a delightful blue-striped rash shirt, frilled tights and matching soft peaked sunhat. The only parts of her that could be burnt were her face, hands and feet and Faith had sunscreened them. They spent so much time at the beach the covering swimwear was easier than catching Chloe for the trauma of sunscreen, which she hated.

For herself she wore a long sleeve cotton shirt and took it off to swim only. It was disquietingly odd to be going on a 'family' outing with Raimondo and her daughter, even if Chloe didn't know that was what it was.

The path swung in narrowly beside the road and Faith chose to follow behind the other two as it gave her time to think, and she could catch snatches of conversation as they floated back. Though, walking behind him, it did draw her eyes to the taut definition of his muscular arm as he swung the basket and the shift of thick muscles on his shoulders through his thin white shirt.

She'd loaded Raimondo with the two folding chairs and the not-feather-light food basket and he'd very happily accepted them. *His arms will have grown by the time he gets there*, she thought with an amused acknowledgement—it was easy to picnic when he carried most of the stuff. Faith carried the umbrella, towels and a blanket and Chloe swung her bucket and spade.

Chloe was saying, 'The beach has a low and a high tide and you have to be careful when you walk on the rocks when the tide's coming in.'

Her daughter definitely wasn't fazed, talking to this big Italian her mother said was a friend.

'Thank you for the warning. I will be careful,' Raimondo assured her.

A small arm pointed to the opposite cliff. 'That lighthouse is so the ships know that the land is there. Especially in a storm. Aunty Trina's house has big windows and in the storm the wind howls.'

A sage nod from Raimondo. 'That must be very exciting in a storm.'

'I don't like storms,' Chloe said severely, and Faith had to smile as Raimondo backtracked adroitly.

'Neither do I.'

Chloe looked at him under her brows as if assessing his truthfulness and Faith suppressed a laugh.

As if reassured, Chloe went on. 'Mummy works at the hospital on the hill and I'll be going to big school next year, which is just down the road from the hospital.' Her daughter could talk.

Faith could also be amused by how mystified Raimondo looked by Chloe's running commentary because he kept turning back to Faith and smiling in pleased bemusement and she suspected he hadn't had much to do with children.

Well, Faith had had a lot to do with children. Especially this one. Twenty-four hours a day and seven days a week for almost five years and still Chloe could stump her.

He had no chance of nailing it on one brief week-long visit.

Chloe had always been included in the conversations between Faith and Izzy and, while a very polite little girl, she was happy to share her views on the small world she inhabited.

No doubt, soon Chloe would ask Raimondo about his town and his life so that he could share things with them—things that she had no knowledge of. Her daughter was thirsty for knowledge of new things. New places. There were certainly opportunities coming up for her there. For Faith too.

Crossing her fingers, Faith hoped her daughter could wait for those questions until they reached the beach so she could hear the answers too.

'The book Mummy is reading me at the moment is called *Chicken Little*. Have you read it?'

Faith smiled to herself at Raimondo's answer. 'No. What is this story about?'

Chloe turned her head to look at him. Faith suspected her daughter rolled her eyes at that point. 'A silly chicken thinks the sky is falling and tells all the animals they have to leave. To run. It's very funny.'

'I am glad that it is funny.' Raimondo turned slightly to look at Faith for an instant. 'Perhaps your mummy could read that story to you again, and I could listen?'

Chloe stopped and turned back to Faith. 'Mummy? Could you read the *Chicken Little* story when Mr Salvanelli comes to visit?'

Faith shooed her on. 'We'll see.'

'So is Italy bigger than Lighthouse Bay?' Chloe's question came as his daughter settled down again on the sand. They were on the beach and had made a small area their own with their things.

Raimondo liked that there was nobody else here. So strange

when it was such a picturesque spot, but perhaps more families would come later.

The chairs Faith had given him to bring were set up and the umbrella she'd carried angled over them all. His daughter played at their feet with a small bucket and spade in the sand and he felt like pinching himself to be sure he wasn't dreaming this moment in time.

He was with his family.

Every now and then his daughter would run on sturdy legs to the water's edge and fill her bucket with water and bring it back to pour over sand so she could plaster the walls of the mound she said was a castle.

It began to take shape. He'd never made a sandcastle as a boy but could see the attraction. Perhaps he could try? To help her. Chloe began to stick shells on the walls. He glanced at Faith but she was staring out over the sea, deep in thought.

'May I join you?' he asked Chloe.

Chloe nodded vigorously. 'We can make it taller.'

So, awkwardly, for he had no skills with children, he crouched down on the sand beside his daughter and began to scoop out the sand in a narrow line to build a moat, putting the sand he removed on the top of her mound. The sand was cool and damp and coarse and felt strangely comforting as he ran his fingers across its salty cleanness to smooth the new walls of the castle.

'I see you build good castles. I am a man. We build forts. So, with your permission, I will dig a moat and build a wall to keep our castle safe from those who might attack while you make it pretty.' Was he being too stereotypical?

She laughed. 'The water will attack it.'

'I will build a diversion for the water.'

Each time she patted on another handful of sand it was as if she had also found a question. He had to smile at her fertile and free-flowing mind.

He had hundreds of questions and couldn't seem to ask any. So instead he thought how to describe his home when she asked about it. 'I live on the outskirts of the city of Florence. It is much bigger than Lighthouse Bay.' He thought about his beautiful Florence and the thousands of people who lived there and the hundreds who visited every day. Unlike this tiny place. 'Our house is part of a very old villa belonging to a nobleman many years ago but purchased by my grandfather and restored. It has several buildings and many rooms and a garden that grows olives and looks over Florence and the Arno Valley.'

He saw Faith look up at that. She raised her brows at him with shock in her eyes but he pretended not to see. They had not spoken of Italy much in the time they'd spent together.

'How many rooms?' His daughter remained persistent.

'There are four other dwellings but the main house has ten bedrooms.' He shrugged. 'My brother's house has nine bed-rooms. Mine has six.'

'That sounds big.' Here she looked at her mother. 'That's big, isn't it, Mummy?'

Faith looked at her daughter. 'Sounds a bit like the size of the hospital, really,' she said, her voice dry. 'You know how it has some separate buildings with other wards in them. Instead of looking over the ocean, his house looks over a city and a valley.'

His daughter nodded and looked much struck. 'You must have a big family.'

He spread his hands. 'And this is our sadness.' He shrugged. 'No. My twin lost his wife and son and I am not married any more. We are the last of our family.'

Chloe lowered her brows and shook her head, her little face serious. 'You should get married and have a family.'

'Yes, I should.' He glanced ruefully at Faith. 'My brother and I both should marry but his love died and mine wasn't meant to be.'

He saw Faith turn away to hide her expression, or to look at something he could not see. He wished she had not turned her face. Then she turned back and there was something in her face that made him pause in his explanation.

Faith said quietly, 'It's not polite for little girls to tell adults what they should do, Chloe.'

'Oh?' She glanced at her mother and sighed. 'Okay. Sorry, Mr Salvanelli.'

Just like that. No angst from either, just a correction. Different to his upbringing, where the emotion always ran high and even the wrath of God was often introduced. So different. He searched for a way to reassure both. 'I am not offended but thank you for your apology. I have a question. Do you always make sandcastles or do you make other things in the sand?'

The change of topic was gratefully accepted by all parties.

'I make sandcastles, though they're not really castles. I've never seen a castle except in books about princesses. I love princesses.'

She could certainly hold a conversation. He was glad English was his second language and he didn't have to translate in his thoughts. She was adorable and he couldn't help considering how his family home was very much like a castle.

He would show her one day, hopefully not too far away in time, and with luck she would be enchanted. But that possibility remained with her mother, who was watching him with an inscrutable expression on her beautiful face. Inside himself he knew that he would also like to show Faith his world, but at the moment that look on her face warned him to be careful.

'Mummy said you are a doctor?'

His eyes returned to his daughter. 'Yes, I work in a part of Florence that is poor and the people come to our clinic because it is free. Sometimes I work in other countries if there is a disaster.' Though he couldn't get away as much as he liked since his brother's wife had died.

'Mummy is a midwife.'

'I know. I saw her at her work yesterday.'

'Do you catch babies too?'

This he didn't understand. 'Catch babies?' He looked at Faith. 'Babies who fall?'

When Faith laughed her mouth curved with amusement, her eyes crinkled and the already ridiculously bright day seemed to grow sunnier to him.

She explained, 'In the past it was said that the doctor "delivered" the baby. Of course, it is the mother who does all the work so here we say we are only there to ensure the safe gathering of the mother's work. So to "catch a baby" as it is born. Chloe has heard me say it many times.'

He smiled at his daughter. 'Yes. Rarely I catch babies but mostly I help those who are sick. Little girls and boys your age. Old ladies and men who are frail. I have come to know many families from the outskirts and it is something I am proud of.'

Chloe was so interested in him. Thirsty for knowledge he could share. He was having a wonderful conversation with his daughter!

For a moment he so deeply regretted the lost time. Maria had a lot to answer for by keeping this news from him... He could feel his mood slipping and Faith's calmness seemed to wrap around him as he considered who really had suffered.

That was not all Maria's doing and bitterness would taint this new promise of a family. He would not do that. No. This was his doing and he would be the one to repair any damage. He had been the one who had flown from Australia into his family's turmoil, into deathbed promises to a man he owed everything, and into funerals. He had been distracted but had not once paused to check, to confirm the safety or check for unexpected complications from his incredible but reckless Australian liaison.

It did not matter that he'd had a marriage to arrange. Then a funeral.

Years he had wasted.

But at the time he'd thought they hadn't been reckless. He had used protection and she also. The thought of this accident of birth occurring sixteen thousand kilometres away had never occurred to him.

It should have occurred to confirm Faith's wellbeing though.

And after Maria had left? Why had he accepted that Faith was in his past and would be settled happily without him? Why had he assumed their amazing connection had meant so little to her when its magic had settled in a space in his heart that it would never leave?

He'd been determined to fill his life with work when he should have returned at least once to Australia to confirm she was happily settled and his own thoughts were the only ones wistful for what had ended. He still didn't know the answer to that question but had yet to be convinced there wasn't hope.

The time after divorcing Maria he hadn't wasted, because he'd given it to others. It had been healing to draw strength from those in poverty wearing quiet fortitude so that he could not feel sorry for himself. Both locally and abroad in disaster zones.

Helping others after the dissolution of his marriage, and the tragic loss of his brother's family, he'd found peace from unobtrusively being present in their need.

But he'd wasted his chance of happiness.

Wasted Faith's chance of happiness.

Wasted time he could have spent with Chloe.

But now he would work towards the challenge of proving himself worthy of Faith and Chloe. This was his new goal for a future that stretched ahead. He stared out over the white sand, over the tumbling shallows, over the rolling waves to the place where the ocean met the sky and prayed that he could be worthy to become a part of their lives.

CHAPTER NINE

FAITH COULDN'T HELP responding to the depth in Raimondo's voice when he told Chloe about his practice in Florence and his aid work, though she knew his simple version was watered down for young ears.

Somewhere inside her a warm gladness expanded that he'd found a vocation he'd been lacking before. None of this passion had been there when he'd spoken of the business side of the pharmaceutical company. It had all been her enthusiasm for her work.

So now she was glad for him. Glad he'd found a purpose in life, even if he hadn't found a happy marriage.

But that didn't change anything. He hadn't looked back to what they'd had in those magical few days. If she let him into their lives now, and she couldn't see how she had a choice about that, it was going to be hard to trust him not to fly in like a comet until Chloe was starry-eyed and then zoom away again.

Certainly she would guard her own heart from him this time.

Looking back, she could see so clearly, his tilted head, his warm eyes as she'd raved about why she loved her job in maternity. He'd watched her as if she'd been the most beautiful, interesting woman he'd ever seen and she, young that she'd been, had been flattered and eager to expound her beliefs.

She even remembered that next day, taking him through the cave, raving about the way water seeped through limestone and dissolved the rocks to form caves. How wonderful it was.

He'd surely known that but she'd been too besotted not to spout all the things that inspired her in her cave tours and dragging him down to the ancient riverbed had seemed the best gift she could give him for the gift he'd given her—a whole new world of wonderful love, sensuality and awareness.

Which, sadly, had ended when he flew away for good.

The warmth in her belly abruptly changed to a chill.

Yes.

Be careful.

And be careful of Chloe falling in love too.

She glanced at her waterproof watch and recognised the sudden need to cool down. She struggled inelegantly out of her beach chair. 'Enough time has passed since breakfast. I think I'll go for a swim. Would you like to come and splash with me, Chloe?'

Her daughter jumped up immediately. 'Are you coming, Mr Salvanelli?'

Faith noted Raimondo's grimace at Chloe's formal address and, yes, she could see this was hard for him. But some of the softening she'd been unaware of had already caught her out.

She needed to stay vigilant and firm on boundaries between him and Chloe until she knew what he hoped for.

He might become the perfect dad.

Or not.

But she wasn't creating storybook fantasies of what daddies were like and wouldn't risk breaking Chloe's heart until she was sure the devotion would be reciprocated. For all she knew, he could be called away again tomorrow and off he'd go to answer a summons without a backward glance at them.

He had the right to leave any time.

She had the responsibility to protect her daughter in case he did.

'*Sí*, I will come.' He rose, a smooth uncoiling of muscles, and she dragged her eyes away from the leashed power of him. Darn him. How could getting out of a folding chair seem sexy? She turned away.

Then he said, 'Are you sure you do not need help with sun-cream on your back, Faith?'

The body part in question was directed to him so he couldn't see her eyes close as she imagined that. Big hands. Powerful fingers with slow movements. Sigh. Sensible was so darn sucky. 'No, I'm fine, thanks, I'll only be in and out of the water.'

She pushed herself forward through the sand, Chloe hopping beside her, as she headed for the sea. She needed to be clear on the boundaries for herself too.

They stayed at the beach for the morning, picking through the basket for food and drinks, choosing topics that sat easily as well, while the solitude of the beach slowly disappeared. Two surfers arrived and ran out into the waves. A lone fisherman walked the beach edge further along the bay.

Soon more families arrived, just as they were packing up. Ellie and her husband and daughter. The new arrivals dumped their chairs and towels beside them to greet them.

'Hello, people. Nice to see you.' Faith had relaxed enough for this to be almost true. Though she did wonder if Ellie had told Sam that Raimondo was Chloe's father. And what they all thought about Raimondo helping in maternity. At least she'd told Ellie about Raimondo.

It was actually neat that she could introduce him to the South-wells after the years of them knowing he'd been briefly in her past. 'This is Dr Raimondo Salvanelli from Florence. Raimondo, this is Ellie, my boss, and her husband, Dr Sam Southwell, and their daughter Emily.'

'Good to meet you, Raimondo,' Ellie said. 'I'm more the paper pusher than Faith's boss. We're self-directed here. Heard you two have been busy already.'

Faith thought of the birth yesterday, and then remembered the man who had collapsed. She needed to phone and find out how he was, but he'd been swept from her mind by Raimondo. How awful.

Raimondo must have read her thoughts. 'He was improving this morning when I rang.' Thank you, she thought silently.

Ellie had carried on. 'Congratulations on the successful resuscitation. Both of them. Faith was lucky you were there.'

Raimondo nodded a friendly greeting. 'Your midwife had it under control. Very nice to meet you both. Faith has mentioned you, Ellie. All good things,' Raimondo said, smiling, and his ease of manner made Faith's jangled nerves settle as he held out his hand to meet Sam's.

'Welcome to Lighthouse Bay,' Sam said. 'This your first time here?'

Raimondo smiled blandly. 'Second. I couldn't believe how deserted the beach was this morning. It is very different to Italy.'

Another family group hailed them. Catrina, another of the midwives and only recently on maternity leave, a month before her baby was due, waddled a little with the weight of her pregnancy. Her husband Finn arrived with his daughter Piper, who'd not long ago turned three, and two chairs. The little girls whooped and ran in circles, excited to see each other, and all the mothers smiled.

Introductions continued as Finn and Raimondo shook hands.

'You should join us for dinner tonight,' Ellie said. 'It's Sam's dad's birthday, and we're having a barbecue. Chloe would be excited to see the girls as well.'

'Who's working?' Trina asked as she shook hands with Raimondo.

'Broni. It's her last shift before holidays and then we have Stacey back from the base hospital.'

Faith, Raimondo and Chloe left the beach a few minutes later, having agreed to meet everyone for the barbecue, and wandered back up the hill with chairs, umbrella, a much lighter basket and a tired little girl with a bucket and spade bringing up the rear.

Faith struggled with herself on whether to invite Raimondo in as they neared the house. Did he need some time to himself? She guessed it had been a pretty big twenty-four hours.

The thought made her almost laugh out loud.

Here she was being a coward at the thought of inviting him in. Scared to be alone with him because Chloe would probably go to sleep for an hour, something she'd been doing lately in the afternoon, and she did need to find out what Raimondo's plans were.

Perhaps better to search for answers, even if he was not ready for more time with her.

She looked across at him. 'Would you like to spend the afternoon with us, though Chloe will probably have a rest now, or are you jet-lagged and want to come back later before the barbecue?'

'Thank you, Faith.' He shook his head. 'Again, you surprise me with your kindness. And yes, please. I would like to talk with you this afternoon.'

She looked at this tall, handsome, serious man outside her door and tried again to think of this from his point of view. 'I don't think I'm being kind. Just practical.' She lowered her voice. 'We need to discuss things.'

She opened the gate, walked to the door and pushed it open.

When she looked back to invite him in his face had paled. 'You do not lock your door?'

She glanced back at the wooden door she'd pushed open off the latch. 'Only if we go away. And that's more to stop it blowing open.' She watched Chloe put her sand bucket down wearily outside the door and kick off her sandy flip-flops. Faith brushed her daughter's dark hair with her hand as the little girl passed in front of them. 'Straight through into the bathroom, Missy.'

She turned back to watch Raimondo remove his beach shoes, trying to ignore the way his broad back rippled and his dark hair curled on his strong neck. Shook her head at herself. 'Come in when you're ready. I'll just get Chloe showered and she'll have a lie down and rest.'

She followed her daughter in but a subtle, sensitive part of her was very aware of the man following. 'There's an album on the table of Chloe's baby photos if you'd like to look at that while I sort Chloe out.'

His face lit when he saw the album she'd discreetly placed this morning before they left.

'Thank you.' Then a quirked brow in her direction and a slight smile. 'And after Chloe will you sort me out?'

She met his eyes. 'That's my plan.'

CHAPTER TEN

WHEN RAIMONDO LOOKED at his watch only fifteen minutes had passed since Faith had left him. Yet his daughter's whole life had passed before his eyes.

His chin felt raw where he'd continually rubbed in deep emotion with his chest tight and painful as he'd slowly turned the pages of his daughter's, and the beautiful Faith's, world.

A life he'd known nothing of while he'd passed his time on the other side of the planet, missing it all completely.

In his mind that first album page still haunted him and he could have wept for the loss for himself and for his Australian family. Could have wept for what might have been if he had known of Faith's pregnancy and Chloe's impending arrival.

Faith had done this alone.

Though no, not alone, for her aunt had been there. He and his family owed an enormous debt to Faith's aunt Isabel.

But he should have been the one to support the mother of his child.

He turned the pages back to the start, not for the first time, and gazed again. A rosy-skinned and radiantly exultant Faith, so young and so smiling up at the camera from a large circular bath, water lapping the swell of her breasts, and a little higher on her chest lay his brand-new owl-eyed baby daughter, staring into her mother's eyes, her tiny body slightly blue, patches of white vernix from the pregnancy still covering her plump baby creases as another woman leaned across to lay a towel over them both.

Dios. His heart actually felt as if it grew and expanded inside him and would explode out of his ribs, tearing his chest apart.

He turned forward the pages to the photos of his daughter's last birthday. The starfish cake, four candles, her baby face maturing into a bigger little girl, her mother's loving smile as she leaned across towards her daughter and helped blow out the candles. Such a moment, captured with love from the photographer. *Sì*, he owed Izzy a great debt. So many wonderful moments to be shared with him even as a future observer.

He heard Faith close the door gently to his daughter's room and then cross the lounge area towards him. Her bare feet whispered on the rugs that covered the wooden floors in circles of bright colour.

Her home radiated the same welcoming charm the woman did.

He looked down at the album and then towards her. Words failed him.

She brushed his shoulder in a fleeting touch of sympathy as she passed to sit opposite. 'You look...upset.' She was giving comfort to him when it should have been the other way around.

'Regretful.' He moistened his tight throat. 'The photographs are very beautiful.' Thankfully his voice remained steady. He pushed the album towards her chair when in fact he wanted to tuck it under his arm and run with it. 'Thank you for showing me.'

She straightened the big album on the table without opening the cover. 'Chloe looks at the photographs a lot.'

He laughed and even he could hear the exasperation. 'As would I. The photographer is gifted.'

'Izzy, of course. She's been good with everything.'

'I can see that I let you down.' Then he leaned forward. The silence stretched between them as he tried to form the words he needed. 'I don't understand. I never dreamed... How did this happen?

'Bah.' He waved his hand at the past, at his ludicrous statement. 'We know how...' And for a brief moment their eyes met and humour danced between them. Then it was gone.

'How do I ask this?' He ran his hand through his hair, anxious not to place blame because that would do neither of them good. 'I am sure we were exuberant, young and excited for this thing that sprang so powerfully between us...' he looked at her and the faint blush on her cheeks only made her more painfully beautiful '...but I thought we were careful?'

'It's a fair question...' she smiled ruefully '...and one I continually asked myself when that pregnancy stick proved positive.' She shrugged. 'We were careful.' Yet he could see she was embarrassed.

Her, embarrassed? A joke. Nothing she could do was anywhere near the moral catastrophe he had achieved and left her to deal with.

'I missed two pills during the conference before we met, though took them when we were together. So must have been susceptible to ovulate.' Her voice lowered. 'Apparently, we had needed that second defence. But by the time I found out it was too late as I was pregnant.'

He thought about that.

Thought about the lovely young woman he'd fallen for in the airport, fresh and vibrant. Almost innocent. So full of life and passion and enthusiasm for her work—and he had left her pregnant and with the heartbreak he'd caused her.

He could have destroyed her with his carelessness if she hadn't been so resilient. He thought about what he'd done to her ordered life and then he'd flown away without a backward glance. No. Even that hadn't been true.

He'd glanced back a lot. But those few days he had shared

with Faith had been dreamlike. A mirage. Something he didn't deserve.

As if she'd read his mind she said softly, 'Maybe it's different for men. I'd like to know how you felt as you flew away.'

He owed her that.

Though he wondered if he could be as honest as she was. Regardless, he needed to be. Such a small price to pay. 'What you gave me in those few days was a gift and I cherished the memories in the months and years ahead. Yet it was strange how little I felt I deserved such happiness. Perhaps that is why I did not make it back. Wedding Marie was a return to the time of my grandfather. Without joy. But my duty. You were the dream I didn't deserve.'

He shrugged. 'Melodramatic, perhaps. You have to understand my family to understand my actions. But, even for my family, I would never have left you to face that alone. I never thought I would leave you pregnant.'

Faith recognised the sincerity. She hadn't imagined a child either or she would have asked for a morning after pill when she'd recovered from Raimondo's departure.

Thank goodness she hadn't or she wouldn't have her darling Chloe.

But Chloe was now a part of Raimondo's family and she'd better at least try to understand the Salvanellis to help her daughter when her time came to meet them.

'Tell me about your family.'

He looked struck by the suggestion. Then he said softly with wry humour as he held her gaze, 'Chloe's other family?'

'So it seems,' she said and tried to ignore the fission of fear that raised the hairs on her arms.

'One day.' No. She wouldn't lose her daughter to them as she had lost Raimondo when his family demanded his return. Nobody could demand Chloe did anything. 'But I do want to know why you didn't feel as if you deserved the happiness we so briefly found together.' They hadn't spoken of his family much at all back then.

'It is fair that you know of my family. Where to begin? Dominico, my brother, is ten minutes older, and with me was sent to live with our grandfather after the loss of our parents. That loss left nothing to soften the already stern man who was my *nonno*. Like our father before us, we studied medicine, despite a lack of enthusiasm from our grandfather, because neither of us had a passion for the business he loved. My brother took over the running of the business when my grandfather became ill. I am grateful to him for that.'

There was a lot there he wasn't saying but she got the general idea. Not the ideal childhood but she'd had loss in her life too, even though it had been later. 'No grandmother on the scene?'

'Gone at my father's birth. Our grandfather's estate was a loveless home, despite the beauty of Florence. Though that altered when Dominico found Teresa.'

She watched his face transform and had a sudden wish that she could have met this Teresa.

'Teresa brought joy,' Raimondo went on, but there was sadness in his voice. 'Soon their son arrived to liven their villa. Finally, my grandfather could relax, my brother was happy, I could stop feeling guilty that I was still furthering my career in medicine and not marrying. Now the family business was secure with two generations of sons to pass it down to.'

'Your brother and his wife were happy?'

'Indeed. Too brief happiness. Again, tragedy struck. We are not blessed with luck.' He stopped for a moment and she saw the shadow of that time as it passed through his mind.

'Not long before I came to Australia for business meetings, and met you, Teresa and my brother's son were killed in a hot-air balloon ride. Broken, my brother withdrew from everyone. I had to travel for the business—the Sydney trip already had been arranged—and suddenly it was back to me to ensure the line when my grandfather became terminally ill. But first I needed to complete the trip to Australia my brother wanted to cancel.'

'And you met me.'

'*Sì.*' His voice dropped and she almost missed the words as he spoke them more to himself. 'My Australian wildflower.'

She remembered he'd called her that. Faith felt the sting behind her eyes, the tightness in her throat, and chewed the inside of her top lip as she struggled to push it all back. This was too important to lose in an emotional blowout. One she'd dealt with years ago and locked securely behind iron gates inside her soul.

Hopefully he missed her struggle as he looked within himself to the painful past. 'You must understand my grandfather's whole world was centred on the pharmaceutical company he'd built. That it must stay in the Salvanelli family. Now, suddenly, my grandfather had days to live. My brother struggled with his demands and called me to come at once—so I went.'

She remembered his sudden departure. The first available flight arranged. The rush.

He looked up and sighed. 'The marriage between Maria and I had been spoken of for a long time and I had resisted. Both my promised wife and I had opposed the match. But my grandfather had so little time, and her father agreed, and it was either I wed the woman he wished or my brother could be persuaded into wedding Maria, and there was no marriage he could face, still grieving for his wife and son. I could feel his pain and would not ask it of him.'

Tough love. She could see his dilemma. And even why he hadn't explained the whole of it when he'd left.

But that was almost six years ago and he'd been free for a while. If she'd been his Australian wildflower, why hadn't he come back to see if what they'd had been real when he had the chance?

She quashed that bitterness. Needed to remember she had let it go a long while past.

But she couldn't help wondering what would happen if his

brother called again. She wouldn't be stupid enough to expect him not to go instantly if he needed him, but what if Chloe was the one left heartbroken—what then?

'You didn't think to come back when the marriage was annulled?'

His heavy sigh lowered his shoulders until he straightened and faced her. 'Who was I to ruin your life again? I had no doubt you would have moved on without me. What we had was a few days on the other side of the world and you were young and not bitter with life like I had become.'

That was true. She had moved on. And she hadn't become bitter. Just thankful for her daughter and occasionally nostalgic for a man who could have been a big part of her life but had told her he would never be back.

She'd made the break he'd told her was permanent.

Raimondo went on. 'I believed you were better without me. Vibrant and passionate about your work. You gave me that. After Maria left I found an area in my work that brought me great satisfaction.' He met her gaze and held it. 'Until someone spoke of you, and your Lighthouse Bay...' a pause '...and your daughter—and suddenly there was nothing that was more important than coming here to see.'

At least the mention of the Bay had jogged him at last. He'd remembered them. 'And here you are.' There was no mistaking the hint of dryness in her tone.

'*Sì*. Here I am.'

Yes. Here stood the major concern. He was very capable of wreaking more havoc. She'd only have to remember the response her body made when he was near. Let alone if he turned the full force of his Italian gallantry and accomplishments her way. Plus, she suspected he had a depth of purpose and strong will he wasn't showing her.

Well, she had that too.

She lifted her head. 'Did you come with plans, Raimondo?' She watched him blink at her direct question. 'If you are here for Chloe's birthday, are you leaving, never to come back again after this week?'

She shrugged as if unable to know what to believe, but all the time her eyes remained on his. 'No evasion, please. Is she to look for Christmas and birthday cards? Or are you hoping for more?'

He stared at her.

Well he might, but she was deadly serious.

Black widow serious.

She would protect her daughter from his charm if necessary. To the death. Nothing in his explanation said he wouldn't leave them suddenly if called.

Now, while Chloe was asleep, they needed to get this sorted and labelled for what it was.

'I understand your concern. You have become a strong woman, Faith.'

Pointless flattery. 'I've needed to be.'

'I have never lied to you.'

Bully for him. 'I've never lied either.' She raised one brow. 'So don't lie now.'

His turn to lift his chin and she saw the narrowing of his eyes, the implacable set to his chin, and now she could see the man he'd become. Perhaps he wouldn't run to do his family's bidding quite so quickly this time, but she wasn't sorry she'd pulled the tiger's tail.

Hopefully she hadn't set in motion the whole attack mode response but he needed to know she was on her guard.

He leaned forward and it was as if he'd flipped a switch because in his eyes shone the force of his personality she'd suspected might be shaded.

Whoa.

Where had he been concealing this man?

His dark eyes glittered and his sensual mouth flattened into a straight line. 'Yes, I have plans. I did not come with them but after seeing you at the cave yesterday, hearing your story, I lay awake and dreamed of the future. Of what could be. Of the possibilities before all of us.

'Not just showing my daughter her Italian family and the world she needs to be now aware of.' His voice was deep. Clipped. Belying the fierce emotion in his eyes. 'I will do what needs to be done to achieve that dream. And other dreams.'

A little more of the strong guy than she needed. But she'd dealt with stressed dads before in the labour ward and she knew where she was going with this. Her end goal. 'Without pain to Chloe?'

He looked at her and then, miraculously, his eyes softened. Even held a glint of admiration. 'Correct. I agree. She is the most important part of the equation.'

'Thank you. More important than you. More important than me.' She sat back and he followed suit. 'That was the point I was trying to make.'

He measured her with an assessing look. 'I can see that now. I will not underestimate you again.'

Well, that wasn't quite what she'd been hoping for but she might as well get the answers she needed.

'And your immediate plans?'

He blew out his breath but in his eyes there was a definite admiration for her. The glint of a smile. The hint of a challenge. 'Three things. I would like to be here for Chloe's birthday. Be a part of her celebration.'

She nodded. That was easy. She'd already agreed.

'I would like to be allowed to buy her a gift.'

Again, Faith nodded. Chloe would be happy with that. And she was only five so he couldn't spend too much on her. 'As long as you don't buy her a house, the gift is fine.'

To her surprise he laughed out loud. 'That house has bolted.'

She blinked. 'It's "That horse has bolted".' The second time Raimondo had mistaken his metaphors. He didn't appear any less amused when she corrected him. Suspicion and disbelief raised the hairs on her arms. 'What do you mean?'

'In this case, I have bought a house, and the gate is bolted.' He grinned a wicked flash of white teeth at her. 'We are off topic and Chloe will wake soon, I imagine.'

Faith glanced at her watch but her head still spun at the assertive man she had definitely underestimated.

No. He did not just say that. 'Bull. When did you have time to do something that complicated?'

Dark brows arched at her. 'It is not complicated if others do the paperwork. Did you not spend eight hours at your place of work yesterday?' He spread his hands in a very Italian gesture. 'I am a rich man. I saw something I liked and it is done. But I can wait to put it in Chloe's name if you prefer.'

That was scary. He had done it. Bought a house for a five-year-old.

Or for himself to have access to Chloe. On his first day back and before meeting her daughter. His actions defied sense.

'What house did you buy?' She guessed that meant he wasn't planning on never seeing Chloe again. She'd wanted that reassurance, hadn't she? But with this new broadside she didn't feel as confident she had everything under control.

He settled back and studied her. 'Which house do you think I would buy? Which house would be useful to me?'

She could feel her own temper slipping and knowing that he was goading her because she'd goaded him didn't help. 'Well, you can't buy mine because I own it.'

He waved the comment away. 'The one beside you. It is nothing. Me dealing with inactivity.'

Next door? Which house was for sale? Only one. The old Sea Captain's house. With the turrets. It was a wreck. She shook off the wild thoughts and concentrated. He had her off balance. That wasn't good. He'd just bought the house next door! That was huge. And had huge implications for him being around more. Her turn to blow out a breath.

How he spent his money could not affect her. She wouldn't let it, or she could try not to let it. But holy heck.

And there was more. What was his third request? What more could he want? 'And the last?'

He paused. 'I would like Chloe to know I am her father before I leave to return to Italy. In fact, I would like her to know now, but...' Another shrug. 'I agree to wait until you decide the time is right, as long as it is before I leave.'

And there it was.

The endgame. She could understand that. And he obviously had real plans to return to see his daughter in the future—he'd started proceedings to become a property owner—she had no valid reason not to confirm his relationship to her daughter. But the thought sat, terrifying her like a black hole of unknown depth just the same.

What if he let Chloe down?

What if Chloe began to want something she couldn't have?

Even more terrifying. What if Faith did?

'I have no control over your second condition except it would have been more sensible to buy her an expensive doll's house, not a real one. Your third request I will consider and let you know tonight. I can understand you wanting her to know.'

'Thank you.' He stood. 'I have given you much to think about.'

Yes. He had given her a lot to think about. And did she want him to arrive with them as a part of their party at the barbecue later? No real choice. He was in their life. Now. Probably for ever.

He looked a little uncertain and, even in their short acquaintance, she could see it sat oddly on him. 'Do you still wish me to join you tonight, at your friend's dinner?'

'Of course.' She looked at him with a resigned expression. Shook her head. He was reading her mind again. 'I'll have to get used to you popping up out of the woodwork.'

'You will.' His eyes crinkled. 'And I will too. Pop up, as you say. Reappear with regularity. Regularity, that I promise.' His brows raised. 'I hope you grow to welcome my arrival.'

Welcome his arrival? Would she? A transference of awareness settled over her, as if from his aura to hers, a melding of
their senses while not touching, as he captured her gaze with
his. 'Let us see where this leads us, Faith. I will not let you
down again.'

Her barriers quivered under the strain but held. 'As you say.
We'll see.'

She watched his eyes narrow at her less than trusting response.

He held out his palm and reluctantly she took his strong fingers in hers and his warmth seeped into her like it had from
the first moment they'd met years ago—until their hands separated, slowly.

She tucked her fingers behind her back. 'We'll leave here by
six. It won't be a late night. Chloe gets tired.'

Instead of stepping away, he stepped closer, his bulk blocking
out the light from the open door. His male scent coated with the
salt of the sea. His strong jaw coming closer as he leaned in and
she turned her head until he kissed her cheek. His breath was
warm on her face, his mouth even warmer, and despite herself
her body softened even with that light touch. His hand came up
and caressed the other side of her cheek, cupping her face with
more warmth and such tenderness that slowly she turned her
head towards him. Towards his full, sensuous mouth, until their
lips were a breath apart. Inhaling the life force between them
as they hovered on the brink of the kiss they shouldn't have.

Yet it was she who leaned forward and offered her mouth,
her first sign of trust, her first forgiveness.

But it was he who propelled them slowly but surely into a
kiss that buckled her knees and sent her hands up between them
to clutch his shirt. His arms came around her with a certainty
and possession that jammed them together until her breasts
were hard against his rock-like chest. She wanted to be lost
like this so much.

She pushed him away.

He stilled at once. Nodded, turned and left before she could make her feet move. Her breath eased out. She sagged against the door she moved to shut.

Phew.

She glanced down at the table and a small package lay there.

Her brow furrowed as she opened the door again and called out to him softly, 'You left something.'

He turned and his smile lit his dark, handsome face and made her knees weaken again. 'It is a small gift for Chloe when she wakes.'

She held the package but almost forgot it in her hands as she watched him walk away. That kiss. They could have ended up in bed if she'd let that go on.

A kiss that had shattered her reserves. Thank goodness she'd managed to cling onto the extremely tattered remains of her protective coat by a few wispy threads. See. This was the problem with the man. Once he touched she became lost on the ocean of his expertise.

She hated that. She'd been like seafoam in his hands until the thought had crashed in that this had happened before. That he couldn't be trusted, despite her body telling her he could. But why did she lean into the kiss knowing this?

She should regret that kiss but in her heart she knew she didn't. And even more worrying was the fact she didn't care that she held no regrets.

She wrapped her arms around her middle and stared at the closed door as if it were the man who had just left. How did this change things for her, for Chloe, for them as a family?

If she didn't know the answer to that, then thank goodness she'd pushed him away.

CHAPTER ELEVEN

WHEN CHLOE WOKE an hour later she wandered out of her room, rubbing her pale face with small fists. Faith saw the moment she realised only her mother was there and their visitor had departed while she'd slept.

'Has Mr Salvanelli gone?'

The sudden droop to her daughter's mouth gave Faith a pang in her stomach.

'Yes, darling. But he'll be back tonight.' She suppressed a worried sigh. Already he was charming her daughter too.

'Oh. Okay. He's nice.' Chloe's gaze landed on the small parcel Raimondo had left. 'What's that?'

'Mr Salvanelli said it was for you. A present he thought you might like.'

'For me?' She hopped up and down and then hurried towards it, just as Izzy came in through the front door. 'Aunt Izzy, I have a present!'

Chloe caressed the tissue-wrapped gift carefully. 'Can I open it?' This to Faith.

'Yes. Open it.'

Faith's eyes met those of her aunt. 'Hello, Izzy. Raimondo left Chloe a present while she was sleeping.'

'Nice of him.' They both watched Chloe burrow through the

tissue paper carefully. Luckily there was only one piece of tape so it didn't take too long.

While they waited Faith asked, 'How's Myra?'

'Good. Looking forward to tonight. I hear we're all going up to Reg's impromptu party.

'Raimondo is coming.'

Izzy's brows rose.

'Oh, she's beautiful!' Chloe's reverent voice interrupted them. She spun to show her mother and aunt the gaily dressed Italian peasant doll. 'Look at her apron. And her scarf and hat.' The red touches did make the little figure glow with colour.

'Lovely, darling,' Faith said and suppressed another exhalation. This was just the beginning.

'She must be from Italy.' Her aunt was watching her. Faith avoided her aunt's eye and looked at her daughter. Forced a gay smile.

'She needs a name and she should meet all your other little dolls.'

Chloe nodded seriously. 'She doesn't have blonde hair but I'm going to call her Elsa. Like in *Frozen*.' Chloe clutched the doll to her chest.

'Elsa is a lovely name,' Faith said. 'Why don't you take her into your room and show her to your other dolls?'

Chloe flashed a brilliant smile at them both and dashed off.

Izzy tilted her head at Faith. 'You look like you need a cup of tea.'

'I think I need two.' She lowered her voice to a whisper. 'He's put a deposit on a house here. Next door.'

Izzy's startled eyes flew to Faith's from the hot water jug she'd been plugging in. 'The Captain's house? Right next door?' Saw the confirmation in Faith's face. 'Good grief!'

Faith nodded heavily. 'Apparently for Chloe. In trust.'

'Did you tell him a doll's house would have been more sensible?'

Faith felt the burden of her worry lighten. She had to laugh. She loved her aunt. 'I did, actually.'

'Well.' Izzy finished plugging in the appliance and came across to hold out her hands for Faith to take. Izzy's warm squeeze of her fingers settled her thumping heart. 'He seems a good man. You wouldn't have been attracted to him if he hadn't been. Perhaps just see where this leads? I guess this means he's planning on sticking around.' Izzy dropped her hands and patted her shoulder.

'I don't see that. He'll return to Italy, leaving us all unsettled again. Including Chloe now. I'm worried this means he's planning on popping in and out of our lives like a jack-in-the-box.'

They both looked towards Chloe's room, where the sound of animated one-sided conversation carried on. Quietly Izzy pointed out, 'She does need a father.'

'And he wants me to tell Chloe before he leaves.'

Izzy nodded. As Faith knew she would. 'I think that's fair. Now that we all know he's invested, literally, but also I believe emotionally in finding his daughter.'

Faith closed her eyes for a second to centre herself. To calm, and be sensible, like she normally was. But again that man had thrown her life into turmoil. She could see where Izzy's usual sense was leading. 'I believe he cares for her already too. And you're right. I know that. I just don't know how to tell her.'

Her aunt laughed. 'Darling. She's five. She'll take to the news as easily as she took to the doll. It's adults who complicate things.'

Izzy was probably right. In fact Faith knew she was. 'How did I get such a wise aunt?'

'Just lucky, I guess.' They hugged and stepped apart. 'Right. Tea.'

'Hold that thought. I should do it now.'

'May as well. Keep it simple.'

'Chloe?'

Chloe's head popped out of the room and then her whole

body appeared. She had a doll in each hand. 'Susan and Elsa said they are going to be best friends.'

'That's lovely. Friends are very special. And I've got a secret to tell you.'

Chloe scooted right up to her mother. 'A secret?'

'Well, after I tell you it won't be a secret but it is true. Come sit with me.' She drew her daughter across to the settee and then onto her lap as they sat. She couldn't help a last glance at her aunt, who waved her on. Her heart thumped in her chest as she smoothed her daughter's hair. Inhaled the scent of her baby beside her.

'Do you remember me telling you that before you were born your daddy had to go away and wasn't ever able to come back here? That we wrote to him when you were born but he still couldn't come.'

Chloe's little brow furrowed and her big eyes blinked as she concentrated on her mother's serious tone. 'Yes.'

'Good.' A quick glance to Izzy and another deep breath. 'Well, he still lives away, but it seems that sometimes he *will* be able to visit us.' And she'd better add one of those big forced smiles here. She actually felt like crying as she watched her daughter process the information. Then the little face beside her jerked up as the penny dropped.

'My daddy? My real daddy? Like Piper has a daddy and Emily has a daddy?'

Oh, good grief, Faith thought, and her heart cracked. 'Yes. Though he won't be living with us like that. But you will be able to write to him. And maybe talk to him on the phone sometimes.'

'And he'll visit. And I'll be able to see him?'

'Sometimes.' Faith thought her heart would break for her little girl, who'd missed out on a daddy like Piper and Emily but liked the idea of a part-time parent zooming in and out of their lives because she knew no better. Izzy must have sensed that because she came and sat down beside them both.

Izzy said brightly, 'I think a daddy who can come sometimes is still better than a daddy who is never here. What do you think, Chloe?'

Chloe glanced at Izzy. 'Yes.' Though Faith thought her daughter didn't sound too sure.

Izzy waved Faith on. 'Simple,' she mouthed.

'Anyway. The secret is…' in a rush '… Mr Salvanelli is your father and he's very excited to finally meet you and know you are his daughter.' The words were out, never to be taken back, and Chloe stared at her.

'Really?' Her daughter frowned, searched her mother's face as if sensing Faith's mixed feelings.

'Yes. Really.'

'That's exciting. It must be why he gave me the doll.' Her hand slipped into her mother's and small fingers tightened around hers. Chloe's big green eyes searched Faith's face. 'But you're still going to be my mummy, aren't you?'

Faith hugged Chloe to her, the soft floating hair surrounded her, the tiny body wiggled in closer. 'Yes, my darling baby.' She smoothed Chloe's silken hair again, the strands so precious under her fingers. 'I will always be your mummy and I will always be here for you.'

Chloe slipped her arms around Faith and squeezed her back and then wriggled away. 'I'll have a daddy here for my birthday. That's lovely. Can I go play with my dolls again now?'

Faith's eyes met Izzy's and she blinked away the emotion that clouded her vision. Her daughter's world was secure. She wished her own world was as simple.

'Yes. Off you go.'

Two hours later, as he strode uphill towards Faith's house, Raimondo knew his life was about to change in ways he'd only ever imagined in weak moments. He was a father. A real family with warmth and joy and he was a part of it.

His axis had already shifted, meeting Faith again and being

forcibly reminded by her beauty and calm how much they had connected so briefly so long ago. And earlier today.

That kiss.

Dios, that kiss.

He must not be distracted.

Because now, knowing of his daughter, he was already growing to love the child. She was such a beautiful young girl and he only hoped Chloe would come to love him when she knew him.

For his daughter was easy to love, like the mother had been almost six years ago, though he hadn't known at the time the indelible imprint Faith Fetherstone would have on his soul.

And on his life. On his future. He should have been here earlier.

His daughter. He crossed his fingers behind his back. Now he was being childish, but perhaps Faith had already told his daughter since he'd seen them this afternoon and Chloe would call him *papà*.

Though he couldn't help but wonder if he deserved such kindness.

He stopped outside the house with the sold sign. Barely saw the neglected gardens and peeling paint on the old weatherboards. *Pah*, it would fix with money. He glanced up at the turret that looked over the top of Faith's house and out to the sea. Remembered his daughter's words and the synchronicity of his purchase before he had even heard them.

A castle for his princess. He imagined his daughter looking though the polished brass telescope he would buy her, perhaps standing on a set of wheeled steps until she grew of a height, but excited and pointing at a passing ship. Yes. He could see that.

And that wasn't all he could see—though this part was more fanciful. He saw her beautiful mother watching fondly, imagined all the things in the wide world he could show them both. The Italy he could show them. The life they could share. If they'd let him. Patience. Already he was bursting with impatience.

It was still difficult to comprehend he had left Faith pregnant, that Maria had hidden the letters Faith sent; that his wife had kept such a secret from him was too petty to comprehend. Too cruel.

He could not imagine the hardships his child's mother, his Faith, had to endure, the judgements he'd exposed her to with his carelessness, but he would not sour this coming evening with bitter thoughts. His daughter waited.

He started walking again and his stride lengthened until he turned into the gate of Faith's house.

As he reached up to knock his fingers on the white wooden door, it opened. His miracle of a daughter stood there, her excited face tilted sideways, her dark hair pulled back and tied with a yellow ribbon, her tiny pink mouth pursed as she studied him. Then she smiled.

'What a pretty ribbon,' he said, more to see her smile widen than anything else.

'Yellow is my favourite colour.' Then, without pause, 'Thank you for my doll. Mummy said you're my daddy. Is that right?'

His heart jumped in his chest and he wanted to lift her and swing her up, hug her to his chest, but instead he was careful not to expect too much and said, '*Sì*. That is right. I am your *papà*, and I am very glad to have found you.'

'So? Can I tell my friend, Piper?'

'Of course. If your mother is fine with that.' He looked past his daughter to Faith as she hovered protectively, as any mother would when an almost-stranger wanted to claim half her child. She was incredible, this woman. Brave. Honest. His heart swelled.

'Thank you,' he said quietly, and she nodded and gestured him in.

'Excuse me,' Chloe's voice piped up. 'Do I have any brothers or sisters or cousins? Or grandparents? Piper has cousins and grandparents.'

'I'm afraid not, Chloe. You do have an Uncle Dominico in

Italy. But he has no family.' He caught Faith's eye and shook his head slightly. He didn't want Chloe to become sad with the history of loss in his family.

'So my Uncle Dominico won't be here for my birthday?'

He smiled. 'No. I am sorry.'

An intense stare. 'But you will be?'

This he could say. 'Yes.'

She nodded once then looked back at him. 'Promise?'

His daughter's head was tilted and she looked suddenly like her mother. He moistened his lips to say yes, and then considered his first ever promise to his daughter. The magnitude of that. 'Unless the sky falls in.'

She nodded and he saw that she understood. Instead she said, 'Is my Uncle Dominico bigger than you?'

'No. We are the same size. But he is older. By ten minutes. He is my twin. Though sometimes he seems much older.'

Isabel stood against the window watching them, a small welcoming smile flashing briefly his way before she turned to give them privacy.

An odd fleeting thought crossed his mind. His brother would appreciate Isabel, if only he could get him here. How incongruous that this place across the world made him think of Dominico and his painful past.

'We're almost ready to leave.' Faith's voice brought him back to the present moment. 'It's just up the hill at the far croft.'

'I am ready. Today I will see one of the little houses on the edge of the cliffs—they intrigue me.'

She narrowed her eyes at him and said very softly, 'They are not for sale.' His purchase had obviously unsettled her. Then she went on, 'The views are spectacular, yes, and they're built from the same stone blocks as the lighthouse.'

He thought of the imposing structure on the far skyline across the bay. 'Your lighthouse is most picturesque.'

Faith smiled. Her tense posture eased a little and he was glad. 'I love it. The first time I saw it I felt like it stood benignly over a place I wanted to live. I came here for the work and found my world.'

He had thought that the first time he'd met her—how much she suited this little bay. Which was a problem in itself, but an issue for later. 'Then you are lucky. To feel at home is a special thing. As I walked here I was thinking that a telescope in the Captain's house would give a fine view as well.'

'I haven't been inside.' She turned to her aunt. 'Have you seen next door, Izzy?'

'Yes. Once.' Isabel gave him an assessing look. As if she too had thought his purchase too impulsive. 'Beneath the wear and tear there's lots of beautiful woodwork and the stairs are lovely. The view of the ocean from the turret is indeed impressive.'

Faith glanced at her watch. 'I'm sorry. Time's marching on.' She picked up a small white-paper-wrapped parcel with a child's drawing covering it and shooed Chloe towards the door. 'Shall we go? We made some Rocky Road chocolate for Dr Southwell. He loves Rocky Road, doesn't he, Chloe?'

'He always has some in a jar.' His new daughter nodded enthusiastically and Raimondo had to smile. 'He says I make the best Rocky Road.'

She looked so pleased with herself and her mother smiled indulgently. He imagined the preparation of the sweets would be a shared task. 'I'm sure you do, little one.'

Raimondo's phone vibrated discreetly and he pulled the instrument from his pocket, frowning at the interruption. Dominico. He glanced at Faith. 'Excuse me, I must take this.' He turned to the doorway and stepped outside into the street.

'*Ciao*, Dominico.'

'Brother. Bad news. The factory has been destroyed. It lies in ruin.'

Raimondo sucked in a breath. His grandfather's legacy, which neither of them had wanted but both felt obliged to continue.

His brother answered the question before he could ask. 'Fire.

I'm sorry. There are questions I cannot answer and I need you to return.'

No. He couldn't. Not yet. He glanced towards the family who were filing from the house towards him. He'd promised. 'This is difficult.' He lowered his voice. 'I gave my word to stay until Chloe's birthday tomorrow. It is only an extra twenty-four hours.'

Dominico's sigh sounded despairing. 'I'm sorry. The police wish to talk to us both.'

Pah. 'How can they expect me to travel so far for their whim? I will be back in two days.'

Another sigh. 'Then don't. It is just my need. This wearies me. Too much.'

Raimondo could hear the despair in his brother's voice. He was not the decisive and upbeat Dominico of old. He knew how hard it had been for his brother to climb back from his heart-break, how he had buried his grief in becoming like his grand-father, lost in the business. Raimondo felt the tearing of himself in two as he wished to be in both places.

Was this the last straw? Dominico had worried him lately.

Yet he needed to stay for Chloe's birthday.

He needed to be there for his brother, who had always been there for him. He could feel his twin's pain across the distance between them. A hint of instability. A risk he could not take.

'If I come, will you travel with me to Australia when I re-turn? A change of scenery may lighten your weariness and I have a young lady who wishes to meet her uncle.'

'I think not.'

'I think so. Or I will not come.'

'You must come.'

'Then we will discuss it soon. Arrange for a friend to stay with you until I arrive. You must promise this.'

'As you wish.' A weary agreement, not a happy one.

'Done. Have Rosa arrange the flights. I will leave in a few

hours to make the midnight flight from Brisbane tonight, use Singapore.'

'*Sì.*' A pause. 'Thank you.'

'Look after yourself until I arrive. Yes?'

'Yes.'

'*Ciao.* Now to tell my daughter I must break my promise I have only just made.' He ended the call.

It was the mother who would be angry on her daughter's behalf, and he didn't blame her. He just hoped the rapport they had begun to enjoy would not be damaged, but he knew it would.

Knew he had done damage to the fledgling trust she had offered him today and he cursed fate and fires and the lack of free will.

CHAPTER TWELVE

FAITH LOOKED UP from straightening Chloe's hair to the man waiting at the gate. There was something in his face that said all was not well. Deep inside she knew she wasn't going to like this and her heart began to pound. 'Everything all right, I hope?'

He looked at her and the worry and frustration in his eyes forewarned her. Her stomach sank. 'A fire. The company head-quarters have been destroyed in Florence. My brother asks that I return immediately.'

And so it begins.

Of course he would go. She'd known that. 'When?'

'Tonight. Later.' Faith sucked in her breath as he finished with, 'I will fly at midnight.'

Hot words wanted to pour out but she wouldn't let them. She'd expected this, hadn't she? She looked at her daughter, who had skipped ahead with Izzy. Instead of berating him, she said calmly, 'Before Chloe's birthday?'

'*Sì.* My apologies.'

'I expected nothing from you.' Her tone said she was un-surprised. She raised her brows and as her heart iced over she shot him a cold look. 'And it is not me you need to apologise to. Perhaps you'd better tell her before she tells all and sundry you'll be at her party.'

Raimondo winced and glanced at his daughter, a few large strides ahead, chatting to her aunt.

Faith seethed. As well he should consider Chloe. Broken promise number one. That hadn't taken long. She felt like stamping her foot and asking if one more day would make such a difference. But of course he would go.

'Chloe?' Faith called and Chloe skipped back down to them. 'Your father has something to tell you. You walk with him here and I'll talk to Aunty Izzy about something she needs to know.' Because if she didn't move away she was going to say something she regretted and Chloe was the important one. She was the one who had told him that.

She turned and walked a little too quickly back to where Izzy was admiring a rose bush in the next-door garden but Raimondo and Chloe's voices carried on the still air. She'd known his priorities so why was she surprised?

'He has to leave for a family emergency.' She could hear the tartness and was glad she'd spoken softly to Izzy. They both turned to see how Chloe took it.

She heard him say, 'Chloe, I am so sorry that I must break my first promise to you. Something has happened in my home town and I have to leave and go back to Italy before your birthday.'

Chloe's face fell and then she furrowed her brows. 'You said you would be here. Did the sky fall in? Like *Chicken Little*?'

He stopped and crouched down to her level. '*Sì*, little one. You are very clever. The sky has fallen in on our factory because of a bad fire and I must help my brother sort the mess.'

Chloe's face creased. 'In the story the sky didn't really fall.' Faith heard the forlorn note in her daughter's words and her eyes narrowed at Raimondo. She hoped she'd done the right thing agreeing to his request of access but she didn't see how she could have done any different.

Raimondo nodded solemnly. 'But in Italy this has really happened. Though when I have finished the sorting I will return as fast as I can. And perhaps bring your Uncle Dominico as well.

But I am very sad that I cannot be here for your birthday tomorrow, little one. I broke a promise, which is not good.'

Chloe sighed and shrugged her shoulders with resignation. 'It's not broken if the sky fell in.'

Faith felt tears prickle behind her eyes as her young daughter behaved so very kindly. Watched Chloe tuck her hand in his. 'But you are coming tonight to the party and I can tell Piper you are my daddy. And you said you will be back.'

Faith heard it all. Tried to be as philosophical as her five-year-old daughter and struggled.

Izzy squeezed her hand and made her walk forward up the hill. 'Come on. Let's go ahead or we'll be late.'

The party was in full swing when they arrived. Reg and Myra met them at the door, and it seemed half of the Lighthouse Bay hospital was in attendance inside. The other half must be working, Faith thought with a forced smile at another of her colleagues.

She couldn't help notice the curious glances Raimondo drew. A stranger and a darkly attractive one at that. Plus he'd actually been present for a birth and two resuscitations as well. He'd been busy in the short time he'd been here. He'd been busy with her too, and even more she regretted that kiss. She sighed.

Of course the first thing Chloe did was drag Piper across to Raimondo and announce in a loud voice, 'He's my real dad. He's from Italy so I call him *Papà*, not Daddy. He has to go home tonight but he's coming back soon.'

And that pretty well sums it up, Faith thought as she felt the heat push past her chest, up her neck and into her cheeks. Piper's mouth fell open, along with the half a dozen people in earshot.

Izzy laughed.

Trina, Faith's friend and fellow midwife, and Piper's step-mother, held her pregnant belly and laughed as well. Then she sent a quizzical look Faith's way. 'Gotta love kids.' She put out her hand and Raimondo took her fingers and shook. 'So, you're Chloe's dad, not just a friend. That explains a lot.'

'It does?'

'It will,' she said cryptically and Faith knew she was in for a grilling. 'Welcome, Raimondo, even though we already met at the beach this morning,' Trina said with a laugh. 'I'm sure Faith will fill us in on the details.' Then she clapped her hands. 'Everyone! Please meet Raimondo Salvanelli, a GP from Florence and a friend of the Fetherstones.'

She turned to the tall man who had come up at the commotion. 'Finn, darling. It seems Raimondo is Chloe's surprise daddy, all the way from Italy.'

Finn glanced at Faith of the red cheeks. Then he met Raimondo's eyes and nodded. 'Kids. I'm the local paediatrician so I understand them a little. I see your daughter has taken my daughter's hand after causing a stir and blithely run off to play dolls.'

'As children do,' Raimondo said with a smiling glance in his Chloe's direction. Then he looked towards her. 'Her mother is equally charming.'

Faith rolled her eyes. Not that easy, buddy, she thought, and was touched when Finn championed her.

'Faith is well appreciated here.' There was no force in the statement but Raimondo nodded at the gentle warning.

'Unfortunately, I must leave tonight, but I will return soon to better acquaint myself with Chloe and renew my acquaintance with Faith.'

Good lord, that almost sounded like a statement of claim and Faith resisted the urge to call him on it. She was the calm one. She was the one in control here. He was the blow-in.

'We look forward to knowing you better.' Finn shook his hand. 'Another doctor in town is always good. And my dad said you did well. We don't have emergencies often here but handy to know when there's extra help in the bay.'

'I'll make sure I'm accredited with your government for such times. The Electronic Portfolio of International Credentials have my CV for the aid work I do, so it should be possible.'

'Excellent. Come, and I'll introduce you.'

Raimondo followed Finn and Faith sagged a little now all announcements of Chloe's paternity were out of her hands. There was no going back from here.

'You've had a wild couple of days. And then he leaves?' Trina linked her arm. 'Come on, I'll get you a nice glass of Sav Blanc even though I can't join you. Ellie said Raimondo popped up at one of your cave tours. Must have been a shock.'

Faith looked at her friend. Saw no judgement, just sympathy. 'Understatement. Apparently, the letters I sent didn't make it to him. It was Sam's sister's Italian guests from your wedding who started the chain reaction. I could say this is all your fault.'

Trina held up her hands and laughed. 'Francesca? My bad. But he is a bit of a dish. I can see how he must have been tempting if he turned all that charm on you. What were you? Twenty?'

'First year out of uni.' Faith took the crystal glass Trina handed her with a nod of thanks. 'He has charm. But the gloves are off if he disappoints Chloe.'

'I'm sure he knows that. Though Chloe is tough like her mother. And her aunt. You've laid good groundwork there for your daughter's coping ability.'

Faith looked at her friend and felt a swell of emotion. For the last twenty-four hours her feelings had been like the waves outside the window. Rolling in one after another. No wonder she was feeling buffeted by Raimondo's arrival. But Trina's belief in her daughter felt reassuring. And similar to Izzy's confidence. 'Thank you. I hope so.'

'Let him do all the work, Faith. You've done your bit. Just enjoy the ride.'

She almost choked. 'The ride? Good lord. I feel like I'm learning to surf and a big wave is going to knock me off the board and pummel me to bits.'

'Not you. You have great balance. Besides, you have plenty of friends to help keep you afloat.'

'Okay. Let's go see what new challenge has appeared with Raimondo loose in the room and my daughter telling all and sundry.'

'You've got this. There's only friends here,' Trina replied as she linked arms again.

Raimondo shook hands and responded to the kindness as he was introduced to many and moved through the room and out into the sunny backyard where tables and chairs were scattered. He had a beer in his hand bestowed by Finn, children played on a swing set in the corner and the ocean stretched away like a tufted blue carpet.

This was so different to the formality of his world in Florence.

The salt air made him breathe deeply, as did the sight of Faith coming towards him with Finn's wife. He knew now he could have done this better with some warning to her and certainly it would have been better not to rush away tonight. He stamped down the frustration his impending journey caused. The sooner he left, the sooner he could come back.

He watched her approach, this woman from the past whom he wanted in his future. So beautiful, and he could see she tried hard to be light and calm when he had certainly complicated her serene world.

'Here you are,' she said quietly. 'How have you survived the gauntlet of Lighthouse Bay medical community?'

'I have been made most welcome.'

Someone called out to Finn and Trina. Trina said, 'See you soon,' and the couple waved and moved away.

Raimondo kept his eyes on Faith. 'Thank you for allowing me to meet your friends.'

Faith spread her hands. 'There was a gathering. We do it a lot and you were here.'

'I have made this very confronting for you, have I not?'

'Yes.' She half laughed when she really wanted to cry. 'Our past relationship is certainly out there for public consumption. But Chloe did need to know her dad existed so I guess I had hoped this would happen at some time.'

'I am truly sorry I leave tonight.'

Her green eyes studied him as if to seek the truth of his words. But she didn't say anything. What could she say?

He was a fool to leave but he would ensure it didn't happen again. The more he saw her, the more he needed to know more. He needed to be with her longer to understand the woman Faith had become and rearrange his priorities. But he'd needed to reassure Dominico that he would be there soon. A frisson of fear reminded him he could not delay this trip—he needed to see his brother for himself. And ensure something had been put in place that would keep Dominico safe until he arrived.

Chloe appeared beside them and snuggled into her mother and yawned. Softly, Faith patted her head. 'You're tired, sweetheart.'

Raimondo shot a glance at his new daughter. Saw her paleness. She had already slept today. 'Always tired?'

Why tired?

Faith met his questioning look. 'Chloe had a nasty cold two weeks ago and she's been easily worn out since then. She's taking vitamins and getting sunshine, and she's been good about resting.'

He heard the tiny thread of worry under the light description of illness. Felt his own concern stir. Grow suddenly huge. Had a sudden memory of his brother's devastation at the loss of his son. No. This would not happen when he had just found them. 'Has she had blood tests for this?'

Faith looked down at her daughter. 'Yesterday morning before preschool. We have an appointment with Uncle Finn on Monday for the results, don't we, Chloe, before I go to work.'

Chloe nodded and yawned again. Faith turned the child away

from him towards the door. He said very quietly, 'This is the first you tell me of this?'

Faith raised her brows at him. 'Yes. Thank you for your concern. Chloe and I will say our goodbyes inside. You don't need to come with us. Have a comfortable flight tonight.'

He bit back an instinctive command it would have been very foolish to issue. Yes, he'd erred in that question, been undiplomatic, but he felt the slap of not having rights and knew it was his own fault. 'I will come with you now.'

Faith paused and turned back to him. 'And if I don't want you to?'

He shrugged. 'I will follow anyway.'

So he shadowed them and nodded his goodbyes along with Faith and Chloe. Isabel, Raimondo noted, was observant of his presence beside them and chose to leave them to continue their departure unaccompanied.

No doubt she would have left with her niece if Faith had been alone.

He truly appreciated her understanding.

While Raimondo waited in the open lounge Faith had ushered Chloe straight to bed.

As he paced the room for her to come back he considered all that had happened over the last two days, the enormous change to his life and his future plans. That shock of seeing Faith again and her effect on him, the way the world had suddenly opened up in the most marvellous and unexpected way with the confirmation of his being a father.

But now the bombshell of Chloe's strange lethargy. All this and he was leaving!

He needed to plan his return, assess his options for gaining further information on his daughter while he was away. Especially as he'd almost alienated Faith with his stupid accusation of her withholding Chloe's illness from him.

So how to approach this new turn sensibly?

He stared at the photo album lying on the table. The urgency of responsibilities he wanted to share ate at him.

Firstly, Faith needed to be able to contact him in any emergency. *Dios*, imagine if something happened to Chloe, something he could help with, and she couldn't access him. It didn't bear thinking about.

Twitching with suppressed urgency, he pulled a business card and a small pen from his wallet and crossed to the table to lean on the surface.

Faith needed his personal mobile number, though that would help little on the flight. Then he wrote his home number as well on the back of the card. The business number was on the front and Dominico would have set up a temporary phone office at least. He thought again and wrote Dominico's details down as well.

Now the numbers he needed. He produced a new card and wrote Faith, Isabel, Finn. He needed the paediatrician's last name as a contact. By the time he'd made his list Faith had returned.

'She's asleep.'

What if his daughter was truly unwell? A surge of panic, a premonition swamped him suddenly, perhaps because he'd seen so much loss and this could not go that way. Unease twisted in his stomach and made his tone more forceful than it should have been. 'Asleep already?'

Faith's brows went up at his doubting tone. 'As I said. I'm not lying.'

He pulled himself back. 'This is not what I mean. I do not doubt you. But her lethargy. What are your thoughts?'

He watched the lowering of her stiff shoulders as she passed a hand across her brow and sighed and now another emotion swamped him. This was not easy and everything had happened very fast for her—he'd had time to consider the impending reconnection.

Suddenly he wanted to take her in his arms and console her.

Tell her all would be well, as any father would console a mother, but he didn't have that right. And they didn't know that.

'Faith, I'm sorry.' He stepped closer. 'For everything.' He put one hand on her arm. 'You have done everything right and I'm not saying this well.'

She interrupted him. 'I'm sure she's fine.' She said what they both prayed. 'We will have the results on Monday and make sure.'

Yes. Monday. Two days' time. When he would be over the ocean and thousands of miles away—though he could email from the aircraft if needed. Even telephone if the conditions were right.

'How will I get the results?' He needed Finn's number. He reached across and placed the business card in her hand. 'These contact details allow you to find me any time.' He handed her the other card.

'Please may I have yours and Finn's numbers? And perhaps Isabel if I cannot contact you?' Had that come out too abruptly?

She looked at him. Cocked her head at his insistent tone. 'I will give you the house telephone number, and my mobile,' she said slowly. 'But I would prefer to share Chloe's results with you myself rather than have you contact Finn.'

More delay. 'That is not acceptable to me.'

Her hand brushed her face again. 'Let me think.'

He lifted his chin. 'Fine. There is no need. I will find out for myself. It is no secret where we are and who the paediatrician in this town is.' He regretted the words as soon as they left his lips.

She narrowed her eyes at him. 'So. Is this the real Raimondo Salvanelli? Are you trying to intimidate me? In my own home?'

'That is not my intention.' Impatience was still in his tone and he tried to rein it back. He could not lose Chloe now.

'Isn't it? Then why are you ordering me around? Laying down laws? You have no say over me.'

He lifted his chin at her. 'My daughter may be unwell and I will not be told at your convenience.'

Her eyes widened. 'Chloe is my daughter and I will let you know the result of the test when I get it.' Her voice held warning and again he saw she was not the diffident girl he'd met nearly six years ago.

'Though—' here a flash of unusual anger in her eyes '—of course you can go behind my back and source them from Finn.'

'Stop.' He held up his hand. How had it come to this? His fault. Doing this wrong. 'You are right.' He ran his hands through his hair, almost pulling it free from its roots. 'My fault. We are friends. Were once more. Your kindness has astounded me and I repay you with this impatience. My apologies.' He touched her arm. 'Forgive me.'

When she looked at him he could see the shimmer of distress, and possibly fear for her daughter, in her eyes and it pierced him with an arrow of protective instinct that surged from his very soul.

Of course she was terrified that Chloe was unwell.

Of course he wasn't helping by being demanding.

Unable to stop himself, he reached out and very slowly, very surely, he drew her against his chest into what he hoped was a comforting embrace. He needed to reassure her he cared.

'I want to be here for you and Chloe.'

'What if when you leave you become caught up in your other life again?' Her voice was so uncertain it stabbed him. 'What if I have to tell Chloe you've forgotten her, like you forgot me?'

It stabbed him again. 'I never forgot you. You have always been a part of a shining star which went home with me nearly six years ago and I tucked that star into my heart and never forgot you.'

She shook her head against him. 'I find that hard to believe.' Her voice was very soft.

'I'm not surprised.' He stroked her hair. 'But it is true.'

His fingers continued to stroke her silky head as she laid her cheek against him, not pulling back as he'd feared she would, and he remembered the feel of her against him from so long ago. The kiss of earlier. The feel of her skin under his fingers triggering memories and transporting him. Her scent was so sweet, her smooth flesh so right in his arms. Perfect.

Too perfect not to act on. His grip tightened with one arm and with the other hand, so slowly, he tilted her chin upwards.

'What if I said when I come back I will never leave you and our daughter again?'

Now he could look down into her face. He waited for her answer as he lost himself in the green pools of her siren's eyes. Could not resist the stretch of his thumb to so gently trace the soft, trembling curve of her pink lips. So beautiful.

'No answer?'

A shake of her head. 'How can I believe that?'

'When I come back I will convince you. For now I must do this task for my brother and tie up some ends that need to be complete. For the moment, begin to trust. At least try.'

'I'll try.'

As her body softened against his he too loosened the bands of the restraint that had been crushing him and lowered his head. Their breath mingled and their mouths touched and finally, after so long being lost, he found the one place for him that was home.

CHAPTER THIRTEEN

Raimondo's mouth against hers felt like a homecoming. Her arms wrapped around him. How had she spent so long without this in her life? How had she spent so long without this man in her life?

That scent of Raimondo against her, something she remembered from the last time they'd kissed, the warmth of his whisper on her cheek as he brushed her face with light kisses before returning to her mouth. The heat in his lips as he gently nudged his tongue against hers and she opened her mouth to him.

Her knees wobbled as he drew her into him and all Faith could do was close her eyes and hang on.

It was just a kiss. Again.

And another kiss. So, with each gentle probe or tender stroke, she forgot more of the world outside his embrace. Took comfort from the craziness of the last few days of turmoil in the last place she'd expected to find shelter from the fear in her heart.

Her hands left his waist to splay against his solid upper body and then curled into his shirt, straining him closer. Her breasts pushed almost painfully into his chest and through their clothes the heat between their skin built into a slow cauldron of need that swirled in on itself, creating a whirlpool of desire drawing her deeper. It had been so long since she'd felt a strong man's

arms about her. So long since Raimondo had taught her the secrets of this place. Too long if she responded like this.

From just a kiss.

Faith dragged her mouth reluctantly from his and searched
his face. His beautiful eyes. Saw the aroused darkness of desire and promise to transport them both to a place she'd almost
forgotten existed. A wisp of fear curled around her. She wasn't
sure she could survive from revisiting the magic if he walked
away afterwards and never came back.

'Should we do this?'

'Should we not?' His voice as bemused as hers.

'What is this between us?'

'Destiny. Tonight I will be gone, but I will be back.'

A cold tendril of foreboding touched her with a chill.

Abruptly it hit her that accidents happened, aeroplanes
crashed, moments were to be grasped. Fleeting opportunities
to be loved by someone were like clouds that you reached for
in the sky and suddenly she didn't want this ray of hope for the
future to pass without grasping the possibilities. If something
happened to Raimondo now, how would she survive if she knew
she could have had this?

'Make love to me before you go.'

Raimondo's eyes darkened even more and bored into hers.
'My most burning desire.'

'Please.' The word floated from her mouth in a whisper,
barely heard, barely believable, and yet brazenly sure. She
needed to feel his arms around her one more time before he
left because inside she still wasn't sure Raimondo would ever
be back and, regardless of the pain to come, she wanted this
from him.

The ground disappeared from beneath her feet as he swept
her up, carried her tenderly, and she rested her cheek against
his chest, listening to the strong beat of his heart to drown out
the voices clamouring in her head.

With infinite care he lowered her to the bed and joined her.

CHAPTER FOURTEEN

ON SUNDAY MORNING, twelve hours after he'd left, Faith lay on the same crumpled bed where she had made love with Raimondo and stared at the fluffy clouds passing in the small gap in the curtains, not seeing them. What she saw was a glorious, tumultuous storm of reconnection, the gentle whispers, the tender caresses—all the reasons they had both been crazy before—the memories now returned to heat her cheeks and make her draw her arms to cradle her stomach as she mourned the loss of Raimondo beside her.

Put simply, wrapped together they made magic.

So she couldn't regret the pure joy of it or the risk to her heart in the making. But where would it end? She had given herself to him before he'd left, their mutual need overcoming their reserve, perhaps each seeking the reassurance holding the other would give. But it had been more. It had been everything they'd found before, with greater poignancy because of the past mistakes he'd made. Their combined worry for Chloe, the risk to the family that was so close to being possible. She saw that it had been hard for him to tear himself away, hard for him to look one last brief time at his sleeping daughter, and she didn't doubt that it would be hard to drive from Lighthouse Bay and catch a plane.

It had been a few days of craziness again.

The upheaval to her life that ridiculously gorgeous Italian man could create in forty-eight action-packed hours. He'd better come back. At least she was sure she was covered for contraception this time.

But he would be back. He'd promised. Chloe would have a dad. And Faith? What would she have?

She shifted to sit up. *That way madness lies...* She couldn't imagine yet.

Now, it was the morning of Chloe's birthday and the sun crept fingers of soft yellow up the wall of her bedroom so she should rise and try to ease the new memories Raimondo had created back into her secret place for later. It was going to be a beautiful November day for a children's party.

How fast those five years had flown since her baby had been born—and hadn't their lives been blessed with the joy of Chloe.

She wondered what the next five years would bring. Which drew her thoughts back to Raimondo.

To their kiss. And the progression from there.

Of course he stayed on her mind.

He would still be over the ocean on his flight, barely halfway to Italy, soon to land in Singapore. So no call had come yet for Chloe on her birthday. She would not think he had already relegated them to the back of his businessman's brain as the drama in Italy came closer. And was it so bad if he did; he'd said he needed to tie ends, sort out his many commitments before he could come back. He'd said he would be back—it was a shame a part of her didn't believe him. But that was for later.

She didn't care if he came back without his possessions. Wealth and assets did not have the same importance in her own life.

Though, she supposed, now she would have to be more vigilant for Chloe to appreciate both sides of the financial coin if her father persisted in spoiling her with extravagant gifts.

Her daughter would not be spoiled by a rich man's whims.

A little voice whispered that perhaps she was being harsh. She didn't want to listen. She'd been so darned unsettled since he'd arrived and even more unsettled since he'd left. Not surprising. Making love with Raimondo before he'd left had been an incredibly stupid, and incredibly wonderful, thing to do. It wasn't fair.

Chloe would wake soon, though, the way she had been sleeping in lately, one never knew.

Surely the lure of the enormous parcel that had arrived yesterday—on a Saturday; who knew how he had arranged that before he'd even known he would fly out?—would have her daughter up early. Obviously from Raimondo, and goodness knew what it would be in all its largeness and expensive express courier, but Chloe had been remarkably patient to wait until today to open it.

Like Christmas, she'd said.

Her little friends were arriving this morning at ten a.m. Faith had decided an early party would be more fun for Chloe than waiting around for the afternoon when she could be weary.

Dear Myra, a pastry chef and cake decorator in a past life before Lighthouse Bay, had made the 'Elsa from *Frozen*' cake and would bring the no doubt magnificent creation down at ten. Because it was Sunday, the adults would come for brunch after the children had been here an hour and done their party games, then they were having a sausage sizzle in the backyard which Finn had offered to cook for young and old.

It would be a typical extended family and friends day, held to celebrate one of theirs. All those coming who genuinely cared...

Raimondo should have been here to see his daughter's pleasure in being the star for the day.

But he wasn't. She shouldn't be surprised.

She shouldn't be disappointed.

Not at all. Really. But she was and not only for Chloe.

Faith pushed away the recently familiar flustered feeling in her stomach and opened the blinds properly to see the day.

Just as she thought. Glorious. She pushed open the window

and the salt-laden air wafted into the room, forcing her to appreciate the good things. Forcing her to smile.

She loved living here. This was her home. Regardless of the ups and downs of the last few days, she was so very fortunate. And here came the footsteps of her precious daughter.

'Mummy, Mummy! It's my birthday!' A pink-pyjamaed missile fired through Faith's bedroom door and into her arms.

Faith hugged the warm tousled body into her and inhaled the tear-free shampoo scent of Chloe's soft hair. Her baby. Her life. 'Good morning, darling Birthday Girl. How exciting. Today you are how old…?' Faith pretended to scratch her chin.

'I'm five! I'm five!' Chloe bounced back off the bed and onto the balls of her feet and grinned at her mother. 'You're tricking.'

'Five? My goodness. So big. Off to school next year. But first—we have a party!'

Chloe's eyes rounded. 'I know! My first party. Piper said she has a present for me.'

'Well, that's very nice. You must remember to thank all the people for coming and also for presents and cards.'

'I will.'

Such a solemn vow, Faith thought with amusement and stroked her daughter's soft cheek. Then she frowned at the small bruise on Chloe's neck.

'Did you bump yourself here?'

'Maybe.' Chloe was peering towards the kitchen and Faith let it go, though unease slid under her skin. 'Let's go and have breakfast and maybe you could open a present from me too. And one from Aunty Izzy.'

'And one from Mr Salvanelli. I mean *Papà*.' The little girl crinkled her forehead. '*Papà* is a funny word.'

'Maybe we can find a different word that works as well. But let's go see what we can find for your birthday breakfast.'

By eleven o'clock, when the adults were due to arrive, the presents had all been unwrapped and the children had begun to settle from the frenzy of pass the parcel. Everyone had a prize and the mood had calmed to staring with admiration at Chloe's wonderful cake and her wonderful doll's house.

Gift-wise, it seemed that Elsa and the *Frozen* story had won the day as well, with a set of *Frozen* dolls, a set of bed sheets, a *Frozen* duvet cover and even a cushion with Elsa's blonde head gazing out from it. It culminated with Raimondo's outrageously expensive *Frozen* castle doll's house, which impressed all the little girls mightily.

Faith remembered she'd suggested a doll's house, more fool her.

She thought of the three-storey, furnished, fantastical fairy tale extravaganza, and wondered how on earth he'd managed to order that and have it delivered in the space of a Saturday afternoon. It had proved well over-the-top but Chloe, of course, was ecstatic. Faith decided she'd need to talk to him about restraint with gifts—and she hadn't told her friends who had bought the Captain's house next door.

Soon enough when Raimondo took ownership, because then everyone would know.

She sighed. The man was turning into a headache of mammoth proportions. And heart-hugging secrets.

Trina and Finn were the parents who arrived last and Piper squealed and ran towards them with Chloe following. Until she slowed.

As if in slow motion, Chloe faltered, stopped and then silently she toppled sideways in a dead faint onto a discarded Elsa cushion, and Faith's heart missed a beat.

Faith reached out but she missed and by the time she knelt beside her daughter Finn was there too, easing her back. Faith didn't understand as her heart seemed to slowly gather momentum in her chest. What had happened?

His voice reached her shocked brain. Calm. Soothing. Like at work when that voice was directed at a patient, not at her.

'She's breathing, Faith. Fainted. Could just be excitement. I'll take her,' he said gently, 'to her bed. We'll look at her there.'

Then he lifted Chloe into his arms and carried Faith's baby away and she couldn't see her daughter's face as she hurried behind.

Once in the bedroom with the door closed, Finn examined Chloe and they found more bruises like the one Faith had seen that morning. Two on her belly and a dozen on her back and both lymph glands under her thin arms were suspiciously swollen.

When Chloe stirred from the faint, only a minute after she'd been put on her bed, she woke slowly, still groggy and vague.

Sadly, there would be no more birthday celebrations for Chloe.

Faith could hear Izzy in the distance as she ushered the guests out with a gentle, 'No, Chloe will be fine,' quietly dispersing the party behind the door as she took control. Her 'Thank you for coming' seemed surreal in the distance to Faith as she watched Finn examine Chloe with growing alarm that she tried to hide. Her anxiety ramped up to real terror as Finn took out his mobile phone and arranged emergency admission to the regional hospital for tests, but she smiled at Chloe and said, 'Uncle Finn knows best.'

But she was thinking, *My daughter is too sick for Lighthouse Bay Hospital.*

The ambulance ride took them to the base hospital and more blood tests were conducted.

Test results that proved serious enough to transfer her from the country to the city, and thankfully Faith was allowed in the aircraft too. So they both travelled by the rescue helicopter down to the Children's Hospital in Sydney.

As soon as they arrived, around three p.m., Faith slipped outside the hospital to leave another message for Raimondo, this time at his place of work, and she jammed her phone up against her ear to try to block the noise of the traffic. She drew a deep breath as finally the long-distance call connected, and a woman's rolling accent answered at the other end.

'Salvanelli Compagnia Farmaceutica.'

Faith prayed the receptionist at his brother's temporary office could speak English. She had no Italian. 'I wish to speak to Dominico Salvanelli, please.'

'Signor Salvanelli is not available. I do not know when he will be back. I am sorry.' The accent was thick but the English perfect. Not that it helped.

That was it then. Raimondo's mobile phone and home number had only accepted voice messages as he would still be flying. She enunciated as clearly as she could, 'This is Faith Fetherstone from Australia. Please try to pass on a message to Dominico to contact his brother. Raimondo must phone me back as soon as possible. It is very urgent.'

So she'd done what she could about informing Raimondo and the forlorn hope that he would immediately begin his return to support her and Chloe through this terrifying ordeal had failed, as she should have expected. She would be alone.

No. That wasn't fair. Isabel would drive down as soon as she'd shaken her slight cold and the unacceptable risk of her infecting Chloe now she was so very susceptible.

Hours later, as visiting hours closed, the sounds of the Children's Hospital in Sydney made resting difficult on the chair beside Chloe's bed. Crying babies, toys being tossed or banged on the side of cots, the beeping of high-tech medical machines that whirred and trilled and the constant swish of nurses checking on her daughter.

At least no more fruitless time had been wasted on unsuccessful phone calls because now her phone was dead without her charger. She would concentrate on her daughter, as she should have been the last few days instead of being sidetracked by a man from her past.

Nine torrid hours after Chloe's collapse, on the longest day of Faith's life, Faith felt like a zombie as she paced the room. It was true that finally, after the terrifying provisional diagnosis, when acute myeloid leukaemia had been suggested at the regional hospital, and Faith had felt as if her body had turned to a lump of ice, things were tentatively looking up. Frozen-faced, she'd nodded, outwardly calm, and clutched Chloe's hand and they had to wait for more test results.

Now, after the bone marrow biopsy in Sydney, some hope for a different diagnosis seemed possible.

An hour ago Finn had phoned Faith on the ward phone with the results.

'The news is better than expected, Faith.'

She'd sagged against the wall, the ward phone clamped to her ear.

Finn went on. 'The latest tests and overall diagnostic pictures have pointed more towards a severe secondary bacterial infection on top of the recent viral infection. That combination mimicked the leukaemia symptoms.'

'Oh, my.' Faith had sagged further down the wall.

She'd almost missed the rest of Finn's news. 'The repeat blood tests still show Chloe's red cells are down and her white cells sky-high. That's why she's spiked that raging temperature.'

'The paediatrician here knows that?' She was trying to understand what this meant for Chloe.

'He rang me. He's been called to the operating theatre until later tonight. Sorry he couldn't tell you himself. We're cautiously hopeful that with the antibiotics Chloe will make a full recovery.'

Faith swallowed again the lump that had seemed lodged in her throat for hours. She hadn't been able to answer Izzy's questions when other calls had been brought to her, her mouth unable to form words as her throat closed. So Trina and Izzy had left messages.

'You need to rest, Faith. Try to sleep so you have reserves for tomorrow.'

She'd nodded and then realised he couldn't see her. 'Yes. I'll try.'

'What of Raimondo?'

'I left messages. He's still flying. Won't land until one a.m. tonight.'

'Hang in there. He'll be back.'

'It will take another two days at least. Thank you for ringing, Finn.'

'Get some rest.'

'Yes.' Then she'd hung up.

Raimondo would be very close to Florence, but that wouldn't help her. He was twenty-six hours' flight in the wrong direction.

But he could have rung the hospital at one of the stops. Despite the fact there was no wife to hijack her messages, he still hadn't answered.

She shouldn't be surprised he was not there for her.

Out of sight, out of mind.

She should have expected that.

The deep disappointment of Raimondo's absence sat in her chest like a stone. Didn't he know she needed strong arms and a chest to cry on at this moment as she watched their daughter sleeping with horror of her childish mortality so fresh in her mind?

Had that two days of upheaval he'd caused in her and Chloe's life meant nothing to him?

Faith stared at her daughter, weary tears she didn't have the energy to wipe as they dripped damply down her cheeks. Chloe's small fingers were tucked under her so pale chin and the other arm lay by her side strapped to the IV line with a bandage and a board to keep her arm straight. Her daughter shone ethereally white against the pillows, and all her mother could do was sit alone, watching, powerless to help her.

Two separate antibiotics were running through the drip she was connected to now the blood transfusion she'd needed was finished.

Still, the news was so much better than it could have been and now that she had allowed the hope to filter in, after the horrific dread that had filled her before, not unexpectedly, exhaustion swamped Faith. She put her head in her hands and closed her eyes.

They would beat this.

She and Chloe. They had to.

The door opened. It would be another nurse to check Chloe and she couldn't summon the energy to open her eyes.

'Faith.' A voice she knew.

Raimondo, looking slightly harried and slightly crumpled, very unlike himself, stood there, his hair mussed, his beautiful warm, reassuring eyes searching hers as he crossed the room towards her, his long strides eating up the distance between them.

Faith struggled to her feet. 'You're here?' Then she sagged and he crossed the last gap to catch her in his warm embrace.

CHAPTER FIFTEEN

Raimondo crossed the room in a rush and pulled her into his arms and she sobbed against him. His strong hands held her as he pulled her against the chest she'd needed so much. Hugged her tighter to him until almost she couldn't breathe but it was so worth it as she felt the warmth of his body warming the chill that had soaked all the way into her bones.

His voice rumbled in her hair. 'I should never have left. I will not leave again unless I take you both with me.'

Faith didn't have the headspace to compute that. Her brain had shut down. She could only deal with this moment. 'She's been so sick.' Her voice sounded thick with tears, and relief, and exhaustion, but it felt so overwhelming that he'd come back. She'd hoped for a call and wasn't sure how he could have arrived but this was so much better than she'd hoped for.

'My poor Faith. The things I do to you without the intention to hurt you. I should never have left.'

'No, I wish you hadn't.' She looked up into his face. 'How are you back so quickly?'

He ran his hand through his hair at the memory. 'I flew back from Singapore. Your message appeared as we taxied in. I sent a doctor friend to sit with Dominico. That is another story. There was some dilemma as I retrieved my bags but it was arranged that instead of flying on I could change planes and fly back.'

'You must be exhausted.' The shadows under his eyes attested to that.

'Not like you. Not like Chloe. I should never have left,' he said again. They turned to stare at their daughter and his mouth compressed as he held back his emotion.

Faith touched his arm. 'You're here now.'

They crossed to the bed and Raimondo sat carefully on the edge and stroked Chloe's free hand at the end of the strapping of IV line. She stirred, mumbled, 'Mummy?' without opening her eyes, and resettled.

Raimondo closed his eyes. Then opened them to stare up at Faith. 'And you have been alone through this.'

Faith nodded.

'She looks so pale.' He compressed his lips and gave her a rueful smile. 'I spoke to Finn. Your phone? He said it was dead, which was better than me thinking you had banned me from talking to you.'

She'd so wanted to talk to him. 'I wouldn't do that.'

He shrugged and squeezed her for a moment. 'How can I know that when I have wronged you again?'

'You did what you had to. And I had no charger. We left so quickly. One of the nurses is bringing me one from home tomorrow.'

'Of course.' He touched her hand. 'But I could not sit in the back of the taxi as I was being driven here from the airport and not find out what was happening. So I found Finn.' He shrugged apologetically.

She had to smile, though it felt so long since she had smiled her face felt stiff. 'I forgive you.'

'You will not need a phone to contact me for I will be here.'

'You're staying?'

'I have said I would never leave again.' His face was intense. 'Believe me.'

And looking at his strong, tired face, his warm eyes that searched to see if she was able to believe him, she did. 'Then I will. Now. With all my heart.'

He squeezed her to him. Then, even with that brief hug, she could feel the recharge of energy she'd stolen from him and straightened her shoulders. There was hope everywhere.

CHAPTER SIXTEEN

Isabel

ONE MONTH LATER, and two days before the wedding, Dominico Salvanelli, the groom's twin brother, stood by Isabel's side in the church as everyone practised for the wedding.

Isabel's hand rested on his admittedly very powerful forearm as they walked together back up the aisle, and she tried not to inhale the particularly divine aftershave he wore. Or glance across at his impressive chest that rose beside her so that she felt tiny.

Seriously, he was there every time she turned around, not saying anything. As if he was trying to understand something. Watching her. Which was ridiculous.

She wasn't one for toy boys and the man was seven years her junior. Though, behind his eyes, she had the feeling he was decades older than her. These Salvanellis certainly knew how to do dark and mysterious.

Look at her niece's man. Though when she did, all she could see was joy. Which made Isabel smile.

Dominico leaned in to say something but paused as another instruction came from the priest. They turned and Dominico reluctantly let her go to return to the altar to stand beside his brother. They did it all again one more time.

'I think he likes you.' Faith was grinning at her as she did her stately bridal walk past, a particularly unfazed, calm bride. How come she, Isabel, the maid of honour, had all the nerves since Dominico had arrived?

Isabel whispered as she and Faith stood together to enter, 'He's too young. And he's got issues.'

Faith rolled her eyes at her. 'Issues are right up your alley.'

'You're being silly.' But she couldn't stop the heat creeping up her cheeks.

'I've never seen you blush before, Izzy,' Faith teased. 'Even when that locum doctor asked you out.'

The next few minutes were blessedly question-free until she was back down the aisle with Dominico's corded muscles beneath her arm again.

'It should be you who brings Chloe over to our villa while the honeymooners tour Italy and France.' Dominico's voice was low.

Isabel raised her brows. 'They will only be away two weeks.'

Dominico inclined his head. 'They could then stay longer.' He shrugged. 'For my new sister-in-law's peace of mind when her daughter is in Europe while she is away from Australian shores, of course.'

Isabel glanced sideways with mild amusement at him. 'And what would Chloe and I do while waiting in Florence?'

'There is much to see.' He lifted his head and smiled. Slowly and with a definitely wicked slant. Quite shocking after all the serious faces she'd seen from him earlier. 'I would show you both around, of course.'

Isabel laughed. 'Thank you for the invitation. We'll see what Faith wants to do.'

'Not what you wish?'

'I always do what I wish.'

Two days later

Raimondo's heart thumped with slow, vast joy at the front of the white church on the hill above the waves. He lifted his face to the light and with infinite patience, indeed he owed his bride that, and with his brother Dominico's shoulders level with his, they faced the round stained-glass depiction of Christ together and waited for Faith and her party to arrive.

To those seated on the pews, waiting with them for the ceremony to begin, they must look like two dark men in this place of light.

Beside him, Dominico's face seemed hewn like the painted granite of the church, inscrutable as he stared ahead in his matching black suit. Raimondo had no doubt his brother was remembering his own tragic marriage and the loss of his family.

He would not have gloom today. 'Brother?' Dominico turned to look at him and thankfully Raimondo noted the strain ease away. 'Today is for rejoicing, yes?'

'Indeed.' Dominico's mouth kinked upwards. 'I rejoice. You managed to wait a whole month before you married her.'

Raimondo laughed quietly. 'It was not possible for more speed or it certainly would have been sooner. Thank you for being here.' It had been difficult to extricate his brother from the many technicalities of an incinerated business, and a lethargy steeped in despair, but even Dominico had known he would have to come if Raimondo married in Australia.

Raimondo smiled internally to himself as he stood, basking in the early afternoon sunshine through the round window, and waited with an eager heart for his beautiful bride. How much time he, Raimondo, had wasted without Faith by his side.

Faith and Chloe. How could a man be so fortunate? He would ensure that he earned it in his care of his wife and daughter for the rest of his life. Perhaps they would be blessed by more family as well.

He had to sympathise with his brother on the irresistible attraction of the Fetherstone women.

At the wedding rehearsal his brother had been unusually taken with the maid of honour, but Isabel had brushed off Dominico's attention as if she were the older, wiser woman fussed over by a boy. It had been amusing to Raimondo when she was only seven years the elder and Dominico... Well, his brother had been markedly ruffled by her dismissal.

His smile kicked at the thought but he knew better than to say anything.

Dominico had reluctantly left Florence with every intention of hurrying home as soon as the nuptials were completed. Though, to Raimondo's delight, it had taken just one evening in the company of Isabel Fetherstone for Dominico to mention to his brother that he might stay 'perhaps a little longer'.

After the honeymoon, he and Faith would return here to live, where the sea breeze blew salty whispers through the open windows of the houses along with the sound of crashing waves and circling gulls.

This bay, this place, held magic the like of which he had never seen before and watching his brother had made him pray for the healing of his sibling's heart as well.

He glanced over his shoulder to see in the congregation Faith's friends and colleagues who would be his associates when he began work here. Yes, he could live here very happily for the rest of his life. There would be many times when he flew home but never again would he leave his new family behind.

But that did not dim the expectation of showing Faith and Chloe his world. The delight of that was for the future.

A car pulled up. He heard the doors open and his heart rate picked up. Soon. Soon he would see the woman he would spend the rest of his life with.

The music started and a rustling at the door and shift of light drew all eyes to the entrance.

Raimondo strained to see his bride.

Ah. The little flower girls. His daughter, his Chloe like a daffodil in her sunshine-yellow dress, the lilac sash so pretty, her dark hair plaited around her sweet, serious face as she solemnly sprinkled yellow rose petals down the aisle for the bride. Little Piper followed her, her own basket of dewy softness on her arm as she copied her friend. They looked like fairies as their glowing faces spread joy like petals among the congregation.

Isabel stepped into view, head up, large eyes excited, yet her face serene, her mouth curved in the happiness of the moment, and Raimondo felt his brother tense beside him. *Sì*, she was a vision. But not Raimondo's vision.

There Faith's aunt waited, the maid of honour who'd refused to be a bridesmaid, the pale lilac dress highlighting the dark auburn of her hair, the silk that slid and slithered over the slim body modestly but with that hint of allure he found abundantly in Faith. Isabel stepped sideways and the music lifted to a climax and there she was.

His bride. Standing in the doorway. Her inner light bathing him with love from fifty feet away as she caught and captured his gaze. His angel. His love. His Faith.

Dios. So beautiful. Glorious. In that moment he swore he would never fall short of her needs again as he stood drinking in the sight of her as she paused in her walk towards him. His swelling heart overflowed with gratitude for this woman, so beautiful inside and out, and the love she offered him made his heart swell.

Faith stopped at the entrance to the church as she reached out and rested her hand lightly on Isabel's arm. Isabel, her aunt, her friend, her rock, was the one to give her away for safekeeping into the arms of the man she loved, as she should be.

She'd never thought this time would come, her at the front of a church, Raimondo waiting at the end of the aisle with such a powerful love shining her way she almost lifted off the ground with it, so it was with surprise she realised her fingers didn't shake. That there was no caution as she threw herself and Chloe into this headlong rush of marriage.

No doubts since the hospital, no doubts since Raimondo had promised his inclusion fully in their future. No doubts since he'd returned to stay by her side.

Now she could imagine nothing else.

The time was here.

She looked ahead to where her husband-to-be seemed to fill the end of the aisle in his black tuxedo and white silk shirt, a yellow rose in his lapel, his eyes on her. Yes, his brother stood beside him but she had eyes only for Raimondo.

Their eyes held and now her belly twitched and came alive. Her heart rate sped up and her breathing increased.

Yes, Raimondo. I'm coming. She lifted her head and stepped forward, Isabel by her side, and closed the distance between herself and the man she would always love.

* * * * *